Bratva Jewel

The Ivankov Brotherhood

Sabine Barclay

OLIVER HEBER BOOKS

Published by Oliver Heber Books

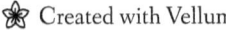 Created with Vellum

Thank you to all of you who have embarked on this journey with me into the world of The Syndicate Wars. This series may have come to an end, but you can get your Mafia fix with the upcoming Italian Mafia, Colombian Cartel, and Irish Mob series.

Happy reading,
Sabine

Subscribe to Sabine's Newsletter

Subscribe to Sabine's bimonthly newsletter to receive exclusive insider perks.

Have you read *The Syndicate Wars*? This FREE origin story novella is available to all new subscribers to Sabine's monthly newsletter. Subscribe on her website.

The Ivankov Brotherhood

Bratva Darling

Bratva Sweetheart

Bratva Treasure

Bratva Beauty

Bratva Angel

Bratva Jewel

Do you also enjoy steamy Historical Romance? Discover Sabine's books written as Celeste Barclay.

Chapter One

Misha

I do not want to do this. The flying commercial part is fine. I'm not so far removed from my early childhood that I can't handle flying on something other than our family's corporate jet. It's not like First Class is truly that much of a hardship. It's the destination. I do not want to be back in Moscow and not for the same reason as last time. It's been nearly two years since my last trip, and that was for a childhood friend's funeral. A friend who'd been an informant for the Ivankov bratva, my branch of the Russian Mafia, and who died for it. I'm leaving New York City to attend another funeral, except this one is for an informant who was one of my father's closest friends in the KGB. You wouldn't think there were such things, but it was often friendships that were the only thing that kept you alive in those days.

"Excuse me."

I'm reaching forward into my hand luggage, so I'm past the

1

little wall to my pod. I shift to lean away from the aisle as a young woman with sandy blonde hair and blue-hazel eyes tries to squeeze between the pod my friend's in and me. We're both broad shouldered, so are the men we're sitting next to. Anywhere but First Class makes it hard for us not to overflow our seats.

"No worries."

I smile at the woman as she passes, and her gaze darts to my brother, Sergei, who sits next to me. Then to my dad and Grigori behind us, then to Anton, who's sitting across from me. She returns my smile, but she's wary. She's also fucking hot. Like super-hot. I know none of the men I'm traveling with will notice, but I do. She's wearing a t-shirt that strains over her tits. They're not huge or anything, but the t-shirt is definitely snug. She has a sweater tied around her waist and jeans on. The damn sweater's hiding a view of her ass, but I can tell she has one. I notice her nose is ever so slightly crooked—the way a broken one often heals. I force myself not to narrow my eyes and demand to know who hurt her. It's none of my business, but I'm still thinking about it after she walks by and heads into the Economy Class section.

"Papa, do you want any of Mama's cookies?"

I'm speaking English as I offer my dad some of my mom's *molochnyi korzhik*. They're shortbread cookies that are delicious when dipped in milk. We may be headed to Moscow, and we may have our accents, but I don't need to make it obvious. I twist to look back at my dad. It gives me an excuse to watch the woman as she heads farther toward to back of the plane. She turns to lift her hand luggage into the overhead bin, and she looks back at me. I pretend not to notice, but I can't help but be pleased.

I reach behind me to my father, Radomir Andreyev, to offer

him the sandwich bag filled with cookies. You would never believe the man is a former KGB operative and a former member of one of Moscow's most ruthless organized crime groups. They conscripted him into the KGB straight out of secondary school, and when his time was up there, the Podolskaya demanded he join within days of returning home to our old neighborhood. My dad is wearing a midnight blue button down with long sleeves that cover his tattoos, of which he and I —and all the men in our family—have many, and black slacks. He looks like a regular businessman, not someone whose sole job description has been violence.

We all look like that. Sergei's four years older than me, but we look so much alike that people often think we're twins. Our hair is blonder than the woman who passed me, and our blue eyes are most often described as icy. We inherited our eyes from our mom, Svetlana. People have a different reaction to her. They say her eyes are kind and maternal. The hair comes from my mom's mom. Mama's hair is a deep red.

Anton is the exact opposite of us, with his dark hair and dark eyes, which he inherited from his father, Grigori Kutsenko. It couldn't be more obvious that Anton and Grigori are father and son. My dad has graying light brown hair and deep blue eyes. Most people would say Sergei and I look nothing like our dad until I smile. Then everyone says I inherited his jokester grin. They aren't wrong. My dad's hilarious, and I like to think I am. According to my family, the jury's still out.

My dad takes a couple cookies and passes the bag to Grigori. Next, my dad hands it to Anton, who grabs four before handing it back to me. Sergei practically snatches the bag from me and takes two of the remaining three.

"What the hell?"

I'm left one—the broken one.

"She's my mom too."

Sergei laughs as he shoulder-bumps me, and I can hear Anton chiming in.

"She's practically my mom, too."

He isn't wrong. Sergei and I grew up with Anton and his younger brother, Pasha. I've known them my entire life. He and Sergei are only a few months apart. Our moms and dads have been best friends since they were kids. As much as my mom is their second mom, I can say the same for theirs.

"Don't cry, little brother."

Sergei dangles his own bag of cookies in my face. I snatch them from him.

"I'll be sure to tell Mama you wiped my tears, old man."

It's a thing in our family. The oldest brother gets called "old man," and the younger brothers get called "little brother." It doesn't matter that there's eight of us, when you include the cousins Sergei and I share with Anton and Pasha. We're all six-and-a-half feet tall and weigh between two-hundred-twenty and two-hundred-forty pounds. We're the size of competitive bodybuilders or American football players who are actually in shape.

"You need a nap. Do you want some milk to go with your cookies first?"

Sergei grins, and I roll my eyes before I tease back.

"Don't be jealous because I can sleep anywhere. And stay on your side."

That's like telling the weather not to snow in Russia. Anton weighs the most in our family, but Sergei is the biggest. He loves nothing more than to lift weights, and it shows. No one would guess that he's an IT genius with an Ivy League education. He's a little broader across the back and shoulders than me, and he likes to remind me when we're in cramped spaces like commercial First Class.

I stand to put my bag into the overhead bin and glance to my right. God, I am so the spoiled youngest child in our family. The seats in Economy remind me of just how far we've come. I have a seat that fully reclines into a bed, and I'll have constant food and beverage service from the flight attendants. And yet I complain that we're not flying in our private jet. If anyone could hear my thoughts, they'd think I was an asshole.

"Humbling, isn't it?"

Sergei reads me too well as I sit back down in my seat.

"We've come a long way from that first flight to America. None of us dared look around. You and I were too scared to even move. Mama and Papa were nervous the entire flight."

We fled Moscow and the Podolskaya bratva. My dad was injured in the Second Chechen War, so he came home before Grigori. He got us out of Russia and onto a flight to America. A few weeks later, his best friend, Kirill Kutsenko—Grigori's younger brother—died in Chechnya. Grigori came home from the war and immediately smuggled my aunt and cousins to St. Petersburg, where they caught a flight to join us in New York. It only took a couple days before the Podolskaya figured out what Grigori did and came after him. He, Alina, Anton, and Pasha hid for two weeks before he got them out of Moscow, too. All of that for what? We still wound up in the bratva, just in New York. Irony is a bitch.

"Now look at us. I know you're grumbling in your head as much as I am, little brother. We've gotten soft."

I snort. There's nothing soft about any of us. We're all senior members of the Ivankov bratva. What we do for a living —being soft gets you killed. But I won't lie. The comforts of being obscenely wealthy these days have their benefits.

My dad and Grigori earned enough to keep us from starving, but none of us were rich when we got here. It took some illegal enterprises when Sergei, Anton, Pasha, Maksim, Aleksei, Nikolai, Bogdan, and I—that's all eight of us, and we range in age from twenty-nine to thirty-two—were in our late teens and early twenties, but now our wealth comes from mostly our legitimate businesses. Our bratva money gets reinvested into our community.

"Speak for yourself, old man. It's just bad timing that everyone else needed to go to Chicago for that deal. Now that Maks and Laura have the twins, and Bogdan and Christina have Lev, it makes sense that they're the ones to take the jet."

We like to keep our legit businesses in the family too. Everyone has a role, including the wives. Laura's an attorney. Ana's her paralegal. Sumiko's an accountant. I cock an eyebrow at my brother as I continue.

"Besides, it's less conspicuous than if we fly into a private airfield. That's what people expect, and I guarantee people have already figured out we're on the way."

"True."

The moment the wheels are up, I'm reclining my chair. I'm asleep before the flight attendant refills my vodka. I'm certain the others will be soon, too. The flight takes the better part of ten hours, so there's no point in wasting it when we all know we won't be getting much rest while we're there. It's hard to fall into a deep sleep when you're keeping one eye open.

The five of us approach baggage claim after a quick stop in the airline's luxury lounge. It's amazing how refreshed you can feel just by brushing your teeth. We've all changed out of our rumpled shirts and trousers into the clothes we brought in a garment bag. We may have flown commercial, but we don't need to look it. For people in our position, first impressions—or first reminders—are everything.

I immediately spy the woman I practically drooled over at the beginning of the flight. Since we were at the front of the plane, my family and I got off well before her. But now we're all standing around waiting for our luggage. Grigori and Sergei see their suitcases first. For all the money we pour into our designer suits, our luggage is understated. I believe mine was like fifty bucks on Amazon. It's less likely to make people wonder what's inside.

I wander closer to the conveyor belt as the woman leans forward. Her case isn't large, but it's immediately obvious that it's heavy. I reach past her and pluck it from the moving belt with one hand. I'm careful not to put it on her toes when I set it down.

"*Spasibo.*" Thank you.

She sounds like a native. She's definitely not a tourist trying out a few phrases.

"*Pozhaluysta.*" You're welcome.

I nearly said no worries again. It's an Americanism that I picked up pretty quickly, but I don't want to sound like I can't think of anything else to say. Even if it's as boring as just you're welcome. I catch sight of my bag, so I lean past her and grab it. I don't really have a reason to linger.

"Do you have anything else you need to get?"

She looks up at me, surprised by my question. She pulls the handle up and shakes her head. She grins.

"I travel light."

I smile back.

"If you say so." I stare a moment too long. "Have a good day."

I force myself to turn away and join my family, who've all gotten their bags. As we head toward the man we know is our driver, I watch my mystery woman walk outside and hail a cab. I want to stop her. I want to tell her not to get in some strange Moscow taxi. I want to offer her a ride. But I can't for so many reasons besides it being completely creepy. I watch her lean forward and speak to the man, and she's clearly a native Muscovite. That does nothing to reassure me.

We have two security cars that are going to follow us, and I'm tempted to tell her to take one. But that'll freak her out even more. A strange man telling a woman to get into a tinted window vehicle in Moscow screams sex trafficker, when that's exactly what I want to protect her against.

"We're going to follow her cab, aren't we?"

My dad comes to stand next to me. I nod. Our drivers will know to be discreet, and she'll be none the wiser, but I'll breathe easier. I don't know why I care. I shouldn't. I'm not worried about any of the other passengers on our flight, and I noticed some other attractive women flying alone. It's not like I have time to chase a hot chick while on a business trip. I don't even do that when I have the time. I don't date. What's the point? It's not like a relationship can go anywhere.

What do you do for a living?

This and that.

Where do you work?

Here and there.

You're emotionally closed off.

Yup. Sure am.

That's pretty much how dating works in my world. I'm not celibate, and it's not like I'm paying for sex either. But I'm not in college anymore and thinking with my dick. Would I like to have more sex? What man in his twenties wouldn't? I don't need it though. My left hand works as well as my right hand if I really get too lonely. I have someone I can hook up with when we're both in the mood.

"Stop staring, or her cab'll be gone before we can follow it."

Anton nudges me, and I realize they've already loaded our luggage into the car. We're in Volkswagen vans, since there aren't that many vehicles in Russia designed for large groups of people. Short of the eight-wheel monstrosity, Avtoras Shaman, even the large vehicles are compact compared to the U.S. These vans aren't the SUVs we usually use that are bulletproof and armored or the town cars and limos that are comfortable with bullet resistant windows. But our connections here reinforced them enough to keep us alive if we're in an accident or shot at.

I watch the city whiz by, and memories flood me from nearly twenty years ago. I can remember winters where the snot would freeze in my nose, and I was sure it would snap off. Winters with hand-me-down coats from Sergei that didn't fit because they were still too big. I also remember kicking a soccer ball around with the neighborhood kids and going to the park with my mom and our friends. I remember just being a kid.

That all ended when we got to America. The haven never existed. By the time I was thirteen, I was already in the bratva. Bogdan and I are the same age, and he got sucked in when he was eleven. It was right after we arrived because he had no father to protect him. Mine and Grigori did what they could for all of us boys, but more would have gotten us all killed. I lasted two years longer than my cousins before they yanked me in.

I'm lost in thought for the next two hours, until I focus on where we're going, and I realize the taxi we're following is entering the same neighborhood as our destination. Even now, nineteen years after leaving the Serpukhovsky District, I can still sense the Podolskaya's presence. This is one of three areas in Moscow where they are the reigning organized crime group. People might call the others organized, but they are nothing like these men. Plenty of former KGB and Soviet Army soldiers joined after the fall of the Soviet Union. They brought their training with them, and the Podolskaya became paramilitary. It's why they sent men to the Second Chechen War. Men who included my dad, Grigori, and Uncle Kirill. It was Podolskaya men who came to New York and joined the Ivankov bratva who trained us. We are what we are today because of the men we thought we escaped.

Chapter Two

Kitty

He may be the hottest man I've ever seen, but nope. No way. No how. Uh-uh. Everything about him that makes me want to run my hands and tongue all over him is what's telling me to stay far, far away. The aura of danger, of barely controlled strength embodies that idea of animal magnetism. But it's also what's likely to get me heartbroken at best and killed at worst. I know this type of man. I grew up around them. My mother says my father was like that. And that means I need it nowhere near me.

But fuck. He's delicious to look at. Those icy-blue eyes remind me of the lakes in Siberia near my grandparents' home. The kind that intrigues you enough to stick a toe in, then you regret it because you just might lose it. They might make me overheat now, but they're likely to freeze my heart if I get too close. It would crumble into fractured shards, never to be put together again.

Holy shit. Okay. I can slow my brain down a notch or two. He smiled at me in the plane—or rather smiled at my tits—and he helped me with my suitcase. It's not like he's luring me into bed. Though... No. I would definitely say no. It might kill me. But then again, he might too. There is no way he isn't bratva. I don't need to ask. No one needs to tell me. I'm a Muscovite from the Serpukhovsky District; I know when I see one. But damn. I could watch him all day. His smile was pure sex, and I don't think he was even trying. God help any woman when he's really trying to charm her.

And the men he was with. Not a dud in the bunch. At least one set was father and son, and the guy next to him was his twin. The other older guy must be his dad. It's easy to tell where the younger guys got their good looks. The older two are on their way to being straight up silver foxes. I spotted their wedding rings. Lucky wives.

I never approach married men. That's why I always look for a ring or a tan line that may as well be a ring. What did I hear that called once? A shadow of shame. Yeah. A guy slips off his ring to pretend he's available, but what looks like a shadow from being paler gives it away. If only Larisa had paid that kind of attention, I might not be back in fucking Moscow. Fuck, I pray she's here.

How am I even noticing hot men on planes and in airports right now? That is the last fucking shit I need to worry about. It's been three weeks since any of us have heard from Larisa. She might be out of touch for a few days, even a week, maybe. But where is my sister?

I swallow the gorge rising in my throat, and I fight back my fear as I take calming breaths. Being here brings back memories I wouldn't wish on anyone. I swore I would never return, but here I am. I keep coming back because it's the only way to see my family. *Where are you, Larisa?*

"*Dve-trista tridtsat' vosem' rubley.*" Two-thousand-three-hundred-thirty-eight rubles. A two-hour cab ride for about forty bucks isn't too horrible, even if I swear this car has no shocks at all. I felt every fucking rut in every road. We basically drove across Moscow from top to bottom.

I step out of the cab as the driver pops the trunk and walks to the back of it. I can't help but notice the three black vans that drive past. My heart races as I look around. Did my taxi driver signal them somehow? Where do I run? I'll have to leave my suitcase. Don't slow down. Don't turn around. Don't stop. Just keep driving. I'm no one.

As the second vehicle passes me, I'm certain I recognize the man in the passenger seat, but he doesn't look in my direction. What the fuck is he doing in this neighborhood? Nothing about his clothing, or that of his travel companions, says he belongs here. I watch as they pull up in front of a building a block away and pour out of the vehicle. This time, he does look in my direction, but he continues to walk. I glance at my driver before pulling money from my pocket. I won't let him see how much I'm carrying in my wallet.

"*Spasibo.*" Thank you.

I pull up the handle to my suitcase and roll it toward the apartment building across the street. When I reach the door, I have a clear view of the building the men went into, and my heart sinks. Nothing has changed. It's a furniture store to anyone passing by. But it's owned by the *pakhan*, or boss, of the Podolskaya around here. I recognize two of the men who greet them at the door. They're carrying rifles.

I dash inside before anyone sees me staring. Nosey means dead if you're looking in the wrong place. I push the button for the elevator and wait for it to arrive. I breathe a little easier when I step out and walk down the hall. The smell of cooking onions hasn't changed in thirty years. The sounds of televisions and people chatting filter to me through the walls. The walls are freshly painted, and the light bulbs are actually the energy efficient ones.

I've had my keys in my hand since I stepped out of the airport. They're the only defense I have right now besides my fists and feet. I unlock the door and walk in as I knock.

"Mama? Papa?"

"*Da. Ya na kukhne.*" Yes. I'm in the kitchen.

My mom hurries out and engulfs me in a hug that would make the world all right if it weren't so horribly fucked-up right now. I cling to her as I steel myself against crying. My mom's already been upset enough lately. She doesn't need to console me too. She kisses my cheeks before pulling me in for another hug. My parents speak only a few English phrases, so we continue in Russian.

"Where's Papa?"

"At the store."

I glance toward the window. He's at *that* store. The one those American men went into. No. They might live in America, but they were definitely Russian. They've just been away a long time.

"Have you heard anything today?"

"Nothing. No one has heard from Larisa at all. The police tried to track her phone, but there was nothing coming back. We've asked the *pakhan*, but he knows nothing. I believe him when he says he's made calls. Papa has been there for some of them. She just vanished."

My mom's tears start again, and she's trembling so much that I guide her to the sofa. I can no longer fight it. Ugly sobs wrack my body as I look around the apartment where I grew up. Everything is exactly the same as it was when I moved out ten years ago and got my own place. It's just as it was five years ago when I moved to New York, and how it's been every time

I've come home to visit. It's a time warp that makes life familiar and could fool me into thinking everything is the way it should be.

As my mom wipes her face, I disentangle myself and grab the box of tissues for her. I stand up and head down the hallway with my suitcase. I put it in my old room before I turn and open the door across from mine. Larisa's room is as much a shrine to her as mine is to me. My parents have changed nothing since we were teenagers. Larisa hasn't lived here in eight years either.

I hear my mom follow me, so I turn my head to look at her. She's aged so much in the twelve months since I last saw her. That was one of the best spring vacations I've had since becoming a school nurse. I've already lined up a substitute for at least a week after this break ends. I didn't get into any details with my principal, but I let her know I might go beyond my ten personal and sick leave days. They're the same thing in my district.

"Are you hungry?"

"Starving. The meal was gross on the plane, and I came straight here."

It makes me wonder what that guy ate in first class. I saw him pulling out a bag of cookies. Now that I think about it, they looked like *molochnyi korzhik*. Those definitely didn't come from the airline or any restaurant in JFK. I enter the kitchen behind my mom and look to the window that faces the street. If he's in that building, then I shouldn't give him a second thought.

There's not much for my mom and me to chat about while I eat leftovers from her dinner with my dad last night. I decide to take a shower and get changed. My bed is so tempting for a nap. My mom suggested it. Who knows when my dad will be back? I'm exhausted from more than just travel. I climb under the covers, and I'm out a few minutes later.

"Papa, I'm going to Larisa's. Her neighbors are way more likely to talk to me than anyone else. They know me, and I'm not a police officer or bratva. They all know I live in America now. They probably think I have some way to help because of that."

"They won't talk at all, Katerina. No one will say anything if they think it might wind up in the wrong person's ear."

"At least let me try."

"So you can wind up missing too?"

My mom never screams, but she just did. She's terrified, and I get it. But nothing has worked so far to learn where my sister went. She left for work and never came home. No one wants to say aloud what everyone's thinking. No one's found her body, so someone sold her somewhere.

"Semyon has already said he'll go with me."

"No. That's even worse." She turns to my father. "Vadim, don't let her go."

I'm not thrilled to see my ex-boyfriend any more than my parents are to hear his name. But he's a necessary evil in this case. I'm fairly certain he'll protect me, and I'm positive he knows the people to ask because they own the type of places pretty and vulnerable young women wind up in.

I can tell my dad is weighing the options. I can tell the moment he relents. He goes to the credenza beside the dining room table and lifts out a box. He puts it on the table and pushes it across to me. I flip open the lid and lift out the gun. I turn away from my parents, pointing it toward the floor. I check, and it's loaded. I lift it and position myself as though I'm about to aim. It feels more natural than it should. I'm wearing my American hiking boots, and I already have a sheathed knife beneath my pant leg and tucked into the shoe. My dad hands me a switchblade that I flick open and closed. That goes into my back pocket. If someone ties my arms behind me...It does me more good there than it would in a front pocket that's too tight to get my hand in easily. It also lets people know I'm armed, and someone trained me enough to know I should carry it there.

My dad hands me the waist holster. I make sure the safety is on before I lay the gun back in its box. I fasten the holster around me, then tuck the gun into my jeans at the small of my back. He gives me another magazine of bullets that I put in the purse I'll have slung across me.

My mother's crying again, and the guilt nips at me.

"Don't do this, Katerina. I'll end up with neither of my children."

"Mama, I have to try. Semyon won't take me to any of those places. He'll just be with me while I'm at Larisa's apartment. He'll bring me back before he goes to them."

I can't bring myself to say brothel in either language. Whorehouse is even worse. The very thing that broke us up may now save my sister. I found out how he liked to spend his time when he wasn't with me or working. We were through before I even told him. I have never been so angry at anyone in my life as I was with him. I told him it could have been his mother or sisters or me forced to live and work in one of those living hells. He'd shrugged and said it wasn't. It took all the restraint I could muster not to punch him. He was—is—the type who would punch back. That wasn't enough to make me leave him, but the whorehouses were.

"I need to go now if I'm going to make it back before it gets dark. I don't want to be out at night."

My dad nods, but I know the warning that is about to come.

"If you aren't back by sunset, I'm asking the *pakhan* to send men."

"No. Don't involve him any more than you have. I don't like knowing we owe him any favors. You know he keeps track despite your position. I don't want any of us indebted, and to be honest, I don't trust him to bring Larisa home if he finds her."

"*Vypolnyayte obeshchaniya, dannyye drugim voram.*" Make good on promises made to other thieves.

It's the last line of the *Vory v Zakone*, the thieves' code. The code also says don't have families, and yet here I stand. They may believe they live by the oath, but it's obvious some parts are selective these days. I don't trust a single person in the Podolskaya bratva to live by any of it.

"The code also says help other thieves, morally or materially. I don't see the *pakhan* rushing to your aid. He's waiting for you to ask, so he has one more way to control you. I'm not ready to give him that."

A knock interrupts what's about to become a heated conversation. I'm not even supposed to know a single word of the bratva oath, and I know the whole thing. It took a few years for me to learn not to be nosey.

I glance at my dad, who hurries to put the gun case away. I sweep my gaze over the living room to make sure nothing stands out before I open the door.

"Katerina, it's good to see you."

I know Semyon speaks passable English because I taught him, but he greets me in Russian for my parents' sake.

"Thank you for coming, Semyon."

There's not a damn good thing about seeing him, but he's a necessary evil.

"Mr. and Mrs. Vasiliev, it's nice to see you too."

I'm pretty sure my mom just bared her teeth at him. She's barely five feet tall, but I wouldn't wager against her in any fight. She can shoot as well as I do, which is like an expert. And more importantly, she has a Russian mother's tenacity. She'll chew him to shreds. He'd do well to remember to fear her more than my dad. It was my mom who made sure he understood he should never hit me again. I was dumb enough to stay with him, even after he learned that lesson. But he never hurt me again.

"Let's go. I want to be back before it's dark."

I lift my purse strap over my head and kiss my mom as she comes to stand by the door. Semyon and I remain quiet in the elevator, knowing voices carry. Once we're on the street, I look around. People are going about their business because things are fine—or at least normal—in their lives. A fresh wave of sadness hits me as I turn left. I see movement down the street, and two of the guards outside the furniture store raise their weapons.

"Stay behind me."

Semyon has his hand at his lower back like I do as he shields me. We continue walking as though we've seen nothing. The men from the flight leave as though no one's pointing a semiautomatic weapon at them as they climb into the cars. I catch only a glimpse of him. Then they're gone.

I exhale slowly as I reach into my purse for bus fare. It's not a long ride, and Semyon fills me on the little he's heard about Larisa. No one can make sense of it. She'd gone on one date with a man who turned out to be married and only visiting Moscow. She blocked his number and didn't talk to him. Two weeks later, she was gone. No one knows who this man was because she told no one his name. She only told me she found out he was married because she saw his phone screen light up, and it said "Wife."

We're headed to a restaurant first that Larisa liked and often went to with friends. I knew if I told my parents I was going to more than one place, they'd be even more upset. I hate lying to them, but I really believe I'm the one who'll learn something. Semyon stops to talk to someone he knows, so I go straight in. The moment I enter, I know I shouldn't have. Semyon's calling my name, and I'm standing toe-to-toe with the blond man. Fuck. He's way bigger up close.

Chapter Three

Misha

I feel like a goldfish in a bowl that's too small. Any and every one can see me, but it's safer inside. We can't wait outside because we're too exposed. But we won't go all the way into the restaurant until one of our guards sweeps the place. He's like a second cousin three times removed on my mom's side. I don't remember how we're related, but we've known each other since we were kids.

"*Katerina, nyet!*" Katerina, no!

I turn as a man calls out. I'm reaching for my gun as I come face-to-face with the woman from the airplane. Katerina. Beautiful name for a beautiful woman. She's staring at me wide-eyed before she takes a step backward, then another. She looks toward the door like she'll bolt, but she doesn't.

"Mr. Andreyev, she didn't know the restaurant is closed for a private party. She's leaving."

The maître d' rushes to explain in Russian as he moves as though he'll step between us and protect her. I glare at him.

"I don't hurt women."

She was about to make her escape, but my tone shocks her. Or maybe it's the tone and what I say. She watches me before she offers a tight smile. The man who must have called her name walks up, and I have a very different reaction.

"What're you doing here, Semyon? Your—" I glance at Katerina and decide better than to be vulgar. Something doesn't feel right. Like I would disappoint my mom if she ever found out. "Your place isn't around here unless you moved."

That's better than saying your balls finally dropped if you dare come around here. He's welcome in a Podolskaya neighborhood as much as we are. The reasons are different, but the welcome would be about as warm. As in frigid. She doesn't turn her head, but her gaze shifts to that walking turd.

"Nothing. We were leaving. We got the wrong address."

"You were a shitty liar when we were kids. You haven't gotten any better." I look at Katerina and switch to English. "Were you planning to have dinner here, and we interrupted your plans?"

"No. I hoped to see a friend, but I don't think they're here, anyway."

She answers in English. I know none of the restaurant staff speaks it, and Semyon only spoke broken English when I saw him nearly two years ago. I doubt it's any better. Only my family can understand us.

"Do you want to look around and see if they're here?"

She looks doubtful, but then she nods.

"I won't take long. I don't want to disturb your party."

She glances around, and nothing makes it look festive. She knows the maître d' meant we intend to eat alone. She's nervous, but she's not suspicious. She's used to this. That piques my curiosity. I think I make her uneasy more than realizing the real reason the place is empty. Is it just because she's from this neighborhood? Or is she the daughter of someone who comes to empty restaurants too?

"Excuse me."

She steps around me and almost runs into my dad. He steps aside. And so do Grigori, Sergei, and Anton. She appears less self-assured than she did when she was only looking at me. She hurries into the kitchen and disappears. I turn back to the others, and the maître d' leads us to a table where all of us can have our backs to walls. It's probably the most popular table in the establishment.

We've already ordered when she steps out of the kitchen. She's pale, and she looks like she's been crying. I'm out of my seat before I realize what I'm doing. I can already hear what Sergei and Anton are going to say when I get back. I step into her path.

"What happened? Who hurt you?"

She blinks away the tears as she raises her chin. She looks down at her arms, and I realize I grasped her biceps. My hold is light, and I don't let go, even when her eyes meet mine.

"No one hurt me, and it's not your business."

"Someone made you cry. I'm making it my business."

"Don't. I need to go. Sem's waiting for me."

My fingers flex for just a moment, tightening to tell her not to move.

"How do you know him?"

"We went to school together."

"And you're friends?"

The skepticism in my voice is heavy.

"That's not your business either."

"You just got off a flight from JFK wearing American clothes, and your English is as perfect as mine. He's a thug who keeps half the whores in Moscow employed."

She narrows her eyes at me and lowers her voice.

"I know exactly who he is and what he does. Let go."

"It's obvious you're from this neighborhood or nearby. But you are not safe with him. I've known him since I was a kid. He will hurt you as soon as he gets the chance."

I cock an eyebrow to make my point. She glances toward the door again, where I know Semyon is watching. Let him. He'll realize she's off limits.

"No, he won't. He's met my mom."

A twitch of a smile gets smothered as she looks around.

"So, he's hurt you before. Your mom wouldn't terrify a man like that unless she had reason to. She'd stay out of his way, and you'd be smart to do the same thing."

Her surprise is clear, and it tells me everything.

"Why would you go near him?"

"Katerina, we have to go if you're going to talk to them and be home before dark."

I glance over my shoulder, then back at Katerina.

"Prince Charming's worried your coach will turn back into a pumpkin."

"And he's announced that he plans to have me home before dark. If I'm not, then everyone here will know where to look."

"It doesn't have to be after dark for him to assault you or turn you over."

"I don't even know your name. Why does this matter to you?"

"It's Mikhail Andreyev. And it was that piece of shit's grandfather who took my friend's mother. You're lucky neither he nor his father have killed Semyon yet because he's no better."

She sucks in a breath and twists to see behind her. She looks up at me, then darts her gaze to Semyon. She's trying to decide, and there is a war going on in her head. I can tell when she decides, and I won't like it.

24

"I know Semyon way better than you do. Believe me. I wouldn't be with him if I didn't need to be. I have to go. Please let go."

I drop my hands.

"Does anyone else know you're with him? Would they know to start with him if something happens?"

"My parents do. I—thank you for trying. I don't think anyone else ever would. But I have to do this."

She steps around me, and I let her go. But I look over her head at one of our guards. I tilt my head, and he knows I expect him to follow her and give me a full report. There's something unsettling about letting her or any woman leave with that douchebag. But we're strangers. Short of holding her hostage, what can I do?

"Be careful."

"I will, Mikhail."

"Misha."

She walks away, and I'm left watching. Semyon looks like he wants to gloat, but he straightens and looks away as soon as he realizes I'm watching him. I offer him my most menacing expression while Kitty has her back to me. I don't return to the table until I can't see either of them.

As I walk back, I realize how I just thought of Katerina. It's a lot of jumps to get to it, but I suppose when you've spent the past fifteen hours thinking about a hot woman, that leapfrog makes sense. Katerina can be shortened to Kat. Kitty cats are also called pussycats. Her pussy is something I'd like to get to know a whole lot better. And I'd like to make her purr. Fuck. Am I sixteen? I suspect no one's ever called her Kitty for any reason. Why do I find the idea of having something that's special to just me so appealing? If I told anyone any of this, they'd think I was a perv. Maybe I am.

My dad raises both eyebrows, and we both look at Grigori

and Anton. To anyone else, they're completely calm. To my dad and me, they're seething. They recognize Semyon too. When Alina was fifteen, Semyon's grandfather and uncles kidnapped her on her way home from school. They didn't see my mom and Aunt Galina a couple blocks behind her. They would have taken them too. My mom is still beautiful, but Aunt Galina is beyond words. I've never met or even seen a woman more breathtaking than my aunt.

My mom and Aunt Galina ran the entire three miles home until they could find Grigori and Uncle Kirill. They were both the same size as Sergei, Anton, and me. Grigori and my dad aren't as bulky these days, but they were. It took them and my dad twelve hours to find Alina. They had done nothing to her except slap her around a little, but she was already at a notorious brothel. If they hadn't found her when they did, they might never have.

"What's she doing with him? She's comfortable with him."

My dad watches me, and I know I can't hide my thoughts from him any better than I can anyone else at this table. The rest of the world might think I'm indifferent, but they know I'm not. I mean, besides me rushing across the restaurant, to everyone else I look disinterested now.

"She said she's known him since they were kids. They went to school together."

"That means you went to the same school. Do you recognize her?"

My dad looks at Sergei and Anton, but they shake their head. Semyon was the same year as them.

"You sent Oleg to follow her."

"Yeah. She might be comfortable with him, but that doesn't mean he won't mistreat her. Her trust is misplaced."

There's not much else to say about Katerina, so we turn our attention to the disaster of a meeting we had. We've been speaking English at the table because we know there's slim chance anyone here can understand us. The place is little more than a hole in the wall.

"They swear it wasn't them. I still call bullshit."

Anton keeps his voice low when he says what we're all thinking.

"After all that shit with Ana, didn't they learn?"

Ana's my cousin Niko's wife. Members of the Podolskaya held a long grudge, and they targeted her. Only an hour or so after they got engaged in Greece, men took her. She's 1990s supermodel thin, so no one expected her to defend herself and our family like she did. I've seen a lot of blood and gore—a lot— but nothing prepared any of us for the sight we found when we rescued her.

It made most things Vladislav Lushak, the old Ivankov *pakhan*, taught us to do as torturers look like a slap on the wrist. She didn't have the fucked-up childhood that the Kutsenko and Andreyev brothers did, but she tapped into a darkness that we've unleashed before. We swore as teens never to allow it to control us, but we understand what drove Ana to such measures.

"You thinking of Ana?"

Sergei's expression says he was doing the same thing.

"Yeah. What happens if Katerina winds up in the same boat? What if that shitbag hands her over to the Podolskaya?" I shake my head. "This isn't what we're supposed to be talking about. Anyway, the Podolskaya broke the truce by killing Matvey. I cannot believe they had the balls to say they didn't do it. We all know they were avenging Gleb and Yaroslav."

Anton listens to me, but he doesn't sound surprised by the circumstances when he speaks. I suppose I'm not really either.

"You know it's only because they were Vlad's brothers.

They didn't do it to avenge Nikita, and he died the worst death. They felt obligated."

My dad huffs a disdainful laugh.

"They didn't avenge Nikita for two reasons. He wasn't Podolskaya, and they don't think dying the way he did at a woman's hand makes him man enough to be avenged. They opened an unhealed wound by going after Matvey. He may have been an informant, but not about them. At least he hadn't been in twenty years."

He'd kept an eye on a different bratva in Moscow. The funeral's in a few days, but we had what was supposed to be a civil sit-down with Timofey Golubev, the newest *pakhan*. He's only been in his position for six months, and he thinks he needs to prove himself. My *pakhan*, Maksim, is my cousin. He sent the five of us here, not only so Grigori and Papa could go to the funeral, and we could all pay our respects to his family, but to remind Timofey what happened the last time the Podolskaya reached too far. It's a dangerous proposition for my dad and Grigori to return to the bratva they fled. That's how much we want to make our point.

I listen to Anton as he speaks a moment later after taking a sip of water. It's the only thing we trust to drink here. We have men in the kitchen watching the chefs. Amazing how someone cooks with exactly the right amount of seasoning when a gun's pointed at their temple.

"Timofey's argument that all's fair here is bullshit. As if they could convince us that's why another branch got him. They did not agree to just leave us alone in the U.S. and everywhere but Russia. They were to leave us alone period. They were already minding their own business for the most part, so why now? They've already seen what happens when they don't."

Sergei looks at Anton as he speaks. As the *sovietnik*, the

head of our Security Group, my brother is our chief information gatherer. He's also a computer genius who can hack
anything, including the most secure government systems.

"When we get to the hotel, I'll pull up all the financials. We
tried negotiating. Now we get them where it hurts. They are
going to suddenly find themselves very broke. Without the
money, no one's loyal to them. The Izmailovskys have been on
good terms with the Podolsks until now, which has kept their
branches from murdering each other. But once the Podolskaya
can't provide for their people, the Izmailovo bratva will move
in. Let those two families and their *boyeviks* fight each other.
With no money, the Podolskaya won't hit us back soon, and
they'll be too busy trying to keep their old friends out of their
businesses. If we have to make it a little more obvious, then we
will."

Anton is his counterpart as the *obshchak*. He oversees the
Safety Group and forms all our strategies for our not so legal
operations, and he's our chief enforcer. They're known as the
Two Spies. If we have to take any real action while we're here,
Anton will plan it. Sergei and Anton have been best friends
since the cradle. They're only a few months apart in age, and
they've been inseparable since they were babies. Maks is the
same age and is super close to them both, but it's not the same.
They've been *together* since high school. Our family has a lot of
secrets we'll take to our grave, but that's the biggest, especially
while we're in Russia. But I'm happy for them. I've never seen a
couple more in sync with each other.

"We—"

Grigori snaps his mouth shut as someone enters the restaurant through the back door. Our left hands slip into our trouser
pockets ready to pull our knives as we all lean far enough away
from the backs of our chairs to reach for our guns.

"Vadim, what're you doing here?"

My dad stands and pushes back his chair. The rest of us look around. We startle him, but it's almost impossible to tell. He approaches our table slowly and tries to keep his voice light.

"I was looking for a friend who works in the kitchen. I thought about slipping in and having a quick chat about him and his wife coming to dinner this weekend. Go back to your meal."

The waiter has just arrived with our plates, but none of us are interested, even if we're all starving. The airline hardly served portions large enough to do more than tide any of us over. We went straight to the meeting after the two-hour drive, so none of us has eaten more than the third bag of my mom's cookies.

"Join us."

My dad makes the offer, but Vadim shakes his head.

"Dariya will have dinner ready soon. I need to head back. It was good seeing you."

He doesn't wait before he hurries into the kitchen. He's aggravated when he steps out of the kitchen, but his expression goes neutral a heartbeat later. Most people would miss it. He meant for whomever he talked to in the kitchen to know they annoyed him. He's my dad's age, and I would bet former KGB too. He's like us because he won't show his emotions unless he wants people to know. But he's not so much like us that we can't read him.

Grigori leans forward to whisper.

"What the hell was that about?"

I have my own suspicions, and they're about five-foot-five with sandy blonde hair and blue-hazel eyes.

Chapter Four

Kitty

It's not like every neighborhood in Moscow is ready for a gang shoot out. There are plenty of nice ones where the word bratva means somebody else's problem. The communities Larisa and I lived in were like that. We were only twenty minutes from our parents, but both areas have next to no bratva involvement. Until three weeks ago, it let my parents sleep soundly at night.

"Do you have her key?"

Semyon holds the elevator door open for me as I walk out. I put my sister's key on my keyring when I woke up for my nap. It's been in my hand the entire time. It pressed into my palm while I clenched my fist throughout speaking to Misha. The caduceus charm with the two snakes coiled around the staff, a symbol of the medical field, left an imprint.

"Yeah. Here."

I have my hand around the pistol grip, ready to draw it if anyone other than my sister is on the other side of the door.

Semyon has been shockingly chivalrous today, insisting that he go first and has been watching my back any time he could.

He eases the door open; when nothing happens, he pushes it open all the way. I step inside, and nothing looks out of place. I search through every drawer and cabinet. I pull stuff out from underneath her bed and look at every bottle in her bathroom. It all seems completely normal. I know I'm not the first person to go through her things. My parents have for sure. But I prayed that somehow, as her sister, something would stick out to me.

"I'm going to knock next door and see if anyone is home."

I try Larisa's first neighbor, but no one comes to the door. I try the one across the hall, and a woman in her early thirties answers. I try not to get my hopes up. I assume she doesn't speak English, so I continue in Russian like I have been with everyone but Misha. *Misha.* For fuck's sake. He's the last thing I need to think about right now.

"Hi. I'm looking for my sister. She lives next door."

The woman's expression grows suspicious. Is it because she doesn't want to get involved? Or she doesn't believe me? Or she knows something?

"I haven't seen her in weeks."

"Neither has my family. We're really scared. Do you remember the last time you saw her?"

"Yeah. It was the day before everyone came looking for her."

"Everyone? Do you mean my parents or the police?"

"I saw your parents several days later, but the others definitely weren't the police. At least not the kind that's been around since I've been alive."

My brow furrows.

"Do you mean like KGB?"

They've been gone since 1991. They were just a history lesson to me.

"Yeah."

The woman looks around me as though she expects someone to jump out at her.

"Bratva?"

The woman's eyebrows shoot sky high. Maybe not.

"No. At least, I don't think so. I've never met anyone who's in the bratva. Possibly."

"Did they have guns?"

"Not that I saw. They dressed professionally, but they—I don't know—weren't men you'd want to get in the way of."

That sounds a lot like bratva, especially since plenty of former members of the KGB basically got conscripted into the various branches. This gives me a hint, but there are still too many possibilities.

"Do you know anything else? She's my little sister, and my parents are terrified. So am I. I came all the way back here from America to help find her."

A speculative gleam enters the woman's eyes, and I could kick myself. Now she's going to bribe me.

"I spent all of my savings to get here."

The woman just nods. So much for her impromptu plan.

"What's your name? I'm Katerina."

"Katya."

"So similar."

"That's what your sister said the first time we met."

"Thank you. If you think of anything, please let me know."

I give her the number to the burner my dad got me while I'm here in case my regular one didn't work. It does. But I'm not giving out that number if I don't have to. I have nearly the same conversation with three more people on my sister's floor. One woman heard Larisa refuse to answer the door two days before she went missing. That was after her accidental and disastrous date with the married guy. The neighbor saw Larisa arrive after work, so she knew my sister was home. But Larisa wouldn't open the door when a man knocked. She said the guy gave up pretty quickly. But who knows if he really did? Did he wait outside until she left? Did he come back? Did he send someone?

I have no real answers as Semyon and I make our way downstairs, but I don't think my parents knew about the men coming to Larisa's place or this one guy. I need to ask my dad if the bratva is moving into this area. Could it be Podolskaya? Did my dad fuck up somehow, and this is revenge? They would have told him by now to make all of us suffer.

The sun's already gone down. My parents are going to flip. I nudge Semyon.

"We have to hurry."

"The bus will come when it comes. We aren't going to miss it."

He points to the bus stop that's half a block away. There's no one there, and I don't see any form of public transportation anywhere. Not even a cab. I look around, and my unease grows. I remind myself that I'm in a good neighborhood where people pay attention to what happens. They'd respond if someone cried out for help.

We pass into a shadow, and all my senses scream, "get ready to run." I reach back and slide my knife from my pocket. I flick it open and keep it pressed to the outside of my thigh.

"Sem, hurry."

I look over at him because he's fallen a pace or two behind. We both hear someone approaching. He reaches for my arm and grasps it as we get ready to run. A massive shape steps onto the sidewalk, and I pull my gun without hesitation. In one fluid movement, I have the safety off, my finger on the trigger, and the pistol pointed at my target.

"At least you have some sense."

What the fuck?

"Misha?"

He steps far enough forward for me to see him clearly thanks to the streetlight that just came on. I don't lower my gun until he's standing in front of me and pushing my arms down. I relent, putting the safety back on.

"I'm glad you didn't shoot me, *malyshka*. But we both know that if I'd been after you, I wouldn't be alone. You might have killed me, but what about the others who would have been ready to catch you?"

I glance around and see the same Volkswagen van from earlier. The sliding door is open, and I can see the men Misha was with are waiting. The two younger ones are grinning, and the two older ones look bored. Are those guys laughing at me or him?

"My brother's going to have a field day with how fast you drew that gun on me."

"Because I was faster than you?"

"No. If I intended to aim my gun at you, you'd already be dead. He's going to say I'm a fool to trust that you wouldn't be as trigger-happy as most men around here."

"So, you are carrying one."

He just cocks an eyebrow. He's not wearing a suit coat now, and his shirt is unbuttoned at the top. It's not just the collar. It's the regular top button too. It shifts as he steps forward, his hands out to his sides. I feel my eyes widen. Oh, fuck. Oh, fuck. Oh, fuck. And not like the kind I wish I were saying while he makes me come. I shake my head and take a step back as he continues to approach.

"Are you Podolskaya too?"

"Too? Definitely not."

There's a hardness to his tone and expression that wasn't

there a moment ago. I point to his right shoulder. He knows what I saw.

"Then who are you?"

"I'm Ivankov."

My brow furrows. I don't know that one.

"*Malyshka*, this is not the right time of day for any of us to stand out here chatting about this." He turns to Semyon and speaks to him in Russian. I hadn't realized we were speaking English until just now. "Go away."

There's such command in his voice that I fear what would happen to Semyon if I wasn't there. But my ex shakes his head and tries to step between Misha and me.

"And leave her to you, Andreyev? Like hell."

He ignores Semyon and keeps looking at me.

"You don't belong at a brothel. A, because you don't look like it, and b, because you're in a decent neighborhood. Why are you with him? If you've known him since you were kids, then you must know he—"

"He's my ex-boyfriend. We dated for five years."

I can't believe I just blurted out all of that. Misha's gazes bores into me, and I wish I could melt into the sidewalk. He takes a menacing step forward, then another and another until he's standing in front of Semyon. He towers over my ex-boyfriend by at least three or four inches, and he's gotta be at least forty pounds heavier than him. And it's all muscle.

"Run."

"I'm not doing shit, you—"

Misha's hand whips out and wraps around Semyon's throat.

"There is only one woman who has stayed with you for that long, and I've heard how you treated her. I heard how you hurt her. You're nowhere near as big as me, but you're still way bigger than her. Run, or I will show you what it felt like to be her. Except I will kill you at the end."

I don't doubt a word Misha's saying. It should freak me all the way out, but it doesn't. The bitter part of me who still hasn't completely healed from my years with the bastard wouldn't mind if someone beat him to death. Lord knows I prayed he would die plenty of times.

Misha releases Semyon, so he can speak.

"Yeah, I was a shit boyfriend to her. I'm lucky her parents didn't kill me and neither did she. I'd have deserved it if they had. But I'm not leaving her alone with you, Misha. She may not trust me with much, but she knows me. Her parents know me. I'm not leaving her side until she's at her parents' place. So, fuck off."

I glance behind Misha to the waiting van. I look at Semyon, then at Misha. Please don't let this be the worst decision I've ever made. I step closer to Misha.

"Go home, Sem. Misha will make sure I get home."

"So, you're suddenly best friends? You going to fuck him the first night like you did me? She gives great—"

Misha's fist flies forward as his other hand goes back around Semyon's throat. I'm a nurse, but it doesn't take being one to know Misha broke his nose and likely shattered his cheekbone. He's already going purple from how tightly Misha's squeezing. I reach out my hand and put it on his forearm. Misha doesn't look at me, but I feel the tension in his arm ease. He punches Semyon again and lets him fall to the ground. He drives his foot into my ex-boyfriend's ribs.

"Do not think for a moment that anyone will defend you. Even if Timofey weren't so fucked right now, he wouldn't give a shit about you. He'd buy me dinner for getting rid of you."

I'm unprepared for Misha to thrust his hand out to me. I'm

unprepared for all of this except for the part where I'm willing to shoot to defend myself. I place my hand in his, and I'm shocked at how gentle his hold is. I let him lead me to the van, but I stop him before either of us climbs in. We need to get off the streets, and I need to call my parents. But I need to know who he really is. Andreyev rings a bell, but it's not that uncommon a last name.

"You said you're Ivankov. Which district is that?"

"It's not here. It's New York."

I'm not sure what to say. Misha's watching me, waiting to take his cues from me.

"I never go to Brighton Beach. I'm rarely in Queens. I—"

"What's your last name, Katerina?"

"Vasilieva."

"Vadim's daughter? He was looking for you earlier at the restaurant."

"You know my dad?"

Misha's expression tells me how stupid that question was. I bite my lip but decide to ask anyway.

"Your star. You're Elite Group. What are you?"

"I'm not part of the Elite Group, but I'm the most senior *avotoritet*."

The authority. A brigadier. Plenty of men move in and out of that position as far as I know. It depends on what they're doing and who's assigned to lead. Even Elite Group members, the senior-most members who advise the *pakhan* directly, can be *avotoritets* if needed. He's important if he got an eight-point star for it. It signifies a high rank and plenty of influence.

"Are they?"

He knows I'm asking about his family. Our gazes lock, but he says nothing. It's a standoff, and I'm suddenly way too tired to do this.

"If you know I'm Vadim's daughter, then you know he's the *derzhatel obshchaka*."

It means the bookkeeper. My dad's an accountant who knows how to do a hell of a lot more than run reports.

"You've already told me which branch you are, even if it is in New York. You're not keeping your tats well hidden, and I get why. It doesn't scare me, but it will scare most people. I'm about to get into a car with you and five other men and trust that you'll take me home. It sounds like things between the Podolskaya and the Ivankovs aren't good, but I'm trusting you right now. I think I deserve to know who's my firing squad or my saviors."

"Firing squad or saviors?"

"You know what I mean."

"Do you know the name Kutsenko?"

I twist toward the open side of the van before I spin back to Misha. I'm more scared now than I have ever been in my entire life. I'm completely unprepared for Misha to wrap his arm around my waist and draw me against his chest.

"Shh, *malyshka*. They're my cousins. We are not going to hurt you. Not my family or our driver. We're going to take you home, and I'm going to walk you to your door. My brother is our *sovietnik*. The other guy his age is our *obshchak*. Our dads are mostly retired."

"Retired? How American."

I can't believe I just made a joke, and he chuckled. He smooths my hair back as he eases his hold on me, but he doesn't let go. He's just told me that his brother is one of the Two Spies, and I recognize the name Kutsenko. They run the bratva in New York. I know that from conversations I overheard before I left Moscow. The story goes the Kutsenkos' dad and uncles were all Podolskaya until their dad died. They left to go to America and got forced into the bratva there.

"I'm too tired to make sense of half of this. Thank you for taking me home."

He leads me to the open door of the van. I notice the two younger guys moved so that the dark-haired one is crammed between the two older men, and Misha's twin is in the front passenger seat. They left the second-row bench for Misha and me. I'm about to step in when Misha stops me.

"Normally, I would always let you into the car first. But I don't want you next to the window. If anything happens, my dad and brother will protect you on the other side."

I take a deep inhale to calm my completely frazzled nerves now as Misha climbs in first. He offers me his hand as I scramble in. I'm too tired to be graceful. It's not a long ride, but I feel myself getting sleepy. If I just take a long blink for a moment. I look up as Misha slips his arm around my shoulder and nudges my head to his shoulder. He kisses my forehead gently before he whispers so quietly, I almost think I've already fallen asleep and am dreaming.

"Sleep for a few minutes, *malyshka*. I'll protect you."

Chapter Five

Misha

I keep my eyes straight ahead for the first mile. Then I'm back to scanning out all the windows. The van is quiet, and I know everyone else is as tired as Kitty, but no one else will nap. *Kitty*. The name's stuck. I glance down at her and tighten my hold around her shoulders. No one told us Vadim was looking for Kitty, but I'd already figured it out. Then she confirmed it. I know enough about Vadim's family and about Semyon to be certain she's the girlfriend he beat up frequently. From what I know, it wasn't all the time. But that doesn't matter to me. It happened even once—he even thought about doing it once.

Vadim hasn't had to let him live because of who he is, but who his grandfather and uncles are. They're the Elite Group. It means he remains untouchable. At least to everyone but me. I'll put a bullet between his eyes. He's a waste of a human being, so it makes me wonder why Kitty went anywhere near him. What does he have or know that she's willing to trust him even an inch?

As I wonder that, I gaze down at her as my thumb sweeps back and forth over her upper shoulder. I'm feeling possessive in a way I never have in my life. As the youngest of basically eight brothers, nothing has been just mine. At least not much. I would make Kitty mine, but this is not the time to be thinking about that. But it's the only thing I can think about. I was mostly just the muscle at the meeting earlier today. My dad and Grigori did the talking. Sergei and Anton were the silent threat to destroy Timofey and the Podolskaya. And I was just there to flex my muscles that even custom suits are tight around when I cross my arms.

I'm protective though. Nothing is more important to me than family. There's nothing I won't do to protect them, whether they're related to me by blood or by marriage. As I glance down at Kitty, I realize I'd do the same for her. Sergei and Anton have been together for nearly twenty years, even if they've never lived together and no one outside the family knows. Maks and Laura have been married for just over two years, and Christina and Bogdan are close to that. Niko and Ana have been married a year, and Pasha and Sumiko aren't that far behind. Aleks and Heather got married just after New Year's. I'm the last bachelor standing.

Our thieves' code says we aren't to have families, but it makes no sense, really. Bratva is often hereditary, so families are necessary to keep the lines going. I swore I wouldn't marry because I wouldn't bring anyone into this life, and I don't want to create a new generation that's forced into the mafia. But as Kitty dozes beside me, her body completely relaxed, it makes me rethink all of this.

She's Vadim's daughter, so she knows what the bratva life is. I'm certain she already knew what I was. It was just the star signifying my senior rank that freaked her out. She was wary before she knew. Hearing the Kutsenko name definitely made her want to bolt. No one outside our world in New York knows for certain what our ties are. But there are plenty of rumors, since all four of my cousins are billionaires in their own right. Sergei, Anton, Pasha, and I aren't there yet. We're merely millionaires. As I watch us enter my old neighborhood, it's surreal to know how far we've come.

When I glance at the furniture store that's a front for Timofey, I see all the lights are off. That doesn't mean people aren't in the basement. I nudge Kitty.

"*Malyshka*, wake up. We're at your parents'."

She looks up at me with sleepy eyes, and I realize she'd slept deeper than I realized. She looks around, her cheeks flaming when she sees my family. The driver gets out and comes around to open the door. A streak of possessiveness courses through me as I watch Kitty put her hand in his as she steps down. I know I'd be pissed if he didn't, but I irrationally don't like it.

"We'll stay here."

My dad's letting Kitty know we won't assume we're welcome in her parents' home. We've already discussed this while we waited for Kitty to come out of the apartment building she went into with Semyon. They all knew I wouldn't back down about making sure she got home safely, so no one said anything against it. I suggested I go up with her and see Vadim. There has to be a good reason for her to be with her shitbag ex and for Vadim to say he was looking for a friend when we know he was looking for her.

"I'll walk you to your door."

"You really don't have to."

I don't respond except to wrap my arm around her again. She tries to step away as her eyes dart around. My fingers press against her upper arm, and my next step brings our sides together. The pressure isn't enough to scare her, but it warns her not to pull away again. Once we're inside, I release her.

"You know people saw us. You may as well have announced to the entire neighborhood that we're fucking."

"But we aren't." *Yet.*

"You claimed me like a whore because no one will believe we're dating."

"Why not? Because you wouldn't be with a criminal? Because you've sworn off bratva men? We arrived at the same time from New York. Plenty of people would believe that's not a coincidence."

She glowers at me as we step onto the elevator. She pushes the button for her parents' floor before she turns back to me.

"*Malyshka*—"

"I am not your baby girl. Why do you call me that? You have no right."

That's a good question and an accurate point. But who am I kidding? I've thought of her this way since the start. I had plenty of time to consider what it would mean to bring her into my life and what that would look like. Surviving the upbringing I had meant being able to deeply analyze a situation or facts and come to a decisive conclusion quickly. I've played out various scenarios already today, and I already know where I want this to go.

"Not yet, maybe."

"Not ever."

I take a step closer and peer down at her. She doesn't step away, and the defiance from a moment ago slips away. I ease my arm around her waist again, and she doesn't push at my chest or tense. I keep my voice low since I don't want anyone to hear us.

"I've never called another woman that in my life. But I think you could do with someone to look out for you. And if you were with Sem for five years, then you definitely deserve someone to take care of you."

"And you think that should be you."

"We both know it will be."

"Your certainty is rather pushy."

"But you aren't disagreeing."

My free hand cups her cheek, and she closes her eyes.

"How are you so gentle? No one your size should be. No one who does what you do ever is."

"Because I will never intentionally hurt you, Kitty."

I'm the one who tenses as that slips out. Her eyes snap open as her brow furrows.

"Why'd you call me that?"

"Instead of *malyshka?*"

I offer her a soft smile.

"That too."

"Would you let me kiss you before I answer that?"

"My guess is I won't like the explanation."

I shrug. She waits a moment, then nods. She tilts her head back before our lips meet. Holy hell. I've kissed plenty of women, but nothing has felt like this. Her lips are plump and soft. Her body feels amazing pressed against mine. She smells divine. Something floral. As she opens to me, I swipe my tongue inside her mouth. I can taste the gum she must have chewed earlier. There's a hint of cinnamon lingering. She sighs as I deepen the kiss.

When she slips her arms around my waist, I don't stop her. I've never let a woman do that while I'm carrying my gun. I've always kept their hands away, so I don't have to explain. But I've already felt her gun twice and seen it. Her hands wander over my back while mine slip to her ass. She's wearing the sweater she had tied around her waist earlier. Her ass is soft and firm at the same time. I don't know how, but I want to do things—dirty, dirty things—to it and with it. I squeeze, but not enough to hurt. She arches her back, so I tighten my grip. Each bit of extra pressure makes her press herself against me.

I slide one hand up her back and fist her hair. I hold her head in place and take control of the kiss. Her fingers dig into my shoulders, and she moves like she can't get close enough.

"Is this what you like?"

"Yes."

It's a breathless answer. I pull away and turn toward the button panel and hit the stop one. I press her toward the wall until her back is against it.

"I've wanted this since the moment I saw you. Every time I'm near you, I want you more, Kitty. Tell me to stop. Tell me this isn't a good idea."

"I can only do one of those. Kiss me, please."

I dive in for another as I slip a leg between her thighs and press against her pussy. It's her turn to pull back.

"I've never kissed a man the day I met him. Semyon lied when he said I was with him the day we met. I was ten. We can't keep the elevator stopped for forever. Do you just want a quick fuck to say you had me?"

"I will not say anything about what we've done to anyone. It's no one's fucking business but ours. A quick fuck. A long fuck. And everything in between is what I want. But our first time will not be in an elevator."

"First time?"

"Do you only want it to be once?"

"I never said I wanted it or agreed with it to begin with, let alone multiple times."

"You haven't said it out loud, but we've both made it clear. Baby girl, right now is probably the worst time for me to think about being with anyone. But it's all I've been able to think

46

about. We both live in New York. Will you let me take you on a date once we get back?"

"A date?"

"Yes. You can feel how much I want you, *malyshka*. But I can wait until you want that as much, too. In the meantime, I'd like to get to know you better. I'd like to take you out."

"And if I want both?"

Her voice is barely more than a whisper.

"A date and to fuck?"

"Yeah."

"All you ever have to do is tell me what you want, baby."

"This is a horrible time for me to be doing this. I can't believe I'm even considering this, let alone kissing you in an elevator. But I can't stop thinking about you, too. I'll go on a date with you. And I want—" Her shoulders slump. "There's no way for anything more right now."

"I'm not going anywhere. My dick and me will be ready when you are."

I flash her a smile before I press the button, and the elevator rises until it gets to her floor. I look around before I step aside and let her pass first. I walk her to her door, and I'm ready to leave as soon as she unlocks it. But she doesn't turn the handle. Instead, she tugs my shirt, so we're not visible through the peephole. She raises her chin again, and I swoop in for a second time. I nip and tug at her lip before my tongue tangles with hers. I squeeze her ass enough to hurt, but she doesn't shy away.

"Is that how you like it? Do you a little pain with your pleasure?"

"I think you could give me that in the only way I've ever wanted it, but I've never gotten it."

Her gaze tells me how earnest she is. It makes me want to murder Sem. She wants it rough—the sex, that is—not the beatings he used to give her.

"I'm not him. I will never hurt you. You will never have to accept what I want at your expense, Kitty. I may like control, and I may insist on leading, but we're equals in all of this. When you say stop, it ends immediately. What you want matters. Always."

"If only I could just follow when it comes to everything else in my life now, too."

I cup her face in both hands and press a soft kiss to her lips.

"Why are you here?"

"My sister is missing, and I think the Podolskaya took her."

Her eyes well with tears, and I pull her against me. She clings to me and tries to burrow closer. But the door swings open, and we both turn to see her father in the doorway. He recognizes me immediately, and he lets me see his anger as he speaks in Russian.

"We heard the door unlock, but you never came inside. What is he doing out here? You never said you knew Katerina when I saw you at the store or the restaurant. Katerina, you never mentioned you knew the Andreyevs. But you seem to know each other pretty well."

"Vadim, may I come in?"

Kitty and I always seem to use English, but I respond to Vadim in Russian. He glares at me before he looks at Kitty. His lips flatten, but he moves out of the way. I wait for her to go ahead of me before I enter. My gaze sweeps the entire living room, down the hallway we pass, and into the fraction of the kitchen I can see. I'm memorizing every detail. It's a modest home with nice furniture and the best TV you can get in Russia.

Kitty walks around to a credenza as Vadim gestures for me to sit. I watch her remove the gun from the holster, check it, and put it back in a case that's sitting on top of the piece of furniture. She handles it with ease, and her stance was expert-level when she drew it on me. I remain standing since my parents would throttle me if I sat before Kitty did. Her mom joins us, but she stares at me rather than sitting in the chair she's standing beside.

"Mama, this is Misha Andreyev. He brought me home."

"It's nice to meet you." She turns to Kitty. "Where's Semyon? I thought he promised to bring you home."

"I decided it was better to stay with Misha once we ran into each other."

"Hello, Mrs. Vasilieva."

I offer her my hand, and she takes it with some reluctance.

"How are your parents and Grigori and Alina?"

"Everyone is well. Papa and Grigori are with me."

"I heard."

That halts the conversation. Kitty comes to stand next to me and looks around. She sits, and her parents follow her. I take the spot beside her on the sofa. It's not very long, so it keeps us close to each other. I pull my phone out.

"I'm going to let my family know I'll be a little longer than I expected."

I pull up the texts and scroll until I see Sergei's name.

ME

Something serious happening with Vadim's family. Staying up here to find out. Go to the hotel. I'll get there later.

SERGEI

What's wrong? And no, you are not going to the hotel alone.

ME

His other daughter is missing. Send a driver back.

SERGEI

Fine. Should Papa come up?

ME

No.

SERGEI

Text when you need the driver.

ME

Will do. Gotta go.

I slide my phone back into my pocket. I look at Kitty who could see my screen as I typed. I wonder if she's pissed that I told Sergei. I wasn't going to at first, but this isn't some inconsequential thing I can mention when I get around to it.

"Papa, I just told Misha that Larisa is missing. He and I ran into each other twice tonight, but I didn't say what I was doing."

"Do you know each other?"

I answer this one.

"Not that well yet. When did your daughter go missing?"

"Three weeks ago."

It's Kitty's mom who answers. She's studying me intently, and I think I may get her approval. But hearing it's been three weeks makes my stomach knot. The likelihood that they'll find her now is next to none. I look at Kitty and try to keep my tone light.

"That's why you were with Semyon."

"Sorta. I would never go to *those* places with him, and he said he would ask around tonight. But I know him, and I knew I couldn't go asking questions anywhere alone."

I look at Vadim, who looks anything but pleased to hear Semyon's name. I glance at Dariya, who I vaguely remember meeting as a kid. She looks pissed. What the hell did Semyon have on them or Kitty that they didn't keep her away from him?

"There's no one else?"

"Not unless I want it to be a Polodsk, which I don't. I don't want any of us to be indebted to Timofey for anything, so I will not ask for any of his men. The Podolskaya stays out of this, especially since I think they did it."

Kitty meets her mother's gaze before shifting to lock eyes with her father.

"They are not involved. They wouldn't take one of our own."

I scoff and shake my head as though he's stupid. He is if he believes that.

"Like they didn't take Alina. Like they weren't after my aunt. Uncle Kirill and Aunt Galina had four kids in four years to keep the Podolskaya away from her. I'll never know all the details, but Uncle Kirill, Grigori, and my dad did things to Yaroslav and Gleb to make sure they stayed away from Aunt Galina. Whatever they did took part of Vlad's finger and kept him away from Aunt Galina for a decade after Uncle Kirill died. And I'm sure you know it was Maksim who made sure Vlad never tried again. He became *pakhan* the next day."

I look at Kitty before I continue.

"Do you know how Gleb and Yaroslav died? They took my cousin Niko's wife only hours after she became his fiancée." I look back at Vadim. "They took a Kutsenko's woman. You really think they wouldn't take your daughter if they were willing to do that."

"Gleb and Yaroslav held a grudge against your family and Anastasia's. It's not the same."

"Maybe not the same. But if they will go up against the Kutsenkos and Andreyevs, then they would take anyone's daughter. You're not part of the Elite Group, but you're close enough. You had to know your *pakhan* gave Gleb and Yaroslav the go-ahead for Ana's kidnapping. You had to know what they planned for her."

"Papa?"

"I did. And if I'd tried to stop them we'd all be dead. I still don't believe it's them. Larisa is beautiful, but she's not like Galina was. They took Alina because of Grigori. They thought they could force him in, but the KGB got to him first. They knew if Grigori joined, Kirill and Radomir would, too. They should have feared Grig as much as they did Kirill. I saw what they left of Semyon's grandfather and uncles after Grig got Alina away from them. Kirill and Radomir just made sure they each waited their turn. I don't know how they survived."

They—Sem's family—ended up forcing my dad, Uncle Kirill, and Grigori to join once the men in my family left the KGB. But my relatives made a reputation for themselves that meant most men wouldn't look in my mom's direction or Aunt Galina's and Alina's. Best friends with rhyming names. They said it was always meant to be.

Vadim's phone rings, and he looks at the screen. Something's wrong. The blankness to his expression tells me he's hiding something. Why doesn't he look relaxed?

"*Privet.*" Hello. "*Da...Da...Nyet...*" Vadim looks at me as he speaks. "*Ya budu pryamo seychas. Ya dumayu, u menya yest' sposob. Spasibo.*" I will right now. I think I have a way. Thank you.

Vadim's gaze doesn't waver as he hangs up.

"I'm going to trust you with Katerina. I will kill you if anything happens to her. I need you to hide her."

Chapter Six

Kitty

"Papa?"

"Vadim?"

My mom and I speak at the same time. What the hell was that call about? Who was that?

"Misha, I need you to take Katerina somewhere safe. You or someone in your family needs to stay with her. Someone found out she was asking around. They saw her with Semyon and assumed he was bringing her to one of the brothels. When he showed up at a few without her, someone got pissed. One call after another got whoever this is enough information to know she's my daughter and Larisa's sister. Then someone saw you walking with her here. I don't know who it is, and neither did my informant. But they want her."

Misha already has his phone out again and is texting his brother. I can see the screen just like before.

MISHA

Get here now. K is coming with me.

There're a few minutes pause while my dad's shooting off texts too, to God knows who.

SERGEI

On our way. Where to next?

MISHA

Hotel for now.

SERGEI

What happened? Injuries?

MISHA

No. Tell you when I see you. Get here now old man.

SERGEI

Coming little brother. Don't be bossy.

Old man? Aren't they the same age? Does Sergei call him little brother because Misha's a few minutes younger?

He shoves his phone in his pocket as he stands.

"My family will be here in twenty minutes or so. You need to leave, too."

"We know. We have somewhere to go. But I don't trust anyone other than you and your family. Do not let that be misplaced. Your family's reputation when it comes to not harming women and defending them is legendary. I'm counting on that with my daughter."

"Papa, won't whoever this is be pissed if you're not here? They'll know you ran."

"They can know whatever the hell they want as long as you and your mama are nowhere near here. Pack."

54

The command is for my mom and me. We both hurry down the hallway to the bedrooms. I hear my dad talking to Misha, but I can't tell what he's saying. It's only a moment later that Misha slips into my room and closes the door behind him. He puts his finger to his lips and comes to stand in front of me. He tucks hair behind my ear and leans in to whisper.

"I don't trust your home not to be bugged. Anything we say, we whisper. Your dad didn't exaggerate. The surest way to wind up dead is for someone to come after the women in my family. Whoever called your dad found out or saw me with you. He knew I'm protecting you. It's why they tipped your dad off rather than letting whoever this is come here. You stay by my side anytime we aren't alone or with my family. If we're in public, you're holding my hand, or my arm is around you. Kitty, it's not just for appearances. It'll be harder to snatch you if I'm holding onto you. And most importantly, the idea of being more than six inches away from you right now may make me go crazy."

"I don't want you involved in this shit. But I'm glad you are. Misha, please don't disappoint me. If this is a set up, then just kill me now. I have money. Probably more than anyone would pay you here."

I'm not prepared for him to spin me around, press me onto the mattress, and spank me. Hard. He lands five stinging blows to my ass before he pulls me upright and into his arms.

"Do not *ever* say something so disgusting to me *ever* again. I don't fucking buy and sell women. I will never intentionally hurt you or disappoint you, *malyshka*. Nothing in the elevator was acting. I didn't lie when I said I want to go out with you. We're about to live together for the foreseeable future. You'll learn just what kind of man I am soon enough."

I wrap my arms around him and burrow against his chest like I did before. I know there's no fucking time for this, but I need it. I'm scared out of my mind, but in Misha's arms, I feel like I might survive whatever is going on.

"Did you already unpack?"

Misha kisses the top of my head before he steps back.

"No. I was going to do it tonight. I'm ready to go."

"All right. I'm going back into the living room. Go spend the last few minutes with your parents, baby girl."

I make to step away, but we both think better of it. I go onto my toes as he presses his body against me. I can feel how hard he is for me. Any other time. Our kiss is short but intense. He gives my backside a light tap.

"Ouch."

But I flash him a quick smile. He takes my bags and heads to the living room while I knock on my parents' door. My dad opens it, and I step in before he closes it.

"Who was on the phone?"

My dad shakes his head but pulls out his phone. He shows me his call log. Holy shit. It's Timofey's son. He's a *shestyorka*. An errand boy who stands look-out or gathers info. It's the lowest position, but it's usually temporary. Either the boy becomes a full member, or he's cast aside. He's fifteen if I remember correctly. He's old enough to understand the consequences if anyone finds out. How badly does he hate his father to risk his life like this? Or how close is he to my dad to be this loyal?

He leans to whisper in my ear like Misha did.

"If it wasn't the Andreyevs and Kutsenkos, I would take you with us. You can trust them, Katerina. After what their family went through to keep the women safe, they'd die before dishonoring their parents or wives. Listen to Misha and the others. They'll keep you safe. I can tell you already trust Misha. I don't know how you know each other or how well, but trust that instinct. If anything happens and you get separated from them, you get on the soonest flight to anywhere in America. I will contact you. Don't call or text. I hate that, but it's the only way we all stay safe."

"All right, Papa. Do you and Mama really have somewhere to go?"

"Yes. It's away from Moscow."

My grandfather's hunting cabin. It's in the middle of nowhere. Truly. There isn't another house for at least twenty miles, and it's probably close to fifty until there's a town. It's tucked into the woods and near a mountain. Considering how my mom's dressed as she steps out of the bathroom, they're ditching the car somewhere and hiking to it. We've had to do that twice in my life. I feel better knowing where they're going.

My dad nods, certain I've figured it out. Our hug is too short, but I know he needs to change, too. My mom and I cling to each other. She kisses my cheek over and over, and I rest my head on her shoulder even though she's so much shorter than me. I don't want to let go. At least not unless I'm going straight into Misha's arms. It's fucking ridiculous that I trust a man that I saw for the first time last night and have only talked to twice.

I rarely do one-night stands, but I have a few times. The kisses we've shared are less than what I've done while barely knowing a guy any better. But I only trusted those guys for a good lay. And I suppose not to murder me or rape me. I'm trusting Misha not to do that either, but it's a lot more. I trust him to protect me and take care of me. He said he would, and I believe him.

A knock on the door makes me straighten. I open it, and it's Misha. He nods, and I know it's time to go. I hug my parents together, and they make a sandwich of me like when I was a kid. Misha and my dad shake hands, and he gives my mom a loose embrace. Then I'm leaving my old home with him. My dad hurries to get changed, then we're getting off the elevator with my parents in the underground parking garage. There's a different car waiting for us. It only has Anton and Sergei in it. Misha jerks his chin to two other cars, and I realize his dad and Grigori are in the others. He and I slip into the backseat, and I twist to watch my parents get into their car. Misha's dad pulls out first, then we follow. Grigori follows my parents out. My parents go in the opposite direction, and I twist again to watch them for as long as I can.

When Misha covers my hand with his, I almost lose it. He laces our fingers together, and the tears start. They just flow silently as I turn to look forward again. He switches hands, and his now free one rests on my thigh. It's just the right type of possessive right now.

"What's going on?"

Sergei glances at us in the review mirror. I don't know if he can see how we're sitting, but his gaze softens when he sees I'm crying.

"Someone tipped Vadim that Katerina got too much attention. Whoever it was didn't approve of her asking questions. Then they saw us together. Either someone doesn't like thinking we're together, or they think they can get to her even though they believe we're together."

"It was Timofey's son. He was my dad's informant."

Misha turns to look at me.

"And your dad trusts him?"

"Apparently. I don't know if it's someone from the Podol-skaya or someone they wouldn't stop. But I'm here because my sister, Larisa, is missing. She disappeared three weeks ago. I think the Podolskaya took her, and now they're after me for trying to find her."

"Do you have any idea where she is? Did you learn anything today?"

"A neighbor said a man came to her door a few days before

she disappeared, but she wouldn't open the door. I know she went on a date with a man she didn't know was married when she accepted. She blocked his number once she got home. The same neighbor said men came to Larisa's door who reminded her of what we hear the KGB looked like. I asked if they were bratva, but the woman doesn't know. I didn't dare ask if she saw any tattoos."

"Are there security cameras at your sister's building?"

I meet Sergei's gaze in the mirror again as he asks.

"Yeah. At the front and service entrances. But I don't think there are anywhere else."

"Do you have the date she was last seen or when these men came?"

"I know when she was last seen. The neighbor said the man who came alone was there two days before Larisa disappeared. I don't remember what she said about the group."

"I'll pull the security footage and scan the city cameras."

"You can do that?"

Sergei shoots me a tight smile as he nods. Misha squeezes my thigh.

"What about at the restaurant, Kitty? Did you learn anything there? You were upset when you came out of the kitchen."

"My sister's high school boyfriend is the chef there. They're still friends and talk all the time. I thought he might know something that he was too scared to tell my dad since he's bratva, and this guy's family isn't. He didn't want to tell my dad that they hooked up the night before Larisa went missing. She went to his place for a while, then went home. He'd tried to convince her to spend the night and that he would take her to her place to get ready in the morning and take her to work. He blames himself."

"Should he?"

Anton looks over his shoulder at me. I shake my head.

"No. They loved each other, but his family didn't approve because of my family. They made their life hell while they were dating. But they're also not the type to know how to make her disappear or know the type of people who can."

"How can you be so sure?"

So, Anton is the real skeptic in the group. He's not wrong to ask, though.

"His brother and uncle are both Orthodox priests. His mother goes to church practically every day, and his father only does what his mother tells him to."

It's Misha's turn to shake his head. His expression is sad, and he's letting me know how he feels. I know it's his choice that I know.

"We were all altar boys even when we got to America. We didn't stop until a year after we entered the bratva. It seemed wrong after a while. But we all did things and still went every Sunday. Going to church isn't an absolute guarantee of a good person."

I get the feeling from Misha and glancing at the two men in the front seat that their relationships with God are complex, deeply personal, and still exist. I can't imagine what their prayers must sound like.

We pull into a hotel parking structure. I reach for the door.

"No. You do not get out of a car unless someone is already standing beside your door. They will open it. It's not chivalry. It's a sign that it's safe. Wait until my dad and Grigori get here. Then Anton will open the door for you. You stay in the circle we make. Keep your eyes down."

I watch Grigori and Radomir—I just remembered that's Misha's dad's name—stroll over as though it's no big deal. Misha and Sergei get out of the car, and once they're both on my side, Anton opens the door. Radomir leads the way. Sergei is behind me, Anton is to my left, and Grigori is to my right, on the other side of Misha, whose arm is around my waist as we walk. Just before the elevator doors open, he whispers to me.

"Keep your head down, so the cameras don't see your face."

I tip my head forward and run my fingers through my hair, so it hangs down each side of my face. The moment we're all inside, all five of them pull their guns. They keep them pointing to the floor. It tempts me to look up at them, and I think Misha senses that. He slides his arm around me from behind and shifts. He must have spotted the camera and is blocking it from seeing me. I realize the others all have their guns where anyone watching the footage couldn't see them. Grigori and Radomir step out first, then Misha and I. Anton and Sergei follow. We're on the top floor, and I only see a few doors.

Radomir opens the hotel room door, and we all walk inside. It's the most enormous suite I've ever seen. It's like an apartment. I can see a living room and a dining room area. There's no kitchen because who would cook for themselves if they could afford to stay here? There are three bedrooms that I can see. Radomir slips into one as the other men move around the suite. Anton draws the blinds and curtains. Sergei gets out six bottles of water. I know that has nothing to do with being too good to drink tap water. They're all sealed. Grigori talks to a guard who was already in the suite.

It confuses me when Radomir wheels his luggage across the suite to another bedroom. I look up at Misha, who's still standing beside me. He guides me into the room Radomir just left.

"My dad's going over to share a room with Grigori."

"Why's he doing that?"

"So you can be in here with me. You can see there are two queen-sized beds in here. Same as in the other rooms."

"Does your dad somehow know we kissed? That we...?"

"No. But I'm almost thirty, and I haven't hidden how attracted I am to you very well. I don't talk to him about stuff like that, but he's not naïve. They also all know that I won't sleep if I'm not near you. Your dad asked me specifically to guard you, and I would have even if he hadn't singled me out. Kitty, I'll respect your privacy and step out any time you want me to. I don't expect anything. I—"

"Why do you call me Kitty? You didn't answer me the last time I asked."

I think he might actually be blushing. He definitely looks uncomfortable, which means he's letting me see he's vulnerable.

"You will not be impressed when I explain."

"You are definitely blushing now. So, it has something to do with wanting to have sex with me is my guess."

"Yes. Kat's short for Katerina. That makes me think of kitty cat."

I wait, but he says nothing else. I cock an eyebrow and my chin falls forward a little, prompting him to finish explaining. He rakes a hand through his hair.

"Kitty cat makes me think about them being called pussy-cats. And there is a particular pussy that—" He tilts his head back to look at the ceiling. "I'd like to make you purr."

I cover my mouth to smother my laughter. His eyes shift to me, and he doesn't appreciate my mirth. He goes back to looking at the ceiling. I walk over to him and pull his hands around me to grab my ass.

"Puuurr, puuurr."

I can't not giggle. He tightens his hold until it lifts me onto my toes.

"Don't tease, *malyshka*."

"I think it's sweet in a very—I don't even know. Such a boy way. But there is definitely nothing boyish about you except for that smile you've let me see a few times. No one else has ever called me Kitty. Some of my American friends call me Kat or Katie. I like it."

I shrug. I do. It's something that's ours. I can't believe that I'm thinking of anything as ours other than this hotel room we're now sharing.

"So, you don't mind me calling you that?"

"I don't mind."

"Which bed do you want?"

I look at both of them. Do I have the balls to say what I'm thinking?

"Which one were you going to take before your dad left?"

"This one."

He looks at the bed closer to the bathroom and away from the door.

"Then I'd like that one too."

Heat flares in his eyes, and he lifts me until I can wrap my legs around his waist. He walks us to where my back is against the wall closest to the bathroom. It's away from the windows and the door out to the living room.

"Do you want me to pick the other one?"

I shake my head.

"Do you want me naked in bed with you?"

I nod.

"Do you want me inside you, *malyshka?*"

I nod again.

"I have to hear you. What do you want?"

"To fuck."

Our kiss is wild and messy. With one arm supporting me under my ass, his other hand tugs up my sweater and t-shirt. I reach behind me to unhook my bra.

"Uh-uh, baby girl. If I wanted it unfastened yet, I would have done it. Take your shirt and sweater off."

I'm eager to obey because I want his mouth on me. But I wonder what his deal is. What guy doesn't want a woman's bra off if they're about to hook up? I drop my clothes beside us, and he dives in. His tongue dips into my cleavage before he kisses the inside of one tit, then the other. I get it now. The bra pushes them up and together. It's sheer, so he licks my left nipple while he tweaks the right. His teeth tug at my wet one as his fingers tug at the other one. I arch toward him, but he lowers me to my feet. He unfastens my pants, and I shimmy out of them.

He drops to his knee before I realize where this is going first. He practically rips my thong off me. He slips his fingers between my legs and taps my pussy three times before he slides two fingers into me. I squeeze my eyes shut and clench my fists. I try not to make a sound as his tongue flicks my clit. He latches onto it and sucks as hard as he did with my nipple while his fingers work me. He reaches up with his free hand and kneads my tits, alternating sides. The moment I try to press his head closer, he pulls away and snags my wrists.

"I'll make you come, Kitty. But I decide when and how. Can you live with that?"

I nod vigorously.

"I need to hear you say it."

"Yes."

He stands, and I groan in disappointment. He kisses behind my ear.

"Don't worry, baby. You'll come more than once before we join the others for dinner. You like a little pain, but do you only like it vanilla?"

"You are not vanilla at all."

"That's not an answer to what I asked. I'll ask a second time, but not a third. Do you only like it vanilla?"

"In the past, yeah. But I'd try all thirty-one flavors with you."

When he grins, I know he gets the Baskin-Robbins ice cream reference.

"You can always tell me if you want more or less of something. If you don't like it and want to stop, we will. No questions asked."

"You've told me that before. It's really important to you that I know I have a choice."

"Very. You know my lifestyle, Kitty. You know I spend my days doing unpleasant things *to* people. I want to do things *with* you that bring us both pleasure. But I also never want you to fear me. That's not—"

"Misha, I don't fear you at all. I should. Any rational woman would be at least cautious around a strange man your size. A man I don't know, but whose job I'm all too familiar with. But for some reason I don't understand, I'm comfortable with you. I've never felt as safe and unscared as I do when I'm around you."

"Do you understand why I like to be in control?"

"It keeps you alive."

"And it protects the people around me. I'm not a Dom, and I don't want a sub. If you've only had vanilla, then I doubt you've ever been one."

"I haven't, and I've never been the submissive type during sex or in any relationships."

"I don't expect you to submit to me other than when we're like this."

I release a sigh that may have come from my soul.

"With how shit went sideways today, I'm not willing to submit to anyone until I know what's going on. But I will listen to you and do what you tell me because you understand all of this better than I do. When it's possible, I want a say in what happens to me until this gets resolved. I trust you, but my faith isn't entirely blind. That said, when we're together and alone, then I will gladly let you take control. I don't want to think beyond the here and now. I'm barely holding my shit together right now."

"You don't look like it."

"You know my family. I can hide my thoughts and feelings, too. It doesn't mean I don't have them. You're letting me lean on you right now, and I can admit I need you. My dad trusts you with my life, and—" I shake my head a couple times and shrug. "—something in the universe is telling me I should too. Maybe it's intuition. Maybe it's the hand of God. Maybe it's fate. I sure as fuck don't know. This is a pretty fucking deep conversation, considering you've barely eaten me out."

"But I think it's an important one to have."

"It is. And I'm glad we're having it. But it's like we're defining a relationship that doesn't even exist."

"It can."

That stops me. I stare at Misha for a long time. Partly because no words want to come out, but partly because I want to see how he handles the silence and me watching him.

"When's the last time you had a girlfriend, Misha?"

"Junior year of high school."

"More than a decade then."

"Yeah. This life isn't conducive to it."

"There aren't any bratva women in New York that you could date?"

"I don't want any of them. I haven't wanted any woman beyond a few quick fucks in a long time, Kitty. I can't bring an outsider into this life without being certain it would be for good. I haven't wanted a woman connected to the bratva because I want at least a few hours out of every day to not revolve around it. You know this world, even if you tried to leave it behind by coming to America. I wouldn't pull you in since I get you don't want a part of it. But it's already sucked you back. If you just want a fling while we're dealing with this because you don't want to be alone, I get it. But if you want more, I want you to know I do, too."

"More?"

"After all of this."

"If I don't find my sister, I don't know what comes next. I can't imagine it. It's too painful."

"Then we take it day by day."

I could fucking fall in love with him right now. I don't get the feeling he's telling me what I want to hear. I don't even know what the fuck I want to hear right now. He must sense that because he's kissing along my neck, as he finally—thank God—takes off my bra. Then his fingers are back in my pussy.

"Do you know how hot it is to have you naked and in my arms while I'm still dressed? While we're like this, you're mine, *malyshka*. You come when I say you do. If you don't listen, I'll edge you, then I'll make you join the others while you're wet and needy."

"It is hot. I like it. But I'd like your cock in me even more."

"Tonight, when we don't have to hurry. We've been in here a long time already. I'm going to make you come twice, then we have to go back out there."

He kisses me, and I suck his tongue, hinting at what I want to do to him tonight. His thumb rubs my clit as his fingers fuck me. My head falls against his chest as he works me.

"Come, baby."

He must be able to tell I'm close. My hips thrust forward, and I'm coming. Fuck. This feels amazing. My eyes are closed, so I sway when I no longer feel him in front of me. But then his mouth is on my pussy. He's sucking my clit, and his tongue keeps sliding inside me. I reach back to brace myself against the wall as another orgasm hits me.

"Misha."

I pant the single word as he stands up again. I want to fist his shirt, but I know I'll rumple it. Then everyone will know without a doubt what we've been up to. My arms tuck between us as he hugs me. I inhale his expensive cologne. I hadn't realized how comforting that scent has been every time he's near me. He leads me to a chair and sits down. He pulls me onto his lap, and I curl against him.

"Do you want something to eat? You can come out to the dining room and eat with us, or room service can bring you something in here. If you're too tired and want to go straight to bed, then I can make sure there's something here if you wake up hungry."

I suddenly feel vulnerable and foolish. I don't want to admit what I want. I try to sit up, but he's draped his arms around me, and I'm just too comfortable.

"Baby, tell me. I can feel you're uncomfortable about something. You were completely relaxed a moment ago. Are you afraid I'll think whatever it is, is dumb?"

I nod. The way he holds me feels different as he eases me back so we can look at each other. We were cuddling a moment ago, but now it's as though he's cradling me. But it means I can look into his eyes, and I'm drowning in the fathomless blue.

"I don't want to get up. I wish I could stay like this until I fall asleep."

"If you don't want to eat right now, then you can. I'll hold you until you're asleep, then I'll slip you into bed."

"I don't want to keep you from your meal or your family. They have to be wondering what's going on. A quickie should be done faster than this."

"My brother would give me shit if he knew just how quick I could be."

"How much older is he than you?"

"Four years."

That makes me sit up.

"Wait. You're not twins?"

Misha laughs.

"No. People think that all the time. I never know if it should insult me because I look old or if I should share the compliment with him that someone thinks he looks young."

"How old are you?"

"Twenty-nine. You?"

"Thirty-two."

"Same age as Sergei and Anton. Do you remember them from school? They remember Semyon."

"I didn't go to the same school as your brother and Sem while you still lived here. I started going to school with him when we were fifteen. But I knew him long before that."

"So, you're a cougar."

Misha's grin makes me wet all over again. I lean forward to whisper in his ear.

"And you've already made this kitty purr. Can you make me roar?"

"Don't doubt it. When you're ready, I'll fuck you until you can't stand up."

"I'm suddenly starving. Let's join the others and eat. Then I'll come up with a reason to go to bed. Maybe you could claim jetlag."

"*Malyshka*, my family are not prudes. I won't flaunt it in front of my dad or Grigori. But we don't have to pretend. If you truly don't want them to think we're doing anything, then we can downplay it. But I don't want you to be embarrassed in front of them."

"All right. I need to get dressed."

"I'm going to take a quick shower. I could hear the water running in the other rooms, so they haven't been waiting around for us. Someone's still in a shower."

"You can hear that?"

"Yeah. You will too if you listen."

I sit quietly for a moment. I can hear the faint sound of running water.

"You have ears like a dog."

"You may be my Kitty, but I assure you, I'm no puppy."

Chapter Seven

Misha

I can hear Kitty moving around our room as she puts things away in the closet. I told her she may as well before I came into the bathroom. I turn on the shower and hop in before the water is even warm. As much as I'd like to linger and rub one off before facing my family with another hard on, I'm done just as the water gets to a comfortable temperature. I return to the room with a towel wrapped around my waist. I know I've caught her attention as much as she had mine while she was naked. She's soft and curvy, and I love the feel of her in my arms. Can I have phantom pains from not touching her?

She gives up not trying to stare as I grab a pair of jeans, a sweater, and boxer briefs. She's looking at my tats, and I'm certain she understands what some of them mean. She knew the eight-point star. I have a cross on my left ribs that signifies the thieves' code, which Vlad forced me to swear when I was thirteen. Jumper cables near your balls make you commit to a life of crime pretty quickly. I have a crown on the other side, that means I have authority within my bratva.

I got it the first time they gave me the duty of being an *avotoritet*. Sergei and I have matching Madonna and baby Jesus on our backs. It's large and one of the first ones I got when I turned eighteen. It signifies that we're loyal to our family and friends, and that we entered this world young. On my upper left arm, I have an executioner. Some would say it declares me a murderer. I only kill when I must, not because I get any joy from it. I got that when I went on my first mission without my dad or Sergei. To me, it means I'm loyal to the thieves' code. Or at least I was until I met Kitty. Now I'm considering breaking the no family pledge. That was the one I was most certain about.

"Do you know what they mean?"

I have more, but those are the ones that hold the greatest significance to me. Kitty walks around me, trailing her finger over the largest ones. When she's standing before me, she shakes her head.

"I've seen some of them before, but the only one I know for certain is the star. I've never wanted to know what the others mean. They scared me when I was younger because I knew most of the men who had them got them in prison."

"None of mine are prison tats, Kitty. I got arrested a few times when I was younger, but nothing ever stuck."

If I got arrested nowadays, I would be on death row.

"They're beautiful. They're like art that should be on a canvas. I suppose you are the canvas."

"Do they bother you? Do you want to know what they mean?"

"They don't bother me. You don't have to explain if you don't want to."

"I will, but later. We should go back out there."

I'm quick to dress but I don't bother with socks or shoes. My hair is wet, but Kitty's isn't. I hope that clues my family in that we haven't been fucking the entire time. No one reacts to us leaving the room together. If nothing else, they may think she waited for me because she was uncomfortable leaving the bedroom without me.

"There's a cheeseburger, salmon, chicken, a steak, pasta, and a chef salad. Which would you like? We didn't know what to get you."

My dad smiles at Kitty as we walk to the table. All of us would eat anything they ordered, so it doesn't surprise me that my dad is offering her the first choice. They wanted to make sure they cover the bases.

"Oh. I don't want to take anyone's dinner."

"You're not. We're all happy with any of these."

If you didn't know my father had been in the KGB and bratva, you'd think he was a nice dad with a warm heart. He's all of those, and it puts Kitty at ease.

"Then the pasta, please."

Sergei hands her the plate, and she moves out of the way. My dad snags the steak before Grigori can, who settles for the chicken. Anton takes the salad, which surprises none of us. That leaves the salmon and the cheeseburger. I use my hip to nudge Sergei out of the way and grab the salmon. He'll eat a cheeseburger, but it doesn't meet his expectations for healthy eating. I grin before taking a seat next to Kitty.

"I'll remember that. Now I don't feel badly about eating most of Mama's cookies."

"You didn't feel badly to begin with. Maybe you would have gotten the salmon if you hadn't inhaled most of the third bag."

Kitty watches me banter with my brother, and I can tell she's amused. It's natural for us, but today's been a lot for her. If it lightens her mood even a little, then it's worth it. I want to bury myself balls deep in her because I suspect they'll be the best orgasms I've ever had. But I wanted to make her feel taken care of and desired earlier. I didn't expect—and wouldn't have accepted—anything in return.

There's a bit of an awkward silence at first since we can't talk business in front of her, and I don't want to bring up anything that will upset her. There are a ton of questions I have for her, but after having my tongue in her cunt, it feels odd to ask her the basic things. Anton comes to the rescue.

"What do you do, Katerina?"

"I'm a school nurse in the Bronx."

That shocks me. The school nurse part and the Bronx. I could see her taking care of kids, but that isn't a borough most people choose to live in. It's—rough.

It's Sergei's turn to ask something.

"Do you live in New York?"

"Yeah. About five miles from the school."

I bite my tongue. That doesn't make me happy. I loathe the idea of her going around on her own. I've seen that she knows how to protect herself, and it wouldn't surprise me if she carries a handgun to and from work. She makes it look like she's adjusting her napkin in her lap, but her fingers brush my thigh then give it a quick pat. She senses my unease, even though I thought I was hiding it.

My dad offers her another smile, and she relaxes again. It's her turn to ask a question.

"Have you been in America long?"

I nod as I consider our time there.

"Eighteen years."

It's hard to believe as I answer. It doesn't feel that long most days. But sometimes, it's an eternity. I was eleven when we arrived in New York. I remember plenty about life here in

Moscow, but I'm glad the majority of my memories are in America.

"That's why you all sound like native English speakers. None of that stereotype of strong like bull. It took me a long time to remember to use the, a, and an. I still forget sometimes, but I try really hard not to sound too foreign."

I get that completely. I know we all tried super hard to blend in. We all speak Russian every day, so we'll never lose our accents completely. But we don't sound uneducated or like recent arrivals. We can't afford to, especially when six out of the eight of us went to prestigious universities. I know we made the effort early on when we were in grade school to fit in.

"How long have you been in the U.S.?"

I'm too curious not to ask my own questions. It's no secret to my friends and family that Kitty and I just met.

"Five years."

"That's not long. You sound as much like a native as we do. We only knew a little when we moved."

Her answer surprises me.

"I took it throughout school, and when I moved to America, I watched a lot of TV to make sure I didn't sound like a textbook."

"It worked. We did the same thing."

She grins as she continues.

"It helps having like five different streaming services. There's always a ton to choose from, so I can keep working on it. The students tease me sometimes because I don't always get it right. They like to point it out, but most are sweet enough to correct me nicely."

This gives me an opportunity to learn more about why she's in the Bronx.

"Where do you work?"

"Beaumont High School."

That's in one of the roughest neighborhoods in the roughest borough. She offers me a reassuring smile, but I don't feel any better about it.

"I've been there the entire time I've been in America. The kids know me and think it's fun to tease me about things I don't know about life in America. There are usually a few of them in the parking lot when I get there, so they walk in with me. Same when I'm leaving. I don't believe I need it, but they like to do it. I tease them it should count toward their community service hours."

"Why the Bronx?"

Anton beats me to it.

She shifts in her seat and doesn't want to meet anyone's eye.

"Considering I'm here because you're protecting me, my reason sounds pretty unappreciative. I didn't want to be anywhere near any mafia, especially not Russians. It meant I didn't want to be in Queens or Manhattan. Staten Island and Brooklyn didn't appeal to me. And I moved here with not much, so the Bronx was where I could afford a place that wasn't a shoebox."

"Do you want to leave?"

I hope so.

"I don't want to leave the school. I like it there, but I wouldn't mind moving somewhere else now that I can afford it."

I knew Sergei and Anton would be curious to hear more about her nursing education. Anton continues his questions.

"Did you go to school in America?"

"No. I trained here and worked in a hospital here for a couple years. I had to pass my certifications in the U.S., but I'm an RN with a BSN."

"Anton and I are both trained paramedics."

Kitty's eyes light up at Sergei's announcement, and she genuinely smiles without reservation for the first time since I saw her on the plane.

"How long have you been certified?"

"Since college. Anton and I took classes in between our regular ones. We keep everything up to date."

Kitty's smile slides as she looks at me then the other men at the table. She nods and grows quiet when she speaks.

"That must be really handy."

It's my turn to give her a comforting pat on her thigh. We all know what she isn't saying. We can't go to the hospital unless we're truly next to death. Gunshot wounds and stabbings require the police getting involved, and that's the last thing we want. Anton and Sergei can patch us up for most things, but if it's beyond their skills, we have Boris. He was a KGB and Soviet Army physician. He saved my dad's life when he got injured during the war. He was also the one who signed off on the papers for my dad to return home. It meant we could emigrate. Boris followed a few years after us when he could get away from the Podolskaya. We helped him get settled, and he's been our doctor ever since. We've all known him our entire lives. I'm surprised he didn't deliver any of us.

"Misha needs someone to put his Band-Aids on."

I scowl at Anton like he truly is my older brother. If it's not one, then it's the other when it comes to Sergei and Anton teasing me. I'm a couple months younger than Bogdan, which makes me the baby of the family. I've milked that whenever I could, but it also makes me the butt of plenty of jokes.

"But I don't kiss his boo-boos."

Sergei smirks at me, and I roll my eyes. I can't tease him back since I can't let Kitty know about his relationship with Anton. He knows it, too.

"I doubt he needs anyone to. Who kisses yours?"

Kitty grins, and we all laugh along with her. We've had conversations too similar to this plenty of times. We all know how to deflect. Our dads usually come to their rescue, and my dad does now.

"He'd have to let someone get close enough to see them. He's the porcupine in the group."

My cousins, Pasha, and I started to figure things out about a year after they moved beyond just being friends. No one wanted to say it out loud because we were scared for them, and we didn't want them to think we were judging them. But it all came out when Aleks joined Maks, Sergei, Anton, Grigori, and my dad on a mission. They were getting their gear on while deciding who would partner. The dads paired up with Maks and Aleks and said no one would cover each other's backs better than people in love. We all froze as we looked around. Alina, Mama, and Aunt Galina were there, too. My dad told us to stop wasting time and help them get ready. And just like that, our family accepted Sergei and Anton's relationship.

There's a lull as we eat. It gives me time to think about what's going to happen tomorrow. We have another meeting with Timofey, but I wonder how that's going to go if he knows we're hiding Kitty. We don't know if he's after her or just condoning it. I can't believe he doesn't know what's going on. If his son's aware, then he must be involved somehow. My guess is Kitty won't be content to sit here all day and not do anything to find her sister. She might be in hiding, but I know it won't deter her.

As usual, my dad eases the tension that's growing with yet another silence, and I can breathe a little easier.

"We know people who can continue to ask questions about your sister, and they won't be obvious. We'll do what we can to help you, but your dad wants you hidden because he's scared for you. If we remain here tomorrow when we came to do business, it will look suspicious. We trust our guards with our lives, so I hope you know you can trust them with yours. If we learn anything, Misha will come back to tell you."

I watch Kitty as my dad explains. I can tell she isn't thrilled, but I can also see she'll be reasonable and accept what he says. I don't bother hiding what I'm doing when I slip my hand in hers and draw it onto my lap before I speak.

"Is there anything else you can tell us about your sister? Things that she likes to do? Places she goes to often? The people she spends time with?"

"She's a lawyer, so she mostly works. That restaurant you were at is a favorite because she's still friends with the chef."

"What type of lawyer? Could it be an angry client?"

"I doubt it. She helps foreign nationals attend university in Russia. There are some rules about attending that differ from in America. She helps them to sign the attendance contract and to translate the documents. She has a translator and interpreter certificate in Kazakh and Uzbek. Kazakhstan and Uzbekistan send the most foreign students to Russia."

That seems like a pretty benign practice, so I can't imagine it would be an angry client. That rules out that theory. I continue to ask questions even though I feel like I'm prying.

"What about ex-boyfriends or men she was involved with?"

She shifts uncomfortably and doesn't want to meet anyone's eye. She bites her upper lip for a moment.

"She went on a date with a man she realized was married. Before that, there were some people. I don't know much."

People? Not men. People.

"Do you mean what I think? We've lived in America a long time, Kitty. We don't share Russian views on many things, that included."

She nods, but she still doesn't look up. Her fear practically vibrates from her. Grigori is sitting on her other side. He gives her shoulder a quick squeeze.

"Katerina, we will tell no one, and it won't keep us from helping you. We don't care about that."

She meets Grigori's gaze before she darts hers to my dad. Her brow furrows for a moment before she looks at me. I know she's figured it out when she looks at Sergei and Anton. I'm certain she's wondering why I was sharing a room with my dad instead of my brother. No one confirms it.

"My sister was involved with someone for a year and a half, but that person moved to Canada. As far as I know, they haven't been back even for a visit in three years."

She won't say it aloud, and I can't blame her. I can hear her sigh.

"I'd hoped she would move to America with me, but she was happy here. Except for that. And that was why I wanted her to come with me."

"Could that be why she's missing?"

She shrugs and her mouth twists.

"I don't think so. They were best friends since they were twelve. No one thought it unusual for them to spend time just the two of them. She also dates men, too."

She leans her elbow on the armrest and rubs the bridge of her nose. I want nothing more than to wrap my arm around her and pull her against me. But I don't know that she'd want that type of PDA. Instead, I rest my hand on her thigh.

"I've already seen her high school ex-boyfriend at the restaurant and gone to her apartment. Sem is checking out places he hangs out. I don't know where else to go. I don't know who else to ask. Maybe at her work. I don't think it's anyone she works with, but maybe some student got too attached. I really just don't have a clue."

She looks up at me, and I can tell she's running out of steam for the day. It's been a long one for all of us between travel and our respective business. We've all finished our meals, so I push back my chair and help her from her seat.

"Do you want to go to bed?"

"Yeah."

"I'll be quiet when I come in. I'm going to talk to them for a few minutes."

She knows it looks better if we don't go to the bedroom together, but I do need to speak to them. She wishes the others goodnight before she heads to our room and closes the door. I puff an exhale before stating my theory.

"Maybe a stalker student, but the date still seems most likely."

Sergei speaks as he pulls his laptop from a bag.

"I agree. Let me see if I can get into the CCTV system from when she disappeared until now. Maybe she's been back to her apartment at night, and no one ever saw her. If she did, she probably wasn't alone."

"That's hours to comb through."

I know that's probably the best thing, but it's inefficient. Sergei shakes his head as he types.

"No. I'll run her through facial recognition. I can put in things like hair and eye color, height, weight. That would narrow it down. Do you know any of those things?"

"No. But I'll ask."

I cross the suite and knock.

"Come in."

"Sergei has software that can scan the city cameras. What color is your sister's hair? Height? Weight? Eyes?"

"She looked a lot like me. Same hair and eyes. But she was about two inches taller than me and ten pounds lighter. I know she was five-eight, and last time I saw her on a scale was a few years ago, but she hasn't changed. I'd say a hundred-and-fifty-five pounds."

I step further into the room and close the door when I see her embarrassment, since she basically admitted her weight. I walk up to her and grab her ass in both hands and pull her against me before I fuse our lips together. I squeeze almost to the point of pain as I grind my hard on against her pussy. When I let go, this spank isn't any more playful than the ones in her bedroom. I squeeze again before I step back.

"I'm going to enjoy every bit of you. It's why I'm hard every time I'm near you. Hell, every time I think about you."

I turn back to the door, but not before she pinches my ass.

"I like yours too."

She grins, and I growl. I don't like her thinking she's inadequate in any way.

"If you aren't naked when I come back, I will shred what you're wearing."

I return to the living room and relay what she told me. Sergei's leaning toward his screen and squinting. He types in the information and sits back. I hope it helps process the videos faster than him trying to search each feed manually. As I walk behind him, I can see he has a copy of her driver's license pulled up, too. Between the picture and the information about her appearance, I feel more confident. I watch as hours of security footage zooms past.

It slows to the day after Kitty believes she was taken. The footage shows one a.m. when three men in dark clothes and caps pulled down to hide their faces enter her apartment building. Five minutes later, they drag Larisa outside. She's not fighting them, but it's easy to see she isn't going willingly. The man behind her crowds her, and I can tell he has a weapon to her back, even if it isn't visible.

"I'm running the plates, but my guess is they're stolen or

fake."

Sergei freezes the frame that shows the Lada Granta. It's the second most popular car in Russia. There are nearly one-hundred-thousand of them on the roads. This isn't a coincidence. They want it to be indistinguishable. She balks when she gets to the backdoor, but a punch to her kidneys from the guy behind her pitches her forward. She's shoved inside, and the door slams. It only takes a minute before the results come back on the license plates. They're fake. They're not even in the system. I grit my teeth and fist my left hand before I wonder aloud.

"Was she hiding for that first day she was unaccounted for? Or was she just staying home, and they caught her there?"

"She was hiding."

We all look up when Kitty comes back out of the bedroom. She has a different t-shirt on and a pair of pajama shorts.

"She didn't call in sick or anything, which is unusual for her. From what I heard right after it happened, her boss called several times, but it just went to voicemail. He texted, but she never responded. Did you find something?"

Sergei's expression is blank, but I can tell he dreads telling her what we just saw.

"Men came to her apartment and took her the day after people thought she went missing."

"Then she was definitely hiding. She would have told someone, or if she didn't want to talk, she would have sent calls to voicemail. She hates hearing a phone ring or vibrate and having no one answer. Can you tell if she logged into anything on her computer?"

"I'll check. It'll take me a moment to verify her IPN."

My dad, Grigori, and Anton move to the sofas and turn on the TV. There's no reason for them to hover, so they get out of the way. They can hear what Sergei, Kitty, and I are saying.

"There's nothing. She last logged in the night before she went silent. The men got her two nights later."

"Are you still running the city cameras?"

Kitty's already standing next to me, but she shifts closer as she asks. I don't think she notices what she's done. I wrap my arm around her waist, and she turns toward my chest, resting her head against me.

The video pulls up an image of her getting out of the car in a neighborhood that's neither wealthy nor poor. It's just typical. She walks inside a house before the camera suddenly stops recording. Sergei pauses it, rewinds, and slows the replay. Something hits the camera, but its source is out of range. Someone shot it. That feed goes black. After that, the facial recognition pulls up nothing between then and now.

Kitty takes a ragged breath as I tighten my arm around her. She wraps hers around me as she cries. Sergei stands as he shuts his laptop.

"Katerina, I will keep thinking of ways I might track her digital footprint or get an image of her somewhere. I'm not giving up."

"Thank you." She sniffles. "I know we're all tired. I don't think we're going to suddenly find something today, even if you search all night. We all need some sleep. I can manage to wait until tomorrow."

I look at Sergei, and I can tell he's unsatisfied with the results. But I can see the shadows forming under his eyes. He's as tired as the rest of us, even if he pushed himself to work throughout the night. If Kitty can accept him taking a break, then it's for the better that he gets some sleep, too. She says good night again, and I steer her toward the bedroom. I gauge her mood as she looks at me once we're alone.

"Get undressed, *malyshka*. I'm going to make you come again."

Chapter Eight

Kitty

Misha's command to undress makes my pussy clench. I'd already gotten naked, then thought twice about remaining in the bedroom. I keep having surges of guilt for considering even a moment's enjoyment with Misha. I feel unsettled that I'm not spending every minute of every day searching for my sister, but to be out this late would just beg trouble. It's safer to wait until morning. It feels so utterly wrong to receive any pleasure while Larisa could be suffering or dead. My mind wars with that and the consuming wish to escape all of this for even a few minutes.

"Kitty, I know you feel guilty. We don't have to do anything if it's going to upset you more. We can just go to sleep."

My gut reaction is that's the last thing I want.

"Make me forget about all of this, even if it's only for a little while. Let me stop being terrified."

I whisk my t-shirt over my head and toss it on the foot of the bed. I push down my shorts until they pool around my feet. I stoop to grab them, and I know Misha's watching my tits sway.

"Do you want it vanilla, after all?"

"Not at all. That won't distract me nearly enough. I just want to focus on what we're doing."

"Lie face down on the bed, *malyshka*. Turn your head to the bathroom."

I listen to him walk over to his suitcase, which is open on a luggage stand. He doesn't want me to know, just anticipate. I see the three ties he grabbed when he walks around the bed. I see the bulge in his pants and reach out to cup it, but he snags my wrist.

"Did I tell you to touch me?"

He cocks an eyebrow as my gaze shifts up to his.

"No."

He raises both eyebrows, and I try to work out what he wants me to say.

"No, sir?"

"That's right, *malyshka*."

I sit up and kneel as I continue to look up at him.

"Why do you call me that in Russian and English?"

"Besides the fact that it sounds hot when the guy on Criminal Minds says it to the IT girl, so it intrigues me? I say it because I will always take care of you, Kitty. I don't mean that I'll just protect you. I'll try to make you happy and give you the things you need from me."

"If I'm your baby girl, does that make you my daddy?"

I say it with a grin, but heat flares between us the moment I do. He tunnels his hand into my hair and clenches enough to tilt my head back.

"Is that what you want me to be? Do you want to call me that as I fuck you until you come? When you're begging me to fill you with my cock?"

My answer is a whisper.

"Yes."

He pinches my nipple and twists.

"Say it."

"Daddy."

"Tell me what you want."

"I want you, Daddy. I want to do it all with you."

He leans to whisper in my ear.

"If you mean that, I'll do dirty things to you, *malyshka*. I'll spank you for pleasure and for punishment. I'll shove my dick down your throat. I'll fuck your ass. You are mine."

I shiver, and goosebumps form on my arms. He looks like he wonders if he's gone too far. When he swipes his fingers between my legs, and his fingers come back coated in my dew, he knows he hasn't. My breath hitches as I eagerly ask what's happening.

"Are we doing that all tonight?"

"We can. Then we'll do it again tomorrow night and the night after that."

"And if I want to spank you?"

He chuckles deeply, and my breath grows shallow.

"That's not how it works. Baby girls don't punish their daddies."

"What if it's just for pleasure?"

"Do you want control, Kitty?"

I sit back on my heels and furrow my brow.

"Not if you're going to call me that when we're like this. It doesn't—it doesn't—feel right."

"If you're spanking me, you're hardly my baby girl, and I'm not your daddy. Do you want me to call you Mommy?"

"No."

I blurt the answer, and he's obviously glad for it. He wouldn't. He couldn't in a million years. He needs the control way too much.

"Can I smack your ass playfully sometimes?"

"Yes, *malyshka*."

"You said you would spank me for punishment. But earlier you said you're not a Dom. I don't get how that works."

He sits down beside me on the bed and pulls me onto his lap. Can I just live right here now?

"I will not treat you like a Little unless that's what you want. Do you know what I mean by that?"

My face flushes deep red.

"I do. I read those types of romances sometimes. I like them, but that's not what I want in real life. I don't want to act younger than I am."

"And I don't think I need to tell you what to do. That's not the type of taking care of you I meant. You know this life. You know the danger and what can happen. If you put yourself at risk, then yes, I will punish you. But this isn't domestic discipline either. I won't punish you if you don't do as I say, or you disagree with me."

"We have some fucking heavy conversations for two people who met today."

I've had sex with more than just Semyon. I've dated more guys than just him. Never have I had such deep and personal conversations—well, ever. I can't remember defining my relationships so clearly and definitely, and not the day that I met the guy. Then again, I've had nothing but regular relationships with vanilla everything.

"I agree. I've never had a conversation like this. I told you, I haven't had a girlfriend since I was in high school. I definitely wasn't thinking about her like this. And even if I had, I doubt I could have said any of it."

"Does it make you uncomfortable to talk about this?"

He tucks hair behind my ear and presses a light kiss to my lips.

"No, *malyshka*. It's definitely odd. I didn't wake up this

morning on the plane thinking this is how I would spend my night. But it feels right to me. I just want to be sure we're on the same page. If we aren't, then we slow down."

"For someone who wants control, you ask for and tell me this is about me giving you consent."

"And I told you I do enough things *to* people that I want this to be *with* you. What you want, like, or dislike is just as important. I will never force you. I may have control when we're intimate, but ultimately you have the control to stop and start everything."

I think I'm falling in love. Who is this guy? I don't think he's telling me what he thinks I want to hear. I think he truly believes this to his core. I've never felt so—I don't even know. He makes me feel desirable the moment he looks at me. He makes me feel safe when I feel adrift. He makes me feel respected when we both come from a culture that isn't always so great about that between men and women. I shift to straddle him.

"Misha, I've never met any man like you. I know you can't be perfect, but you sure as fuck seem like it right now."

He chuckles, and this time it's much lighter.

"I am definitely not perfect, and there are four men in this suite who will gladly prove it. But I want this. It doesn't mean I'll lie. I won't tell you what I think will fool you into being with me. We both know there are plenty of things that I can never tell you. You know not to ask. I hope you don't because I never want to lie to you—whether it's by my words or omission. I will be honest whenever I can."

"Is this just until we return to America?"

"No." He's quick to answer that. "*Malyshka*, you are mine. I told you that already. I won't make you stay with me, but neither do I plan to let you go."

"Are you mine?"

"Do you mean is this monogamous? Absolutely. I only want you. I swore years ago to never get involved with someone, and I haven't. I'm not going to fuck anyone else for the sake of getting laid, and I don't want to date anyone else. Do you want to be monogamous?"

"Yes. I don't want anyone else. And the idea of sharing you —" I swallow. "I don't like that."

"You are mine, and I am yours."

I cup his cheeks and lean forward, but I wait for him. I expect him to kiss me, but he nods his head instead. I press our mouths together and open for him immediately. He does nothing except press his lips back against mine. I slip my tongue into his mouth and swipe it along his inner cheek. The moment I do, he pounces. He let me lead for a moment. I think he sensed I wanted to show him I meant what I said. But he's back in control, and I revel in it. He twists until I'm lying on my back, then he pulls away and stands.

"I told you I want you face down. I meant it."

Fuck. The timber of his voice might make me come before he touches me. It's smooth like a fine whiskey, and it heats me to my toes the same way. Fuck. It's the sexiest thing I've ever heard. He calls me Kitty, and my pussy is ready to purr. I follow his command. A stinging slap lands across my ass. I peer up at him.

"I will not punish you for needing to talk to me about how you feel. I never will. But that will remind you when I tell you what to do during sex, I expect you to do it. Close your eyes, *malyshka*."

I obey immediately as excitement and nervousness and curiosity make me giddy. He slips one of his ties over my eyes and knots it snugly behind my head. Not a single bit of light peeks in, and it's obvious he's an expert at blindfolding. I don't allow myself to think about how he gained that skill. The same as when I feel him bind my wrists behind my back. He's careful and gentle, but it's tight. There's not even enough space to attempt to tug them apart.

"Spread your legs wide, *malyshka*."

I'm just as quick to obey again. What must be his right hand massages my shoulder as his left fingers thrust into me. I can't stop the moan that escapes. The pressure in his hands is in opposition. His right hand squeezes with the lightest hold, his thumb sweeping over my spine, soothing my tension. But his left hand pistoned in and out of me with enough force to make me pant. He has three fingers buried in me as he presses and twist before he pulls back. I kick my feet.

"Too much, *malyshka?*"

"No. More. Harder."

God, how I love that chuckle. The deep, dark one. The one that just made my pussy clench around his fingers. He leans over me and whispers.

"Do not come until I tell you, or there will be nothing pleasurable about the spanking I give you. Do as I say, and I will eat you out while I spank you."

"That. The second one. I won't come."

But it only takes a minute to realize he's testing me. He turns his hand and strokes my g-spot while his thumb rubs my clit. His other hand moves to knead my left shoulder. It's a blend of erotic and comfort, and I'm ready to explode. If he wants to spank me, then I want to fulfill that desire as much as I want to come. I let myself relax until I can feel the impending release...Fuck. It's going to be strong. Now I don't want to stop it no matter how he reacts. The tidal wave crashes over me, and my pussy spasms as I grind it into his thumb.

"You came, baby girl. I think you did that on purpose. I would have spanked you either way. Why a punishment?"

"Because I want to give you what you want. You were

trying to make me fail, and that must have been because you want that kind of spanking. You gave me what I want, and now I want to give you what you want."

"Fuck, you're perfect."

I barely hear him, but his tone sounds reverent. But I have no time to ponder it because his hand cracks down on my ass, and I suck in a breath to keep from howling. He alternates sides until I'm certain my ass has gone from pink to apple red. It burns, but I have never felt more aroused.

"Your cunt aches for me, doesn't it?"

"Yes."

It's a ragged confession.

"Does it burn with an unbearable need for me to be inside you?"

"Yes, Daddy. Please."

"Pull your knees up and go on all four. I want to see your soaked pussy while I undress."

"Are you going to fuck me doggy-style?"

"Is that what you want?"

He pulls the blindfold from me, and I watch him hurry to undress. It's not, but again, I want to give him what he desires.

"Do not lie to me, *malyshka*. Do you want me to fuck you that way?"

I can only whisper as I admit how I feel.

"No."

"Do you want to face me? Do you want me to hold you while I'm so deep inside you, you'll think I'll come out your throat?"

Not the most romantic sentiment, but it's true. I nod as I answer yet more demanding questions.

"Yes."

He's naked now, and he pulls the tie from my wrists faster than I imagined possible. He flips me onto my back and follows me down to the mattress. He slides his arms beneath my shoulders as I open my legs for him to settle between.

"I know I wasn't gentle when I fingered you. But how long has it been since you had sex? Do you need me to be more careful?"

"More recently than I want to admit, Misha. Let's just say I'll be fine if you're rough."

"Do you have a boyfriend?"

"No. And it wasn't a recent break up or a one-night stand. I have an arrangement."

"A fuck buddy."

"Yes."

"Will it bother him to know that arrangement is over?"

"Yes. But he'll get over it."

"I haven't been with anyone in more than six months, and I've tested since then. I'm clean."

"And I haven't had sex without a condom since I was with Sem. I still test just in case. I'm on birth control too. I'm doubly cautious. I took it while I was brushing my teeth earlier."

"Do you want me to get one? I can't remember how old it is, but there's one in my wallet."

I laugh. Do condoms have expiration dates? I feel like, as a high school nurse, I should know that, but I don't.

"I've had sex more recently than you, and you're trusting me. I trust you too, Daddy."

He surges into me, and I arch off the bed. Holy fucking shit. This is amazing. Fuck. I saw he was big, but he's unlike anyone I've been with before. As he moves, not only is he huge, but he fucking knows what he's doing. He kisses my throat as he drives into me over and over. We realize pretty quickly that he's too tall to bend down and suck my tits unless he shifts position. Then he's kneeling and sucking so hard, I think my nipple could come off. He suddenly bites, and I can't stop. I come as I claw at him to come closer.

"I will let that one go because I didn't tell you, you can't come. But you will wait next time."

"Daddy, I can't. I don't know how to make myself stop. Not when it feels like this. I don't want to think about anything else or pretend this doesn't feel better than anything else I've ever done."

"Delayed gratification can be learned, little one. I will teach you. But for tonight, come when you want. I want you to enjoy this, not get frustrated by it."

"Fuck. If I enjoyed this any more, I'd float to heaven. Goddamn."

Our kiss is sloppy, and my nails sink into his shoulders as I come yet again.

"I'm going to fill you with my cum, and you're going to keep it there. There's no question that you're mine now, *malyshka*."

"I want all of it."

Fucking brand me if you want.

He's the hottest man I've ever met, and he wants to keep fucking me. He's also the most thoughtful and kind, which seems so at odds with the man I know he can be. But I like that he's complicated. And fuck. I like that he's coming in me.

Fuuuck.

I clench around him as I come once more. I'm too spent to do anything but lie here as we both struggle to catch our breath. If it was this good the first time, I might die when it gets better as we get to know each other. Is he going to give me a heart attack?

Chapter Nine

Misha

I might not be banging someone on the regular, but I do have sex. I have something sorta like a fuck buddy with two women. But it's definitely not often, and they aren't late-night-can't-get-anyone-else kinds of deals. Hearing that she has someone that she's fucking, and probably only last week, creates a jealousy and possessiveness entirely foreign to me. There were practically eight brothers growing up, not just four brothers with two sets of cousins. We've shared everything, including the torture Vladislav Lushak inflicted upon us when we got trapped into this fucked-up life. Sergei, Anton, Pasha, and I managed to stay out two years longer than our cousins. Their experience during those two years is enough to make anyone wonder how the fuck they survived and aren't insane. Mine wasn't much better. What we survived is why our bond is indestructible.

That's why this consuming need to claim Kitty and make sure every-fucking-one knows she's mine is—alarming. Nothing has ever felt better than the moment I slipped inside her. Well, nothing but the moment she made me come. I don't think there's a drop of cum left in my balls. If she weren't on birth control, I'd be seriously nervous. I'm still inside her as I roll us, so I don't squash her. I like that she has meat on her bones, but I still weigh nearly seventy pounds more than her. I'd crush her.

All of us look like we could be the starting lineup of a Super Bowl winning NFL team. We could be pro bodybuilders if we wanted. None of us looks like we weigh what the scale says, though. Anton's the healthiest eater, and Aleks eats the most. I'm right there in the middle with the rest of us. As her hand trails over my ribs, and the way she touched me while we were fucking, I can tell she likes what she finds. The things I do —the way I have to be—has never made me feel like a "real" man. Inflicting pain and dominating other people has never made me feel superior. But the way she looks at me and touches me—I've never felt better. I hope I do the same to her.

"I don't even know what to say, Daddy. That was—you took my breath away. I feel..."

"How do you feel, baby girl?"

"Special. Really feminine, I guess. You're so much bigger than me. And I think you liked it."

I don't care for the uncertainty in her voice.

"I more than liked it. It's never been like that before."

"Same."

I curse my body when it decides my dick's done. She rolls to her side, and I follow her. I abandoned the third tie and my plan to bind her ankles. I preferred what we did. It was more intimate than anything I've done before. We caress each other with tenderness I've never felt or received. Our kisses are short pecks until she nestles against me. I stroke her hair as I feel her body go lax. This is where I belong. I finally found it. But what the fuck is next? Something is going to shit on my parade.

The past six days were a whole lot of nothing. We got next to nowhere with Timofey. He's still claiming what happened to Anastasia was entirely unsanctioned. Bullshit. My dad pointed out that if that's the case, he's not doing much as a leader if he can't control his men. That was ballsy, but true. The funeral came and went three days after Kitty came to stay with us, and I feel horrible for my dad and Grigori. They showed no emotion at the cemetery, but that's no surprise.

None of us will ever show how we feel unless we want outsiders to see it. But at the hotel, they let their guard down more. Kitty saw their sadness, but they grieved once she was in bed. They commiserated together over an entire bottle of vodka. That's the same as about three cups of water to any of us, but it was the sentiment that mattered. However, their eyes were both red-rimmed when they came out to breakfast. Eye drops soon remedied it.

It's the seventh morning, and Kitty and I are in our bedroom after taking a shower. I know she's going stir crazy not leaving the suite, and I can't blame her. It doesn't feel like a week has passed because I've been busy dealing with the Podol-skaya, meeting with informants who're watching the Podolsks and searching for Larisa, and, best of all, fucking Kitty. But I know it must feel like an eternity for her. I hope this helps.

"Get a hoodie and your tennis shoes."

I'm slipping into mine. I'm wearing jeans and a fitted sweater instead of my usual suits. She's in yoga pants and a tank top. Her tits look divine and make it hard to concentrate on anything but ripping that shirt off and mauling her. The sex is still as earth shaking as it was the first time. We've done it against the walls and doors, on the bed, in the shower, and on the bathroom counter.

"Are we going somewhere?"

"I know you're bored out of your mind, so I'm going to take you out for a bit. You have to keep your hood up and this hat on while we're out. We'll leave through the basement garage and drive north for a bit. But there's a park about three miles from here. At least you can get some fresh air. It can't be for long, but it's better than nothing."

"Thank you. It's killing me to stay here and not be looking for Larisa myself. I know it's safer using your informants, and I appreciate the little info they've found, but I feel like I'm failing my sister."

Once she has her shoes on, I wrap my arms around her. I feel a tenderness toward her that's lasted past that first day and the first time we had sex. I enjoy holding her, and she accepts my hugs whenever they're offered. She even seeks them out when I can tell she's overwhelmed.

"You're not failing her, *malyshka*. The last thing we need is for someone to take you, too. You know that's what'll happen. My family and I have resources you don't, and that'll keep you safe. I don't think your parents would survive losing both of you."

I wouldn't survive it.

"I know. I still feel guilty not spending every minute searching. I'm here in a penthouse suite in the nicest hotel in Moscow, and God only knows what hellhole my sister is in."

"Neither Semyon nor any of our informants have seen her at any of the brothels, and no one's been bragging about a new girl at some private establishment."

"But they might have sold her to someone. She might not even be in Moscow."

"I know. We've got our people working all the known and suspected traffickers. They're asking around discreetly."

"And beyond finding out they took her to that house before

the camera broke, we know nothing. I want to question some people she worked with, some people she might have been closer to than I realized. They might be more willing to talk to me than someone they suspect is bratva."

"Do people know your father is?"

"I don't think so. Larisa did everything she could to keep that quiet. Anytime my parents visited her apartment, they went inside alone. They attended events with her and left their guards outside. They did their best to look normal. She could have come with me. I didn't try hard enough. I should have insisted."

"*Malyshka*, she's as much an adult as you are. If she didn't want to move, then it's not your fault that she didn't. As far as we can tell, she wasn't involved in anything that could explain why this happened. For all we know, someone spotted her one day and decided they had to have her. No rhyme or reason beyond that."

"Misha, tell me the truth. You can't stay here forever. When are you going back to America? I need to plan for when you're gone."

"I am not leaving until either you're ready to go back too, or you can go back to your parents'. I am not leaving you alone here."

"But you can't just hang out in Moscow indefinitely. You have a life and I'm certain responsibilities back in the States. I doubt your family would let you stay here alone, either. They have shit they must need to do, too."

She's right. I had this conversation with Sergei and my dad last night while she took a shower. I wasn't thrilled to miss that, but we had to talk. Now that the funeral is over and Timofey is stonewalling us, there is no reason to stay. Remaining here will draw too much attention, but I can't leave Kitty. I won't insist she comes either. I feel fucking stuck between a rock and a hard place. More than anything, I don't want to disappoint her or leave her feeling abandoned when I keep swearing to protect and support her. But I can't ignore my duties at home. It's not just bratva stuff. I run Bear Enterprises, an import/export company, with Pasha. I have six gas stations and convenience stores I own and oversee. They're a front for our less than legal endeavors, so I can't ignore them for long. I work security at the nightclubs and casinos my cousins own. And I'm a bodyguard for our family. I don't just while away my days killing people.

"You know Pasha and my cousins are handling things."

"Yeah, but they have lives and work, too. You told me the other night that Radomir and Grigori are basically retired from the bratva, but they guard their wives. Helping me is leaving your mom unprotected. What about Alina? It's the same for her."

"My mom, Aunt Galina, and Alina are not unprotected. They probably feel more suffocated than when my dad and Grigori are home. They have Maks, Aleks, Niko, Bogdan, and Pasha all breathing down their necks and probably locking them in a basement or attic to keep them from going anywhere. We're all just the right amount of scared of my dad and Grigori to make my cousins and Pasha not want to let those three women out of their sights."

I'm not exaggerating. Dad and Grigori know every move and tactic we do with twenty-plus years more experience. They don't go on missions unless it's personal to our family, but they have forgotten nothing. They come to the gym with us several times a week, and they have their own home gyms for when they don't. They still go shooting on the weekends together and take my mom, aunt, and Alina. It's no exaggeration that they could kill someone with their little finger. I sure as fuck wouldn't want to face off against them.

"Fine. But guarding them means your cousins are away from their own families."

"Do you want me to leave?"

"I want to stop feeling guilty about every breath I take."

She tightens her arms around me like she's afraid I'll push her away.

"Let's go for that walk. If you want to talk more, we can. Or we can just enjoy the sunshine. Whatever you want, baby girl."

She inhales deeper than I could ever imagine before she releases it in the slowest exhale. She's not giving up, but I can tell she's resigned to what I'm offering. We head out to the living room and find Sergei and Anton ready to go, too. They look like they're going for a run, so they don't stick out too much in the park. When she spots them, she turns to me.

"Could we go running? It would make me feel better. I haven't worked out since we've been here, and that's part of why I feel so anxious. Do you run?"

"Like a fucking gazelle. Fast and dainty."

I flick off my brother as he laughs. I'm the fastest of all of us and have the best endurance. But I worked on my stride and form when I ran cross-country in high school and college. I don't go barreling down the road like Sergei, and he loves to tease me about it.

"At least I don't look like a fucking ox charging."

"You just wish you were as strong as me, little brother."

"Try not to drag those knuckles on the ground, old man."

I roll my eyes and duck back into the bedroom to change. I'm back out in a couple minutes ready to go. Kitty's eyes skim over my tank top and basketball shorts. I haven't been running in Moscow in years—decades. I don't know what the fuck men wear here or if men even go running. We've used private gyms in hotels during our sporadic visits. My tats will either scare people away or make a rival bratva think they can take me down. My guess is the former since nothing about Sergei, Anton, or me says come close enough to find out. We say goodbye to our dads and head down to the parking garage. There's a Lada Granta waiting for us, and three guards get into another one.

"Lean down and keep your face covered while we leave the hotel. There are cameras, and I don't want anyone seeing you until we're in a different district."

Kitty does as I say, and I know she can't be comfortable. But it's one of the few ways I can try to guard her while we're away from the hotel. The hat and hoodie should help, but they're not the best disguises. She remains in that position for five minutes before I ease her back to sitting. No one talks as we make our way to the park. Sergei and Anton can tell no one wants small talk, and there's nothing the three of us can discuss in front of Kitty.

We park near the entrance to the park and wait for our men to do a sweep. It isn't large, so it doesn't take them long. There's a path that wraps around it we can run. It's not as far away from the main road as I would like. None of us realized that when we searched it online. It makes me have second thoughts, but one glance at how eager Kitty is, I grin and bear it.

It's only a few minutes of stretching before we're off. Anton goes first and gets a head start before Kitty and I start our run. Sergei's about a hundred yards behind us. My brother and Anton go running together most days, then they work together. After nearly twenty years, I don't know what the fuck is left for them to talk about. But they always seem to come up with something. I glance at Kitty and wonder if we would ever run out of conversation. Maybe we wouldn't. I hope we wouldn't.

That's a jarring thought. Spending the next twenty years with her and twenty or thirty more after that. Who am I kidding? She might not have made up her mind yet, but I have.

A normal person wouldn't make such a life altering decision in the space of a few days, but when you've lived as I have, you do. My tomorrow is far less guaranteed than most people's. I've had to make life-changing decisions with not even minutes to spare. We've all gotten good at assessing situations, deciding, and sticking to the choice. I've mulled over things with Kitty nearly every spare minute I've had since I found her outside her sister's apartment building. This isn't me being rash. It's me considering every option and angle, then being decisive.

"Do you go running in the Bronx?"

"Hell, no. At least not unless I'm with someone. It's not like there's a crime everywhere I look at every minute of the day, but I knew better than to risk that when I first arrived as a foreigner. I found a gym, and that's where I go. Do you live in Manhattan?"

"Yeah. Most of my family is back in Queens, but I've stayed there."

"Back in Queens?"

"Yeah, when we were all old enough to leave Queens, we did. We wanted to put distance between our home lives and the bratva neighborhoods. But now that almost everyone is married, they've gone back to Queens. They live in the same neighborhood and within walking distance of each other."

"That sounds really nice. I wish I had family near me. I know I could have lived in Queens and been around people who—I don't know—get me. But I wanted nothing to do with that. If they weren't strangers, though, I suppose it would be really nice."

"Are you lonely?"

"Sometimes. I'm not a serial dater or anything, but I've had a few relationships in the five years I've been in America. But how do I explain I can never take them to meet my parents? How do I get around not having normal holiday stories? How do I keep them from asking about my family photos in my place? They never last long."

"I get that. I've felt all that and more. Maks's wife, Laura, studied in St. Petersburg while she was in college. She speaks Russian like it's her mother tongue. She knew who and what we were before we met. It's taken her time to adjust, but very little surprises her. Aleks's wife, Heather, is the newest member of our family. She grew up in Queens, and we went to school with her. She and Aleks reconnected, but they'd only known each other in passing in high school. She'd heard the rumors about us growing up. So, our life didn't entirely shock her."

I glance at Kitty to see how she's doing with the pace. She doesn't look any different from if we were walking.

"I never share this sort of stuff."

"I'm surprised you are. But I appreciate it. I want to know."

"And you're the only person I've ever wanted to tell. Niko's wife, Anastasia, is half Russian on her father's side. She's Laura's paralegal. Laura worked for a big corporate firm before she and Maks got married. Now she's our in-house attorney. She handles only non-bratva business. Same for Anastasia. Bogdan's wife, Christina, was a city building inspector. They met one night and didn't realize they'd end up working together on a project. Kutsenko Partners, my cousins' company, poached her from the city. She's now the head of their construction division. She doesn't speak Russian fluently yet, but she can be as stubborn as any Russian woman. Pasha's wife, Sumiko, is an accountant. Pasha has the same position as your dad, so it's funny that they wound up together. They're—make that she's— the least boring accountant I've ever met."

Pasha is hardly boring, but he gave her a gift that yelled stuffed shirt when they were on vacation. She loved it, so I guess that's all that matters.

"Sumiko? That sounds Japanese."

"It is. Her parents are a hundred percent Japanese, but they both grew up in Brazil. Their families went there after World War Two. Sumiko and her two brothers were born and raised in California."

"Wow. Your family is huge."

"And noisy. And fun. And close. There's twenty-one of us."

"Do you have to rent out a reception hall to all get together?"

She's going to find out eventually, but it's not easy to just blurt out.

"Kitty, my family aren't starving immigrants anymore. Some of our money in the beginning came from being bratva, but now we all live off our legal incomes. Bratva money goes back into our community. Kutsenko Partners has made my cousins billionaires. Sergei, Anton, Pasha, and I aren't quite where they are, but—we have a lot of money."

"What's a lot?"

"Millionaires. The houses they all have in Queens are practically mansions. There's plenty of room in each of them for our families to get together and for each of the wives' families to join us."

"And I live in a one-bedroom apartment in the Bronx."

"You also left your home and moved to a foreign country entirely on your own. Got yourself certified in a challenging field and got a job helping other people. You've lived on your own for five years. I'd say you're pretty damn successful in your own right."

"That's generous."

"Do you think I'm patronizing you? That's just how I see it. I've never been on my own. I mean, I live alone. But I've had twelve people to help me with everything my entire life. What you did takes courage, resourcefulness, and determination. I'm not kidding when I say I'm impressed."

"Thank you. You might have had a big family around you, but I know I've had it way easier. Misha, I've seen and felt your scars. I won't ask you to explain. If you want to tell me, I'll take those secrets to the grave. But I know how you got them—the gunshots, stabbings, restraints, and burns. Your tats cover everything unless you know what to look for. I know what I touched. I'm proud of my accomplishments, but they are nothing like yours. I couldn't have survived."

"You do what you have to for your family, especially when they're doing the same for you."

"I'd do anything for Larisa. Same for my parents, but it's different. She used to get picked on a lot when we were kids. She wore the thickest glasses I've ever seen, and she was short and pudgy. You'd never guess it now. I got suspended for a week in fourth grade because I kicked a kid younger than me in the balls for pushing her and making fun of her. I broke another guy's nose when I found out he touched her after she said no while they were on a date. I'd do a fuck ton more if I had to."

"I don't doubt that. When we find her, will you trust me to handle whoever did this? I can't agree to putting you in danger, and what I will do are things you will never watch. Never."

She looks up at me. I can tell she doesn't want to agree, but neither does she want to lie to me.

"I'll think about it. That's the best I can offer."

"Fair."

We run in companionable silence for at least a mile before I have more questions.

"What made you want to be a nurse?"

"I wanted to do something as far away from what my family does as I could. I wanted to save lives instead of taking them."

That almost makes me trip. I guessed as much, but the disdain in her voice makes me wonder why she even looked in my direction.

"I know what you're thinking, Misha. Your face doesn't show it, but I can tell. I'd call it irony."

"Me too."

She wipes the sweat dribbling along her temple as we continue at a pace that tells me she's an experienced runner. She's keeping up without a struggle even though my stride is longer than hers.

"I wanted out because I felt like I had no choices, and I wanted to prove that they couldn't force me into anything I didn't want. It's different with you. It's entirely my choice."

I hope it's one she never regrets. I'm still waiting for the shitstorm. I can tell it's coming.

Chapter Ten

Kitty

Misha's taken me running or walking ten days in a row, and it's been fantastic. But the rest of the time, I'm still holed up in the suite. It feels like house-arrest, but it's certainly not somewhere I can complain about. When we're here, Misha helps me make the most of it. Last night comes to mind.

"When we get home, malyshka, *we have some shopping to do on Amazon. That fine little ass of yours is missing something."*

There isn't a chance in hell either of us is looking for a sex shop in Moscow.

"And what could that be, Daddy?"

"A butt plug with a nice sparkly jewel. Your ass is mine, just like your pussy."

"Is there anything else you want me to wear?"

"Nipple clamps wouldn't be a bad place to start. I'll lick and suck away the sting once I take them off. Do you like it when I suck your tits?"

"*You know I do.*"

"*Take your bra off,* kiska."

It means pussy, but only like the feline.

I was in the middle of getting undressed when he came into the bedroom. I'm quick to follow directions. I discovered my ass and pussy aren't the only things I enjoy being spanked. His hand lands on my right nipple before he pulls and twists. The pain shoots straight to my pussy. He does it three more times quickly. Then he's sucking as he does the same thing on the left one. He alternates his attention until I'm panting.

"*I thought I told you no more panties. Was I not clear?*"

"*You were. But it's just odd not to wear them.*"

"*But you knew what I expected, didn't you?*"

"*Yes, Daddy.*"

"*Come with me,* malyshka."

There's a chair in the bedroom, and he settles me across his lap once he's seated and I've slipped off my thong. He rubs my ass and squeezes as he talks.

"*I told you I would only punish you if you endangered yourself. I expect you not to do that. But I will also punish you if you know my other expectations and don't follow them. Can you live with that?*"

"*Doesn't that make it domestic discipline? Or like you're a Daddy Dom?*"

"*I don't think so. I'm not going to punish you for not wearing a coat if you don't want to or not putting laundry away. I'm not going to punish you for talking back to me or disagreeing with me.*"

"*Does that mean I get to spank you if you don't meet my expectations?*"

He does that hot chuckle again.

"*I thought we already decided on that. How about you make me watch you take a shower naked and don't let me fuck you?*"

I huff.

"Sounds like a punishment for both of us. But I can live with this."

The moment I consent, his hand rains down four smacks across both cheeks. The sound of his hand hitting my flesh fills the room. Then his fingers are teasing my pussy, sliding along so slowly and lightly. I want to shift to get them inside me, to wiggle from frustration and eagerness. One of his wide fingers rubs my clit, and I don't smother my moan. He loves hearing me, but I'm careful that he's the only one.

"This is why Daddy says no panties. I couldn't do this with them in the way."

I close my eyes and focus on his hands. His fingers keep working my cunt as the other hand strokes my sore ass.

"May I come?"

"Yes, malyshka. *You took that spanking well."*

It's only a moment later that I feel that tightening in my core, then the pleasure radiates out as my thighs clench around his hand. The moment I relax, Misha puts me back on my feet and stands. We cross the room, and he grabs my bra from where I left it on the bed. He backs me against the bathroom door, and before I know what's happening, he's used my bra to not only bind my hands together but secure them to the doorknob. He drops to his knees and draws my left leg over his shoulder. His teeth graze my still-sensitive clit before he licks me. He pulls my hips toward him, sliding his tongue over my asshole to my clit. I'm uncertain how I feel about that.

"You don't like that."

"Mmm. Maybe it's the nurse in me, but I can't not think about that being unhygienic."

He laughs and nips at my inner thigh.

"Very well, kiska. *But I'm still fucking your ass."*

"I know."

He laughs again at my eagerness. I've never had anal before, so he's insisted that we start me with a couple plugs to prepare me. I don't think I need them, but I can tell he's really concerned about hurting me. I didn't argue.

His tongue slips inside me, and he flicks it back and forth. The sensation makes the knee that's supporting half my weight shake. He practically inhales my clit as he moves back to suck it. His teeth graze over it again. I tug at my wrist bindings, wishing I could run my fingers through his hair, hold his head to my pussy, push his tongue deeper. He knew that's what I would want, and that's why he secured my hands behind my back. He knows I hate not being able to touch him. He loves the control that gives him. And I love that more than I dislike having to wait to touch him.

"May I come?"

"Yes."

I can barely understand him since his mouth is still between my thighs. He keeps working me until I squeeze my eyes shut and press my lips together. I release a muffled moan as I come. My eyes flutter open as I take a deep breath.

"Daddy, I want to suck you off."

I never really enjoyed giving blowjobs in the past. I did it to get what I wanted in return. Small price to pay. But I crave the feel of his cock against my tongue. I want to suck him off. I love watching what it does to him. How he'll fist his hands to keep from touching me, mastering his desire. Or when he presses my head forward and fucks my mouth, completely in control of what I take. For someone who's never been submissive during sex— like ever—this is not only new to me but fucking fantastic. I've never felt more desirable.

He releases my hands, and I fall to my knees. I practically rip the basketball shorts off while he yanks his t-shirt over his head. He's abandoned the boxer briefs, and now he smirks at me.

"Fine, Daddy. You win."

I told him not to wear them, and he listened. I gotta admit, it's nice having his dick spring free right away. I pounce. I lick him from stem to stern before I deepthroat him. His hands fist my hair, but he does nothing to hold my head in place or push deeper into my mouth. I suck him like I'm trying to get a milkshake through a straw.

"Mmm-mmm."

I try to keep him in my mouth when he pulls back. I wrap my hand around him, but he pulls my wrist away. I squeal when he scoops me off the floor and carries me to the bed. He practically tosses me onto the mattress, then grabs my ankles and drags me back to him. My feet are over his shoulders before I know what's happening. Then he's in me.

Holy fuck.

He supports my hips and holds them up as he plows me.

"Is this what you want, malyshka? Is this how you like to be fucked?"

"You know it is, papochka."

And it is. We've done it slowly and tenderly, and I love that as much as this. But these moments when he lets go of some of his restraint make me feel like the sexiest woman alive. It's like he needs to be in me so much, he can't help himself. I'm happy to oblige.

"You're so deep."

It almost hurts, and I'm here for that. The moment he rubs my clit again, I'm done for. I clench all my muscles, and it raises my hips. He thrusts into me two more times before I clamp down enough to hold him inside me.

"Fuck. I don't know how I still have cum after each time. I feel like there can't be anything else. I've never come so hard as when I'm fucking you."

"Good. Remember that."

He picks me up, so I straddle his lap as he sits.

"I will never forget, Kitty. You are my alpha and omega."

I shake myself back into the present as I get dressed. I'm soaked remembering last night, and I ache for another round even though we just had shower sex. I've never been this horny in my life. I calm myself as we get ready to join the others at the table for breakfast.

I know Sergei's still been scouring every digital clue he can find, but nothing's shown up. Today's Monday, and I've convinced them to take me to Larisa's office. Everyone's background check came up clean, but I can't stop thinking maybe someone knows something, and they'd tell me rather than the police or the bratva.

"Are you ready, *malyshka?*"

Misha keeps his voice low when he calls me that. I'm certain the others have overheard him, but no one reacts. He admitted the other night that, while he's never called another woman that, he's heard his cousins call their wives that. He has a hunch they all have pretty kinky marriages, but he'd never ask.

"Yeah. I guess."

I'm suddenly nervous, and I think I might be sick. Am I making a huge mistake? Will whoever this is come after me next? Will they find out and punish Larisa? I'm having second thoughts about this.

Misha and I are in the bedroom, and we haven't heard anyone else moving around yet. But from the time on the bedside clock, I know they will come out for breakfast soon. He comes to stand in front of me, his right arm going around my waist, and his left hand fisting in my hair. He has me pinned against him.

"If you don't want to do this, say so."

"I do, but I don't. I don't even know anymore."

His hand slides down to grab my ass. Hard.

That surety. That sense of command. Like he can control any situation. It's reassuring in ways I never imagined.

"You will go nowhere alone. No one speaks to you unless I'm with you."

"That defeats the point. I don't want anyone to think it's the bratva there to intimidate them. They'll clam up."

"I'll relent on you speaking to them alone, but I won't give in on you going anywhere alone. I need to be able to see you, even if I have to deal with you being out of reach. I don't like it, but I think you're right."

"I do feel better knowing you'll be nearby. I need to do this, but I'm scared."

"Of what you might learn, or of what someone might do to you?"

"Both. I feel jittery, and I'm not used to it. I just want to get this over with."

"You don't like things being out of your control."

"Not like this. It feels like no one has any control. There's too much unpredictability."

"Do you think I'm predictable?"

What? Why is he asking that all of a sudden? That makes no sense.

"In some ways, yes. I know I'm safe with you. I know you'll do whatever you have to. I know you won't get angry if I disagree with you. I know you listen to me."

"If you can't have control of things, do you want me to?"

"Yes. But—"

"Come here, *malyshka*."

He leads me to the bed and sits down. I'm about to sit next to him when he stops me.

"Pull you pants down and lay across my lap."

"You're going to spank me? Is this because I disagreed with you after all?"

"This isn't a punishment, baby. This is purely for pleasure. Concentrate on your spankings. Think about how wet they make you, how much you need me to make you come by the end. Relax and let me be in control."

I don't know how a spanking is going to make me feel better, but if I can come...Fuck. I'll take that any time. I push my pants and panties down to my ankles before he lays me across his lap.

"We are going to have a conversation about your panties."

"We are?"

"Yes. You aren't wearing them anymore."

"You want me to go commando? Are you going to free ball it?"

"Yes, and do you want me to?"

"I like the idea that I could wrap my hand around you or suck you off at any moment if you don't have those tight boxer briefs on."

"And now you understand why I don't want those fucking panties in the way."

The first slap lands, and I'm not prepared for it. It's not as hard as it could be. It's not as biting as the first night we were together. As he lands more, he aims for my sit spot and pushing my clit against his solid muscle thigh. His hand goes down the collar of my shirt and grabs my tits that are hanging past his other leg.

"That's only been five, and I can see your cunt is dripping."

If it were any other man saying that to me, I'd be mortified and definitely turned *off*. But all it does is make me want to ride his cock. He lands two more blows, one on each side before his fingers delve inside me. He pulls his hand free from my shirt, and I kick my feet with displeasure. But next thing I know, he's still fingering me while his now free hand continues my spanking. As three more come in quick succession, I focus on how good it feels to have my ass warmed while he buries his fingers in me. I feel myself relaxing, and my body loosens. My shoulders and back don't feel tense, and my arms feel heavy.

"Daddy, am I allowed to come?"

"Yes, baby. Whenever you want. Are you close?"

"No. I don't want to come yet, but I was wondering."

"Are you liking this?"

"Very much. It hurts. I mean, I don't need you to spank me any harder, but I actually feel calmer than I did before."

"Do you need a fuck, or is this enough?"

I laugh. His voice is so casual, as though he's asking if I need more mashed potatoes at Christmas.

"I'll always take a fuck, Daddy."

I can't stop another laugh as I continue to think how ridiculous this conversation is. But I do feel better for it. I kick my feet again though when he pulls his fingers out. I awkwardly look up at him as he licks them. He savors them as though he were licking chocolate from them, not my pussy juice. He eases me to my feet.

"Take me out."

Hell, yes. I waste no time pulling his belt loose then unbuttoning and unzipping his trousers. He spins me and lifts me high enough to bring my knees under me on the mattress.

"Ughmm."

With a grunt, he's inside me. He's pounding me, and I can feel my ass jiggle. Even though I run often, it's not firm like you'd expect. I mean, it is under all the extra meat. But he's made it clear he loves that. He spanks me on each cheek as he drives into me even harder.

"Whose cunt is this?"

"Yours."

"And what do I get to do with it?"

"Whatever you want, Daddy."

"And if I want to make my baby girl come?"

"Yes, please, Daddy."

His hand spanks me on my horizontal crack one last time before sliding around to rub my clit. My head hangs down between my arms as I clutch the bedcovers. But the moment I feel my orgasm start, I fling my head back, forgetting that his might be in the way. He dives in to kiss my neck, nipping and licking as he doesn't let up.

"I will fuck you to make you come. I'll fuck you to make me come. And I'll fuck you to make you sure you know that I'll always give you what you need."

"You think I need your dick inside me?"

"We both know you need it as much as I do."

"You're right. Fuck, Daddy. I want to come again."

He slams into me, harder and faster. I don't know how he does it. I press my hips back as his other hand fists my hair.

"Do you understand how much I want you? I will never get enough of you, Kitty. Never. You are mine."

"Don't let go."

"Never."

This isn't just lust and passion talking. The sex is mind-blowing, but it's so much more. The way we move together. The way we understand what each other needs. No couple that's been together a week should be this close, this in sync. It's insane. It's marvelous. My pussy clenches around him as my body goes stiff. He pulls me back, so I'm kneeling upright.

"I want to make you come, Misha. I need to."

"You are. You don't have to prove anything. I've never wanted a woman the way I want you. There's no comparing this to anyone else. Fuck, baby."

I feel him tremble behind me as he shoots his load inside

me. I reach back to wrap my arms around his waist as he kisses my jaw, neck, behind my ear, and my shoulder through my shirt. His hand soothes my ass as he strokes it.

My body feels completely boneless, and my mind is clear. This wasn't just a distraction. This was me truly accepting Misha being in control. He did everything I needed and wanted without me having to ask. He just got it, and it made it simple for me to let go. I wonder if this would make sense to anyone other than me, other than us.

"*Malyshka?*"

"*Da, papochka.*"

We switch back and forth between English and Russian all the time, and so does his family. Sometimes even within the same conversation. But my mind is so blank, I don't even think about what I'm saying. I could curl up and go to sleep, but then reality rushes back in when I remember why I can't. All the tension comes right back.

"Shh, baby. You gave up control to me because you wanted me to take care of you. You relaxed and let that happen. I know how much your trust means, and I won't break it. Can you trust me beyond the bedroom? Can you believe that I'll take care of you out there the way I just did in here?"

"It's not automatic, but I want to. I'm going to try to. But I can't change how stressful this is just because I know you're on my side."

"I know, and I don't expect you to. But I don't want you feeling like you're bracing for war the moment we aren't m —fucking."

I heard that mmm sound. He caught himself, but I heard it. Was he going to say making love? That was rough sex. There's no doubt about that. If I weren't stopping to think about it, I would say we just fucked. But maybe not. It went a lot, lot deeper than just getting off. Part of me wants to believe my intense feelings are ridiculous and won't last once this fucktastrophe of my life is over. The other part of me is telling me I'm a fucking idiot if I don't see how special this is and that he's committed to me as much I want him to be and as much as I want to be committed to him. I know he didn't exaggerate when he said he's been thinking about this. He's not even remotely impulsive. He's hinting at permanence and fuck me if I don't want the same.

I hate the feeling of him pulling out, but I pull my pants up high enough to dash into the bathroom without waddling. I'm quick to clean up, and we're headed into the living room as the others sit down to breakfast. I'm in a blouse and nice slacks, but I feel underdressed compared to their tailor-made suits. There is no way there's a piece of off-the-rack clothing in this room except for mine. Everything fits them too well, and they're all too big but trim to wear shit that isn't custom.

I glance at Radomir, but he's busy uncovering the room service plates. My dad tends to be gruff and insensitive even though I know he doesn't mean to. He wants to be as loving as Radomir clearly is. I know it's wrong to wish Radomir was my dad, but he's so much more reassuring and daddly—that's not even a word, but it fits—than any other man I've ever known. He hugged me the other day, and it was like an enormous, muscular teddy bear engulfing me.

If I were five, I would have crawled on his lap and asked for a story. Misha was right about his family not being prudes. Sergei and Anton have said nothing about me, but I've heard their off-color jokes about Misha's balls finally dropping. Radomir and Grigori act as though Misha and I have been a couple since the beginning of time. I just seem to fit in like I'm family.

We're all quick to finish our breakfast before we head out.

We're in one of the big vans again, and I wonder why we aren't going for more subtle. Misha leans over and whispers.

"Asking questions may piss people off. Someone might squeal. We need to be in the cars that are bulletproof and reinforced against impact."

I nod my head. Makes sense, but shit just got really real. The men chat around me about some soccer game they watched last night after Misha and I went in our bedroom. When we get to Larisa's office, I remember to wait until someone is outside before I get out. All five of them walk me to the door, but Radomir pulls out his phone and looks like he's casually waiting in the lobby. Grigori and Anton stand between the elevators and the fire exit, chatting. Sergei rides the elevator up with us, but he stays right outside it. I lead Misha to the office suite door.

"I have my gun in my purse, and my knife is in my belt beneath my cardigan."

"Good. Your cardigan is too thin to hide a gun, but I wish it were there instead."

"I know. Me too. I wasn't thinking about that when I packed. I can get my hand in and out of my purse without a problem."

"If anything happens, you have the alert in your purse, too. Press it, and we will all come. I can't see the earpiece at all. We all have ours in. We'll be able to hear everything."

"I know. I better go in before someone sees us."

"*Malyshka*, I'll be right here."

"I know, Daddy."

He gives me a quick kiss, then steps back and turns halfway like he's going into the suite across the hall, but I know his gaze is sweeping everything he can see when I open the door extra wide. I turn back to make sure it closes without slamming. He shoots me a confident smile, and my racing heart slows. I turn back and walk to the receptionist. She greets me in Russian.

"I was hoping to speak to the director."

"Is there a problem? Do you have an appointment?"

"I don't have an appointment, but I need to see him about an employee's handling of a contract."

I came up with that excuse last night because I couldn't think of anything better. I still can't. The woman stares at me before she nods.

"What's your name?"

"Katerina."

I know she expected me to give her my last name, but my tone makes it clear I don't plan to say more. She picks up the phone and speaks quietly while pointing to a chair I can sit in. I look around for any familiar faces. I notice a man and woman looking in my direction, but they avert their eyes once they catch me watching them. The man hurries to walk away, and I'm certain they must know who I am, or at least have a solid guess. Larisa and I look enough alike to be sisters. But our height and weight differences are usually enough to make people doubt themselves.

"I understand you wanted to see me."

A middle-aged man approaches and speaks to me in Russian. Larisa said her boss was a douche, and his patronizing smile confirms it.

"It's an employee matter, so I'd prefer to talk about it in your office."

He leads me along the hallway until we reach his office door. Since he goes in ahead of me, I leave the door open partway. I want to hear anyone approach, and I'm not comfortable being closed in and alone with him.

"I don't think it has anything to do with a contract, does it? You're Larisa's sister."

"I am. Did you recognize me from a photo on her desk?"

"Yes."

What the fuck has he been doing that close to her? The way the work areas are divided, I know he would have spoken to my sister from across her desk. Unless he needed to do something on her computer, he shouldn't have been able to see the photos on her desk. I know because I've stood across from her before.

"Have you heard from your sister?"

"No. That's why I'm here. I know people have questioned you and your employees, but I'm her sister. I'm not the police, and I'm not my father's employers. I just want her back. I'm not looking for justice or to prove a point. Larisa is all I need."

For now. Then I will tear whoever took her to shreds. I told Misha that I would let him handle it. Maybe I'll be rational enough to let him. But I doubt it.

"Miss Vasilieva, I truly know nothing about what happened to your sister. She was an excellent employee, and honestly, she wasted her skills here. But she enjoyed helping the students."

"Did any of the students pay too much attention to her? Seem too eager to see her?"

"No. None. They were always respectful, and she kept a professional distance between them. She never got too personal, but they all knew they could trust her to help them. I really don't think it had anything to do with work. I know you were close. She spoke highly of you to others. I can't imagine how you must feel, but I told your father and the police the truth. I don't know anything more than she stopped showing up to work with no explanation."

I still think he's a douchebag, but he's an honest douchebag. That or he deserves an Oscar. He has no tells. Nothing about his body language or inflection hints that he's lying. I watch all of him as he speaks, and there's not even a twitch to hint that he's deceiving me. The sincerity is forced, but he's honest.

"Thank you, Mr. Golubev."

I stand and shake his hand. I heard someone walk past and stop while we were talking. I'm quick to turn on my heel and cross the room. I see the woman from earlier hurrying away from the office. Why was she eavesdropping? If she wasn't, she wouldn't be rushing away.

"May I say hi to a few people I recognize?"

"Of course. I'm sure they would like that."

I doubt it, but at least he didn't refuse me. I make my way over to the woman, who's now back at her desk. I strain to hear every conversation I pass, but very few people are talking. I offer the woman a warm smile even though we're strangers. I don't want people suspicious about why I'm talking to her. I'd rather they think we're old friends.

"I'm Larisa's sister, Katerina."

"I know. We met before you moved to America. I don't think you recognize me since my hair used to be brown. I'm Sofia Golubev."

I glance toward the office I was just in.

"He's my father. Nepotism is nice."

She offers me a quick smile before it drops, and she straightens to sit taller.

"I know other people have already been here, but is there anything you can tell me? I'm desperate to find my sister. Whatever happened. Even a guess. This is killing my mother, and I'm ready to quit my job and stay here. I can't think straight in America, and I'm terrified here."

"I know nothing. She was here one day, then not the next."

I watch her swallow twice. She cocks an eyebrow.

"I miss her."

Oh, shit. Were they...?

"She told me you'd understand, but I can tell she never told you..."

"No. We never talked about that over the phone, in texts or emails."

"Smart. If you find her, I want—need—to know, Katerina. I—"

She snaps her mouth shut as the man from earlier joins us.

"Katerina, this is Oleg. He worked with the same universities as Larisa and processed her paperwork."

He worked beneath her. Interesting. Smug bastard. I take in every detail I can about him, including how worn his shoes are, his soft looking hands, and his scrawny build. I wouldn't underestimate him, but neither do I think Larisa couldn't defend herself against him. But if this guy is some great criminal mastermind who sent those men for her...My mind is running wild.

"Hello, Oleg. It's nice to meet you."

"Same."

No one says anything for a minute. No condolences or well wishes. No suggestions or warnings. Just silence.

"Is her desk still the same?"

Sofia flashes me a frown I know Oleg can't see.

"No. Your father collected everything after the police came by."

"Can I see it?"

Oleg answers for Sofia.

"Sure. Follow me."

I like him even less than a minute ago. It sounds like a command and an inconvenience at the same time. When we get to my sister's work area, I run my fingers over her desk. I look on the floor and in the drawers. I don't expect to find anything, but on the off chance...I'm not passing up the opportunity. There's nothing. It's obvious they wiped things down, and the computer is gone. I force myself not to let my shoulders slump.

I nod to Oleg and head toward the door. As I pass the receptionist, I glance back to find Sofia observing me. She dips her chin, but I don't know what that means. Oleg is talking to another woman and clearly flirting. Misha's leaning against the wall when I step into the hallway, and I've never been so glad to see anyone. I saw the security cameras, so I don't dare collapse against him. It's not until we're back in the van that I sink against him.

"Could you hear everything clearly?"

No one spoke that loudly in the office, so I didn't know if my earpiece picked up everything.

"Sort of."

"Her boss claims he knows nothing. A man was watching me when I arrived, but he wasn't forthcoming during the few minutes I was with him. But the woman he was talking to admitted she and Larisa were more than just friends. It makes me wonder if she got pissed that Larisa went on a date with a man. Did someone find out? If that's the case, Sofia's fine, so why isn't Larisa? It also makes me wonder if it wasn't actually a date but something else entirely. I couldn't get any details, so I don't know how close Sofia and Larisa were or when they were together. Her entire work area was bare. I feel like it was one step forward and two steps back."

I sigh as Misha kisses my forehead. I'm almost ready to tell them to take me back to the hotel, but I won't give up yet. There's somewhere else I want to go first. Maybe I'll have better luck there.

Chapter Eleven

Misha

We arrive at the hair salon, and I immediately wonder if Russian hair stylists are pseudo-therapists like the stereotype in America. Kitty adjusts her earpiece after she insists she go inside alone. I hate it, but five men walking into a salon is nothing but suspicious. Even if I went in as her boyfriend or husband, it would be weird. And I doubt the conversations would flow as openly if a man my size sat and browsed a fashion magazine.

All of us still have our earpieces in when I hear Kitty's voice speaking Russian. I almost don't notice her accent anymore when she speaks English because she practically sounds like a native. But hearing her speak Russian just reminds me of how little either of us still fits in here and how much more American we've become. More so me, but I can see —hear—it in her too.

"Do you have any appointments for a trim open? I know you're busy."

A trim? We didn't agree to that. Someone will see the listening device in her ear. Then what?

"It'll be about ten minutes. Then Vera can see you."

"Is Yulia working today? I've heard she's very good."

"Um, let me see if she can fit you in."

There's silence for a few minutes, then the receptionist's voice fills my ear.

"She can. She actually thinks it'll be about twenty minutes. Would you like to have a seat?"

"Thank you."

There's nothing but background noise for five minutes. Then I hear Kitty walking.

"Could I use your restroom, please?"

"Sure. It's straight back past the shampoo bowls."

"Thanks."

Women's voices get a little louder, so there must be more people there than I thought. That makes the situation even less controlled. I don't like it. Kitty's is the next voice I hear.

"Oh. That looks so good on you. Wow, your eyes look so bright."

"Thank you."

That's a stranger, but the woman sounds thrilled.

"I wish I could pull off a cut like that. I don't think I could go that short, but my friend who recommended this place has a style like that. It's tempting."

"I think you could. It's just hair. It'll grow back if you don't like it."

"I don't know. I work in a law firm, so everyone's kinda serious. I don't think it would fit in."

It's a new woman who speaks up next.

"I have a client who's a lawyer, and I just cut hers like this about two months ago. She texted me to tell me how many compliments she got."

"Does it take a lot of maintenance? I'm pretty wash and go. Has she come back to get it touched up?"

That's true. Kitty wears her hair in a ponytail most of the time. I love taking it out and watching it fall loose around her shoulders, then running my fingers through it.

"No. I actually haven't heard from her in a while, which is odd. She comes every month to get highlights or some color treatment."

"Do you have a photo, so I can see what it looks like on someone else?"

There's a long pause before the woman who must be a stylist answers.

"Sure. Hang on."

The woman must be unlocking her phone and pulling up the gallery because no one says anything.

"Oh, fun! You two went out clubbing. Her hair looks great. Was this right after she got it cut?"

"Yeah. About two weeks after."

"Her hair looks kinda like mine. How long do you think hers is by now if she hasn't been back?"

"Mmmm. It's only been about eight weeks, so maybe two or three inches longer. It couldn't be much more than that."

"So, like, halfway down her neck."

"Yeah."

"This looks so good. I'm really tempted. Where is this? I don't recognize this club. It looks cool."

"Bar Disko 50."

"I wonder if my boyfriend would take me."

There's another long pause, and it's the client who speaks next.

"It gets kinda wild there. How serious are you and your boyfriend?"

"Really."

"That might not be the right place. People—it's a good place to find someone else to go home with, if you know what I mean."

A fucking swingers' club?

"Oh! Um, yeah. I don't think he'd like that. Does everyone do that? I mean, could I go with my girlfriends and just have fun without hooking up?"

"Sure. The guys can be kinda pushy though, so just be warned."

"Do you have any photos of the place?"

What Kitty means is: do you have any more pictures of her sister at a club for random sex partners?

"Sure. Here are a few more from that night."

There's silence for a while, so I assume she's swiping.

"Damn. He's hot. Your friend got a good one."

The stylist releases a disdainful exhale before she continues.

"Yeah, no. He turned out to be an asshole. She told me she went out with him once but found out he was married."

"That sucks. Maybe that's not the right place to find a guy for a date."

"That's what she told me. We were supposed to go out a couple weeks ago, but she hasn't texted me back."

"Weird."

I know Kitty's trying to sound casual.

"It's actually kinda fucked up."

Now we might get somewhere with the stylist. Kitty doesn't drop a beat, and she sounds normal.

"What is?"

"That she hasn't texted me back. I left her a voicemail. I thought we were close, but she disappeared. From what I've heard, no one's talked to her or seen her recently."

"I'd be freaked out if I were you. Do you think...I mean, maybe she's on vacation."

Kitty sounds doubtful as she hints at what we all understand, then she tries to play it off. This might be a good tactic.

"I really don't know. But I—I—"

"I'm sorry. I didn't mean to make you cry. I was too nosey."

"It's all right. I'm really worried about her. I tried finding out where she lives or find her family, but I only knew her first name. Larisa. She said she was a lawyer, but I don't know where."

"Did you try the police?"

There's a tiny waver in Kitty's voice, and I wish I were there to hold her hand or hug her.

"You know they're not reliable. They won't care about one woman who goes missing."

"But maybe someone else has reported her too, and they gave more information. If you were one of the last people to see her...You never know."

It's the client who speaks next. I almost forgot about her.

"She's right. Maybe it could help. You could just report it without asking them to do anything. And not all of them are corrupt. Most aren't."

"I guess."

The stylist sounds no more convinced than a moment ago.

"I wish you luck. I hope your friend is okay."

"Me too...You're right. I'll go to the police after work."

The stylist sounds more confident this time. It's time to get her out of there, though. I'm about to call when the client must have bumped into Kitty because she apologizes. I dial her number like we planned.

"Hello?"

"Ready?"

Kitty doesn't respond right away like she's still listening to someone talk.

"Yeah. I can be there in five minutes. I was going to get a haircut, but I guess I can do that later."

I say nothing else, but Kitty remains quiet for a moment.

"Okay. See you soon."

She hangs up with me.

"My boss just called me back into work. So much for an hour off for lunch. I'll have to try another day. I hope everything works out with your friend."

"Thanks."

The client is standing closer to Kitty since she's louder when she speaks next.

"Weren't you headed to the bathroom? I know I have to go, then you can blow dry me."

"Yeah. I was."

I hear Kitty and a door opening. Then it's the client talking.

"You look too much like her not to be her sister. I know Larisa. Put my number in your phone. Call me tonight. I didn't know her last name either, so I didn't know who to call. I think your dad's bratva, so I didn't go to the police."

"Tell me now."

There's a bite to Kitty's voice.

"This is a private conversation, and this is not a private place. Call me."

"Fine."

"I'm glad you came here. I hope I can help you find your sister. I hung out with her and Yulia a few times. She was really nice."

"What's your name?"

When there's no answer, I wonder if something happened.

"Valeriya Ivankov."

Everyone in the van freezes. I swallow as I wait to hear

anything else. Ivankov isn't an uncommon name, but Valeriya Ivankov was once married to the man who started our New York bratva branch. Roman Ivankov was a well-known criminal here before he moved to America. He spent ten years in a Russian prison camp, then ten years in an American prison. This woman could be the original Valeriya's granddaughter or something. The likelihood of two unrelated women having that name is slim.

"Solntsevskaya?"

"*Da.*"

Holy shit. They're the bratva that sent Roman to America to take control of the bratva in New York. They're the same bratva that fought the Chechens like the Podolskaya, which is the branch my family belonged to, and that Timofey now leads.

"Did you know?"

From Kitty's tone when she asks, I know she means did Valeriya know someone took Larisa.

"*Da.*"

These one-word answers are all Kitty will get for now. I whisper to her.

"Tell her to come to the hotel instead."

"I'm staying at a hotel downtown. It's safe there. We can talk, and no one will know."

"I have to get there."

I whisper to Kitty again.

"Get her address. We'll send a car."

"I can send someone I trust to get you. What's your address?"

I'm not certain Valeriya will give it to her, but when she speaks, Anton's ready to type it into his phone. Kitty gives her the hotel name too, and I'm certain Valeriya has to be wondering how the fuck Kitty is staying there.

"I can come after dark. Say seven-thirty."

"I'll have someone there for you. You'll come into the hotel through the underground parking garage's elevator and come up to the top floor."

"Penthouse? Who's going to be there, Katerina? You better not—"

"I'm not. It's my boyfriend and his family. They're bratva, too. But don't live here. They aren't tied to anyone here. They're helping me find Larisa."

"You know who I am. What's your name?"

"Katerina Vasilieva."

"I don't know that name."

"I'll tell you what I can if you'll do the same tonight."

"Fine. I'll see you then."

"Same."

By the time Kitty climbs back into the van, Sergei has his laptop open and is running Valeriya's name. Everything from articles about Roman and his wife, Valeriya, to this Valeriya's driver's license pops up. She's their granddaughter, after all.

"Do you think telling her you're Ivankov will make her more willing to share everything she knows?"

She directs the question to me, but it's my dad who answers.

"Yes. We fought alongside her uncles in the Second Chechen War. I saved her father's life when he got drunk and picked a fight with my brother-in-law after he insulted my sister-in-law."

Uncle Kirill married my mom's sister, Galina. Grigori was going to let his younger brother kill Valeriya's father. If it had been any man other than Roman Ivankov's son, my dad wouldn't have stopped Uncle Kirill. I'm not sure how old she is, but if Uncle Kirill had killed her father, she might never have been born.

"Can you explain how you're all related again?"

Kitty fastens her seatbelt, then I take her hand. I point to my dad first.

"My dad married my mom, Svetlana, and had Sergei and me. She has a sister, Galina, who married Grigori's younger brother, Kirill. Uncle Kirill and Aunt Galina had four sons. Grigori married Aunt Galina's best friend, Alina, and had Anton and Pasha."

"Alina and Galina?"

"Yes. They said they were meant to be best friends just because of that."

"Why didn't your uncle come with you?"

Grigori turns to face forward, and Kitty turns questioning eyes to me.

"Uncle Kirill died in the Second Chechen War. My dad came home with an injury, but Grigori and Uncle Kirill had to stay. Grigori was there."

I keep my voice low. It's no secret, but it's still something no one likes to talk about. I can't imagine being almost within arm's reach of Sergei and watching him be blown up by a land-mine. Uncle Kirill was saving Grigori's best friend. Bogdan was ten, Niko was eleven, Aleks was twelve, and Maks was thirteen when they lost their dad. I know it's been a blessing and a curse to my cousins that Grigori looks exactly like their dad.

"I'm sorry. I shouldn't have been so nosey. I know better than to ask—"

"Katerina, it's all right. You had no way to know, and I'm not upset. It's just a painful memory. I miss my brother."

Grigori turns back as he talks and offers her a fatherly smile, and I can tell she breathes a little easier. When we were all younger, sometimes my cousins would slip up and call Grigori *papochka*. It's hard to imagine how something so painful can also be so comforting.

"Are you really okay with her coming to the hotel?"

It's my dad's turn to offer her a fatherly smile as he nods.

"It's for the best."

It really defies the imagination how two men who were KGB and bratva and did everything they've done for the past thirty-odd years can be so kind. If no one ever saw their tattoos, they'd never guess they were Russian mafia.

Kitty's sitting between Anton and me this time. I wrap my arm around her shoulders, and she leans against mine. My thumb rubs over her shoulder and the top of her arm. I kiss her temple as her eyes close, but I know she's not falling asleep.

"Could she really know something about Larisa? Could her family have done this?"

"I don't know, *malyshka*."

I keep my voice to a whisper, and I press a soft kiss to her lips when she tilts her head back.

"How much danger is she in coming to see us?"

"I don't know for sure. I don't know where she usually goes or what she does. But if she went to that nightclub, then she must have a lot of freedom."

A lot of freedom to fuck who you want and get drunk all night is a lot different from going to a hotel to speak to bratva members from another branch. But I won't say anything because I don't know how things stand between the Solntsevskaya and Podolskaya. Last I heard, they were okay. But who the fuck knows what Timofey's done, or what his members have done if he can't control them enough for them to know to leave my family the fuck alone?

Sergei's still working as we pull into the underground garage. A car backfires, and I push Kitty down as I release my seatbelt and lean over her. I hear the safeties flick off on four guns while the driver speeds down the ramp. When nothing else happens, I slowly sit up.

"Are you all right?"

"Yeah. Was that a car or a gun?"

Anton's leaning forward to peer past the driver. He shakes his head.

"It was a car. That old piece of junk down there."

The car somehow survived the Soviet Union, and the man popping the hood could be my grandfather. We don't discount him, but the threat lessens. The driver pulls us close to the elevator, and Anton hops out to punch the button. No one says anything until we get to the hotel suite.

"I think I'm going to take a nap."

Kitty's worn out, and I can tell she needs the rest. But I'm not sure if she wants to be alone. We stand away from everyone else as we whisper.

"Do you need space?"

"No, but I don't want your family to think I'm needy."

"They don't, *koshechka*."

I call her pussycat, and she offers me a tired smile. I think she likes it in English and Russian.

"I like it when you call me Kitty in public. But will you call me *koshechka* in private like you do *malyshka*?"

"Of course. I've called you *kiska* before. Do you like it better?"

"Either. I like both, *rodnoy*."

Darling. I can't help but grin.

"Never in a million years did I imagine anyone calling me that."

"Nobody else better. You're *moy rodnoy*."

My darling. I sure as fuck am.

"Do you want me to lie down with you?"

She closes her eyes and shakes her head.

"You must have work to do. There's no way you don't. Just make sure I'm awake in time for Valeriya's arrival. I don't want to be coming out of a bedroom the same time as she's walking in."

"You told her you have a boyfriend. Is that who I am? Or am I a brother or cousin?"

"You better not be my brother." She winks. "If you're all right with going by boyfriend right now..."

I cock an eyebrow and wait.

"Is that what you are, Misha?"

"I thought we agreed to a monogamous relationship. That sounds like I'm your boyfriend, and you're my girlfriend. Does it mean something else to you?"

"That's how I think of you. I just wasn't sure how you'd feel once I said it."

"Fucking proud, *kiska*."

She beams and bounces on her toes to kiss my cheek.

"Just wake me before she gets here."

I watch her until the bedroom door closes. I go to the room safe and retrieve my laptop. Not that it's foolproof, but we keep our computers there when we're not here. I sit on the sofa across from Sergei. He finished screening all the city cam footage, and I think he's done looking up Valeriya. Just like the rest of us, he has work to do for Maks and his brothers, who make up our Elite Group. The next few hours pass as Anton joins us and makes phone calls to check on our various men who ensure people have squared away their debts. My dad and Grigori are watching soccer in their room. We all seem so fucking normal. Far fucking from it.

Is Valeriya going to be the shitstorm I've been expecting?

Chapter Twelve

Kitty

I didn't think I would fall asleep, but exhaustion is catching up with me. Between the stress from the three weeks before I arrived, the trans-Atlantic flight, searching for Larisa, being stuck in the hotel for days, and hours of sex every night, I'm more tired than I imagined. I wake to Misha shaking my shoulder gently. I look at the clock and see it's seven-ten. I relax back against the pillow and shut my eyes for a moment before I force myself to sit up.

"You slept through dinner, *malyshka*. I tried to wake you an hour ago, but you just kept rolling over. Do you want to have something to eat before she gets here?"

"A snack. Can I have dinner after?"

"Of course. I'll eat with you."

"You haven't had dinner? Is everyone else waiting? Shit."

I scramble to get out of bed, but Misha stands in the way.

"No, baby. They ate. It's fine. And before you worry if you

wasted any food, we didn't order for you when I couldn't wake you."

"Thanks."

I hurry to put my blouse and slacks back on before we join the others. Misha's family is spread out around the suite, hoping it won't appear so intimidating when Valeriya arrives. Five large men plus three guards don't scream welcome. I grab some nuts and fruit before I join Misha on the sofa. I'm just swallowing the last bite of my snack when there's a knock on the door. Dimitri opens the door, and Valeriya walks in with two guards of her own. The ten men look at each other, her guards assessing Misha's as his family watches them.

I walk to the door and smile.

"Thanks for coming."

"You didn't mention that your boyfriend is a Kutsenko."

Misha walks over and extends his hand. She glances at it before taking it.

"I'm not. I'm an Andreyev. I'm Misha. The blond is my brother, Sergei. The man standing next to him is my father, Radomir."

"They're Kutsenkos."

Valeriya's looking at Grigori and Anton. I don't know if she's heard stories about them or seen pictures or something, but she sounds certain. Anton walks over.

"We are. I'm Anton, and my father is Grigori."

Her eyes narrow at Grigori before shifting to Radomir. Her chin notches up. So, she has heard of them. I wonder what her father's version of the story Radomir told me is. She turns back to Misha.

"You worked for my grandfather."

"No. He was already away when we arrived. He wasn't still *pakhan*."

Boss. Godfather. Whatever you want to call the man who

leads a bratva. Misha's told me he would have preferred Roman Ivankov over Vladislav Lushak one hundred million times over. Vlad was a fucking psychopathic, sociopathic demon spawn from the depths of hell. Apparently, Roman was in prison when they arrived. Misha only met him once when he was still a teenager before someone shot Roman.

"You weren't Solntsevskaya before you emigrated, were you?"

Radomir answers for him and Grigori.

"Podolskaya. None of our boys were bratva until after we arrived in America."

Valeriya nods, but she's taking in everything in the suite. Every man, every piece of furniture, the room service trays off to the side. She meets Misha's gaze before she looks at me.

"Would you like to sit down? Would you or your men like something to drink?"

That makes Valeriya's lips twitch. There isn't a chance in hell Valeriya, or her men, are accepting anything to eat or drink from us. But my good manners insist I offer.

"We're all right, thank you."

She follows Misha and me to the sofas. Radomir and Grigori join us, but Anton and Sergei station themselves where they can hear us but aren't part of the conversation. It's clear they're guarding me, which is exactly what Misha wants, but didn't have to ask for.

"How did you know my sister?"

I jump straight into it, and without looking at her guards, Valeriya switches to English.

"I met her through Yulia, her hair stylist. Yulia's my sister."

I try to mask my surprise, but I think Misha can tell I hadn't realized that.

"She and Yulia went out a few months back, and my sister

invited me. I met them for a movie. Then I went for drinks a few times, then that club."

"And neither you nor Yulia ever heard my sister's last name?"

I sound skeptical. And from the tension I sense from Misha, he finds that hard to believe, too.

"We're Ivankovs. I suspected your sister was from a bratva family. No one asked anything. We just guessed about each other and ignored it."

"It is what it is. Was the night from the photos the last time you heard from or saw Larisa?"

"It was. The man she met wasn't Russian. We spoke English with him and his friend. Yulia and I are already involved and have boyfriends, so we ignored his friends. But the man had an accent that wasn't American or anything English sounding. But his English was definitely American."

"French? Polish? Spanish?"

I'm ready to grasp at any straw.

"I think probably Spanish, but not from Spain."

I look at Misha.

"Latin America?"

He frowns before he answers.

"Yeah, but from where?"

Valeriya's brow furrows before she speaks again.

"He might have been Italian. But his accent didn't sound like someone truly from Italy. That's why I thought Spanish."

Misha looks over at Sergei, and he nods. While I ate my snack, Misha said Sergei started hacking to see if the nightclub stored any of their security footage on a cloud. He found something right before Misha woke me. Sergei goes over to his laptop and wakes the screen. He clicks a few things and brings the computer to Valeriya.

"Is this him?"

Sergei turns the laptop toward her.

"Yes. That's the guy right after he started dancing with Larisa. You can see a tiny bit of her right there."

She points, and I lurch forward. Valeriya's guards are ready to draw their guns, but they realize I just want to see anything that might be my sister. I squint, then tears come to my eyes. Misha moves slower than I did, but he stands beside me. When I straighten, he slides his arm around my waist as we watch Sergei toggle over to another image. I turn and bury my face against Misha's chest. His other arm wraps around me. It's a freeze frame of the men pulling Larisa from her apartment.

"Do you know who they might be?"

My voice catches mid-sentence after I turn my face to look at Valeriya.

"Can I see the whole video?"

Sergei plays it for her, and Misha goes rigid. He knows the instant she recognizes someone or something. She has a good poker face, but I think Misha sees recognition in her eyes. She looks up at me with regret.

"I'm pretty sure I know that neighborhood."

We wait, and I can tell she's dreading whatever she's about to share. Her shoulders slump as she exhales deeply.

"We only speak English until I leave."

Even though we already are, she clearly doesn't want her guards to know she's talking about their bratva. I know she won't name any names, even in English. Those are the only words the guards will understand, and they'll call her father before they get to the car.

"That neighborhood is one of ours, but not under my father. It's Eastern and Central Europeans who use that area when they travel here. I don't know for sure who these men are, since they could be Czech or Hungarian, maybe Polish or

Albanian. They could even be from other parts of Europe or America. The Ivankovs aren't the only bratva in the States."

Misha's terse as he responds.

"We know that from the trouble we had with a branch from Chicago not so long ago when the Podolskaya took Niko's wife, Anastasia. My guess is these are actually Americans in the video. But what's with the man with the Spanish accent?"

While Misha seems to mull that over, I have another question.

"Why did they take Larisa?"

"I know she's careful about not letting people know her ties. But maybe something came out during that dinner. If I had to guess, they knew who we were and targeted us that night. The guy who tried to talk to me hinted at buying drugs. He wanted to know if we knew where to get some. Yulia, Larisa, and I aren't dumb enough to tell them from our own damn families. But maybe the man she went on the date with figured it out and wanted to use Larisa to pressure your family."

I wonder what it means when Misha glances at Sergei, who gives his head one shake. Have none of their informants heard anything about the Podolskaya dealing drugs with Latin Americans? As far as Sergei's been able to learn, no one's tried to trade a young woman for a deal. Valeriya continues with her hypothesis.

"Katerina, if I had to wager another guess, I would say this Spanish-speaking man is from America, and he's trying to bring drugs into Russia. Either he's doing it through branches of our organization from other countries who'll then smuggle it here, or he brought Americans from our organization to convince us. Since he spoke American English, my guess is the latter. Larisa speaks English really well, so I think they took her to the States."

"Why? There's been no ransom demand, so why have they kept her? I know this is all assuming she's still alive."

"If one of them—the Spanish speaker or the ones from our organization—thought she might convince my organization or yours through a marriage, then...It wouldn't be the first arranged one."

"Arranged."

I snort the word as I stare at Valeriya then the computer. Sergei's already stepped out of the room. I think he'll have their cousins looking for her within the next five minutes.

"Katerina, I really wish I knew more. I can't imagine what I would do if someone took Yulia. I couldn't start asking various organizations if a girl was missing."

"I know."

"That's why I couldn't go to your family. If it would have been safe for any of us, I would have."

"You've helped more than anyone else has."

"I'll see if my father knows anything about Americans being here. If I learn anything, I'll get in touch with you."

Valeriya stands from her chair and looks like she's not sure what to do next. I let go of Misha, and we embrace. The enemy of my enemy is my friend. Or maybe Valeriya has a good heart. Whatever it is, at least we can keep moving forward. Once she and her guards leave, I collapse onto the sofa. Once again, Misha doesn't know if I need space or want him nearby. I appreciate he respects that. When I move a pillow, he sits beside me. Anton slipped into their dads' room, but he comes back out as the suite door closes.

"The jet'll be here in ten hours. We can meet it at the airfield. As soon as they refuel and the other pilot takes over, we can go."

"Go?"

I look up at him, and my eyes fill with tears as my heart races.

"I'm not leaving you, *koshechka*. You're coming back with

us. Chances are these men are from Miami if they're Russian with a Spanish speaker. I think the Spanish speaker is Colombian. Do you think Valeriya could have confused a Spanish accent for Italian? They're not the same, but similar. She even wondered about it."

"Maybe. I don't know."

I can't think straight. I don't want to have to muddle through everything Valeriya just told us. I just want to get on a flight to wherever Larisa is, torture and kill the fuckers who touched her, then get her home—which is with me in New York. Fucking ironic. New York is hardly ever considered a safe option for anything.

"What about my parents? They need to know. How am I going to tell them I'm leaving because we learned something?"

"We'll get the message to them. Anton's already working on it."

"How?"

"Because that's his job."

"Is he your *obshchak*?"

"Yes."

Anton heads their Security Group if that's the case. He must be a brilliant strategist, and at that size, a fucking terrifying enforcer. I glance over at Sergei, who's still on the phone. My guess is he's their *sovietnik* and leads their Support Group since he's already proven to be a master at collecting intelligence. I feel better with them around. My dad already told me Misha is an *avotoritet*, or brigadier. That means he leads their missions when they're doing their less than legal dealings. I know anyone can be one, no matter their other leadership positions. But Misha said he's the head one because he's the best at adapting plans and overcoming challenges on the fly.

"Kitty, my brother and Anton are computer science geniuses. Both of them, and I'm not exaggerating. They studied at UPenn and graduated top of their class. If the information exists, they will find it."

I nod as I look around the suite. Grigori and Radomir are on their phones now, too. I can't hear what they're saying, but it looks like they're speaking to people who are irritating them. I turn back to Misha and meet his gaze. He sees my uncertainty and kisses my forehead.

"Dad and Grigori are tying up things here with Timofey. I loathe the fucker, but I think he finally understands that allowing any Polodsk to reach all the way to America and to our family is a suicide mission. The Podolskaya is done with us, and we're done with them."

"We have nine hours?"

"Yeah. Do you think you can sleep some more?"

"I know I should, but I don't think I can until I'm certain my parents know what's going on."

His arm is wrapped around my shoulders, and he strokes my hair as he drops kisses on my head.

"Just rest then, baby."

Rest? I can rest when I'm dead. That won't be until after the motherfuckers who kidnapped my sister are ash.

Chapter Thirteen

Misha

Anton tracked down Kitty's parents, and she was able to talk to them for a couple minutes, but neither line was secure. They were still hiding and will remain wherever they are for at least a week after we leave. Part of the reason her suitcase had been so heavy were the things she'd brought from America to give to them. But she never had the opportunity since she didn't unpack at her parents' apartment. I promised the items would make it to them. She wound up falling asleep on the sofa, so I carried her through to the bedroom and packed for both of us before I climbed into bed beside her. The alarm on my phone went off way too soon.

Stefan, one of our most trusted men, picked us up from the airfield in New York, and we're headed to Maks and Laura's now. It's where we tend to congregate whenever we need to meet as a family or as the Ivankov leadership. As we pull up to their door, I can tell the house flabbergasts Kitty. I said it was practically a mansion, and I wasn't exaggerating. If anything, I was minimizing. There are enough bedrooms for each couple and me to have our own room, plus all the parents. It's enormous.

She glances down at her rumpled clothes from being on the plane for nine-and-a-half hours. I slide out of the SUV's second row, then offer her my hand. I entwine our fingers as we walk inside. I know this is going to be intimidating and over-whelming as fuck. I spot my mom as she hurries forward, prac-tically pushing Pasha over. His mom is on the other side of him. I swear he just took two elbows to the ribs.

I laugh as my cousin tries to protect himself. Alina huffs at him.

"*Dvigaysya*, Pasha." Move, Pasha.

My mom reaches out for me. She holds her left arm out, and Sergei steps into her embrace. She's nearly a foot shorter than us and half our size, but no matter how old we get or how big we grow, she can still hug us both. We can't each sit on her lap like we did when we were little, but we'll never stop wanting our mom.

Alina has engulfed Anton in a hug that surely cracked a couple vertebrae. Our moms release us and greet their husbands. None of us watch. They're fucking indecent for people in their fifties.

"Welcome home."

Aunt Galina kisses my cheek before I return the favor. My parents' kiss is intense but short.

"*Mama, eto Katerina*." Mama, this is Katerina.

"*Dobro pozhalovat'*." Welcome.

My mom embraces her, but it's not as tight as how she hugs Sergei and me. But she smells like roses and fresh air. I can tell it eases some of Kitty's nervousness. When they step apart, I slide my hand back into Kitty's. It's time for the formal introductions, and she's glancing down at her clothes again.

"*Malyshka*, they know you've been traveling. You look beautiful. You could wear a trash bag and still be the most gorgeous woman in the room."

She sucks her lips in and glances up at me. I know she thinks I'm exaggerating, but I'm not.

"Kitty, this is my family. This is Maksim and Laura's house. They're holding their twins, Konstantin and Mila."

Mila chooses that moment to wave her hand as though she knows who we're talking about.

"Bogdan and Christina have Lev."

The baby is still a newborn, but he has hints of Christina's red hair. The name means lion, which has some private significance to them. Christina wears a pendant with a male lion, and Bogdan wears one with a lioness. They never take them off.

"This is Anton's brother, Pasha, and his wife, Sumiko...This is Nikolai and Anastasia. Ana's father is Russian. She and Laura both speak fluent Russian."

I see it still surprises her when I say Laura speaks the language.

"Laura studied it in university with a man who was a former Soviet instructor. He made sure she sounds like a native. She spent a year in St. Petersburg while she was in college."

I turn to the last couple and grin. My cousin looks as dour as ever, and his wife is a ray of sunshine.

"Eeyore over here is Aleksei, and the angel who puts up with him is Heather."

He scowls at me until Heather bounces onto her toes to kiss his cheek. He snags her lips and gives her a quick but heated kiss. He's grinning from ear to ear when they pull apart. Then he's back to scowling at me. I roll my eyes. He's doing it to goad me.

"Kitty, this is my aunt Galina. Those miscreants belong to her. Alina's sons aren't any better, but there's only two of them."

I know she's trying not to stare at Aunt Galina, but it's impossible not to the first few hundred times you see her. She is easily one of the most beautiful women in the world. I think Kitty is the end-all-be-all, but I know I'm biased. Aunt Galina is beyond breathtaking or stunning. I don't know a word in Russian or English to describe her.

"Mrs. Andreyeva, you and Mrs. Kutsenko are sisters, right?"

"Yes. And I'm Svetlana."

"And you'll confuse everyone if you call me Mrs. Kutsenko. There are seven of us by that name now."

I watch her brow furrow as she looks at my mom then me. My mom's hair is a deep red, but we share the same features. Sergei and I got our blond hair and blue eyes from our mom's mom. Sometimes people assume Aunt Galina is our mom because she has blonde hair and blue eyes too. People don't know what to make of my mom and Alina when they're with my cousins. People can't figure out who they belong to.

"How...How do you all look so much alike yet so different?"

Bogdan laughs and speaks up.

"We're the best of both our parents. Pasha and Anton look just like Uncle Grigori, who could pass for our dad. Mama looks so much like Aunt Svetlana, except for their hair. My brothers and I got the dark hair from our dad, and our blue eyes from Mama. Somehow, their genetic influence was equal, I guess. It means that while Anton and Pasha look nothing like Sergei and Misha, we look like both sets of cousins."

"It's incredible...and disconcerting. You could pass for quadruplets. I thought Misha and Sergei were twins and almost didn't believe Misha when he said he's four years younger than Sergei. But Pasha, you and Anton could be twins, too. How many years apart are you?"

"Almost four."

She looks up at me again, and this time her smile is pure mischief.

"And you're the baby of the family?"

I cock an eyebrow in playful warning. Lev wails at that moment as though to point out he's the baby of the family now, and everyone laughs. Christina looks at her son in disbelief before shaking her head as she talks to the newborn.

"How are you hungry again? You ate like twenty minutes ago."

"How old is he?"

I see how Kitty looks at all three kids. The twins are just over a year-and-a-half old, and Lev is clearly still a baby.

"Three months."

Kitty's eyes widen.

"You had a baby three months ago? I would never guess. Does he sleep through the night already? My friends have all looked like death warmed up at this stage. And I can't believe he's only three months. I would have guessed five easily."

"He's this big because his father is a giant, and he eats around the clock. So, no, he doesn't sleep through the night. Do you, you little stinker?"

Bogdan offers to take him, but Christina sighs.

"I may as well feed him because he sounds like you when you're hangry."

Kitty tries to smother a giggle, and it almost sounds like she's choking. Laura steps forward after giving Mila to Maks. He was the most cantankerous of the group before he met Laura. Uncommunicative is what she called him. But you would never guess that about him since he turns into a big bowl of jelly when he's holding his kids. He makes faces at them and blows raspberries on their necks and bellies. It's insanely cute... considering he's often doing that only hours after—well, doing his job as *pakhan*.

"Welcome to our house, Katerina. There's no point in pretending we don't know about you or your background. All the wives know who our husbands are, so don't fear letting that slip. We know who your family is, and we know what's happening. Is there anything we can do to help? Do you want to sleep? Are you hungry? One of us could go to your place to get some stuff. Or one of the guys could take you."

"Thank you. Um..."

It's too much. Too many people and too much noise. I can tell. I pull her into my arms and smile at everyone else. They understand since each wife has gone through this when she meets the entire family. Most of them move into the living room or the kitchen. I keep my voice soft.

"How about something to eat and maybe a nap? Heather and Aleks could go to your place and get some of your things if you want. We're going to stay here tonight, then we can go to my place tomorrow. Is that all right?"

She nods as she takes a calming breath and straightens.

"If it isn't an imposition, I would love to have something to eat."

Laura's genuine smile gives Kitty a boost of confidence as she steps away from me.

"It's never an imposition. With this many people coming in and out, there's always a ton of food. Would you like me to make you something? Or would you prefer to rummage? Take whatever you fancy. If you want to shower, Misha has a room upstairs."

"Thank you..." She turns to me and whispers. "Could you

take me to my place to get some stuff? I don't want to impose on your cousins, and I—well, I have nothing to hide, but it's a little embarrassing to ask someone I've known five minutes to pick out my underwear."

"There's an easy solution. They don't need to bring you any."

"Shh."

Her cheeks go bright pink.

"I promise you we aren't any different from the rest of them."

Her face goes beet red when she glances at my parents then Grigori and Alina. We can see my parents at the other end of the kitchen, and I'm pretty sure my dad's hands are on my mom's backside. Grigori and Alina are off to the corner of the living room, and she's sitting on his lap, her fingers in his hair, as they kiss again.

My parents pull apart and shoot me a stare like I'm interrupting and inconveniencing them. My dad chuckles when he turns toward us, but now I'm positive his hand is on my mom's backside as she speaks.

"I made a pot of *solyanka* and brought it over." Beef stew.

"It's delicious. It's Mama's best dish."

"That sounds lovely. Can I help with anything?"

"No, no. *Moy lisichka* will help."

"Little fox? That's cute."

Kitty grins at my mom. Something passes between them, and I can tell they'll grow close in no time.

"Yes. I would call Misha and Sergei that because they could always find trouble, but I could never catch them in the act. They still do."

"I'm easily led astray by my older brother and cousins. It's not my fault."

I feign the same innocence that hasn't worked since I was

five. I was always guilty by association, and Mama was never wrong when she assumed we were involved.

"Get the bowls while I heat this up."

My mom moves around Laura and Maks's kitchen with the familiarity of someone who is here often. Then again, so do I. I don't need to look for anything, so I soon have six bowls lined up on the island with spoons next to them. Once the food is warm, and my mom is serving it, I let the dads, Sergei, and Anton know there's food ready. In the time it takes Kitty to eat one hearty bowl at a normal pace, the rest of us have devoured two.

"So much for anyone else having this."

Sergei kisses our mom's cheek as he moves to the sink to wash his bowl.

"I guess you'll just have to make more, Mama. It's your fault for making it so well."

He flashes her a smile and winks. Kitty giggles. It's a reassuring sound.

"They called you the porcupine in the group, but I think you're the charmer."

"He's the porcupine, all right." Anton mutters around a spoonful of food. "We're just all mama's boys."

That makes Kitty giggle even more. We're all nearly six-feet-five and weigh between two-hundred-and-twenty to two-hundred-and-forty pounds. None of us have any fat to spare. I take my bowl and Kitty's to the sink and give my mom a kiss and wink too.

"That just means we all still have a healthy fear of our mothers."

Kitty shakes her head with a smile.

"She's Russian. You should be. My mama is *way* scarier than my dad."

Her smile falters, and I wonder what happened. She looks at me before she explains.

"My boyfriend before I left Moscow didn't treat me well. My mom is the one who made sure he finally understood that wasn't okay."

Knowing that piece of shit, Semyon, I'm glad Dariya scared the shit out of him. She should have killed him for laying a finger on Kitty with anything but love and affection. Even when I spank her, the goal is never to harm her.

Her exhaustion settles on her, and she seems to shrink on her barstool. I offer my hand when she slides off, and we head upstairs.

"I didn't mean to be a downer just now."

"You weren't. That's just what moms do."

I know that wasn't exactly what she meant, but I try to put her at ease. When we get in the room I use when I stay here, she plops down on the bed and rests her elbows on her knees as she covers her face with her hands. I sit next to her and lift her into my lap. She curls in my arms.

"I feel guilty for laughing at all right now. It feels wrong to be happy, even for a moment. It's not like I forget about Larisa. It just gives me a moment's reprieve before I have to think about this again. It makes it easier to face reality when I have a break for a few minutes."

"None of us would ever think you've forgotten about your sister. If making you laugh gives you that break for a few minutes, then we all want that for you. Believe me, my family has been through heavy shit my entire life. It was Semyon's grandfather and uncles who took Alina when she was fifteen. My mom and Aunt Galina saw it happen and ran to find Grigori and Uncle Kirill. My dad helped them, and they found Alina before the men did anything beyond terrifying her. They were all the same age, and they made sure those men could never hurt another woman and could never come back for Alina."

Alina's abduction isn't something we talk about often. But it was what sparked the protectiveness that is the heart of our family. We will always do anything and everything to keep our family together. The wives who married into our family are sisters and cousins. There's no "in-law" attached to it. Their acceptance and belonging aren't conditional. They're absolute. I know my family knows Kitty is the one for me, so that extends to her, which extends to her family.

"Being part of this family has brought danger to Laura, Christina, Anastasia, and Heather, with people targeting them. Pasha was the target, but that didn't mean Sumiko wasn't in danger too. We understand, Kitty. Konstantin, Mila, and Lev have all been born amid turmoil and these dangers, but we find joy with each new marriage and each new baby. It's not wrong to find moments of happiness among hours of sadness."

"But I doubt the weddings or conceptions took place while someone was missing. Our lives aren't that different, so I under-stand and believe what you said. I really do. This isn't just our regular sadness about a life none of us chose, though. This is a gaping wound that's festering. It's not something I should ignore or pretend isn't there."

"No one is saying that you should, Kitty. You're not out partying, and you haven't abandoned your sister. We both know the reality of the situation is that there's no way you could spend every minute of every day searching for her. You're not choosing this over searching for her. So, if you have to stop, then fill that time with something that lightens you enough to have the energy to start the search again. You aren't being selfish."

"I know what you're saying makes sense. I even agree with

you because that's what I've done. But it's not so easy to turn off the shame and guilt."

My heart aches for her because if anyone understands shame and guilt when someone else suffers, it's me. The fucking shit Vlad made us watch while he tortured each of us created a helplessness that none of us have ever recovered from.

I carry her into the bathroom and put the plug in the tub before I turn on the water. I squeeze bubbles into it before I undress her. Once I'm undressed too, we embrace until the tub is full. I can't help and don't want to help my body's reaction to us being skin-to-skin. I turn off the water before I step into the tub and help her in. She moves to turn around and sit between my legs, but I stop her. I keep her facing me and lift her to straddle my hips. Thank God for huge soaking tubs. I ease into her and press her head against my shoulder.

We simply soak while our bodies are joined. I stroke her hair and back, pressing kisses to her forehead. She kisses my shoulder and neck. It's not sexual. It's affection and comfort.

"This is helping, Daddy. I needed to feel this connected to you."

"*Malyshka*, you are my one love. I will always do whatever you need and hopefully most of what you want. I told you from the start that I would take care of you. It's like I found that last part of me I thought would never appear. We're one. It's us against the world."

"I keep warning myself that when this is over, and I don't need you anymore and when the crisis no longer has us pushed together, I need to be ready to let you go."

"Why?"

"Because this is so extreme. Who meets someone and almost three weeks later has this kind of connection? But every time I try to prepare myself for that, all I feel is wrong. I don't want this to be over, Misha. I feel like the reason I'm trusting you so much is because there's more than just situational necessity."

"This is how my family is. None of us has an explanation. When we meet the right person, it just is. Every couple has known almost immediately that they've found their soulmate. Uncle Kirill and Aunt Galina fell in love when they were five. She still loves him and always will. There will never be anyone else. My parents met through them, and so did Alina and Grigori. Both couples were in love within weeks and only waited to marry because they weren't old enough. The moment they were, they did."

"So, you believe in soulmates?"

"Absolutely. I just never believed I would find mine."

"Is that what we are?"

I hear the timidity in her voice. I press her back, and our lips meet. I infuse all the emotions I feel into that kiss. It's as much sexual desire as it is emotional longing. When we pull apart, Kitty sits back to look at me. I slide my hands into hers before I speak my answer. I think I already showed her.

"Yes. I told you. You are mine. I'm yours, Katerina. Only yours. You will never know the details, but you know what it means when I walk out the door. You know none of us trust easily. We can't afford to. But it also means we've become experts at reading people quickly. Our life almost always depends upon it. It's why I've known since the beginning. I want our future to be together."

"I want that too. I will never ask for those details. I won't ask where you go or what you do. I don't want to know. I know sometimes you don't want *me* to see *you*, but it's never the other way around. I know your loyalty is hard-earned and to receive it means the world to me. I see honor and duty along with loyalty, and I know family is everything to you. Those four qualities are everything to me. That's why I know I want my future with you. I just don't want to imagine this is more than it is."

"What it is, *malyshka*, is two people from different paths meeting and walking the rest of the way hand-in-hand."

I want to tell her I love her. I believe I do. But that really will freak her out. I just keep asking myself, when will the time be right to tell her? And does agreeing that we're soulmates mean she loves me too?

Chapter Fourteen

Kitty

Misha and I remained in the bath last night until the water turned cold. He didn't stay hard the entire time, but the intimacy remained. We stepped into the waterfall shower, and he washed my hair and body. I returned the favor. By the end, neither of us could help ourselves. He lifted me, and I wrapped my legs around his waist. It was slow and emotional. The whole experience from start to finish was. I always knew that my future wasn't with Semyon, even though we talked about it so many times. I couldn't be more certain with Misha. Last night's non-sex, then real sex proved it. That feeling that we are one with no start and no finish. He told me once that I was his alpha and omega. I get it. We lived it last night in that tub.

But morning has come, and reality is a fucking bitch with a broom up her ass. We'd curled into bed, and Misha held me the whole night. We're in the same position this morning, but someone's knocking. Misha rolls over and hurries out of bed. He grabs a pair of basketball shorts from the dresser. I hadn't guessed he actually keeps clothes here. It's Maks. He keeps his gaze on Misha after giving me a quick nod.

"We need to go."

I've heard that single sentence at least a thousand times, but it was always said to my dad. It's a different set of emotions when it's toward the man I want to spend my life with. That's a jarring realization when I only just accepted the idea last night that we're together for good.

"We're leaving for the gym in ten minutes. If you're coming, be downstairs. Laura's arranging for Dimitri and Stefan to take her and Katerina to Katerina's place for whatever she needs. The twins are staying here with my mom. Laura says it'll be a couple hours. She thought Katerina might want to sleep in."

The gym?

"What the fuck, Maks? I wanted to sleep in."

"Since when?"

"You are one of the most intelligent people I've ever met, so how are you so fucking stupid right now?"

Misha tilts his head in my direction. I'm just trying to get my heart to slow down.

"Maks, I'm not leaving my girlfriend alone with a bunch of strangers the day after she arrives."

"We're not strangers. We're family."

Maks's tone is so certain that it almost sounds like Misha's the one being dumb.

"It's all right, Misha. Go work out. I might go back to sleep or get caught up on emails. I couldn't open any of mine on my phone while we were in Moscow. I also need to talk to my principal and let her know that I'm going to be out longer than I planned."

"Fine. I'll be there in ten minutes."

Misha shuts the door and comes back to the bed. I watch as

he climbs in and pulls the covers over him. I just stare at him. He pulls me to lie next to him.

"It'll take me all of two minutes to brush my teeth. I can put on my shirt on the way downstairs. They'll be putting their socks and shoes on too. That leaves me eight more minutes to hold you. Come here, *kiska*."

Who am I to refuse? I snuggle closer to him.

"If you don't feel comfortable going to your place with Laura and our guards, I can go with you."

"They must be the most trustworthy men you know if someone like Maks will let them guard his wife."

"They're our second cousins or something like that. To be honest, it'll probably be Sergei and Anton who go with you. They'll end up volunteering, and Maks won't say no. None of the wives goes anywhere if one of us isn't with them. The husbands just feel better when someone within our immediate family is there."

"But—"

"Do not argue, *malyshka*. If neither Sergei nor Anton offers, then I'm not going. It's that or you wait until I get back. Now I'd rather be kissing."

"Why should they give up working out to babysit me?"

Misha sits up.

"Are you serious right now? You live in the fucking Bronx to begin with. Laura's going with you, so automatically that not only means guards but someone from our family. She's our *pakhan's* wife, so she'll always be a potential target. And considering why you went to Russia and why we came back when we did, you're lucky I'm not such a control freak that I don't let you stick your nose outside without two guards."

"But that's what you want."

"Yes. But I won't. You are not a prisoner anywhere. I won't force you to stay here or anywhere else. That said, I will insist that you're properly protected. Kitty, you may have been invisible for five years, but that's assuming we're right about that. Who knows who's watched you? And if we're together, then that comes with its own risks. That's something you have to consider. Are you willing to live with those risks again after you left this life behind?"

"I already have considered that, and I know what I'm getting into. Better to be here than in Moscow if I'm accepting this life again. I'm not arguing against a guard. But your family has other things to do and other people to protect. They don't need to be stuck with me when I'm just going to get a couple pairs of jeans and t-shirts. Laura doesn't have to go either. I appreciate her offer to keep me company, but I'm all right."

I'm not ready for his swift move when he rolls on top of me and pins my arms above my head.

"You are one objection away from a toasted ass. This is an expectation, and it's not negotiable. You are not and never will be an inconvenience or a burden. Each person in my family knows what it means for any of us to trust the people we love most to be out of our reach, to be out of our control. When Maks and Laura trust me to protect Konstantin or Mila, that's the highest form of respect. They know I would do anything for their children. Are they still babies who each have their own bodyguard if they leave the house? Yes. Do I care that they're babies? No. They're my family, and I love them. We all feel that way about one another. Argue with me if you want that spanking, but I'm not sending the most important person in my life out into the world without protection. You will not convince me otherwise."

Fuck, I'm wet. The set of his jaw is pure determination. The look in his eyes is a blazing fire. And the feel of his body pressing into mine, keeping me where he wants me, is enough to send me up in flames.

"I want the spanking, Daddy. But I won't disobey you. You said you..."

"I know what I said, *malyshka*. And it was about the most unromantic way to blurt that out. I'm sorry. You deserved a better declaration, but I love you. There's no one more special to me than you."

"I love you, and I don't want to drive you crazy with fear. I'll accept a guard, and I'll deeply appreciate that it's someone in your family."

"*Kiska*, I want to take you to my place to see it. If you like it, then I want you to move in. If you prefer your place in the Bronx, then consider whether you'd want me to live with you there. If you want somewhere different from either of those, then we find it together. This isn't about having you close, so that I can protect you or control you. We already said we see our life together. I want to start that now."

Holy shit. I didn't expect that. I am fucking crazy to say yes. Like so fucking wackadoodle it's ridiculous. But it took me a month of Semyon asking to me to live with him after we'd already been together three years, and he'd already proven to be an abusive asshole. It took me six months to decide which university I wanted to attend to become a nurse. It took me five fucking years before I came to America. No other decision has ever been so clear and so easy to make.

"My home is with you. It doesn't matter where."

A sense of calm settles over me that I haven't felt since my second night alone in my apartment when I moved here. The first night alone had been scary. But the second night was like all my worries evaporated for a few hours. I was away from Semyon. I was living alone. I'd successfully moved to America and got into a program to get my American credentials. I was free.

I don't feel any less independent agreeing to live with

Misha than I did before I woke this morning. Just the opposite. That sense of hope is back. I sigh as someone else knocks on the door.

"*Ukhodite.*" Go away.

A deep laugh comes through the door after Misha's command. I guess he isn't going to the gym after all. I raise my head to give his lips a peck, but he snares my mouth, and the kiss explodes. I'm already naked. Of course. I hurry to push Misha's shorts down, and he kicks them off. Who knows where they land? Couldn't care less.

"Do you want to fuck me, *Daddy?*"

"Yes."

He thrusts into me and groans. I grin.

"Do I feel good?"

"Fucking better than anything in the world. Do you like my cock filling your cunt?"

"Absolutely."

"When I get you home tonight, when we're truly alone, I'm going to fuck you until you beg me to stop. I'm going to make you beg and scream."

"Can we go now?"

"You're going to take my cum after I get you off. Then we are going home. And on the way, we have some online shopping to do. We are going to get every toy you want and might be curious about. You are going to think about your fantasies and what you want us to do. Kinky or vanilla. Whatever you want."

"I thought I had a spanking coming."

He flips us, and I grab his shoulders, unprepared for how easily he can move us. I should be used to it by now, but I'm not. His hand lands across my horizontal crack, pushing me upward. It grinds my clit against his pubic bone. He continues to spank me, each one getting harder than the last. His other hand fists my hair and holds my head in place.

"This is for pleasure, Kitty. Do you understand? I'm not upset that you didn't know how I feel about you or your protection."

"But I was prepared to argue with you."

"Because you didn't know. This is to make you come."

It's as though the explanation is the detonator to my pussy. The next slap drives me over the edge. I release a silent scream, wanting no one else to know what we're doing in his cousin's home. He sits up abruptly and holds me tight. I ride his cock as we kiss. Our bodies are still fucking, but our kiss is about making love for the first time after sharing our feelings. It should be so contradictory, but it's just us.

"You're so fucking perfect, *malyshka*. I can't hold on. I need to come."

"Then do it. I want your cum inside me and on my thighs."

"You want to know that you made me come."

He grins at me, and I nod. It's my form of control. I know he wants me and making him come proves it. And I'm the only one he's letting ride bareback on his dick. I'm the only one riding him, period. He's the most gorgeous man I've ever met, and that's saying something, considering his family is filled with Armani model kinda hot men. I could be fearful, and I could get jealous if I saw him talking to another woman. But I know family, loyalty, honor, and duty are so ingrained into his soul that he would never imagine being unfaithful. I also think his family would kill him—or at least beat the shit out of him. There's a euphoric power that comes with that, that makes me feel more special than anyone in the world.

He holds me in place as he grinds me on him. My head falls back as I come again, doing a Kegel that surely squeezes every drop from him. He growls as his teeth sink into my shoulder. His hands squeeze my sore ass.

"If you keep doing that, then my needy little pussy is going

166

to become a very greedy little pussy that won't let you do anything but fuck me."

He chuckles as he carries me into the bathroom. Once the shower is warm enough, we step in. He immediately spins me, pulls my hips back, and thrusts into me.

"You keep me harder than a nineteen-year-old."

He wraps an arm around me, his elbow on my belly, his forearm between my tits, and his hand around my throat.

"*Malyshka*, your greedy little pussy can have me any time it wants. I'll gladly oblige."

"Thank you, Daddy."

I brace my hands against the wall, arms outstretched, as we go a second round. I give as good as I get until the mirrors and shower doors are completely steamy, and my knees shake. We finish our shower and go back in the bedroom. There's a note under the door.

Didn't want to bother you. Suitcases are outside the door. Breakfast whenever you're ready. L

Laura. That was so thoughtful. I appreciate she didn't disturb us. Misha opens the door and brings our cases inside. I'm happy for some clean clothes, but I look forward to going to my place to get something more casual than the blouses and trousers I took with me. The only really comfy clothes I took were what I traveled in and the yoga pants I wore to go running.

It doesn't take us long to get dressed, have breakfast, and make our way to my apartment. I guess I didn't expect to have a driver today too. I just assumed someone was picking us all up from the airport. I didn't think about whether Misha would have a car at Maks and Laura's. We live in the capital of public transportation. I guess I didn't even think about whether Misha has a car. I don't. Students meet me in the parking lot to walk with me, but I still ride the subway to get there.

"That's it on the left."

I point to my building since the privacy partition is down, and the driver—Stefan—can hear me. I glance at Misha, and I can tell he isn't pleased. He's scanning the area, and I know he thinks it's too dangerous for me to live here. It's not a question about whether my building is nice enough. It's not about the types of cars parked on the streets. It's not about the clothes people wear. He doesn't enjoy thinking of me being alone in a neighborhood that's known for crime.

I'm about to reach for the door handle when Misha puts his hand on my thigh. Oh. That rule applies in the U.S. too. Okay. He gets out on the sidewalk side and reaches his hand in to help me out. A town car with two men in tailormade suits stands out, oh, just a wee bit. It's drawing more attention than any of us want.

"I'll circle the block a few times. Text when you want me to come back."

Stefan's watching a group of teens approaching us as he speaks. Misha's hand is at the small of my back as he nods. We hurry to cross the street just before Stefan pulls away. We're about to walk up the steps to my building when a teenager calls out.

"Hey, Ms. V! You're back!"

I hiss to Misha.

"Don't."

I'm certain he's about to reach for his gun. I recognize the voice immediately. I turn back and wave as the group of boys approaches.

"Hi, Dante. Hey, guys."

"Ms. V, we was wondering when you were coming home. Ms. Fletcher said it might be a few weeks. Something about your family. We was wondering if everything was okay."

"It may be a few more days before I'm back. Shouldn't all of you be at school right now?"

Another boy, Alfred, speaks up.

"Don't you remember, Ms. V? It's teacher in-service or whatever today. We get the day off."

Shit. That seemed like a million years in the future before I left. I completely forgot. I see them eyeing Misha and trying to get a read on him. He's relaxed as much as he's going to be. His hand is still at the small of my back, and his other hand is in his pocket. I know he has a knife there. I'm not worried that he's going to pull it on any of these kids. It's just being here that makes him so uneasy. I have to remind myself that we're back in New York, and while people might have known he was bratva in Moscow, nothing was as personal as it is here. We're out in the open, and that makes him anxious.

"Guys, this is my boyfriend, Mr. Andreyev."

"Hi."

"Hey."

"What's up?"

There are a few more mumbled greetings as I smile at them.

"These are some of the young men from my school. Dante, Alfred, Duane, Tom, Gio, and Chris. I'm certain they must be on their way home or to the library to use this extra time to study for midterms."

I cock an eyebrow, and the boys laugh. They know this expression.

"We ain't coming to ask for Tylenol, Ms. V."

Gio grins as the others laugh.

"And I have no ice packs or Band-Aids to give out. What are you doing in this area?"

It's several subway stops from the neighborhood where the

school is and where they live. I narrow my eyes when no one answers.

"Boys?"

Dante shifts and looks around. Gio nods encouragement.

"Look, Ms. V. My sis was spilling the tea to her friend, and I heard them. This guy came round, looking like he got guap for days. They be like he got real drip. I think he sounds real extra. But he was asking about a Russian woman. That's like real sus, Ms. V. The only Russian lady 'round here be you."

I try not to smile because this isn't funny, but I know I'm going to have to translate for Misha later. Apparently, Dante's friend gossiped with her friend about some hot, rich guy who was a little too flashy. It sounds like he was looking for me. I'm not the only Russian in the Bronx, but I'm the only one these kids know.

Gio continues to explain.

"This was a few days ago, but it didn't sit right with us. We came by to check your spot. You know, make sure it was a'right."

Any good humor evaporates.

"How'd you know where to look, Gio?"

"That's what was real sus. The guy asked about the woman living on this street. We didn't know which place is yours. We was gonna ask around. We just happened to see you."

Misha's hand presses against my back, and I know he's about thirty seconds from dragging me inside. But I still have questions.

"Did your friend hear why he was looking for me?"

All the boys get really uncomfortable, and none of them want to look at Misha.

"Boys?"

I put more command into my voice. They've heard it before at school. I'm not an authoritarian or a disciplinarian, but I don't take bullshit from the kids. They trust me and know they can come to me, whether or not it's medical. But they know Homie don't play. That was a phrase a teacher taught me for how I am. No nonsense.

"My sis is gonna be pissed if she finds out I was listening to her. I ain't trying to catch those hands, Ms. V."

"Dante, I'm not going to tell anyone that you gave me this heads-up. I have some friends who moved here from Moscow recently, but I haven't had time to see them. It was probably one of them."

"No offense, Ms. V, but this guy was like your boyfriend. He didn't look like he belonged in the Bronx. His whip was real new. Ain't no subway tokens for him. Why didn't he just hit you up rather than coming all the way down here? Is he that new that he don't know this ain't a place to be asking questions about nobody?"

Alfred pushes Dante aside and steps closer.

"He wasn't from Moscow. He didn't sound like you. This guy was like OG New York. It was my girl who heard them. They said he had an accent when he spoke English, but he could speak Spanish too."

Misha's fingers squeeze my waist, and I'm scared enough now to want to get off the street. A rich man with a new car who sounds like an Original Gangster isn't cool. Is this the same guy Larisa met?

"Thanks for telling me all this, guys. I appreciate it. It'll be awhile before I'm back, so good luck on those midterms that I know you're going straight home to study for. Right. Now."

I cock that eyebrow again, and the boys laugh.

"Sure, Ms. V."

"Nice meeting you."

"Bye."

I can't tell who says what, but they head back the way they

came. I pull out my keys as Misha and I go up the stairs. I have to unlock an outside door, then an inside door. We take the elevator up to my floor, but as we move farther down the hall, Misha pushes me behind him and draws his gun.

"Is 8D yours?"

"Yeah. What's wrong, Misha? I can't see past you."

"Someone's been here."

"What?"

We get to my door, and I peer around him. Nothing looks wrong, but Misha pushes the door, and it swings open. What the fuck? I locked both the doorknob and deadlock.

"How'd you know?"

"I could see it wasn't closed completely. There was a little gap between the door and the doorframe."

Fucking eyes like a goddamn eagle. Now I'm freaking the fuck out. I pull the gun Misha gave me before we left the house in Queens.

"Stay behind me, *malyshka*."

"Yes, Daddy."

We aren't even remotely close to having sex right now, but it comes out without thought. I'm terrified, but I feel safe with Misha here. I know he'll protect me. I guess that's why I said it. Calling him Daddy clearly goes beyond just kink. It's our dynamic, and it's just about the only reassuring thing happening right now.

We move to the spare bedroom, then my bedroom and finally the bathroom. We could see into the kitchen when we walked in. It's not exactly spacious, so it wasn't hard to tell we're alone. We both put our guns away. I hurry back into the bedroom and start yanking dresser drawers open, then I push the closet door open. I flip through my clothes. I look at my bedside table. Nothing is out of place, but I know someone's been here. I'm not OCD or anything, but I know how I left everything since I had to get clothes from my dresser and closet when I was packing.

I walk over to my desk, which is in the corner of my living room. I like the sunlight when I work. I move slower as I examine each drawer. I take things out and stack papers on my desk. I don't think anything is missing. I put everything back, but as I reach for my computer, Misha stops me.

"Sergei's coming over. I want him to look at your computer before you touch it. He'll know if anyone's tampered with it. Get whatever you want to take to our place that isn't furniture. Anton's driving one of the SUV's and bringing Sergei. We load up, then you and I leave. Stefan is still here. He'll drive Sergei and Anton when they're ready to go. Hurry."

He must have been texting them while I was going through everything.

He's freaked out. He's letting me see that. He and his family hide their emotions better than anyone I've ever met. When I know what he's thinking and feeling, it's because he wants me to. I think he reveals to me far more than he ever has to anyone outside his family. If this bothers him, and he wants me to know it, then I need to move my ass. To be honest, I don't want to be here any longer than we have to.

I have a few large suitcases in the spare bedroom's closet. I wheel those into my room and open them on the bed. I cringe that I didn't put anything down on the comforter first. My mom taught me to always do that since suitcases are inherently filthy on the outside, so you don't want to ruin the bedcovers or transfer the dirt to something that touches your whole body. But I don't have time to grab bath towels first.

"Can you put everything from the dresser in this one, please? I'll empty the closet."

Misha does as I ask. I watch him out of the corner of my eye. He grabs photos from my bedside table, dresser, and off the wall. He uses my t-shirts and pajamas to wrap them before he puts them in the case. He says nothing when he goes into the living room, and I'm too frazzled to do anything more than hurry to pull things off hangers, fold them, and toss them into the luggage. I glance over my shoulder when I notice him coming back with his arms full.

He's collected all my photos and all my ornaments. He slides them into more of my clothing to keep them from breaking. My heart swells at his thoughtfulness. I can't help myself. I step over to him and press a hard, quick kiss to his lips.

"I love you for more reasons than I count, but right now, I love you even more for being so considerate. Thank you for being careful with my stuff."

"*Kiska*, we already planned for you to move, which is a big step. Now we're doing it in a rush. I don't want anything to happen to the things that will help make you feel like where we live is *our* home."

I pinch his ribs.

"Ow."

"Just making sure I'm not dreaming."

"You're supposed to pinch yourself. I'll remember that, *malyshka*."

"I had to be sure you're real."

I shoot him a quick smile before I finish packing my room. I suppose I don't need to take any linens or kitchenware. I move through the rest of the apartment to be sure we aren't leaving anything behind that I need or want. When I'm certain we have everything, I look at the two suitcases by the door. Granted, we jammed them full, it almost seems sad that I have little more than what I arrived with five years ago. I mean there's still stuff in the apartment I'm leaving behind, but there's not that much more that truly has meaning or sentimental value to me. I haven't really purchased much in the way of new clothes or shoes. I wear scrubs and sneakers or clogs to work most days just because they're comfortable, and I don't care if I get blood or vomit on them. It happens sometimes.

I move to sit beside Misha on the sofa, but he pulls me onto his lap. As I always do, I curl into him. I close my eyes as he strokes my back.

"Baby girl, we'll figure all this out. We'll go to the condo in Manhattan. Once my brother does whatever he does to hack, we'll possibly know more. You weren't in my life before we went to Moscow, so we don't have informants near here. But we do have people on the payroll in the Bronx. We'll see if we can hear any of that same—what was it—tea as those kids."

"Yes, tea, Daddy. They spilled the tea by sharing the gossip."

"And I take it a whip is a car. What the hell is guap?"

"Money. The guys thought he was being too flashy when they said he was real extra. Apparently, the girls—though technically, apparently, sis can refer to a guy too—thought he was sexy. That's what drip means—I think."

"I didn't know you spoke so many languages. This is foreign to me, and I speak five."

"Five?"

"Yes. Russian, English, German, French, and Spanish plus enough Polish to get by. We do a lot of business overseas."

"I speak Russian, English, French, passable Spanish, and apparently Gen Z."

"Do you think they were really coming to check on you? Or could someone have sent them?"

"They're good kids. If it had been just about any other group of boys, I would question it. They all work really hard and, for the most part, have good grades. They're going to have choices for their futures. They don't hang out on the block. They do their best to stay out of trouble. Whatever the full version was—because we definitely got the abbreviated one—it got to them enough for them to come out here. If teens in this neighborhood found out which one they were from, it would be a problem. It was pretty brave of them, actually."

They risked getting jumped to make sure my place was all right. They wouldn't have gotten into the building, but they would have asked around. Being too nosey isn't good for your health here either, but they risked it.

Misha and I fall into silence until Sergei knocks and walks in without waiting. He walks straight to my computer but looks at me before he sits at my desk.

"Do whatever you have to. I just hope you find something, anything. I left my passwords on the desk."

They're in Cyrillic since there's little chance people could read it. But now I wonder if whoever came here could.

"It might take me a few hours depending on what I find."

"Then take it with you."

"I'll do a little preliminary looking while Anton sweeps the place."

Fuck. They must think someone is listening in. That's why Misha was basically whispering to me. I thought it was just because of how close we sat. He didn't need to speak any louder. I glance at the sofa.

"You were where you belong, *malyshka*. It just made it easier to talk. It wasn't the other way around."

"I'm not sure that I like your mind-reading."

"I'm not always fond of your ability to do the same."

He kisses my cheek with a smile before Stefan comes to the door. He and Misha carry my stuff down to an SUV. There's a guy standing beside it, clearly unwelcoming to anyone who gets too close to the vehicle, or the town car parked behind it. My suitcases go in the back before Misha opens the door to the rear passenger seat. Stefan and the nameless man get in the sedan, but they just sit there. But when Sergei and Anton come out a minute later, the nameless man gets in the SUV's driver seat while Stefan drives Sergei and Anton in the town car.

We pull away from the curb, and I settle next to Misha as he pulls out his phone. He opens the browser and immediately searches for sex–devices. I don't even know what to call the category that encompasses toys, restraints, paddles, whips, clamps, and whatever else pops up. There's no privacy glass in the SUV like there are in the town cars. We point to things that interest us, and the items in the shopping cart seem to grow exponentially by the minute. With the way we're going, we're going to buy out the entire online store.

As we approach the bridge to leave the Bronx, I sense Misha looking up far more often. I shift my attention from his phone to him. He keeps looking at our driver, who I notice keeps looking in the rearview mirror. I twist to look behind us, but Misha squeezes my thigh.

"What's happening?"

I keep my voice to a whisper as though it would matter.

"We're not sure, but someone has been following us since we left your place."

"Are they behind Sergei and Anton?"

"Yeah. For now. They keep trying to get between us, but Stefan is a better driver than they are."

"Who do you think they are? Is this about me?"

"I don't know, *malyshka*."

As Misha answers, our driver—whose name I still don't know—accelerates. It's not like he just speeds up a little to make a light. I mean, he guns it.

"Get down, Kitty."

Misha pushes my back as he reaches behind him to draw his gun. I can lift my head just enough to watch the driver pull his own handgun from the center console. The driver maneuvers and takes a series of unexpected turns.

"Unfasten your belt and get onto the floor."

I don't hesitate to obey Misha. This is act now, ask questions later. I've never been in a high-speed car chase and never imagined I would be. How the hell is there room in any part of New York City for high-speed anything?

There's a gunshot, but I don't feel anything hit the car. There's no sound of metal on metal. There's no sudden swerve of a punctured tire. Was it just a warning? I don't know what I expect Misha to do. Duck with me? Shoot back? I turn my head to see him. He's sitting cool as a cucumber with his gun pointing toward the window, but he does nothing else.

"Kitty, I'm not opening this window and making you a target unless there's absolutely no other choice."

"Can you see who it is?"

"No. The windows are too tinted. Whoever shot at us only opened the window enough to get a rifle barrel out. They probably had a periscope attached, so they didn't have to look directly out of the window. They're turning off."

I wait for Misha to tell me I can sit up. When he does, I glance toward the window, and I recognize the car Anton and Sergei are riding in. Misha puts the handgun back in its holster. He helps me back onto my seat, and I sink against him. Before I can fasten the seatbelt, he lifts me onto his lap. He holds me tightly, as scared to let me go as I am for him to let me go.

"Who was that?"

"I don't know, but my guess is whoever came to your apartment before us was watching the place."

"Just waiting in case I came back? Or could they know I stayed at Maks and Laura's with you? Did they follow us?"

"I don't know, baby girl."

"We're back to an unknown man with a Spanish accent. That's millions of options in New York. What the hell?"

"Sergei will be on it."

"Those plates aren't real. Even I know that."

"The city cameras. He'll work backwards to see if he can tack the car that way."

I feel a little better, and my heart is no longer racing. Misha rubs my back and eases some of the tension from me. But it doesn't disappear completely since I can feel his legs tensed beneath me, like he's still on full alert. I lift my head to whisper in his ear.

"Daddy, I'm safe. You're safe. It's over."

"It's not over until I find out who put you in danger."

"Daddy, please let it go for now. I just want to get into Manhattan and behind a locked door."

I'm still terrified, but I need Misha to calm down. Otherwise, I'm going to freak the fuck out. I take my cues from him, but he understands better than I do. I feel completely in the dark other than knowing that someone was after us. Maybe it was about me. But maybe it was just about him. Maybe someone saw an opportunity and took it, and it's one of their regular rivals. This is the closest a threat has gotten to me. It's not just some ominous figure in the distance that has no face or shape. This was someone who could have killed us. Then what would happen to Larisa? Who would keep looking for her?

I feel Misha's body relax, and he kisses my head over and over. He knows what I need. I feel like a selfish bitch because I have nothing to offer him. That I'm just taking right now. I don't know what to do to help him, and I can barely think about that.

"Shh, *malyshka*. Knowing your fear is easing is what I need. Protecting you is all that matters to me right now."

"There's that mind-reading again. It's uncanny."

We sit in silence and just hold each other until we pull up to a building in a chic part of Manhattan.

"Are you ready to see your new home, *koshechka?*"

"So ready."

I sure as shit wasn't ready for the place I walk into when we get to Misha's—our—building. Holy hell.

Chapter Fifteen

Misha

I watch as Kitty's gaze sweeps throughout my massive Manhattan loft. It's a far cry from the tiny apartments my parents, Sergei, and I shared in Moscow and Queens. Vlad's training forced us into this life. He demanded that we knock off liquor stores, run illegal gambling rings, and steal vehicles and motorcycles. While he didn't pay well, he did pay. All of us—my cousins, my brother, our friends, and I—saved everything we could. What we didn't use to help support our families, we tucked away, literally, under our mattresses. With no father and a mother struggling at first to get all her pharmacist certifications accepted in America, my cousins hustled the most.

But we all shared the same desire to never be under anyone else's thumb, to never depend on anyone outside our family to provide for us, and to prove to that fucking psychopath he shouldn't have trained his monsters quite so well. Except for Maks and Aleks, the rest of us went to college. We got scholarships and grants to help pay, but by the time we left, we were all on our way to being millionaires. We were also rising in the ranks among our bratva.

Maks was being trained to be *pakhan* one day, and everyone knew his brothers would join him as the Elite Group. They're the men who guide and counsel the *pakhan* and supposedly rein them in when needed. The old Elite Group never reined in Vlad. So, the day he forced his way in Aunt Galina's house and tried to force himself on her was the day Maks killed him.

Vlad didn't realize my cousins were all in the backyard with my aunt for dinner. Maks had just come inside and heard his mother's scream. Vlad was dead before he knew what was happening. They swore Maks in as *pakhan* the next day. Within two years, we all filled the senior-most positions within our organization. We ousted the old Elite Group by coercion and manipulation—just the way Vlad taught us. After that, we began our legal operations. Without Vlad there to stop us, we ventured into investing, imports and exports, construction, bio-pharma, and various other things. It's not that Sergei, Pasha, Anton, and I aren't as driven as our mutual cousins. We are. But being *pakhan* and the Elite Group entitled the four brothers to resources the rest of us couldn't access. None of us —Anton, Sergei, Pasha, nor I—are struggling. We're million-aires in our own rights, and it wouldn't surprise me if we caught up with our mutual cousins within the next decade.

And that not struggling is obvious to Kitty as she takes in the high-end electronics I love. I watch the most television among any of us. None of us are going to clubs unless we're working security at the ones Kutsenko Partners owns. We don't have huge circles of friends to go out drinking with. None of us has ever touched a single drug, not even when Vlad thought we did. There's always someone willing to test shipments of cocaine for us. When I have a quiet night at home, I like to watch movies on my ridiculously enormous television in my living room or the not quite so over-the-top one in my bedroom. I also have a state-of-the-art stereo system.

My kitchen would make any chef jealous. I love to cook. I love to eat. Therefore, I love to work out. My eight burner stove catches Kitty's attention after she notices the practically industrial size fridge. Before the family started filtering back to Queens as everyone started getting married, my cousins and friends usually gathered at my place at least twice or three times a week for dinner. I had to have a fridge that size to accommodate the amount of food I needed to feed the eight of us.

"Do you enjoy cooking, *kiska?*"

"I do. But I've never seen anything like your kitchen, except on those house renovation and real estate shows. It's —impressive."

I slip my hand into hers as I guide her into my haven.

"Feel free to eat whatever is here. We can go to the grocery store tomorrow and get what you like."

Kitty grins, then chuckles. I raise my eyebrows.

"I just have a hard time imagining you pushing a shopping cart."

"Aleks met Heather at the grocery store when their carts nearly collided."

"Really?"

"Yes. That man is at the grocery store like twice a week. He hands down eats the most of any of us. Anton eats the healthiest, and I cook the most. The others tease them and come to my place to keep from starving. Or so they said before they got married and could no longer blame bachelorhood for why they needed someone else's home cooking."

I roll my eyes as Kitty's smile broadens. I pull open the fridge door and watch as she inspects what's in there. Since I've been away, there isn't any produce or the usual containers of leftovers. It looks a bit sparse compared to normal. But I suppose to most people, it would still appear pretty full. We walk through to the dining room with the table that seats eight. It seems tiny after seeing the table that seats twenty at Maks and Laura's. For years, it was enough.

As we pass the living room again, Kitty releases my hand. I know what she's spotted even before I see the surprise register on her face. She glances back at me over her shoulder as she crosses the room.

"Who is this?"

She smiles so broadly as she leans toward the cage that I can't help but join her.

"This is Mr. Bun-Buns. He's a miniature lop. He stayed with Heather and Aleks for a few days because she has a guinea pig named Gloria and knows how to take care of him. Pasha's wife, Sumiko, has a chinchilla, so Mr. Bun-Buns stayed with them too. Pasha brought him back while we were out."

She's careful as she sticks her index finger through the metal cage and runs it along my rabbit's back.

"I never imagined you'd have a bunny rabbit. You're so large, and it's so—mini. How'd you wind up with him?"

"I had a stuffed rabbit I adored as a kid."

That's all I want to say. I don't want to give the entire reason. The anger it sparks has died with the passage of time. But Kitty's expectant face turns wary as she straightens, glances at the cage one more time, then turns toward the hallway that leads to the bedrooms. I feel like an ass for shutting her out. There are so many fucking things I can never tell her. I can share how I got my damn rabbit.

"I carried that stuffed rabbit everywhere until I was seven. Then he had a special place on my bed until I was eleven, and we moved to America. In our first apartment, I had a dresser that sat in the corner of the room I shared with Sergei. He got a spot where the walls could prop him up. I forgot he was there when I had some supposed friends over when I was fourteen. They were bratva like I was. We were still young enough to be *shestyorka*—" Errand boys. Not yet full members but on our way. "—so we still had time to hang out. They spotted my rabbit and teased me. I thought it was the end of it once they left. I should have hidden him."

Kitty steps closer to me as I explain. My eyes are locked on Mr. Bun-Buns. It's all so vivid, even though it's been fourteen years.

"They told Vlad."

That's all it takes for Kitty's eyes to widen and for her to freeze. I can tell she fears what I'll say next. She's gearing herself up for a story about torture. She wouldn't be far off.

"He sent them to break into our apartment while Sergei and I were at school and my parents were at work. Then he demanded all eight of us appear before him. He had my stuffed rabbit and a real rabbit both strung up and hanging from nooses. He'd put the real rabbit in the noose as we walked in, so it was still flailing and panicking. He told me to choose which would survive. I admit I had a moment's hesitation, but I picked the real rabbit. He laughed as he stabbed his knife into my toy and cut from the top to the bottom. Then he slashed it as stuffing fell to the ground. When he'd pretty much eviscerated my toy rabbit, he moved to the real one. By now it was already dead, but he gave it the same treatment as we all stared in horror. But we'd been around long enough to know not to show a single reaction, a single emotion. Vlad knew he didn't have to restrain me. I would never run forward and do something so stupid as to try to stop him. That was the first part of my punishment. I had to battle my emotions and hide everything I thought."

"Misha, you don't have to tell me the entire story."

"I won't hide what I don't have to."

"But that doesn't mean you have to scratch at an old wound. You like rabbits, and that's why you have this one."

"Kitty, this is your home now. I want to share my life with you. That also means as much of my past as I can. I don't want you to ever feel like you're living with a stranger. That you're fucking or making love to a man who refuses to let you know him."

She nods.

"He left both rabbits swinging as the boys who betrayed me grabbed me and wrestled me to the ground. Another lesson we'd all learned was never to intervene. If we did, all eight of us got the shit beaten out of us. We always wanted to, and it nearly killed us inside when we didn't. But we all agreed that none of us wanted to cause someone else's torture, so we had to watch each and every fucking time. That was part of the first pact we made as a family. Part of how we swore we would endure Vlad and all the fucked-up shit he put us through. My brother, cousins, and friends witnessed the worst beating I ever got. Vlad swore every homophobic, vile curse he could think of. He had them strip me to make sure I was still a man. By the end, I wasn't sure that I still was. I took a lot of boots to my junk that day."

Kitty doesn't realize she's taken hold of both my hands and is squeezing with more strength that I ever imagined. It's like those scenes in movies where the woman is giving birth and practically crushes her partner's hands. Kitty giving birth. A family. A new generation of bratva. Holy fuck. That's enough to give me cold sweats. I never imagined children with anyone before I met Kitty. Now I think about it all the time. But picturing bringing another generation of bratva into the world is like a knife in the chest. I know Maks and Bogdan have both started families, but it terrifies me.

"Sergei sneaked Mr. Bun-Buns into the apartment two days later. We knew our mom would know in a heartbeat, but my parents also knew what happened. God. I can't imagine how all of our parents felt back then. The uselessness of not being able to protect us without risking getting us all killed. We weren't supposed to have pets, but my parents never disagreed. I loved Mr. Bun-Buns from the minute I saw him. He looks so much like my stuffed rabbit. But I thought I had to be tough, so I smirked and named him Mr. Bun-Buns. It stuck. And Sergei knew how much I appreciated him and the rabbit. There have been plenty of days when he's felt like my best friend."

Wow. I didn't plan to admit that last part. That's how comfortable and trusting I feel with Kitty.

"How did you come up with his name?"

"I was joking, and it stuck."

"Did your stuffed rabbit have a name?"

"*Morkov'*."

"Carrots. I like that."

It's not pity in Kitty's eyes. It's empathy. It makes me wonder how much of a childhood she got. I think back to her room at her parents' house. It was comfortable and likely hadn't changed since she moved out. But nothing at all said a little girl once lived there. Maybe she changed it as a teenager, but I don't think so. She smiles when Mr. Bun-Buns twitches his nose at her, so she walks over and strokes between his ears before taking my hand, turning toward the hallway that leads to the bedrooms.

"The guys and I usually go to the gym a few times a week before work. A couple years ago, it was pretty much every morning. But for some reason, they don't like to get out of bed and come into Manhattan at four-thirty in the morning. My home gym is getting more use than it used to."

I wink at her. I can't blame them for not wanting to leave their wives in bed alone. It's down to Sergei and Anton going to the gym every morning now that I'm with Kitty. But I like the idea that my brother and friend will have the place to themselves. It's another chance for them to snatch a few hours alone before putting on their public faces.

"You cannot tell me that you didn't use this place. Everything is in terrific condition, but it's clear it's all been used plenty of times."

"I only worked out in here once a day. Now it's usually twice, unless I meet the others at that gym my cousins own. It's really a boxing gym, but there are weights and cardio, plus the ring and punching bags."

Kitty's eyes meet mine for a moment before she nods. I burst the happy bubble that was forming again. She must know part of my training was learning to fight. She doesn't want to think about it.

"Maks was a golden glove prize fighter for years. Bogdan is the only one who really enjoys boxing. The rest of us enjoy letting off some steam and taunting each other."

I hoped that would ease her sudden tension, but all she does is nod again. I draw her into my arms, and she doesn't hesitate to wrap hers around my waist. I gaze into blue-hazel eyes I love.

"What's wrong, *malyshka?*"

She shakes her head and tears well in her eyes.

"Do you not like the idea of me boxing? Worried it'll ruin my pretty face?"

That has the opposite effect from what I wanted. Tears slide down her cheeks.

"Baby girl, what's wrong?"

She shakes her head again and burrows against my chest. I abandon the rest of the tour as I scoop her into my arms. She's unprepared for that and yelps. I carry her back into the living room and sit on the sofa. It feels entirely natural for her to remain on my lap. She slides her hand beneath the collar of my shirt, but she doesn't like how that limits where she can place her hand. She unbuttons the top one and slides her palm onto my chest. I feel her sigh.

"I won't push you to tell me what you feel, but I'd like to know. I didn't mean to upset you."

"I know, Daddy."

Her voice is soft when she answers. I wait for her to say more, but she remains quiet for a long time. I realize she's marshaling her emotions, so she can talk. Her hand remains on my chest, and I glance down to find her eyes closed.

"I just had a flash of you fighting someone in the street, then Sergei is telling me you're dead. I don't know why knowing you box bothers me. It's not like I don't know you've been in fights before. I've told you I know the types of scars you have. But for some reason, that just made it feel even more real that you might not come home one night."

"Is it too much?"

"Of course, it is. Everything about the bratva is too much. Too much greed. Too much violence. Too much death. I have newfound respect for my mother and what she's endured while loving my dad. I remember how scared I would get as a little girl when my father would be late coming home or when he left at night. On those late nights, my mom would let Larisa and me crawl into bed with her. We'd fall asleep next to her, and we'd magically wake in our beds in the morning. It's how I always knew my dad came home."

"I would leave this all behind in an instant if I could."

"I know, Daddy. I don't doubt that. But it would be far

more dangerous for you if you did. And your family would never leave you unprotected. None of you can walk away."

I'm glad she understands that. One of many fears I've had about dating is keeping my bratva life away from the woman I'm with. If the woman found out, I feared trying to make her understand why there's no choice in this. I know the others have had to explain these things to their now wives. Part of me is relieved that I don't have to explain it all to Kitty. But it also breaks a part of my heart that she already understands. The fear that her loved ones won't come home and knowing they can never leave is something she's lived with her entire life. It's why she left. I've sucked her back in.

"Kitty—"

"No, Misha. I'm not leaving. I love you more than I fear your death. It just hit me for a moment."

She kisses along my collar bone and up my neck. She tugs on my earlobe with her teeth before she whispers to me.

"Take me to bed, Daddy, and do all those unspeakable things to me."

She doesn't have to tell me twice. I'm off the sofa and carrying her to a room I've never shared with anyone else. The few women I've hooked up with and brought back here never spent the night. I've never made space in my closet for someone else. I can't wait to do that for Kitty.

I place her on her feet once we're in our bedroom. I sit on the end of the bed and school my features to keep from grinning like a schoolboy because I'm so excited to have her in what's now our home.

"Strip, *malyshka*. Slowly."

As she inches her shirt up, exposing her stomach and ribs, I wonder if I should reconsider the hell I've just put myself in. When her tits appear in her push-up bra, I'm ready to stop her so I can maul her. She lets it drop to the floor before she kicks off her shoes and unbuttons her pants. I know what I'll see when she pushes them over her hips. I threatened to shred every pair of underwear she owns since she won't need them anymore. So instead of a thong, which I know she prefers, I see the bare strip of skin above her pussy.

Her pants hit the floor, and she reaches back to unfasten her bra. I fist my hands as she eases the straps down her arms but holds the bra in place. She's in no hurry to peel it away from her magnificent tits because she knows what she's doing to me. She can see it from the bulge in my pants.

"Come here, *malyshka*."

She drops the bra and walks over to where I'm perched on the end of the bed. I reach around her and grab her ass. My fingers dig into her flesh as I pull the cheeks apart. I press my index finger against the puckered flesh, tapping it twice.

"All of you is mine, baby girl. By the end of tonight, you'll have my cum down your throat, dripping from your pussy, and filling your ass. You will not come unless I tell you, you can. If you don't obey, I will edge you all night while I get off. Do you understand?"

"Yes, Daddy."

Her breathy voice tells me how eager she is. If I couldn't tell from that, the way her nipples have tightened proves it. The room isn't cold. I slide my fingers between her thighs, and her pussy definitely can't hide how much she likes my command. I ease her back two steps before I stand.

"Undress me, *malyshka*."

She opens my shirt, moving quickly from button to button, before she shifts her attention to my sleeves. She hands me each cufflink, and I put them in my shirt pocket. I better not forget to take them out before I send this shirt to the dry cleaners. They're twenty-thousand-dollar diamond cufflinks. I'm not so rich that I'm flippant about that. She pushes the shirt off my shoulders and down my arms until it drops on the bed. I toe off my shoes as she unfastens my belt. She pulls it free from the loops and folds it in half, then stares at it.

"Are you afraid that one day I'll use that on you?"

"I'm not afraid of anything you will do to me. I know you'll give me the pain I want without harming me."

The pain I want...

"Baby girl, we've barely touched on kinky. You've only had vanilla in the past. We've had rough sex, but we haven't had *rough* sex. Is that what you want?"

"Yes."

She answers without dropping a beat. We're going to have to define some terms then. I'm not sure that I can do anything that would make me think I'm torturing her. I know I sure as shit will never restrain her wrists with anything other than handcuffs, a tie, or maybe a scarf or something. I will never put rope around any of her. I can't. I want nothing I associate with work to ever touch her. I don't want any part of that man to come near her.

"Daddy, breathe. I don't mean torture me. I want to be restrained, but only how *you're* okay with. The last thing I want to make you think of is work when we're like this."

She reads me too well. I held my breath for only a second longer than usual. I know my face gives nothing away. I didn't want her to know that's what I was thinking, but I should have known she's already learning to read me.

"Does the belt intrigue you?"

"Yes. I—I—think I want to see the lines you leave on my ass. I—I want to know you put them there because you can. I want to think of you every time I try to sit. I want to remember that I'm yours."

"And I'm yours because no other woman will ever bear any marks I make. Do you want to try this now?"

192

"Yes, to both. I think it's hot that I'm naked, and you're in your pants."

"You need a safe word, Kitty."

She frowns at me. At first, I think she doesn't know what I mean by the term. Then I realize she really doesn't like me using her name when we're like this. I pull her into my embrace again.

"You don't want to be called Kitty, do you?"

"It's jarring when we're like this. I know you did it to make sure I know how serious you are. But I don't like it, *papochka*. It feels distant and cold. I don't want to be a sub, Misha."

I agree. It feels cold and disconnected to use our names like this. I hate hearing her say mine right now. I know she didn't do it to prove a point. It was the same reason I used hers: to make it clear this is something serious. But I don't enjoy it.

"You are not my sub, and I am not your Dom. That isn't the dynamic I want between us. I don't want that distance. I want an emotional connection in other parts of our life that we wouldn't have if that were our relationship. You said you read DDLG romances sometimes, but that isn't what you want. Have you changed your mind? Do you think you're a Little?"

"No. I'm not. I don't want stuffies or blankets. I don't want to color. I don't feel younger than I am. I like it when you take control, especially when something is upsetting me. It means I know I can rely on you, and I can trust that you will take care of me like you say you will. But it's not the type of taking care of that I think of when I think DDLG. It's more like I feel like I have someone to help me, not take over because I can't or don't want to."

I believe I understand what she means. I'm not a Daddy Dom. That isn't what I want, but I would learn if that's what Kitty wanted. I realized that a while ago. Even if it's not something that I'm naturally inclined to, or it's something I don't know, I would do it if it provided the type of emotional connection she wants. I think she would do the same. I think she would at least try to be a Little if I truly was a Daddy Dom.

"What's your safe word, *malyshka*?"

"Beets. I'll eat them, but I'll never ask for them."

I can't help but laugh.

"Aleks loathes them. Like with the strength of a thousand suns. But he eats them since they're in practically every-fuck-ing-thing. When we were kids, he thought they only grew in Russia. When we moved here, he thought he'd escaped them. The first meal Aunt Galina cooked in their apartment was borscht. He was thirteen and cried. He's never lived it down."

"Poor guy. I'll eat them if someone else makes them, but I won't volunteer."

I consider my options for how to position Kitty. If I spank her over my lap, I'm afraid that I'll land them too hard but can be more exact in where they land. If I have her lie on the bed, I'm more concerned about the angle that I strike since I will keep the belt folded in half, and I'm tall.

"Lie across the side of the bed, *malyshka*."

I think that'll give me the right position. I'm having cold feet now that it's my girlfriend's ass in front of me and not some fucker from my world that deserves whatever he gets. I refuse to think of it as her world too, even though I know...Anyway.

"Yes, *papochka*."

She quicks to follow my command, and I relish the sight of her upturned ass, knowing that in a moment it'll blossom red. I angle myself beside her.

"Put your hands beneath your cheek. Do not reach back, *kiska*. If I hurt you by accident, I will not be pleased. The next spanking will not be for pleasure."

"I understand."

She angles her head to look at me as she speaks. But she closes her eyes, and I see her body relax. I wonder what she tells herself as she gears up for the first blow. I caress my hand over the loveliest ass I've ever seen. Temptation to toss the belt aside, plunge into her pussy until my dick is soaked, then fuck her ass is almost too much. Why was I giving her this spanking again? Because she's curious about the belt and because she trusts me.

"I will warm your fine little ass before the first spanking with the belt. I will give you five with the belt. Do not ask me for more. I won't do it the first time. If it's too much, then use your safe word. It won't disappoint me if you do. I never want to harm you, *malyshka.*"

"I know, Daddy. That's why I want to do this with you."

We've told each other the same thing enough times that we both have to accept it. I crack my hand against her soft flesh and watch the waves as her ass jiggles. Fuck. That's hot. I land five more before I switch the belt from one hand to the other. I realize I need the inhale I take. I've never done something like this without the intention of inflicting severe pain. I almost back out. I fear my own strength; that it'll be inadvertent, but I'll be too rough. The idea makes me want to throw up. Maybe I'm the one who isn't meant for kink. God, do I want it. But I don't know if I can do it.

Kitty's eyes open as she waits for me. Her brow furrows in confusion, then she reaches out her hand to me. I take it and give it a squeeze, but she won't release it when I'm ready to let go. She nods, and I realize she's offering me support and will hold my hand through this entire thing. I'm certain I love her even more than a minute ago if that's possible.

"Count them, *malyshka.*"

I raise my arm to only mid-thigh. Normally, it would be well over my shoulder. I snap it down, listening to the brief whizzing sound. It lands where I want it. The first red welt blooms across the middle of her ass.

"One."

She takes a fortifying breath and nods. I land the next one slightly lower.

"Two."

The next two land across her horizontal crack. She lurches forward for both. I know her clit is rubbing against the side of the mattress. I can see her getting wetter with each blow. I raise my arm to my waist for the last one. It welts the most.

"Five."

I help her to her feet and look into her eyes. She's trembling, and I'm afraid I've done exactly what I feared. But she throws her arms around my neck, and her kiss devours me. She can't seem to get close enough. I'm careful when I rest my palms on her ass. I don't apply any pressure. She reaches between us and unfastens my pants before pushing them down. I agreed to her demand that I stop wearing boxer briefs if she has to give up her panties. The moment I kick them free, she sinks to her knees as I yank my socks off. She rests her hands on my thighs and opens her mouth. Her bright eyes are half closed in the sexiest fucking way. I brush the tip of my cock against her lips, and her tongue darts out.

I press forward until the head rests against her tongue. She tries to lean her head forward, but I pull back. My hands fist her sandy blonde hair, holding her head in place before I thrust into her mouth. She gags, but her lips tighten around me, sucking before I can withdraw. She sets to work, sliding her mouth along me as I loosen my hold on her head. When her shoulders droops, and her eyes close all the way, I hold her head in place once more and fuck her. The hands resting on my thighs slide around to the back and up my legs until she grips my ass. She presses me into her.

"*Kiska*, I'm in control. Try to push me into your mouth again, and your hands will be behind your back during a spanking that isn't meant to make you wet."

I love it. I love that she wants to pleasure me as much as I want to do the same for her. But I don't think I'll ever not want to be in control. It's what keeps me alive. It's not that I fear Kitty as a threat. It's just monumentally stressful not to be. It sends me into a panic.

She no longer presses against my ass, so I sweep my thumbs over her cheekbones.

"Do you have any idea how sexy you are? Do you feel how fucking hard I am for you? Fuck, *malyshka*. I won't last as long as I wanted. You're too fucking hot and feel too fucking good."

She hums her approval, and her lips twitch into a smile for a second. I thrust hard three more times before I explode. Thank fucking God. I fill her mouth with my cum, just like I promised. My dick can't stop twitching until I'm almost certain there isn't enough cum to leave in her pussy and ass like I also promised. I pull out, my cheeks flushed and chest heaving. I watch her lick her lips, then smile like a Cheshire cat. How did I get so lucky in such a fucked-up situation?

Chapter Sixteen

Kitty

I never imagined a month ago that I would want a man to spank me, let alone spank me with a belt. That's actually not true. I did want a man to spank me. I just didn't think I would find one who would. Some of the worst fights Semyon and I had were when I suggested ways to spice up our sex life. Little did I know he was having all of his spicy sex at brothels. He just wanted a sweet little woman to come home to. He went so far as to stop at a friend's house every night to shower and change clothes before he came home to me. Fucker.

As I kneel in front of Misha, I realize a few things. The way I feel about him is unlike anything I felt for Semyon, and I was certain I loved him and that's why I stayed with him. I loved who I thought he was, and so I forgave who he truly was. I feel sexually fulfilled in a way no man has ever made me feel before. And I've never wanted to please someone in reciprocation as much as I want to do so for Misha. I want to make him happy.

"Stand up."

I hurry to obey. I'm eager to know what comes next. My pussy aches with a need to have him fill me. The spanking hurt like a motherfucker, but it also made me so wet I was dripping down my thighs. I can't believe that doesn't embarrass me, but I know Misha loves knowing he has that effect on me. He likes it as much as I enjoy seeing how hard he is even though he just came. The man can go more rounds than Mike Tyson. Misha would put any nineteen-year-old in his supposed prime to shame.

"What we bought in the car will arrive tomorrow. Until then, we improvise."

He walks to his closet, and I enjoy every step he takes. A view of his fine ass as he walks away, and a view of his massive cock as he walks back. Too bad, bitches. He's mine. He grabs three ties from his collection and returns to where I'm now standing beside the bed. He kisses along my right collarbone and up my neck until he draws his teeth against the skin behind my ear. My pussy clenches.

"If you don't like something, tell me."

"Yes, Daddy."

He slips a tie over my eyes before knotting it against the back of my head. He helps me onto the bed face down. I can hear him moving around, but I don't know what he's doing. Then I hear what I'm certain is a lighter flicking. I can smell sandalwood and know that he's lit a candle. I find the scent soothing as my anticipation builds. The second tie binds my left wrist to my left thigh, and the third does the same thing on my right side. My mind is running wild as I wait for something else to happen, but there's at least a minute where nothing does. Then I feel the slow, hot drip of wax down my spine.

The hot sensation makes me shiver. It's almost too much heat, the pain a shock each time a drop hits my skin. But it soon cools, leaving me eager for the next. He must have been waiting for enough wax to melt before he started, because he trails it over my lower back and between my ass cheeks. I can't help but clench at the foreign sensation. That earns me a loud smack. I kick my feet, and he laughs.

"How're you doing, *malyshka?*"

"Fine, Daddy."

I thought I sounded breathy, but he's satisfied with my answer as his hand skims over my ass before his fingers dip between my checks just like the wax did. It's a fucking good thing I had a Brazilian right before I went to Moscow. It doesn't take the wax long to harden, and he rips it free. I kick my feet again as I squeeze my eyes beneath the blindfold. I suddenly feel something cold dribble onto my backdoor. I realize he just spit, and now he's using it to lube the tip of his finger as he presses against the opening.

"Do you remember what I said?"

"Yes, Daddy. You said you'd come in my mouth, pussy, and ass tonight."

"Why?"

"Because it'll feel great."

"Sassy, baby girl. Try again."

He presses his finger a little deeper, but only so the tip is inside me. The nurse in me wants to ruin the moment, but I press my lips together as I let myself enjoy.

"Because I'm yours, Daddy."

"Is that what you want? For Daddy to fill you with his cock? To be the only man who ever gets your ass?"

"Yes, to all of that. Anything you want, I want to try."

He feathers his well-trimmed fingernails up both sides of my spine before using his index finger and middle finger to slide back down. He pours a little more wax across my back, starting on my left side with a slow trickle to my right. The heat from the candle flame intensifies the brief burn from the wax. Every time I think I can't be more aroused, Misha tops it.

I hear him place the candle on the bedside table, then he's massaging my shoulders. It's not just the wax that melts tonight. His strong hands work my shoulders and upper back. The stress from the past month won't leave my body, but his ministrations ease it. My mind jumps to thinking that Larisa is suffering and may never meet someone who loves her the way Misha loves me. Tears threaten to leak from my eyes and ruin his silk tie.

"You're getting tenser, *koshechka*. Are you thinking about Larisa? Or do you not like this? Is it too much?"

I inhale a ragged breath and shake my head against the pillow.

"It's not too much. It's amazing. I was enjoying it until I thought about how Larisa will never have someone to love her and take care of her like you do for me."

Misha gently peels the wax off me as I speak. It's the first time I've really let myself think that Larisa is dead. It's been so long. How can she not be?

"What do you need right now? Do you want to stop, and we call Sergei to see if he has any information or ideas?"

"Yes...No. I don't want to stop, and that's why I feel so guilty."

"Sergei will call the minute he finds anything, but if you'd feel better pausing this, we can call him."

"I believe you that he'll call. Calling him won't make him find anything or make it happen sooner."

He unties my wrists and legs as we continue to talk. He nudges my legs apart, and I feel him climb onto the bed. He links our fingers together and draws our arms up and under the pillow. He shifts and brings his chest to my back. He doesn't put all of his weight onto me. I doubt he ever would because I

know he'd fear crushing me. But it's enough for me to feel shel-
tered with him at my back and the mattress beneath me. Like
nothing can get to me. As comforting as this position is, it's also
erotic as hell. I tilt my hips and push them up. He understands
and reaches between us to align the tip of his dick with my
pussy. Then we're both sighing as he slides into me.

"What do you need, *kiska*?"

"Just stay like this for a minute, then make love to me,
please."

Never in my life did I think I'd enjoy being connected to
someone like this. Yeah, I felt an emotional connection to
Semyon when we slept together, but it was mostly about
getting off. With the few other guys I've slept with, it was
always about having orgasms and feeling satisfied. This is a
whole other level. He kisses my shoulders and neck and cheeks
before moving back to my shoulders. He slowly rocks, and I
follow the rhythm he sets. He doesn't stop his smattering of
light kisses, and I curl my fingers over his as we still hold hands.

"I don't know any man like you, Misha. The lives we have
aren't ones that breed gentleness and tenderness, yet you
haven't made me feel anything less than precious to you."

"You know men like me. I'm related to all of them. You are
precious to me, Kitty. I cherish the trust you put in me to help
you and love you. You know what my life is like the moment I
walk out my door. When I'm with you, I don't want any of that
to touch you. You're a refuge for me from what I've known for
the past eighteen years."

I release his right hand and pull mine out. I push off the
blindfold, having forgotten it was on until I felt this need to
look into his icy-blue eyes. There isn't the ice in his veins I
assumed there was. They're vibrant, like a spring sky. I turn my
head to look back at him and pucker my lips. He gladly accepts
the offer of a kiss. I move my hand, so it's back where it belongs.

As the heat builds in our kiss, so does the speed of Misha's thrusts. I moan as each surge presses me into the bed and rubs my clit.

I'm unprepared for him to pull out, flip me over, and lift me to straddle him. The moment he's inside me again, he sucks on my tits. He moves from one to other as I ride him. My head falls back, my hair brushing his knees.

"So fucking beautiful."

I look up at him when he whispers his declaration. My hands cup his jaw as I kiss him again. He shifts us once more, so I'm lying on my back. We're looking into each other's eyes as we come. Sweat glistens on his brow, and I can feel it roll from my temple. He lowers himself, always careful. I pull him down, so we're chest to chest. I want to hold him and be that refuge he seeks.

When the moment passes, he rolls onto his side, and I follow him. He tucks hair behind my ear as I rest my hand on the arm beneath him. I feel like I'm one existential question after another. What does it mean to have met a man under these circumstances? Why do I feel so certain about something that should be completely uncertain, considering we barely know each other? Can this really last? Is he real?

I can't help the smile that makes my lips twitch. He's definitely real, and it's his cum I feel on my thighs.

"Are you hungry, *malyshka*?"

"I am. Starving, actually."

He rolls off the bed and walks to his closet once again. He pulls one of his button-down shirts from a hanger before he hands it to me. I slip it on as he pulls a pair of boxer briefs from the drawer.

"Ahem."

His cocked eyebrow matches mine. He will not Daddy me on this one. My gaze darts to his underwear, and my eyebrow goes up even higher. He may scare the shit out of grown men, but I deal with teenagers every day.

"I'm not putting anything on over them."

"Then I should be able to wear a thong if I'm not putting anything over them."

He doesn't walk over to me. He prowls. I yelp when he squeezes my ass with his left hand. Holy fuck. I forgot all about my hot ass because I was too focused on all the other sensations he created.

"Who makes the rules?"

"You, Daddy. But I told you what I expect, and you refuse to follow through on what you agreed to."

I'm quick. My arm shoots out, and my hand slips between his arm and ribs as I take a step forward. My hand lands on his ass with a slap that fills the air. Before I know what's happening, I'm over his shoulder as he stalks toward the window. There's a full-length mirror on the wall perpendicular to the one with the window. He puts me on my feet and grabs each side of his shirt and yanks. Buttons pop as he practically tears it from me. He spins me to face the mirror, but I realize that anyone looking up from the street can see us.

"Misha."

"Oh, baby girl, that was a poor choice."

His deep voice rumbles beside my ear. He grasps my wrists and pulls them to my lower back, then holds them with one hand. His other hand pinches my clit, and I go onto my toes, only to have him pull me back down by tugging on my wrists.

"What do you see in the mirror, *kiska*?"

My mind flashes to my faults, but I doubt that's what he means. If I list them, I'll likely not be able to sit for a month. Somehow I don't think he sees them the way I do, and I don't think he'd take well to me putting myself down.

"*Papochka* and *malyshka*."

"Who has control?"

"*Papochka.*"

"Is that what you want?"

"Yes. I was just joking."

"Were you though?"

Maybe not entirely. Maybe I did want to have a moment of control and demand he obey me instead of the other way around.

"*Kiska.*"

There's a clear warning in his tone.

"Not entirely joking."

"Do you want me to submit to you? Do you want more fluid power exchange?"

"No. Definitely not. I cannot think of you as someone who obeys, and I cannot think of myself giving you commands. I did want a little control for a moment, but I don't want to change our dynamic. I..."

"What do you...?"

"This sounds so hideously old-fashioned that I'm embarrassed to say it."

"You never have to be embarrassed to tell me anything you're thinking. Never."

He eases the pressure on my wrists, and his other arm wraps around my waist. I close my eyes with a sigh as I lean back against his chest. This. Him being bigger than me and stronger than me. So fucking masculine in every way. I crave it.

"I don't know that I could see you the same way as I do now. I—" I puff a sigh. "—it's not that I would think less of a man if I knew he submitted to his partner. If that's the dynamic for a gay couple, then one of them submits. I wouldn't judge the guy for it. But I just can't see it with you. It wouldn't feel—" Fuck. I'm so embarrassed to say this. It's like I'm saying fuck feminism and bring on toxic masculinity. "Manly if you did that."

"Do you mean it wouldn't feel like I'm as self-assured and assertive?"

"Yes."

"I think you would feel off kilter if your partner changed, regardless of whether it was a man or woman. I get what you mean about it seeming manly. But I've seen you self-assured and assertive. It makes you neither manly nor less womanly. That's just not what you want between us when we're like this."

I nod.

"So, I'll ask you again: who's in control?"

"You, Daddy. And that's how I like it."

"I don't mind your teasing, and I get why you'd do it. Just remember that with your teasing comes my response."

"Yes, Daddy."

"And since I already promised more than once to have your ass, this seems like as good a time as any."

He turns me toward the window, and I look at the people below before I look across at the building in front of me. Holy shit. Can they truly see in? No. Misha would never have windows that allow anyone to see into his home. This is probably bullet-proof glass, too. But the thought that they could is both nerve-wracking and exciting. With his arm around my waist, he draws my hips back.

"Watch us in the mirror, *malyshka*."

With an arm still wrapped around my waist, the other grips my hip. He slides his cock along my pussy, then thrusts into me. I wasn't expecting it, and I feel like I'm falling forward. His steel band of an arm supports me, and I shouldn't have doubted for a moment that he wouldn't let that happen.

"Put your hands on the window, then watch us."

I'm quick to follow his instructions. I stretch out my arms and places my hands on the glass before I turn my head to the left and once more watch us. This is an entirely different angle and seeing us like this is the fucking hottest thing I've ever seen. It's almost like watching a porn, then realizing that you're the ones in the movie. The arm around my waist lets go, and his hand slides down to my pussy. He rubs my clit and brings me so fucking close.

"Do not come, *malyshka*. I haven't given you permission."

Orgasm denial. I would have been pissed if Semyon tried that with me. I would have taken the slaps and even the punches, but I would have told him how I felt. And believe it or not, he would have listened to me. But with Misha...I'll wait a fucking lifetime if I get to enjoy the wait.

When he pulls out of me, his cock glistens with my cream and his cum that coats him. He spreads my ass cheeks and spits. Every time I've seen that in a porn, I've thought it was disgusting and stupid. Now I love it. I whimpered when his fingers left my clit, but seeing his hands on my ass as he looks at my backdoor makes my pussy ache.

"If this is painful rather than just hurts at first, then you tell me. I don't think you can imagine the level of pissed I'll be if you take this, and I harm you."

Oh, I can imagine. And I have no intention of finding out for sure. I nod.

"I need to hear you."

"Yes, Daddy."

I see the concentration on his face as the tip of his cock presses against my puckered hole. I take a deep breath and relax. I try not to tense as the head pushes past the rim. The invasion hurts, and I love it.

"*Kiska?*"

"I'm all right, *papochka*. I promise."

He presses further, and I watch as he slides into me inch by inch. Yet again, the nurse in me flashes thoughts that could kill the mood if I let them. But the sex-hungry—no, sex-crazed—part of me is *way* stronger. I moan with each added inch until he's completely inside me.

"Lean back against me."

He doesn't have to ask me twice. His arms wrap around me, and it no longer looks like he's balls deep inside me. But I know he is. Our eyes meet in the mirror as we both enjoy the picture we make.

"All of me is yours now, Daddy. I want to make you come."

"You will. That's not in question. Your pussy is so fucking tight, but this is incredible. It's almost too much, and the need to come is unreal as your fine ass squeezes my cock."

I press my hips back, and he groans. He moves the hair away from my left ear, pushing it over my other shoulder. He leans to whisper in my ear.

"Is that my cue that you want me to fuck your ass? Do you want me to leave my cum in the last spot I had to claim to make you entirely mine?"

"Yes, to both."

"Just like I'll fuck your mouth and pussy whenever I want, your ass will take it too."

"Yes, please."

He chuckles at my eagerness.

"And I thought you only had a greedy little pussy. I can't wait to get a plug in your ass. Something with a jewel. You will wear it everywhere we go. It'll be our secret."

The idea of sharing something so intimate with only him makes me need to move. I want to feel him surging into me, pushing me toward the window before pulling me back. I want to feel his hips slam into my ass.

"You like that idea, don't you?"

"So much. So, so much."

"I think I'll put a vibrating egg in your pussy at the same time. I'll turn it up or turn it down as *I* please. The next time we have dinner with my family, I'm going to watch you try not to come in front of twenty people. And when you do, because I'll make sure you do, I'll take you into the closest bathroom, eat you out, and stick it right back in to do it all over again."

These aren't just words uttered during sex for a little dirty talk. I know he'll follow through. I watch my nipple harden, and he sees it too. He pinches each of them and tugs.

"I'm looking forward to those nipple clamps, *malyshka*. I can't wait to see your hard nipple stretched, then the grooves when I take them off. I'll suck your tits as the sensation comes back into them. I wonder if I can make you come just by doing that."

"I've never gotten off that way."

"I'm particularly looking forward to the under-the-bed restraints. I've been fantasizing about that, *kiska*."

"So have I."

"Mmm? What's your fantasy, baby girl?"

Once more, so much for feminism. But I can't help my sexual fantasies with Misha. I don't want to. They don't reflect how I think about the rest of life.

"I want you to restrain me and leave me there, wondering when you'll come back. After maybe an hour or so, you come in. You say nothing. You fuck me hard and leave your cum in me. Then you leave. I don't know when you'll come back, and as part of the fantasy, I'll make myself wonder *if* you're coming back. When you do, you fuck me hard again without a word. Maybe this time, your jiz lands across my tits and stomach. You leave me again. You keep doing this until I'm too sore to take any more. The only relief to my fear is that you let me come.

But you also don't let me touch you. That's worse than being restrained for an unknown length of time."

"You want me to keep you captive and fuck you like a sex doll rather than my girlfriend?"

"Something like that."

"Something?"

"For this fantasy, I want you to do whatever you want with me. You don't ask my permission; you just take. Like I'm your sex slave."

I can't believe I just said that. We're fucking Russian, and I'm trying to save my sister from becoming just that. What the fuck is wrong with me? I suck in a ragged breath, so completely and utterly ashamed of myself.

"Shh, *malyshka.* Shh. It's a fantasy. It doesn't mean you want that every day or that you believe in that kind of relationship. It doesn't mean I'm truly stripping you of your freedom. It's all right to want this. Baby, I have the exact same fantasy. That doesn't mean I want to go to a whorehouse and rape a woman. It doesn't mean I have that fantasy about anyone else."

That makes me feel worse. I hang my head, squeeze my eyes shut, and press my lips between my teeth. Misha watches me in the mirror as he speaks.

"You've had the fantasy before, but it's never been fulfilled."

"Yes." It comes out a whisper, so I try again. "Yes. But it's never been with a specific man. It's the idea of it that appeals to me."

"It's the same for me. I've thought about it hundreds of times, but the woman I'm with in the fantasy has never been specific before you. I'm not wanting it with someone else, just you. Lean forward, baby."

I listen and put my hands on the glass again. I watch as he pulls almost all the way out before easing back in.

"*Kiska*, what we do in private is our own business. What we desire and how we fulfill those fantasies is just about us."

He flexes his hips forward before drawing back out. This time he thrusts harder, and it pushes me toward the window.

"Daddy, as embarrassed as I am about someone seeing us, I enjoy fearing that."

He's moving faster as I speak, and the concentration on his face tells me he's enjoying fucking me and hearing my wishes.

"Do you want people to watch us, *malyshka*?"

"As long as no woman can touch you, then yes."

"No man is ever touching you, *malyshka*."

The certainty and possessiveness are everything. It's not the type of possessiveness that'll keep me prisoner. It's the kind that makes me want to live out any and every desire right this minute.

"And if a man jacks off while watching us?"

"You want to make men wish they were me?"

"And make women wish they were me, too."

"Have you been to a BDSM club?"

His thrust is extra forceful with that question. I think he's wondering who I've been with, not if I've been. And that idea pisses him off. His pace increases, and he's no longer gentle. He's jealous, and by taking my time answering, I'm only adding fuel to the fire.

"Answer me, Katerina. Have you been fucked in a BDSM club before?"

When I don't answer immediately, he yanks me back against him and pinches my nipple mercilessly. His other hand rubs my clit.

"You will fucking answer me, or I will edge you for days. I will make you cry with the need to come."

"Are you that jealous?"

"Yes."

He barks the answer as he presses harder while rubbing my clit. I still don't answer. He lets go of my nipple and fists my hair.

"You're taunting me by not telling me. Do you really want to find out how possessive I can be when it comes to thinking about some fucker fucking my girlfriend? Do you really want to know how much that makes my skin crawl, how much I want to wrap my hands around these men's throats and squeeze?"

With hair still in his hand, he wraps it around my throat. It rests heavy, but he's not squeezing.

"Have you been to a BDSM club, Misha?"

"Yes."

Okay. Now I get how he feels. I glower at him in the mirror. He'd stopped fucking me for a moment, but now he presses my entire body against the window before he fucks me hard enough to bring tears to my eyes.

"Say your safe word if it's too much. If I hurt you, I'll be even more pissed."

"I know, Daddy. It's just the right amount of pain. Don't stop. Please."

"Have you done breath play before?"

"No."

"If it gets too tight, tap the glass."

"Yes, Daddy."

He tightens his hold on my throat as he goes back to rubbing my clit.

"You will answer me. I told you the truth. Now it's your turn. Have you been to a fucking BDSM club?"

I shake my head. I haven't. I'm curious, but I've never wanted to figure out how to join one to go fuck random men.

"Did that bastard let his friends watch?"

My eyes widen, and I shake my head furiously.

"Semyon suggested it, and I threw a vase at his head. It was the only time I was ever violent toward him."

"I will take you to one if you want. We can fuck out in the open if you want to be an exhibitionist, or we can fuck in a private room and let people be voyeurs through double-sided glass. But we are not swapping partners."

"I would lose my shit if you suggested it or let it happen. Misha, I am just as possessive and jealous as you are. Believe me when I say I will put her body somewhere no one will ever find. Do not cheat on me. Ever."

His teeth dig into my shoulder as he thrusts one last time before his cock twitches inside me. He presses hard and rubs my clit faster until I can't hold back. The look in his eyes. The feel of him inside me. The way he touches me. It's too much. My eyes drift closed as I come, but they're wide open when he speaks again.

"Do not *ever* doubt me, *kiska*. I will never betray you. There will *never* be anyone but you. I'm going to marry you. You are going to wear my ring, just like I'm going to wear yours. I told you I'm yours. I'm ready to prove it."

Chapter Seventeen

Misha

Fuck. I hope Kitty doesn't think that's the best proposal she's going to get. Why the fuck am I so inarticulate when it comes to how I feel about her and find it so it easy to issue commands when we fuck? Did I really just ask myself that? For fuck's sake.

I watch her in the mirror as I pull out. I see her clench her ass as she turns toward me. I'm not sure what I'm going to see when our eyes meet. I think I might faint from relief when I see acceptance, even eagerness, in her gaze.

"Do you want that kind of commitment, Kitty?"

"Yes."

"In general, or with me?"

The way her expression changes could make me whither. She looks duly insulted.

"Just checking, *koshechka*. When the time is right, I will ask you properly."

Her face softens, and I believe she's genuinely happy for a moment. I press the softest kiss to her lips.

"I love you, Daddy."

"I love you, baby girl. Let's shower, then I'll make you some lunch. I believe you told me you were starving."

"For your dick. Now I'd like some food."

She shoots me a saucy smile before she walks past me to the bathroom. She stops at the door and looks over her shoulder. When did she become such a temptress? It takes all my restraint, and I think most of hers, for us to make it through the shower with no kind of sex. I go months upon months without fucking, but I can barely go five minutes without having my dick in some part of Kitty. I'm hornier than a fifteen-year-old.

I playfully scowl as we get dressed once more. I don't like it at all. I'd have her walk around our place naked all the time, and from the frown she's wearing, I think she would prefer me naked too. We walk into the kitchen as someone knocks on the door. I glance at the screen next to the door and see it's Sergei. Kitty starts pulling things out of the fridge while I let Sergei in. I glance toward the kitchen when I see Sergei's expression. It's fucking inconvenient that Kitty speaks Russian because Sergei can't warn me about whatever shitstorm is about to blow in. Kitty pokes her nose out of the kitchen, looks at me, then at my brother.

"Hi, Sergei. Misha looks like he's about to freak out. Why don't you tell him whatever you're going to tell me first? Do you want a sandwich?"

She tries to sound confident, but I don't miss the waver in her voice. She tries to appear chipper, but her smile is tight, and her eyes show her fear.

"Hi, Katerina. I've already had lunch, but thank you. You can tell Misha's stressed?"

She nods. I know my expression is completely blank. I know my body is relaxed. I know no one outside my family has ever read me when I don't want to be read.

"How do you know I'm reacting to anything?"

I'm curious to know what my tell is.

"When our eyes met, you kept your eyes open a little longer than usual. You wanted to watch me and gauge my mood when I saw Sergei."

My eyebrows shoot straight up. I let her know my shock without any question. That's exactly what I did. Then my brow furrows.

"How do you know to look for those kinds of signs?"

"Because I was always watching Semyon to judge when he was going to lose his shit and beat the crap out of me."

She walks up to me and places her hands on my waist. She stretches onto her toes and kisses my cheek. She whispers to me so low I'm certain even Sergei's dog ears don't hear her.

"Breathe, Daddy. It's over and has been for five years."

I wrap my arm around her waist, and she steps closer. I rest my forehead against hers for a moment before I give her forehead a peck. She rests her head against my chest as she looks at Sergei.

"How bad is it?"

"I know she's in America, Katerina. She arrived in Miami three days after they took her. I can't account for two weeks, but she went to Texas for at least a week."

I'm shocked.

"Sinaloa?"

They're a Mexican Cartel that runs drugs into America across the entire southern border. They're violent and don't hide it. They run Tijuana and have made it the most dangerous city in the world. Rarely do people believe that unless they know about the public executions and beheadings the cartel uses to persuade people to comply. Once upon a time, there was an alliance among three cartels, but that didn't last. Now the Sinaloa battle each other for control of the Mexican-American border from the Pacific to Texas. It was their fucking El Chapo who got a tunnel dug from his prison in Mexico to near San Diego. He fucking escaped. That takes balls and resources.

I'm dreading what Sergei tells us next if those bastards got hold of Larisa. I can tell Kitty is confused, and I hate to explain what Sergei and I already know.

"Texas is part of the Mexican Sinaloa Cartel's territory. If they sold her to someone in Texas, then she may be in Mexico now. They sex traffic along with drug traffic. They could force her to do either. They keep the women drugged, so they're too fucked up to know what's happening."

"So, she could be tied to a bed and getting raped around the clock, or she could swallow bags of coke to bring into the States. Either way, she won't live long. Sergei, you said she's in America. Do you think they're making her cross back and forth?"

"No. I think someone in the Sinaloa wanted her and planned to buy her, but she's not in Texas anymore. I think she's somewhere between Boston and New York."

I watch Kitty as I speak to my brother.

"What makes you think that?"

"We got a tip."

My head whips toward Sergei before he continues, and Kitty trembles.

"*Tres J's* of all people."

I expect her confusion.

"Who are they?"

What the holy fuck? I stroke Kitty's hair as I answer.

"Enrique Diaz heads the Colombian Cartel. He has several nephews. Pablo is the oldest and his heir since Enrique has no kids. That's through his younger brother. Our family has a complicated history with Enrique, Pablo, and Pablo's younger brother, Juan. Laura grew up next door to Pablo and Juan, and she was extremely close to Enrique. She called him *tío* for most of her life. Some shit went down with Juan, and he crossed way too many lines. He's no longer a threat to Laura and the twins."

Kitty's expression doesn't change. I know she understands what I didn't say. She doesn't really care. She wants to know the important parts.

"Enrique has three more nephews through his younger sister. Javier, Joaquin, and Jorge. They're fucking certifiable. They grew up Colombia and saw shit way younger than any of us did. Pablo is Enrique's enforcer, and we suspect he does the things all eight of us divvy up. But the *Tres J's* take care of things on the street. They fuck up businesses that don't pay Enrique on time. They beat the shit out of guys who won't buy drugs or stolen goods. They hold people hostage and extort ransoms. They keep Jackson Heights in line basically, and they enjoy it all. Pablo handles the more serious issues, but they like terrorizing people. It wouldn't surprise me if they get off on it."

I keep to myself what Sergei already knows. They kidnapped me after conspiring with another set of enemies to take down Aleks while he and Heather were still dating. They were there when a person connected to the Irish mob broke into my mother's house and shot at Heather, her sister and brother-in-law, her nephew, her mom, and my mom. I want to know how those fuckers are involved.

"What tip did you get, Sergei?"

"It was Javier who texted, but he said he and his brothers saw Larisa in Miami. They didn't know who she was, but once they saw you, it didn't take much to know you're Larisa's sister."

"They've seen me?"

"Kitty, we were in the Bronx for more than an hour. We stood on your building's steps talking to those boys for at least five minutes. Then we left with suitcases. Someone chased us through most of the Bronx. You know people saw us. Someone probably took photos and sent them to Enrique or one of his nephews. Someone else probably sent them to Salvatore, the *Cosa Nostra's* don. It wouldn't surprise me if Dillon doesn't know too. He heads the Irish."

The sheer terror in her eyes as she looks at me breaks my heart. She's not just scared for her sister. Now she's scared for her own life.

"I thought that could have been one of your rivals. I didn't really think that there could be so many."

I cup her cheek and brush her lips with mine before I press a soft kiss to hers.

"*Malyshka*, you are as well protected as any of the other women in our family. You go nowhere without guards. We can't stop people seeing you unless you never leave here. None of us wants that. If they're giving us a tip, it's because they want something badly enough to dare try to bribe us."

"Sergei, what are they asking for in exchange for information about my sister?"

"Something to do with one of our businesses."

She nods, understanding he means something illegal. Sergei pauses for a moment, waiting for her to ask for more details, but she remains silent.

"Misha, they want to meet Katerina."

"No."

I answer before Kitty can even open her mouth. My gaze bores into her, but I can tell she's going to resist. I can't blame her.

"If they know a single thing about my sister, and they want to meet me in order to share that, then I'm meeting with them. Either you help me and keep me protected, or I find a way to do it on my own."

"Kitty, let me try with them first. If that doesn't work, then I'll arrange a meeting."

"And if they back out and won't tell you anything because

they wanted to meet me first? Then I lose the only hint of where my sister is. No, Misha. She's my family, not yours."

She snaps her mouth shut as she realizes what she said. Her eyes are enormous, and there's fear in them. I hate that I see it. I know she doesn't fear me. She fears the consequences of what she just said. But I hate having it directed at me in any way.

"I'm sorry."

"Shh. I get it."

"But she's your family now, too. I shouldn't have said that. I'm sorry."

Sergei looks out the window rather than at us. I'm certain he's wondering if we fucking eloped in the few hours since we left Kitty's place.

"Kitty, I don't trust the *Tres J's*. Until I'm certain it isn't a trap to take you too, I don't want you anywhere near them. There are too many unknowns right now. Let me talk to them in an environment where my family and I have control. Once I check out whether they're bullshitting us, then we go from there. I'm not saying you'll never talk to them. I just don't want you to talk to them before I do."

"How soon can you meet with them?"

I look at my brother who turns back toward us. He glances at me before he looks at Kitty.

"In an hour."

"Where?"

I think I know the answer to my question, but Sergei's answer still surprises me even though I knew it.

"Jersey."

Kitty's brow furrows as she looks up at me.

"Why Jersey?"

"Enrique's brother, Luis, has a house there. Laura grew up next door to it. Enrique must have sanctioned this meeting, and he knows that everyone but Sergei and I will be at Laura's parents' house because we'll meet with them in Luis's house. It's supposed to be neutral ground."

"Doesn't that put Laura's parents in danger?"

"Laura's family has a complicated connection with the Diazes, but they know what Luis and his family are, just like they know what we are."

"Where will I be during this meeting?"

"At Maks and Laura's. All the wives and all of our parents will probably be there too. Besides the security Maks already has set up at his place, my dad and Grigori will guard all of you."

Men in paramilitary tactical gear patrol the grounds. They're in all black with earpieces and semi-automatic rifles. It's better security than money can buy. It's bratva men trained by former KGB agents and Soviet Army soldiers who were almost all Podolskaya bratva before they arrived in America. They don't just look paramilitary; they are paramilitary. It's the only way any of us would feel comfortable leaving our women and children behind. All of our homes in Queens have that much security. Plus, I know what my dad and Grigori would do to protect our family. If I cared enough about their lives, I would pity the men who've underestimated either of them now that they're middle aged.

"*Kiska*, I need to take you to Queens. I'm not going to this meeting until I know you're at Maks and Laura's. They can fucking wait for me for all I care. I'm not leaving until Grigori and my dad are there, too."

"How long do you think it'll take?"

"I don't know, but estimate at least an hour each way. The meeting could take five minutes, or it could take an hour. Depends on what games they think they can play and how much they actually know."

"Misha, I really don't like this. Something feels so wrong

about not hearing what they have to say for myself. If they won't talk to you, then we've wasted more time. Would Enrique let his nephews murder all of you in his brother's house?"

I cock an eyebrow and shrug one shoulder. She looks at Sergei, whose expression matches mine. I almost don't hear what she mutters.

"How are you not twins?"

"Kitty, we'll go to Maks and Laura's. We'll talk to the others and decide what to do."

"We'll? You'll talk and decide, and I'll listen is what you mean."

"No. When I said 'we'll,' I meant we'll."

She looks at me as though I'm a simpleton or like I'm lying to her.

"Sergei, we'll meet you downstairs. Kitty's going to get a few things in case we spend the night there."

My brother offers Kitty one of his rare genuine, sympathetic smiles. I think it takes her aback. If he weren't committed to Anton and had ever been interested in women, I might worry that he was trying to steal my girlfriend. I'm no idiot. I know how attractive women find him. He grins at me as he reaches the door. He was being kind to Kitty, but now he's taunting me.

"Go wait in the fucking car."

I take Kitty's hand and lead her into the living room. I ignore how she drags her feet. I sit on the sofa and wait for her to sit next to me. She does, but I can tell she's irritated that we aren't leaving. I won't make this long, but it's a private conversation between us.

"Kitty, this isn't Mother Russia. Have I treated you like I think you're less than me? Like I don't respect and value your thoughts and opinions? When I say 'we,' I mean that. I'm not going to ignore your wishes. I may not be able to make them happen if I think it's unsafe for you or your sister. But I will listen to you and take what you say into consideration. So will everyone else in my family. Maks is *pakhan*, and my cousins are the Elite Group. My brother and Anton are the next most senior members. Pasha and I are highly ranked, too. We are the people who decide. But we don't do that without listening to the women in our lives. We value the knowledge, insights, and wisdom all of you bring to our family. You aren't giving up your voice by being with me. That's the last thing I want."

"That is so different from how I grew up, Misha. I know we're in the States, but we're all still Russian. You may have lived here longer than you did Moscow, but everything about your community and life is basically still Russian. I thought you were just saying that to placate or dismiss me. I shouldn't have because that isn't how you treat me at all. But this is now your bratva's business, so I thought you'd see it differently than when it might have been the Podolskaya's business."

"I understand, baby girl. That's why I'm explaining this to you. I know this is yet another foreign dynamic for you. But I really want you to understand that I respect your wishes and your thoughts. I want your opinions, Kitty. I don't have all the answers, especially not for this. There are going to be times when I need your advice, and I trust it."

"I know my dad trusts my mom, and he listens to her. But she would never attend any type of meeting, and she definitely would never speak up at one if she went. I only know what I know. I'm sorry I doubted you, Misha. You haven't made me think you don't value me or my opinion, or that you'd ever keep me from expressing them."

"This is new territory for both of us. I'm not upset, and I didn't want you to be. We will figure this out together."

"Thank you, *papochka*."

She leans forward, and our mouths meet. It's a tender kiss

that ends way too soon. But we know Sergei is waiting, and Stefan is probably with him in a town car. We make our way out to the car. I can tell Sergei is in the front passenger seat while Stefan stands with the rear door open. Kitty slides in, and I follow her. I wrap my arm around her shoulders, and she nestles closer to me. Her eyes drift shut, and I know she must be exhausted. We're both jetlagged, and it's been yet another intense day. It feels like a million years ago that we were at her apartment. I suppose a car chase with a gunshot and mind-blowing sex with the woman you love can warp your sense of time.

"Baby girl, why don't you nap? It'll take us at least half an hour to get to Queens. Unless those dipshits are already at their *tio* Luis's house, it'll take them at least an hour to get to Jersey from Queens. I doubt they've set off yet. We don't have to worry about making a stop. And if the fuckers have to wait for us, then let them fucking wait."

"I am exhausted all of a sudden."

As always, the privacy glass is up. It's the default with any driver, regardless of who's behind the wheel or in the front passenger seat. I reach across her and unfasten her seatbelt. I know I shouldn't take for granted that we're safe enough in these town cars to not have on our seatbelts. But I lift her onto my lap and unfasten her pants. She wiggles them down her hips as she looks at me questioningly.

"Rest your head against my shoulder, *malyshka*."

"All right, Daddy."

When her head is against my chest, I slide two fingers into her pussy. She's wet but not dripping.

"Close your eyes."

I stroke her g-spot as my thumb rubs slow circles over her clit. Nothing about my movements is rushed. I'm heightening her arousal, but I'm also soothing her. I can feel her pussy clench around my fingers, but her body is relaxing. I keep the same pace until I feel the first spasms around my fingers. She's half asleep as she comes.

"I love you, Daddy."

"I love you, *malyshka*."

She's out by the time I withdraw my fingers. I reach for the tissues and clean off my fingers. I watch her sleep for a few minutes before I lean my head back and close my eyes.

If these fuckers do anything to threaten Kitty or lead her on about her sister, I'll make them pay in ways even their fucked-up life in Colombia never taught them.

Chapter Eighteen

Kitty

I can't believe I fell asleep while getting fingered. I never imagined it could be such a relaxing experience, certainly not when a man as gorgeous as Misha is doing it. But I just woke up as we pull up to Maks and Laura's house.

"I'm glad you got some sleep, *malyshka*."

"Me too, Daddy. I was out like a light."

"I know. I wish we had time to tell Stefan to go around the block a few more times. You need the rest, and I don't want to stop holding you."

This man is so sweet, yet I know there's a good chance he might beat the shit out of someone in an hour. With the top two buttons of his shirt unfastened, I can see some of his tattoos. There's no forgetting that he's a mafioso, but I can put that aside when he's like this with me. He helps me adjust my pants back into place before he opens the door, gets out, then reaches back in to offer me his hand. I don't recall seeing any man do that other than in an old movie, but one of them always does it when I'm getting out of a vehicle.. That is definitely a family trait, not just something they do for safety.

A lot has happened today, so it doesn't feel like we left this house only a few hours ago. Misha opens the front door for us, and we enter to find everyone gathered in the main living room. Yes, that means there is more than one. The first thing I notice is Lev sleeping in a swing, and Mila and Konstantin toddling across the carpet as though they're in a sprint to reach Misha. He squats down, his muscular thighs straining the material, as he encourages the twins to come to him. They take a moment, but it's pretty much a tie. Misha scoops both up and blows raspberries on their necks. They howl with laughter as Mila snatches a handful of Misha's blond hair. I reach up and gently pry her fingers loose. She shoots me a look that I'm absolutely certain she inherited from Maks. I've never heard a girl described as dark and brooding, but this little one just shot me a death stare. Konstantin is clapping and laughing...and I think it's at my expense. When they both wiggle to be put down, Misha gives them each a smacking kiss on the cheek before lowering to them to the floor, his arm wrapped around each of them until he's sure they're stable on their feet.

Fuck. I love this man.

"*Kiska?*"

Misha slides his arm around my waist and draws me close enough for me to rest the back of my head against his chest as we watch Mila and Konstantin make their way to Niko, who does almost the same thing as Misha. I keep my voice low as I continue to watch family members tease and play with the twins as they waddle past.

"Do you want this too, Daddy?"

"With you, yes. Anyone else, no. Do you want this?"

"Yes, and only with you. But you have to know why this terrifies me, too."

"I do, baby girl."

"It's not just because I'm scared you won't come home one night. We're here because my sister—the daughter of a bratva member—is missing. It's our children who could be in danger. I don't know how your cousins do it."

"Because we're finally finding joy. None of us imagined meeting our soulmate and settling down. We definitely didn't picture any of us having children. Not even Maks, who technically should have an heir. Nothing has been decided about Konstantin, and it won't be for many years. But I know Niko, Aleks, and Pasha are all thinking about starting families soon. Ana loves her job as Laura's paralegal, but she's also expressed a desire to be a stay-at-home mom. Heather left her teaching position because it just wasn't realistic with the amount of times she's had to come here for protection during the day. She does some kind of curriculum something, but she's said it would make starting a family easier. Sumiko only works from home these days. We're all entering a new phase, and it includes a different version of our family."

"I'm scared, Misha. But I also have this consuming want to have this with you. I'm thirty-one. I'm not getting younger. In four years, I enter what's considered advanced maternal age. They call it that for a reason. The risks increase for mother and baby. I hadn't given it much thought until now. I was too focused on making my life here and being happy to be in America."

"Do you feel pressure for us to start a family?"

"Not right this second. Though I'll never turn down the opportunity to practice. But soon. How do you feel about that?"

Misha places his other hand on my belly before sliding his arm around my waist.

"There was a lot of time in Moscow spent waiting around. I thought about our future a lot. Every time I picture it, it includes a family with you, Kitty. When you feel ready to try, then we do."

I twist to wrap my arms around his waist and look up at him.

"Thank you, Daddy."

"I love you, baby girl."

"I love you, too."

"Katerina, Misha, let's go in the office."

I look over my shoulder at Maks before I release Misha. He slips his hand into mine and leads me to an office Maks and Laura clearly share. There's a rocking armchair in the corner and two Pack 'N Plays along one wall. The other men follow us in, and the room is a tight squeeze with the eight leaders and me. Sergei has my laptop and hands it back to me.

"It's clean, but I would hold off using it for a while. A new one would be best."

Wonderful.

"Thank you."

What else do I say? Misha squeezes my hand, and I look up at him.

"You can use mine whenever you want, *kiska*."

"Thanks."

Sergei sets up another one and looks at Misha. I don't know what's happening. Is this a strategy meeting? Are they going to tell me something Sergei didn't? Misha pulls his phone from his pocket and unlocks it. I watch him pull up a contact that says "*Pinche* Javier."

I look up at Misha in confusion.

"*Pinche* literally means the cook's assistant, but it basically means fucking."

"Fucking Javier?"

"Yeah. I have a friend Javier from college. I don't want to get them confused."

I watch him hit the call button, and it only rings once.

"*¿Qué está pasando, ruso?*" What's happening, Russian?

"*¿Dónde está ella, hijo de puta?*" Where is she, fucker?

Clearly, Misha is out to make friends. I'm following so far since it's really basic.

"*¿Quién?*" Who?

"*No tengo tiempo para lo estúpido que eres. Sé que tu tío está escuchando. Pásamelo. Enrique, no estoy jugando. Ahora mismo.*" I don't have time for how stupid you are. I know your uncle is listening. Put him on. Enrique, I'm not playing around. Now.

"*Está aquí, pero este es mi trato. Tú tratas conmigo y con mis hermanos.*" He's here, but this is my deal. You deal with me and my brothers

"*Adelante, o no tendrás nada más que ceniza para volver a casa esta noche. ¿Tu mamá no vive contigo?*" Get on with it, or you won't have anything but ash to go home to tonight. Doesn't your mom live with you?

My eyes widen as I listen, grasping almost all of it. My gaze sweeps over all the men assembled in the office, and none of them seem fazed by Misha's threat.

"*Vete a la mierda. Todo el mundo sabe que nunca tocarías a mi madre. Ustedes, los rusos, no lastiman a las mujeres y los niños.*" Fuck off. Everyone knows you'd never touch my mother. You Russians don't hurt women and children.

I breathe a little easier.

"*Pero sabemos que ustedes, los colombianos, sí. Por eso Laura no habla con Enrique ni con Pablo. Deja de hacerme perder el tiempo o pondré a Laura al teléfono.*" But we know you Colombians do. That's why Laura won't talk to Enrique or Pablo. Stop wasting my time, or I will put Laura on the phone.

A voice I don't recognize speaks next. Maybe we're getting somewhere. I'm guessing this is Enrique.

"*Basta de medir pollas. Hablaré con Laura si quiere, pero no quiero que ninguno de ustedes, cabrones, la moleste más de lo que estoy seguro de que ya lo está. Katerina, estoy seguro de que estás escuchando. No tenemos a tu hermana, pero tenemos información sobre ella.*" Enough measuring dicks. I'll speak to Laura if she wants, but I don't need any of you fuckers upsetting her any more than I'm sure she already is. Katerina, I'm certain you're listening. We do not have your sister, but we have information about her.

I look up at Misha again. Am I supposed to respond? Misha nods.

"*Estoy aquí. No me interesa el tamaño de la polla de nadie más. Solo quiero a mi hermana.*" I'm here. I'm not interested in anyone else's dick size. I just want my sister.

"Is English easier, Katerina?"

The heavily Spanish-flavored accent is one I'm used to. English is easier since I'm only proficient in Spanish.

"Yes, please. What do you know about Larisa?"

"*Habla y no jodas.*" Speak and don't fuck around.

I can hear Enrique's muffled voice, then someone I don't recognize starts talking.

"Katerina, I'm Joaquin. I got a message from a Cuban associate a few weeks ago about a Russian woman who was about to arrive in Miami. He wanted to know if I wanted her to ransom to the Kutsenkos. I was in Colombia, so I didn't get it right away. Because I didn't answer, the associate arranged for someone else to take Larisa. We got to Miami right after she arrived, and we saw her in passing while we were at a hotel conducting business with this associate. None of us got a clear look at who took her to Texas. She may have gone to Mexico at some point, but I don't know for sure. The name my Cuban associate gave me didn't lead anywhere, but I watched security footage from the Dallas Airport."

I'm not even going to ask how he or they got their hands on that. I don't want to know.

"I saw her arrive, and she looked exhausted but not drugged or injured. Same for when I saw her pass through TSA three weeks later. I don't know what flights she boarded since her legal name shows up on no manifest in or out of Dallas. But she was in the domestic terminal the last time I saw footage of her."

"Why were you watching her? Did you plan to kidnap her and ransom her to Misha's family?"

"The thought crossed our minds, but we've had enough shit go down with the Kutsenkos and the rest of the Ivankov bratva. We don't need any more trouble with them. So no, we weren't going to do that. I figured they'd want to know if a Russian woman was being trafficked. Tracking her and giving you the information is an olive branch after the fucking shit-storm Juan caused. We know we only made it worse with Misha."

I furrow my brow when I look at Misha. He shakes his head and mouths, "Later."

"How did you know she was my sister? And how did you know what name to look for on the manifests?"

"My associate told me her name. Turns out, it was her legal one. I only learned that once you arrived in New York, and we learned you and Misha are together. *Felicidades.*" Congratulations.

This doesn't feel like much of a celebratory moment.

"What're you going to demand to tell me where she is now?"

"I wouldn't demand anything. I won't hold you being with Misha against you. If I'd known Larisa had a sister in New York, I would have reached out to you, regardless. I admit, I might have taunted the Kutsenkos for having rescued a Russian when they didn't know what was going on under their noses. I won't now. But this is for your sake, not theirs. I just wish I had more to tell you, Ms. Vasiliev.

"Vasilieva. But thank you."

My shoulders slump as the moment of hope dissolves. I shut my eyes, forcing the tears to remain unshed. I'm not embarrassed or ashamed to cry in front of Misha's family. I fear that if I start, I won't stop. I don't realize I'm trembling until Misha pushes the phone toward Maks and pulls me into his arms. I lose it. I sob. I try to do it silently, but I can't. My breath hitches over and over, and I whimper. I give in. I don't even recognize the keening sound coming from me. I haven't let myself cry like this since my parents called me and told me Larisa went missing. I cling to Misha as the sobs wrack my body.

"*Razberites' s nimi.*" Deal with them.

It's Misha who snaps at someone in the room. He tries to lead me away, but I refuse to budge. I take a deep breath, trying to slow the rhythm and slow my racing heart. I pull away from Misha and swipe at the tears. They don't stop, and my breath still hitches, but I'm not quite sobbing anymore.

"*Mne nuzhno uslyshat' vse eto.*" I need to hear all of it.

"Maksim?"

Enrique's voice is clear, so he must have the phone now.

"I'm here."

I look at the man I hope will be my cousin-in-law sooner rather than later. He's an impressive man. The air of authority and command that radiates from him is constant, whether he's in this office acting as *pakhan* or while playing with his children. Laura said this morning that he's much more communicative than he used to be. If this is chatty, what the hell was he before?

"Take me off speaker."

"No."

"Maksim, take me off fucking speakerphone."

"No."

There's a long pause before I hear a sigh.

"Shockingly, Katerina, Laura has softened Maksim's rough edges."

I didn't expect Enrique to address me. But he continues.

"Maks, my nephews will help you as the olive branch Joaquin mentioned. I don't expect this to make you or Laura forgive us, but I hope it solidifies our truce that we don't target women and children. You and I will still have our differences when it comes to business, but I'm committed to Laura knowing that I've never lied to her, and I won't start."

"I will let Laura know, but I make no promises. If my wife isn't ready to forgive, then neither am I."

"I'm not ready to forgive or forget, Enrique."

My head snaps around when I hear Laura. She walks into the office and directly to the phone, which she picks up.

"I heard your voice, so I decided to join the call. Juan is gone, but you let all of that shit happen. I suggest you fucking figure out whatever Katerina needs and do it fast. If you don't, you better laser Maddy's and my initials off your arm. Because if they're there the next time I see you, I will cut them off with whatever knife I can reach. Chances are it'll be butter knife, so it won't go fast. You will never be a *tío* to me or my sister ever again, but you have a chance to not remain my enemy."

I think my eyes are ready to fall out of my head. I have never seen a woman attend a bratva leaders' meeting before me attending this one. I never imagined a woman speaking during one, and now Laura and I have. I sure as fucking holy hell never imagined a woman speaking to another syndicate leader. And I most definitely didn't believe there was a flying fuck's chance of a woman issuing commands and threats to another syndicate's leader. What the hell kind of family and bratva will I marry into?

"I don't doubt every word you speak is the God's honest truth, Laura. We're doing what we can. I may never be like family to you again, but you have never stopped being like a niece to me."

Laura snorts.

"Prove it."

The steel in Laura's voice would make any man's balls shrink. It's like a nine-iron to the groin.

"Laura, it's Javier."

"I assume your shitbag brothers are with you, too."

"Joaquin and Jorge are here. We know what everyone thinks of us, but you've known us since the day we arrived in America. We have never done anything against you and never would. Juan saw the three of us approaching that day in the park. We forced him to a place where you could see him, so you would know he was back. Who do you think arranged for Juan to be on that street corner when Maks and the others got him? We set him up to join the Mexicans to deal drugs for them. We got him to that corner by having that hooker tell him she wanted to buy rock off him. I know your husband and his family think we should be committed to some insane asylum, but maybe they should think a little harder. We all play our roles. We just play ours better than anyone realizes. If we can find Larisa, we will."

Laura's face has drained of all color, and Maks pulls her onto his lap. She buries her face against his chest. I don't really understand everything Javier said, but from everyone else's expressions—which are unguarded when they're with each other—what Javier revealed shocked the shit out of them.

"Like we already said, we don't harm women and children."

This is a new voice, so it must be Jorge. The third of the *Tres J's*. None of them sound psychotic. They actually sound really kind. But then again, Javier said they're the consummate actors. I won't believe anything until Misha tells me I should. I've calmed enough to speak again.

"So, what happens next?"

"We help you find your sister, Ms. Vasilieva."

Four voices speak at once. Maybe this Diaz family is as in sync as Misha's. Nothing that I learned today makes me think they are. But that was fucking uncanny. But if they're dicking me around, Laura's threat of a butter knife will be merciful compared to what I will do. I'm ready to tell them as much.

"I grew up in Russia. If you know so much about my sister and me, my guess is you know I grew up in a bratva family. I'm now with a bratva *avotoritet*. Violence has surrounded me my entire life. I'm sure you know how that teaches you things. I was a quick learner. Men may be malicious, but women can be vindictive. Play me for a fool, and you will rue the day I stepped off that plane from Moscow. I am not forgiving to those who fuck with my family. If you follow through and do as you say, then we have no problem. Your issues remain with the men, and I won't be involved. But just be forewarned and understand me well."

"If you and Laura aren't already best friends, you will be."

It's Enrique who speaks, and I could swear he sounds proud. Again, what the fuck kind of family am I marrying into?

I recognize the next voice as Joaquin's.

"I'll reach out to the Cuban contact again and see if I can press him for more. We have some people in Texas I can ask too. I'll be in touch in the morning."

I have another question that I can't believe I haven't asked. It should have been the first.

"Wait. Who took my sister?"

There's a long pause that makes me shift uncomfortably before Javier responds.

"Does the name Yuri Preobrazhensky mean something to you?"

I can't breathe. I'm completely frozen except for my eyes, which dart to Maks. But it's clear he doesn't recognize the name. I look around, and none of the men recognize it. They're all looking at me. I don't notice my fist rubbing at the burning sensation in my heart. I think I'm going to vomit the acidic bile rising in my throat. My ears are buzzing.

"*Kiska?*"

I hear Misha as though someone stuffed cotton wool in my ears. He says it again, and I hear the urgency this time, but I can't make my mouth work, or my throat produce any sound. I turn my head and look at Misha. I know my eyes are huge, and my mouth hangs open, but it's as though I have no control over them.

I finally snap out of it when I hear Enrique. His voice is gentle, and I'm not sure if it soothes me or irritates the shit out of me, but I turn toward the phone.

"Katerina, does your silence mean you know who this man is?"

"Yes."

I croak and swallow.

"If the devil exists, he's Yuri. He—"

I don't want to reveal all my secrets, especially not something I haven't told Misha. But they need to understand just how dangerous Yuri is.

"Larisa and I had a younger brother. When I was twenty, Pyotr was only eight. There was a big gap between him and Larisa. Yuri and I were at the same university, and he noticed me. I wasn't interested. It was before I started dating Semyon, so I was single and just wanted to focus on my studies. He cornered me one night on my way home from class. He—"

I can't say it. I'm reliving every moment of him assaulting me, but I can't share any of it out loud.

"To make sure I wouldn't tell anyone, he killed Pyotr the next day. He warned me he would do the same thing to Larisa as he did to me. My parents were out of town, but I didn't stay quiet. I told them everything. My father made sure Larisa and I had three times the protection we had before. They retaliated, and I thought Yuri was dead. I heard nothing about him for three years, then one day on the way home from work, three cars boxed mine in on the road. They forced me off, and five men with metal poles smashed the windows. Yuri was the one to pull me out. His face and hands were scarred from whatever my father and the other Podolsk did, but not enough to disfigure him. I recognized him immediately. He held me at gunpoint and dragged me by the hair into a building."

I don't want to do this. I don't want to talk about this. I don't want to imagine this motherfucker doing the same things to Larisa that he did to me.

"He kept me there for four hours. He beat me worse than Semyon ever did, but unlike Semyon, he didn't go near my face. Then he assaulted me again. He strangled me in the middle of it until I passed out. When I woke, I was alone. The police arrived to investigate the car, and I stumbled outside once I got my clothes back on. They took me home, but I couldn't talk. He'd almost crushed my windpipe on purpose. It took me a day before I could produce enough sound to be intelligible. Podolsks searched, but he was gone."

I run my hand over my face as I explain why he was able to disappear.

"Preobrazhensky is his mother's family. He took the name so he could move to Russia. His father is Roel Elezi."

I wait to see if that rings a bell. The men's expressions immediately change. It does. Enrique breaks the silence.

"Do you mean as in the Albanian Osmani?"

"Yes. Albania's organized crime isn't that vastly different from the bratva. Instead of a *pakhan*, they have a *krye*. Yuri's father became that when he murdered the previous one. Yuri was to become a *kryetar*, or underboss, but his father sent him to Moscow for an education first. Clearly, he didn't remain in Albania after the last time he and I met."

I look at Misha finally. Shame for what happened and guilt for not telling him wash over me. He cups my cheeks and presses the gentlest kiss I've ever received on my lips. He tucks hair behind my ears and leans in to whisper to me.

"Nothing changes unless *you* want it to."

I shake my head. I need him more than ever. I whisper back to him.

"Please don't let go, Daddy."

"Never. You're mine, *malyshka*. The only way I'm letting you go is if you tell me to."

I nod before I close my eyes and lean into his chest. I feel safe. From my haven, I continue to talk.

"Those weren't Russians from America we saw in the video. They were Albanians."

I hear curses on the phone, then Enrique sounds pissed.

"Those *malparidos*—" At my confusion, Misha mouths "motherfuckers." "—are doing business in Honduras as a way to get into Colombia. They're laundering money and supporting the local gangs. They're paying government officials big money in Central America to make it easier to traffic coke back to Europe."

Maks looks ready to explode, but his voice is calm when he speaks.

"And they've been making noise here. They're so far up

Salvatore's ass he could blow them out his nose. The Albanians have a history of sucking off *Cosa Nostra* dicks to get what they want. Fuck, Salvatore."

"Wait, Maks." It's Javier. "Nothing at all points to the Mancinellis with this. I thought the same thing, but none of them have been in contact with the local Albanians in months. Ever since the Sulas attacked that bar in Queens and tried to take it over, things have been hostile but quiet between them and the Mancinellis. Salvatore let them have that bar because he burned down three of their warehouses full of guns and product. The Sulas decided they weren't the match for the *Cosa Nostra* that they thought."

I'm certain that's old news to Misha and the others, but it's news to me. It also sounds like they won't protect each other either.

"If the man Valeriya met in the club was Albanian, she would have known. She wouldn't have confused the accent. Larisa wouldn't have gone near them. She knows what happened to me. The men who took her may have been Albanians and working for Yuri, but who was the man she met?"

Jorge has been mostly quiet through this call, but he speaks up again.

"The man's Cuban. It's not our contact. It's possible she briefly stopped in Cuba, then they handed her over to someone else. But we suspect the man is a Cuban operating in America part of the time. Whether or not it's well-publicized, Cuba is notorious for human trafficking."

"Sex trafficking."

I point out the obvious. If we find Larisa—and God, I hate how I'm now thinking *if* not *when*—what the hell kind of condition will she be in? I rub my fingers between my eyebrows.

"Is there anything else you know about my sister?"

As Javier answers, I realize Misha probably doesn't need to

go to Jersey after all. Whatever they would have talked about, they've done on the phone. I guess it's a good thing I heard the conversation. I don't even know at this point.

"No, Ms. Vasilieva, there's nothing else. But as soon as any of us hear something, we will let you know."

The call ends, and I bury my face against Misha's chest. I feel like I need to scrub myself in the shower all over again like I did after both times Yuri hurt me. I want to crawl out of my skin, and I don't want to look at anyone.

"I'm taking Kitty upstairs."

"Can the rest of you leave and give me a moment with Katerina, please?"

I lift my head and look at Laura. She offers me a kind smile, and I know she hopes I'll say yes. Part of me wants Misha to stay because I don't want to let him go. I can admit to myself that I'm scared that what I confessed will push him away. But Laura's smile is so encouraging that I nod.

"It's all right, Misha."

I can tell he doesn't want to let go of me any more than I want him to let go. He steps out of the office with the others, leaving me alone with Laura.

"I won't presume to guess how you feel after this call or about what you shared with us. I'm certain you hadn't planned to tell anyone what you did, and that took a shit ton of courage to do it in front of a room of men and over the phone with strangers. All I want to say is that you're family now. The moment you and Misha decided to be together, you became family. We don't use the qualifier 'in-law.' There's no distance between those by blood and by choice. We're bonded by love. I saw the shame in your eyes, and I won't tell you not to feel that way. I have no right. But I can tell you that the men in this room will defend you to their last breath no matter what. They don't pity you. They don't judge you. They don't see you any differently from how they did thirty minutes ago. They already know you're brave. You're one of us, and that's all that matters to anyone."

"Thank you. Misha will probably tell me the same thing, but I admit it's a bit more convincing coming from you."

"That's what I figured. I'm not saying this as the *pakhan's* wife. I don't see myself as the *de facto* leader among the women because I married Maks. I'm saying it as someone who wishes to be your friend and someone you consider family."

"I know, and I do. That's why it means so much to me."

Laura's tentative, but she reaches out and hugs me. It's almost as good as hugging Larisa. It's fortifying, and I feel ready to face the world again.

"We better go out there, or Misha is likely to break down the door to get to me."

"You jest, but I think you know that's the truth."

"What will they do if they find these men?"

"I guarantee you don't want to know. You'll never stop having nightmares if you do."

Chapter Nineteen

Misha

I forced myself not to fidget when I waited for Kitty to come out of the office with Laura, and I've forced myself not to fidget for the past three days. Kitty and I have tried to have some semblance of a normal life, but it's not even close. I've gone back to work since I really couldn't ignore my businesses for much longer. Pasha has been handling much of the import/export business we own, and that's helped. I've worked security at Ivy and Envy, two nightclubs my cousins own, but I hated being away from Kitty. I knew there was no way she would want to go to either, so Anton and Sergei kept her company. Kitty claimed it was a sacrilege that they'd never seen *Dr. Zhivago*. The movie is like nine-hours long. Okay, maybe only three-and-a-half, but good God it felt that long the one and only time I watched it.

My brother and Anton were good sports and have been the last two mornings when they took Kitty running. I left for work early, hoping it would mean I could be home early. Unfortunately, that hasn't been the case. We discovered we had three men within our brotherhood stealing from us. They were skimming off the top what they extorted from some local business owners for us. That's a major no-no.

We have a warehouse in Queens where we deal with our less savory business. It appears on no city plans, and there aren't any city cameras within miles of it. The neighbors ask no questions, and they're paid exceptionally well for their silence. They're all Russian, anyway. We choose to pay because we feel it's right, but everyone knows we don't have to.

It's also where we control the environment and have easy disposal. Anton's team picked up the men and brought them to the building beside Flushing River. I worked them over the first day, then left them to dangle overnight. I went back the second day to see if their memories worked better than they had when I took a tire iron to their ribs. Go figure, they did. I learned what I needed to—which was they worked alone because no one else was dumb enough to join them—then I switched on the meat grinder, which whirred loudly enough to drown out their screams. They're part of the silt on the riverbed now.

Now I'm in my office catching up on work when Kitty walks in.

"Misha, there may be nothing for them to find. I've accepted that."

I know she's talking about her sister. I hate that those words even crossed her mind, let alone that she said them. I refuse to accept it. If we can't find Larisa alive, then I want to know where her body is. Her family deserves to know that. And I want these motherfuckers to pay.

"Will you please shut your laptop and come sit with me?"

I snap it shut. She doesn't have to ask me twice. I push back my chair and walk around the desk to where she leans against the doorjamb. I slide my hands over her hips and cup her ass.

We've been pretty vanilla since the call with the Diazes. I won't push Kitty, but I can tell she's growing more anxious about us along with her fear for Larisa.

"Baby girl, what's wrong?"

"Besides everything to do with my sister?"

I deserve her testiness. That was an asshole question.

"I'm sorry. That wasn't well said. What's wrong between us?"

"Nothing."

"Kitty."

"What, Misha? Don't patronize me with that tone of voice. Nothing's wrong."

"We both know that's not true. What do you need?"

"Besides everything to do with my sister going away?"

She's hurting and afraid. I remind myself of that.

"Do you need space? Do you need me to just sit quietly with you? Do you need to work out? Do you need a good rough fuck? I don't know what to offer you, Kitty."

"You'll never be able to accept that there are some things you can't control, can't fix, will you?"

"Probably not. But you figured that out about me from the very beginning."

"But it's not perpetual optimism. What happens when you fail? Will you be resentful that you did? Will I be disappointed that you promised something you couldn't deliver? You're a control freak who doesn't get that most of life is uncontrollable."

I know why she's lashing out, and my shoulders are broad enough to take it.

"I know what you're thinking, Misha. You may as well say it out loud. You think I'm lashing out because I have no other outlet for my fear and frustration. I want to know what reality is going to look like when you have no reason to be my knight in shining armor. Because there is a very strong likelihood that your arrogance and stubbornness won't get me my sister back."

"You're right. There is a strong likelihood that my sheer will won't be enough. That the resources we have won't be enough. I thought you saw more in me—in us—than what I can do to help you now. I thought reality was going to be building a life together because we love each other, not what I can do for you. You make it sound as though we're only together because you need me to help you with this, and that I only want the glory of solving this. Is that how you feel about us? How you feel about me?"

"It's not like we met at the library, or someone set us up on a blind date. We met because of this fucked up situation. If you weren't bratva, and I wasn't a bratva member's daughter, we wouldn't have done more than look at each other on the plane. It's just circumstance that brought us together."

She steps back and turns away. As she walks to the living room, I follow her.

"Are you admitting that you're just using me?"

"Or are you and your family using my situation to prove a point to the other mafias?"

I snag her arm and yank her to face me. I'm pissed.

"That's bullshit, and you know it. It's fucking disgusting to accuse my family of that. You really think that little of them. You think Laura's kindness is just an act. You think we let you near my cousins' children just so we could use you to further our position in the city. You think my father and Grigori risked staying in Moscow, staying right in front of the very bratva they escaped, just to make us look better in front of our rivals here. You are not stupid, so stop acting like it."

We've both gone too far.

"You just like someone to fuck regularly who already knows the fucked-up life you have. I'm just the easy choice."

"What exactly is easy about this?"

I glower at her as I pull her closer to me. She tries to maintain her resolve, but I see it waver for a moment. She uses her free hand to push me away, and I release her immediately. I take a step back and sweep my hand to point around my loft.

"I'm not good enough and neither is three-thousand-square-feet. Go back to your shithole in the Bronx if I'm such a horrible and impossible man to love."

I step closer to her and wrap my arm around her waist. I pull her flush with me and fist her hair as I pull her head back.

"Or admit that you're scared of all of this. Admit that you have no outlet for this, so you took it out on me—on us."

I see she wants to fight me on this, wants to push me away again. But I also see when she crumbles. My mouth descends to hers in a punishing and claiming kiss. I squeeze her ass with both hands until she comes up onto her toes and yelps. I squeeze harder, then I spank her. I heft her over my shoulder and carry her to our bedroom.

"Strip, *malyshka*."

"Yes, Daddy."

She doesn't hesitate to answer or obey. When she's standing in front of me naked, I open my arms to her.

"Kitty, you're terrified and angry. You have no other way to vent because we don't know who's truly behind this. You want your sister back, and nothing is moving fast enough. There's too much uncertainty. I understand. I shouldn't have said the things I did. I should have been more patient."

"No. I goaded you. I was cruel just because I could be. Misha, I didn't mean those things. Please don't send me away. Don't dump me."

"I'm not going anywhere, and neither are you, *koshechka*. I think you were egging me on because you knew the outcome would be a spanking. I think that's what you want and what you need. I think not having any control right now is wearing you down. The one thing you can control is surrendering to me and letting me take care of you for a while. I think if you can't have control, then you at least want me to."

"How'd you know?"

She speaks at little more than a whisper.

"Because I'll always take care of you."

"I'm ashamed of how I spoke to you, *papochka*. I really am sorry."

"We are going to argue, and it may not be pretty. But don't pick a fight again if what you need is my attention and my love. I give that freely."

"I didn't really understand why I was doing it until I'd already started. But the more I said, the more I wondered if you would spank me. I wanted that. I wanted to rile you up enough for you to punish me, so I could think about that instead of all of this."

The things we ordered arrived yesterday. There is plenty to put to use, and several things are getting opened right now.

"Lie over the edge of the bed."

She swallows and keeps her eyes on the floor between us.

"Daddy, I'd really like to make amends first. I know that makes no sense before a punishment, but we both know the spanking is only partly a punishment."

"What do you want to do, *kiska*?"

"I want to suck you off until you come down my throat."

"You don't have to pleasure me to earn forgiveness. Never."

I've always liked rough sex and dirty talk, but I've discovered I much prefer praise kink with Kitty.

"I know. I want to do it because I've made you feel bad, and now I want the opposite. Daddy, please let me."

"Unfasten my pants, *malyshka*. Then get on your knees.

Suck me however you want, but when I'm ready to come, I'm fucking your mouth, and you're taking all of it."

She relaxes and even appears eager. The relationship we have would make most people believe we're fucked-up. Like entirely dysfunctional and unhealthy. But it works for us and gives both of us what we need.

She drops to her knees as she undoes my pants. She grins when she sees I'm going commando. She already knows since she saw me get dressed this morning, but I know she likes it as much as I like her not wearing panties. She swirls her tongue around the tip of my cock, and I leak. I pull my tie loose and unbutton my shirt as I watch her lick me over and over. Her hand rolls my balls before she massages my taint. It makes my cock twitch. I hurry to toe off my shoes and kick my pants free. She knows I hate the idea of fucking with my socks on. She pushes them down before I balance on one foot, then the other, to pull them off.

She opens her mouth wider and takes me into it, letting my cock rest on her tongue. Our eyes meet, and she closes her lips around me. Then she goes to work. Holy Mary. I can't stop my groan, and my eyes might already be rolling back in my head. Fuck. I'm too close way too fast, but I don't care. I want to get off and get on with pleasuring her until tomorrow morning. I tunnel my hands into her hair and hold her head in place as I fuck her mouth. After the first squirt of cum hits the back of her throat, I pull out and jerk myself off. My cum covers her lips, her chin, and her tits. I pull her onto her feet.

"You are mine, *malyshka*. It's my cum you taste, and it's my cum marking you. Don't think you can push me away so easily. Don't think I'll let you go without a fight. You are going to beg me to fuck you, and you're going to beg me to let you come. Tonight, I'm going to test you beyond what we've done in the past. You know my one rule."

"Yes, Daddy. If it goes from pain to really hurting me, I tell you immediately, and we stop."

"And if you don't obey that rule?"

"A spanking, and we stick with vanilla."

"Why, *malyshka?*"

"Because you love me, and the thought of really hurting me is something you can't stomach. I know that, *papochka*. I was cruel today, but I don't really want to hurt you. I know you wouldn't forgive yourself if you really harmed me."

"I wouldn't. You're everything to me. I love you."

"I love you. I'd really like my spanking now, please."

Gladly. I steer her toward the end of the bed and press between her shoulder blades until she's lying with her tits on the bed.

"Stay there."

I walk to the dresser drawer where we put everything. I pull out lube and a butt plug with a glittering sapphire-looking stone. I return to her and pour lube onto the plug, letting it drip between her ass cheeks. I spread them, and I watch as she relaxes enough for me to pour lube onto her hole. I snap the lid shut and toss it on the bed. I ease the plug into her and step back to admire how it looks.

"Turn around, *malyshka*."

I'm making this up as I go along. I go back to the drawer and withdraw something else. I hold it up for her to see, and I see her belly flex. I take out one more item before stalking back to her. I thrust my hand between her legs and press three fingers into her. I already know she's dripping.

"Whose pussy is this?"

"Yours."

"And what do I get to do to it and with it?"

"Whatever you want."

I pull my fingers out and roll her clit until she squirms. I hand her the clit clamp that's connected to nipple clamps.

"Put this on."

I watch her examine the two-piece chain with the three clips. She loosens it until she can snap it open around the protruding little nub. She grimaces with discomfort. How I'm going to enjoy sucking it as the sensation rushes back into it. I'll make her scream. She attaches the nipple clamps next and screws them tighter than I expected.

"Daddy, my safe word is beets. I haven't forgotten. I want this."

I hand her the massive dildo that she jokingly pointed out when it arrived and said was still smaller than me.

"Go stand in front of the window."

No one can really see in. The windows are too tinted on the outside for that. I like my privacy too much for anything less. She knows that. But the idea that someone could see her arouses both of us. I'd fucking gouge a man's eyes out if he really tried to watch without my permission. I'm still on the fence about a sex club and letting people watch Kitty. I don't like that kind of sharing, but I know the idea excites her.

"Fuck yourself on it. Come without me inside you, and I will punish you even more."

She follows my instructions without looking back at me. I wrap my hand around my dick and stroke myself until I'm rock hard again. I walk over to her and slap my dick on her ass.

"Watch us, *malyshka*."

"Yes, Daddy."

We turn our heads to see ourselves in the mirror. I put it there for the natural light, but now I see it has another purpose. I wrap my arm around her waist and slide my cock between her legs.

"Daddy, I can take both."

"I know you can, baby. And you're going to."

I nudge her legs apart and draw her hips back. She moves the dildo inside her cunt, and I thrust into her. She cries out at the burst of pain she must feel. She's plugged plus a dildo and my dick shoved inside her. Her head falls back on my shoulder. She's so unbelievably tight right now that I'm not sure I can move.

"Your tits, your clit, your pussy, and your ass are all mine, *malyshka*."

There's nothing gentle about my tone. I'm insistent. Demanding. Possessive as fuck.

"Good."

I reach between us and twirl the plug in her ass as I command her to fuck herself with the dildo. I don't move my dick, but I'm pulsing inside her.

"Daddy, I'm really close. Please let me come."

I withdraw.

"Take the dildo out."

"Daddy!"

She whines, and I grin as we watch each other in the mirror. I pull a chair over and face it toward the mirror. With my dick still hard and coated in her pussy juice, I pull her over my lap. I take the dildo and slide it inside her cunt. Before she can settle herself, my hand cracks down.

"The first ten are punishment. The second five are to make you come. Do not. If you make it through those without an orgasm, then the last five are to let you come as many times as you can. You will count each one."

Her hands wrap around my ankle as she braces herself. The sound of my hand hitting her ass fills the room.

"One."

I continue as she counts to ten. I'm not gentle. I cover her ass from top to bottom and side to side until it's cherry-apple red.

"Open your legs."

It's awkward, but she does it. I slap her pussy, pressing the dildo all the way into her, and she yelps. My middle finger taps the clit clamp in the process, and she moans. Her hips drive forward, and I know she's trying to rub her clit against my leg. She needs relief.

I slap her pussy again, and she stomps her feet.

"Do you need to come?"

"You know I do."

"Only three more. Can you make it?"

"Yes."

That answer comes out through gritted teeth.

"Count these."

"Twelve."

I slap her again.

"Thirteen."

I pull the dildo from her and dip my fingers into her and stroke her g-spot until I know she's close to crying. My hand lands again.

"Fourteen."

For the last one, I use both hands to spank her pussy and her ass. She howls before croaking.

"Fifteen."

I pick her up and stand. I seat her in the chair as I go down on one knee. I pull her hips to the edge of the chair and tilt them up. I release the clit clamp and dive in. I suck before I slap her inner left thigh. I slap her right one next.

"Daddy, please."

"You don't come until my dick is inside you."

"But you said…"

"I said they're to make you come as many times as you can. I didn't say while I was spanking you."

I suck her clit again until I know I've pushed her to the point of frustration rather than pain and pleasure. I release her nipple clamps, sucking each nipple until she's writhing in the chair. I trade places with her and lower her onto my cock. She wraps her arms around my neck and clings to me.

"Will you come inside me now?"

"Don't enjoy being marked, *kiska*?"

"I do. I love it. But I just want us to be one."

I stroke her hair back from her perspiring temples. I rock my hips beneath her, and she rides me. She squeezes me with every thrust. She's moving fast and hard, and I know she's close because I am too.

"Come, *malyshka*."

"Uhhh...Uhhh...Ohhh...Yes...Harder,   Daddy... Fuck...Harder."

As I feel her spasm around me, I grasp a handful of her hair and wrap my other hand around her throat.

"You are fucking mine, *malyshka*. You want to end things, then you end them. But goad me like that again, I will fuck you raw just to remind you of who you're playing with. Do you understand me?"

"Yes, Daddy."

I see the spark in her eyes. Despite my words and my tone, she knows that I'm really giving her permission as long as she understands the consequences. She comes on me, and I explode. As our hearts race, I stand and carry her to the bed. I groan as I slide out of her when I toss her onto the bed.

"Stay there."

I bark the command as I retrieve handcuffs, a spreader, and a blindfold. I attach the cuffs to the headboard and her wrists.

Then I widen the spreader as far as it'll go and fasten it to her ankles.

"You told me your fantasy once. I haven't forgotten. I'll be back to fuck you a few more times. You won't know when. You won't know how I'll do it. And you won't know if I'll let you come. Your cunt and ass are mine to fuck. Do you accept that?"

"Fuck, yes, Daddy."

I slide the blindfold over her eyes and walk to the door. I open and shut it, but I remain in the room. I creep to the chair that I silently turn toward her. I watch her for the next thirty minutes before I open and close the door again. I say nothing as I climb onto the bed. I fuck her hard enough to make her scream. I make sure she gets off before I shoot my load.

We play the same game for another four hours. Sometimes I wait thirty minutes, sometimes fifteen, sometimes an hour. I make it unpredictable to her, but it's every time I stroke myself until I can't stand not being inside her. When I make her come the last time, knowing she must be getting sore, I lift off her blindfold. She lifts her chin for a kiss, and I gladly oblige.

"How do things stand, *kiska?*"

"My home is with you, Misha. I can't promise I won't lash out again, but I don't want to. I won't say the cruel things I did today. I'm sorry."

"I know, baby. And I'm sorry I lost my patience with you when I understood what was happening."

I release her wrists and remove the spreader before I roll to her side and place my hand on her belly. If she weren't on birth control that I see her take every morning, I would think it odd if she weren't pregnant. One day, and hopefully not too far in the future. I just need to figure out who these motherfuckers are, take them to the warehouse, and punish them for every second they've upset my *malyshka*.

Come out, come out wherever you are.

Chapter Twenty

Kitty

I'm not proud of my outburst yesterday. It was petty and immature, but I couldn't help myself in the moment. The words just vomited from my mouth before I knew what I was doing. But Misha got it. He really did. He knew why I was doing it and what I needed. By the time we had dinner and climbed into bed for the night, I felt like the weight of the world had finally lifted. It's back today. But I had a little break, and during it, I realized I will never piss away what we have.

I stretch in bed and roll toward Misha, who I know is already awake. I haven't figured out if he wakes the moment I do or if he barely sleeps. Maybe it's both. He's always ready to pull me into his arms the moment I stir.

"Good morning, *malyshka*."

"Good morning, Daddy."

"Did you sleep well, baby girl?"

"I think so."

"Are you sore this morning?"

"A little, but it's what I like. A reminder of being with you."

"Do you feel better than you did yesterday?"

I consider that question. The best I could say is sorta. I'm glad we resolved things after I picked the fight. I'm glad I had one of those brief reprieves from all of this. But it's not like anything other than being with Misha is good. Everything's still fucked-up shit. As I think about it, I feel myself growing testy again.

"*Kiska?*"

There's that delicious commanding voice. I know he's concerned, but he's reading my mood. I shrug one shoulder. He wants an answer, and I'm being defiant. He deserves an answer, and I'm being reticent.

"I will ask you a second time, but not a third. Do you feel better than yesterday?"

I shrug that shoulder again.

"Sure."

I don't expect his gentle touch as he rests his hand on my waist. It slides down my hip and over to my ass. Then he grabs it mercilessly. It makes my back arch.

"Do you need more of last night?"

His voice is as gentle as his touch was a moment ago. But he hasn't eased his grip on my flesh. If anything, he's holding me even tighter. I love the pain. It's soothing because it's taking my mind away from what was, and will soon, stress me out.

"Yes, Daddy."

"Ask."

"Daddy, will you take control?"

"Do you need a rough fuck, *malyshka?* Is that what you're asking for?"

"Yes."

"Do you need me to punish that ass?"

"Yes."

"Do you want to obey my commands?"

"Yes."

I'm practically begging.

"Daddy, I need you. Last night, I shouldn't have taken things out on you. But I'm already feeling testy again. I need you to take over."

He releases my ass, but only long enough to spank it. Hard. Then he grabs it again.

"You're very lucky I don't have a traditional nine-to-five job. Do not move."

I watch him climb out of bed naked. He walks over to the dresser and pulls open *that* drawer. He made space for me in the dresser and his closet, but we set aside that drawer for everything we ordered. It needs a drawer of its own because we bought that much. I can't tell what he's gathering, but it seems like a lot. My eyes almost fall out of my head when he turns toward me. Holy fuck. He isn't messing around.

"Roll onto your back, *malyshka*."

"Yes, Daddy."

This time I'm quick to obey. The sooner I do, the sooner we can start. He places most of what he was carrying on the bed, but he has something in his hand that I can't see. I can see the ball gag he has in the other.

"You aren't saying what I want to hear, *kiska*. Last night, you couldn't say enough. This morning, you won't speak. I have something better to do with your mouth right now. Open for me."

I do. Immediately.

He fits the ball gag, careful not to catch my hair in the buckle. I still can't tell what he has in his hand, though. He leans over and sucks my left nipple. He always wakes up hard, or at least he's hard by the time I'm awake. But he has a fucking tent pole pointing at me right now. I'm so fucking tempted to jack him off. I give into it. I wrap my hand around his cock and stroke. He bites down on my nipple, so I tighten my grip.

"If you make me come, it'll be all over your face and tits. I will make you wear my cum all fucking day."

"Mmm."

I nod. He grabs my wrist and pries me loose as he leans to whisper in my ear.

"I fucking decide. Not you. Do that again, and I will leave you needing to get off so badly that you can't think straight. I'm going to come in your pussy, and you are going to keep it there. When it drips down your leg and keeps you wet, you will remember I'm fucking you. Not the other way around, *malyshka*."

"Ymm dmmm."

I try to say, "Yes, Daddy," but the ball gag garbles everything. While he was whispering to me, I didn't notice his hand moving between my legs. He thrusts all four fingers into me, and I scream. He doesn't hurt me, but I was completely unprepared. Maybe not completely. I'm wet, and his fingers slide inside me as he strokes my g-spot. But I feel something else. He pulls his fingers out, but I still have a full sensation. Then my pussy buzzes. My eyes widen as I look up at him.

He holds up a small remote. He presses something with his thumb, and the vibrator pulses faster. Oh, fuck. I writhe on the bed, and that earns me a slap to my pussy. My belly flexes as need shoots straight from my clit into my core.

"Roll over."

I obey immediately. I'm too fucking excited. I want to know what's coming next.

"Spread your arms and legs out."

Misha's quick to fasten me into the under-the-bed restraint system we picked out. I'm left spread eagle. His hand cracks down on my ass as I watch his cock again. His wicked grin tells me he knows how much I wish I could touch him. I'd take him in my hand or my mouth if I could. The denial only makes the desire stronger.

He flips open the cap on the bottle of lube. I watch as he preps the butt plug. It's big, and I'm going to feel full. I'm also going to feel the fucking vibrator pressed against my g-spot. He's methodical in everything, even with how quickly he picked things. He didn't just grab whatever caught his eye. He's planned every choice.

Once he's eased the plug into me, he picks up a rope paddle. It wasn't very heavy when I unwrapped its packaging, but the rope's braided to make a thick enough paddle to be both thuddy—I learned that word for impact play tools while we were on the website—and create a sting. He slides his free hand between my shoulder blades, calming me and reassuring me. I'd like to say the anticipation is the worst part, but when the rope paddle lands across my ass, the impact is definitely way, way worse.

"We've never used this before, and you're still new to this, *malyshka*. I will only give you five spanks."

Only?

"Do not come."

You'd think the searing pain would be a distraction, but it only heightens everything. Each time the paddle lands across my ass, it presses the plug into me, which presses against the little vibrator, which presses against my g-spot. It also makes me grind my clit against the firm mattress. I feel the sweat break out across my brow as I breathe through my nose.

The spanking is over quickly, and Misha tosses the paddle aside. He releases the ball gag, and I work my jaw. His fingers ease into me this time, careful how he removes the vibrator he turns off.

"I'm tempted to fuck you doggy-style, baby. But I don't think that's what you need, is it?"

My ass burns so badly I can't think about what I need. I don't realize that I'm even answering until I hear my own voice.

"That's not what I want."

"You want to see me, and you want me to hold you, don't you?"

"Yes, *papochka*."

He releases me from the restraints and carefully rolls me onto my side enough to lift me off the bed. He does it with such ease that it's still disconcerting. He guides me to the chair that remains in front of the mirror and window. He sits before he pulls me back toward him. We're looking into the mirror, watching ourselves, as I slide down his cock.

"Rub you clit."

He kneads my tits and tweaks my nipples as I rub my finger in circles. As I get close, his hands slide down my ribs until they grip my hips. He moves me, so I rock on him. His thumbs sweep over my punished flesh.

"Did I hurt you, *kiska*? I didn't think to tell you to snap if it was too much. You couldn't say your safe word."

"It hurt, but it wasn't more than I can take. I would have found a way to let you know. May I come?"

"Yes, baby."

I watch as my stomach flexes as my pussy squeezes his dick. Seeing us like this is fucking hot.

"Are you close, *papochka*?"

"Yes. But I'm not ready to come yet."

"I want to make you come. I don't want you to wait."

"Not until you have at least two orgasms."

I squeeze my eyes shut as I explode. I rub harder as my toes curl. The moment I relax, he plucks me off his dick and turns me toward him. I grab his dick and guide it into my pussy.

Fuck. That feels amazing. He cups my tits and sucks both of them before I lean forward, and we kiss. He has one arm wrapped around my waist and the other across my ass. I ride him as I hold on to the chair back.

"May I come again?"

"Yes. I'm barely holding on."

I rise and fall faster until he grabs my hips and rocks me. He knows I like that better, but I know he likes it the other way. We struggle against each other, both wanting to make the other come.

"Daddy!"

He sucks hard on my tit as I come again. I switch my pace, once more rising and falling, until he pins me in place.

"Malyshka!"

He roars the endearment as he fills me with his cum. He wraps his arms around me again and rests his head on my chest. I run my fingers through his hair as the other hand roams over his shoulders and upper back.

"I love you, Kitty."

"I love you, Misha."

The aftercare is as important to us as the roleplaying. We share soft kisses as our hands caress. Nothing has ever been like it is with Misha.

I've just finished running on the treadmill in our loft. That still feels funny to think. Misha's been gone all day. He said something about going into Queens again, and I got the distinct impression that it had nothing to do with seeing family. I've known all along that there's somewhere they go, and I assumed it was Queens, but that was the closest thing to confirmation I will get. It's more than enough for me.

I was listening to streaming music on my phone while I ran, so I'm about to close the app, but my phone rings. It's a New York City number, but I don't recognize it. I hesitate to answer, but I don't want to send it to voicemail either. I bolt out of the home gym and down the hall to Misha's office. I slide my finger to answer the phone as I burst into the room.

"Hello?"

There's a pause before a heavily accented voice responds.

"So breathless, Katerina. Did you have a good run?"

I know that voice. It's my nightmare on the other end of the phone. How does he know I was running? Is it because I'm breathless answering the phone? Is it because he saw me on the treadmill? Did he see me running down the hallway?

I feel all thumbs as I open Misha's laptop and hurry to enter the pin. I search for anything to record the call as I respond.

"Spying on me, Yuri?"

"Just a lucky guess."

I pull up the program and start the recording before I switch the phone to speaker. I keep it close to my mouth, so the volume of my voice doesn't change for him.

"Where's Larisa?"

"How would I know?"

"Those men are yours."

"Doesn't mean I know where she is."

"You don't deny that you took her."

"Katerina, why deny what you already know?"

"Who was the man she went on the date with? It wasn't you."

"An associate."

A fucking associate. That's what the *Tres J's* called the Cuban who snitched to them. I fucking hate the word.

"A Cuban associate. Raping women isn't enough for you.

Now you sell them to be raped. Did you touch Larisa?"

"As tempted as I was, she's not you. That purple sports bra doesn't do much to hold those magnificent tits in place, does it?"

I force my expression to remain neutral. How the fuck does he know what color sports bra I'm wearing? Without turning my head, I look toward the window. Can he see me now? Has he guessed I'm recording the conversation? I don't know who's with Misha, so I don't know who'll get any message I send. I place my hand on the desk next to the laptop and twist, so my back blocks the side closer to the window. My fingers move to the mouse pad, and I open an internet browser.

"What do you want, Yuri?"

"You. But I've already had that twice."

"You asked how would you know where my sister is. You didn't tell me you didn't know. Where is she?"

I shift again, so I can slowly type in my email provider. I don't want him to hear the keys if I type too fast. When I'm logged in, I force myself to remember Laura's and Sergei's emails. I already have it set to switch easily to Cyrillic.

Subject: сейчас

I type the word "now" and pray they get it means urgent.

"Somewhere in this hemisphere."

"You killed Pyotr, and now you've sold Larisa. Why do you care about me enough to hurt me over and over?"

"Because I can. Because I wanted you, so I took you each time. The Russian you're fucking needs to do more than just playfully spank you, *kiska*."

I want to hurl when he calls me that. I hurry to type. I don't care anymore if he hears it.

По телефону с Ю.П. Верни М домой сейчас же.

I'm on the phone with YP. Get M home now. I keep the

message short since who the fuck knows if he's hacking my shit. I don't sign my name or anything. What's the point with my email address attached to it? I just hit send. What he said before the nickname I won't let him ruin sinks in. How the hell does he know this shit about me?

"Are you jacking off while you watch Misha fuck me? Are you trying to figure out why he gets me off, and you didn't?"

"I was never interested in your pleasure. Why would I care if you enjoyed it?"

"You forced me because you knew I would never want you. You forced me because you knew that if I had said yes, you wouldn't have satisfied me."

This recording is going in a direction I don't want. I need to get it back on track.

"Yuri, what do you want in exchange for Larisa?"

"I don't have her, but I might convince the guy to give her back for a trade."

"You want to sell me. You took Larisa nearly two months ago. Why have you waited so long?"

"To make sure you're desperate enough to agree."

"You can't or won't tell me where she is, so why should I believe you enough to turn myself over to you?"

"Because you love your sister enough to give up your life for her. You don't care where she is as long as she goes free. Her location doesn't really matter."

"I want proof of life."

Larisa will know what to do if someone comes to take her photo. Maybe people already have, but as long as she's conscious, she'll communicate through the photo.

"I want her holding today's newspaper within the next ten minutes, Yuri, or I will believe you're lying to me."

"Testy, *malyshka*."

How does he know these things about my private life with Misha?

I look up as the loft door starts to open. I yank the top desk drawer open and pull out the gun. The safety is off, and my finger is on the trigger before it opens another inch. The gun's pointed at Sergei as he slips into the apartment. He puts his hands up, and I lower the gun. I click the safety back into place and put a finger to my lips.

"Our time is up, Katerina. Sergei is there now. Try not to blow his head off."

"Proof of life, Yuri. That's the only way I'll consider it. Ten minutes or you're lying and get nothing."

The call ends, and I click the computer program to stop recording.

"How'd you get here so fast?"

"I was downstairs. I'm your bodyguard today."

I should have known Misha wouldn't leave here without a family member somewhere in the building.

"I know his phone won't be on. Can someone get a message to him?"

"Anton's on his way from Pasha's to pick him up. It'll be at least an hour, though."

I walk around the desk, so I'm facing him, and our shoulders are nearly touching. I whisper to him.

"I know. Sergei, he knew private things about Misha and me. What Misha calls me. What we do in private. He knew what I'm wearing right now. That I was running."

Sergei's gaze sweeps the office before he rips the plug from Misha's laptop. He shrugs out of his suit coat before flinging it around my shoulders. He grabs the laptop in one hand and mine in the other. He practically drags me across the apartment. I snag my purse from near the front door while he pulls his phone from his pocket. He presses a single number on the keypad, and I hear it ringing.

"My place."

That's all Sergei says. I don't know who he just called because I couldn't see the contact before he put the phone to his ear or after he hangs up.

"*Priyti.*" Come.

He snaps the single word at the guard outside the loft's door. The man presses his earpiece and tells whoever is on the other end to be ready for us to come out of the elevator in the garage. The car is to meet us at the elevator. Whose car?

We round the corner, and there are four men already waiting at the elevator before we even get in it. They're quick to surround me, making me practically invisible. My hands are trembling as we ride down to the underground parking garage. When the elevator pings, all the men pull their guns. The doors open, and I see a town car waiting. As a one, the men move forward in lock step, like they're soldiers marching in a parade. I don't even know the man's name, but one of them opens the door for me. The driver is inside, and the privacy glass is down. Sergei slips into the front passenger seat as I get in the back.

"*Podpisyvaytes' na nas.*" Follow us.

Maybe Sergei is the porcupine in the group. He barks the orders as his eyes constantly survey everything around us. I see his head moving against the headrest. I want to believe the tinted windows will protect me from anyone watching the building, but Misha's windows reflect, and Yuri still saw inside. That's assuming he doesn't have the place bugged with listening devices and cameras.

My phone pings, and I look down. I unlock it and open the text that just came in. I clutch my chest and gasp. Sergei spins in his seat. I hold up the phone and hand it to him.

"I demanded proof of life. I told him he had ten minutes to

get a picture to me of Larisa holding today's newspaper. Look. It's the *Boston Globe*. If it were the New York Times, then she might be anywhere. But the *Boston Globe* isn't exactly an international news source. If she's not actually in Boston, then she's somewhere in Massachusetts. See how she's holding it?"

I lean all the way forward and reach through the divider. I point to Larisa's hands.

"Do you see how her left hand has her middle finger and pinky showing? The middle finger signal there are less than ten men wherever she is. The pinky tells me they're all armed. Do you see how she has her thumb wrapped around the front of the paper? It's like a thumbs up. It means whoever comes for her should be able to get inside. Her right thumb isn't showing."

I swallow as my chest pinches. I take a deep breath.

"That means they've either been drugging her or beating her. She's telling us she's not okay. She's hiding her ring finger and pinky on that hand. It means they aren't giving her enough food and water."

I take the phone back and zoom in as far as I can. Larisa's left eyebrow is raised. She would always do that to me when she wanted to prove a point. It was her way of saying "see." I follow her gaze in the photo. There's a door open, and I can see a street sign, but it's blurry at this magnification. I zoom out, but it's too small to read. Whoever is there doesn't fear her bolting or anyone seeing them inside.

"Is there anything you can do to see more details?"

I offer the phone back to Sergei. He texts the photo to himself before giving my phone back to me. I sink against the seatback and watch our progress through the front window.

"I'll see what I can do. This should help a lot. Between what's in the picture and you decoding your sister's message, this should give us somewhere to start."

"Thank you."

I turn my head to look out my window, but I shut my eyes. I just want Misha to magically appear by the time we get to Sergei's. My future brother—I remember what Laura said about no qualifiers, and I like it—is comforting because of his size and silent confidence. But he's not Misha.

When the car stops for longer than a stoplight, I open my eyes. I'm unprepared for the gorgeous townhouses along this street. Sergei gets out and opens my door for me. I assumed he lived in some penthouse or enormous loft like Misha. I heard about the other guys' places before they married.

"I just moved."

I glance at Sergei and nod. He leads the way up the front steps and quickly unlocks the door. We're entering on what must be the second floor because there's an ornate set of stairs that leads up and leads down. As we move past the foyer, I glance up. The stairs go up three more floors. Then I look down and see only one floor below us. Normally this would be a two or three family building, but I get the impression Sergei isn't sharing.

I look around as we walk farther into the townhome. It's not ultramodern or minimalist, but it's not exactly a cheery family home. It's comfortable and suits a bachelor.

"It's beautiful."

"Thank you. It's a good investment. So good that Anton bought the place next door."

I stare at Sergei for a long moment before I nod. I want to ask if that's safe. I wonder if it'll raise questions, but then I remember that the others not only live in the same neighborhood in Queens, they live only a couple blocks from each other. I can't remember who, but two couples live across the street from each other, or something like that. I guess it makes it plausible for Anton and Sergei to be neighbors. I smile as I feel more reassured.

Sergei's just offered me a bottle of water when the front door bursts open. He and I both draw our guns and raise them. I kept the one Misha gave me, and it's always in my purse now.

"Kitty!"

I hear pounding footsteps.

"Kitty!"

"Misha, I'm in the kitchen with Sergei."

We put our weapons away as Misha storms in. He lifts me off my feet and nearly crushes me against him. I have to tap on his shoulder because I can't breathe.

"What happened? All Anton said was that you emailed Sergei and Laura saying you were on the phone with Yuri, and you needed me."

"He called me, Misha. He knew things about us and what we do in private. He knew what I was wearing. He didn't deny taking Larisa, but he wouldn't tell me where she was. He wants me in exchange for her."

"No."

"I didn't say I would do it. But I will, Misha. If that's the only choice, then you will not stop me."

"It won't be the only choice. I'll kill the fucker before that happens. Did he say where she was?"

"No. But I made him send proof of life."

I pull out my phone and open the text. I quickly explain what I learned from the photo. Sergei disappears, saying he's going to examine the photo on his larger computer screen.

"How do you know all of that from the photo?"

"It was a system my dad taught us in case someone ever took either of us. I don't know if it was something he came up with on his own or something he learned in the KGB. If it was the latter, then he changed the meaning of the code, but not the premise."

"I'll ask my dad later."

"Wait. Didn't Vlad ever teach you anything like this?"

"No. If any of us were ever taken, he would have written us off. He wouldn't have asked for proof of life. He would have said dying was what we deserved for getting captured."

Fuck.

"There's more code than what I shared. I want to teach it to you at some point. I will always demand proof of life, and I will always demand someone go after you."

"Baby, no one in my family is leaving someone to die if they're captured. We just don't have that system. When this shit is over, ask Pasha what happened when someone took him while he and Sumiko were dating. I was outside when Grigori went in the building to find him. And I missed his reunion with Anton. But I could hear it. Believe me, no one gets left behind in this family."

What the ever-loving fuck? That doesn't reassure me. Does this shit happen often?

"Misha? Sergei?"

I turn toward Anton's voice. Misha answers for us.

"Kitty and I are in the kitchen. Sergei's in his office."

Anton joins us and sweeps his gaze over me as though checking for injuries.

"I'm all right, Anton. Just freaked out."

"Come to my place. People must have seen all of us arrive here. If they send someone in, I don't think you should be here."

"You think someone is going to break into Sergei's place?"

"I'm not putting anything past Yuri after what Sergei just told me on the phone."

I didn't know Sergei called Anton. What the fuck do I know at this point? I follow Anton, and Misha follows me. I'm ready to head for the front door, but Anton takes the stairs up. I glance over my shoulder at Misha, but he's texting something.

"Don't trip. I'm not in the mood to set your nose."

I don't know how Anton saw Misha texting, but I force myself not to laugh. Misha huffs but puts his phone away. I wonder what it's like to basically have seven older brothers. Maybe six since Bogdan is barely older than Misha. They're more like twins age wise. I follow Anton into what must be the master bedroom. I'm completely confused when he opens the closet door. He pushes clothes aside and pushes on the back wall. A door springs open, and my eyes almost fall out of my head. I follow him through and find myself in what must be his townhome.

I look back as Misha closes the hidden door. The significance isn't missed on me, even if it's a horribly perverted cliché. They come out of the closet to be together. Our lives are so fucking fucked-up.

"We all worked construction when we were teenagers. It wasn't hard for them to do that."

Misha doesn't lower his voice as he explains, and Anton doesn't seem to care that Misha's telling me. I really am part of the family because it's obvious neither of them fears me spilling this secret. Once my initial surprise passes, I smile like an idiot. I'm happy they figured something out. They deserve whatever joy they can get.

Anton leads us to his kitchen, and immediately, Misha rummages through the fridge. It's obvious he's been here plenty of times because he gets out pots, pans, the chopping board, and knives. It looks like we're spending the evening here because he starts making dinner that's like a fucking feast. Then I realize he's making enough for Sergei, Anton, and him. I might be lucky to keep all my fingers and catch some scraps.

"Don't worry, *kiska*. I'll serve you first. That way I know you get enough."

He kisses my cheek before taking vegetables to the sink to

wash. He's trying so hard to act like everything is normal, but we all know it isn't. I ask him to give me some tasks to keep me occupied. Dinner is almost ready by the time Sergei appears. We move to the dining room table.

"I was able to enlarge the photo and make it crisper. I did some searching, and it's an old restaurant that's been closed for like twenty years in South Dorchester. Not surprising near Blue Hill Avenue."

I stare blankly at Sergei. I don't know what he means. Misha hands me the cubed and seasoned beets, and winks before he explains what his brother said.

"South Dorchester isn't a great neighborhood. It's a high crime area known for shootings and drugs. There are a lot of distressed properties in that area, making it a good spot to hide."

"But you know which one it is, Sergei?"

"Yes."

I wait for more, but nothing is forthcoming. I raise my eyebrows at Misha.

"There's an Albanian community in South Boston, so it's not surprising that Larisa is in the area."

"You don't think this is Boston bratva?"

Misha shakes his head before he answers.

"We don't have a large presence in Boston, and they wouldn't be foolish enough to accept a kidnapped Russian woman and think we wouldn't hear about it. After what our family's gone through to protect our moms, every bratva leader in America probably knows that'll piss us off. Some of the Chicago bratva thought to get involved with the Podolskaya and made Anastasia a target. It didn't work out well for them. That sent a message loud and clear. Yuri's relying on his Albanian connections, not his Russian ones."

I'm trying to keep it all straight in my head, but it's

confusing adding all these other syndicates with roots in so many foreign countries.

"I never thought the Albanians in America would have connections to the Cubans or the Mexican Cartels."

"They don't. That's all Yuri."

"In Russia, the Russians and Albanians get along well enough. It's not bad, but it's not great. I think Russia tends to side with Serbia a bit more since that war, but as best I know, there's no love or hate between us. Is that the case in America?"

"They're here, and they run their own smaller operations, but they generally stay out of our lanes."

Anton swallows his milk—apparently, even into your thirties, milk does your body good—and offers his thoughts.

"Chances are the Albanians helping him here have no idea who Larisa is. I doubt anyone's told them. They're just doing what Yuri says. They may not know Larisa is Russian if they've gagged her most of the time or Yuri's threatened her if she speaks. Even if they know she's Russian, they probably don't know who she's connected to. He's probably using people not even connected to organized crime. My guess is he's intimidating them into doing what he wants."

"Which makes them completely expendable. None of them will help Larisa."

My stomach hurts from the three bites of salad I've taken. I don't want any more. I put my fork down and look in my lap. Misha's hand covers mine, where they rest on my thighs.

"Misha, what happens next?"

I don't like how he glances at Sergei and Anton before he looks at me.

"I'm going to Boston, and you are staying here, *kiska*. You are not coming."

"Misha—"

"No. Sergei and I will make the trip. There's a woman I know who will help."

I narrow my eyes, and my teeth clench. Misha looks at me and doesn't blink.

"Yes, I have a past with her. No, I'm not interested in fucking her. No, I will not fuck her to get what I need."

"I don't care if it's a man, woman, or dog. I don't like how cagey you sound, Misha. What aren't you telling me?"

Sergei and Anton slip away from the table, and that only infuriates me. Why the hell do they think we need privacy?

"I was supposed to marry her, Kitty. The old Elite Group wanted Maks to marry her cousin, and they wanted me to marry Yelena. I was too young to want to get married, but she agreed to it. I didn't know that until things blew up in my face. I thought I had a fuck buddy. She thought she was house-breaking a future husband. She manipulated me with sex to get what she wanted. Or at least tried to. Because I didn't care that much about her, I never gave in. We slept together for six months, then I discovered the Elite Group's plan. I refused. I told her she could fuck half the Eastern Seaboard before I fucked her lying ass again. It was ugly."

"And you think she'll help you?"

"She will if she wants me to keep her secrets."

I stare at him.

"Kitty, they're her secrets, not mine. I'm not adding hers to what I already can't tell you. I won't tell anyone outside our family because, as long as I don't, I control her when I need her. But I'm not hiding things from you. Part of the reason she agreed to marry me was because she was already involved with someone. If she got pregnant, she wanted to make sure the child had a father. She was going to use me. She was fucking her father's best friend. I didn't know this until after we'd been together, but she was sleeping with Vlad."

I shiver.

"By choice?"

"Yes. She thought she would marry me to ensure her safety once Vlad was gone because everyone knew it was only a matter of time. He was making poor decisions, and his health wasn't what it once was. But she's twisted enough to have actually cared about him. And in his fucked-up way, he cared about her. But they never wanted her father to know. Needless to say, he found out anyway when I told him I wouldn't marry a woman who slept with Vlad. I didn't say it outright, but I hinted heavily that she was only good for one thing as far as I was concerned. She moved to Boston right after Maks killed Vlad. She was like Vlad's Eva Braun. No one knew they were involved, but they loved each other in some sick and twisted way. She'd like to keep that part of her past buried. To do that, she owes me any favor I call in."

"Wait. Do you mean Yelena Petrova? I know Nadia Petrova. She's Timofey's girlfriend."

"Yes, and we all know Nadia's involved with Timofey. The Elite Group wanted her to marry Maks and pushed them to be together for a while."

"She disappeared for a while. I heard she came here to get back together with someone she dated after high school, and it was as a disaster. Timofey has had her pretty much under house arrest for the past year."

"It was a disaster. She tried to ruin things between Maks and Laura. Yelena is cut from the same cloth."

"I know. Nadia talks a lot when she's drunk. I went to parties with Nadia when I was still with Semyon, but after things must have ended with Maks. I didn't know it was you Nadia was talking about. I guess Yelena used to tell Nadia that she controlled Vlad and was stringing along some guy—you—while Nadia was fucking half the Ivankov bratva underneath her boyfriend's nose. Nadia was bitter that she hadn't become the *pakhan's* wife here in New York, so she was determined to be a *pakhan's* wife in Moscow. Did she come back here with one last hope to convince Maks?"

"Yeah."

"Clearly, that didn't work."

"It didn't. Pasha and I were in Moscow for a funeral during Maks and Laura's wedding. We met Nadia at the airport and delivered her to Timofey. We did the fucker a favor, and he repaid us by letting Vlad's brothers terrorize Niko and Ana."

"No government's politics will ever beat the shitshow that is the inner workings of a mafia."

"Not likely. Do you understand now that I'm not doing anything with Yelena other than getting information?"

"I do. Will she?"

He hesitates, and I shake my head as I push back my chair.

"When's the last time you fucked her, Misha? Tell me the truth."

"Seven years ago—nearly eight, actually—right before Maks became *pakhan*."

"Okay. Not fucked, hooked up with. When was the last time?"

"Kitty, I haven't touched her since I called things off. But she's the perpetual optimist. She'll think I've come crawling back. Believe me, I will set her straight immediately. The idea of her touching me makes my skin crawl. She's useful for this. I will never betray you or be unfaithful to you, but I will manipulate the fuck out of Yelena if it helps us find your sister."

"Do you think she knows we're together? Would she have heard?"

"Maybe. I don't know. Why?"

"Because I know Yelena."

Chapter Twenty-One

Misha

I didn't expect Kitty to know this woman from my past. A woman I wish I could forget ever meeting.

"How do you know Yelena?"

"She, Nadia, and I went to grade school together before they moved here. She and I were in Moscow at the same time during my last trip, and she felt it necessary to share a little piece of info I could have lived without ever knowing. Misha, she wasn't just fucking Vlad while she was with you. She fucked Semyon while he and I were together, and she came to visit Nadia. I didn't know she lived in Boston now. I assumed she was still somewhere here in New York."

I don't know what I expected to see in Kitty's gaze as she tells me about her ex-boyfriend being unfaithful. I already knew he had been, but I assumed he'd only been fucking whores. The ones at brothels, not bitches like Yelena. Kitty's completely emotionless as she tells me. It's like she's telling someone else's life story, not something that happened to her personally.

"Misha, are you certain she'll talk to you just because you knew she was fucking a guy who's been dead for eight years? Would she talk to me either to gloat that not only did she fuck my boyfriends, but she also knows who took my sister? Or does she have enough of a conscience these days to tell me who took my sister because she fucked my old boyfriend?"

"She and Nadia are basically the same person. She wants me to keep her secret because she's got some guy she's fucking these days who thinks she's next to perfect. And her grandfather still supports her now that her dad's dead. He's in Moscow, and as far as I know, never found out about her relationship with Vlad. She doesn't want either of those things ruined."

"We talk to her together, Misha. I start with her. If I can't convince her, then you have a go."

"I'm not saying no, Kitty. I'm asking you to let me think about it for a moment."

"Fair enough."

Kitty's brow furrows.

"I just realized I don't know why you think Yelena would know anything. I got irritated too fast. Why would she?"

"The man she's fucking is the Boston *krye*."

"She's with an Albanian? Her grandfather's still supporting her, and she's in a relationship with the head of the Boston *fis*?"

Bratva means brotherhood in Russian. The equivalent in Albanian is a *fis*, which translates basically to family clan. I think I've heard it called a *fare*, too. I learned what I could about any other syndicate years ago.

I shrug before I answer Kitty.

"She's not in Moscow or here, causing trouble. That's all her grandfather cares about. He'll do what he has to, whether it's sending money or turning a blind eye, if it keeps her from causing shit with us or the Podolskaya."

"I suppose one thief is as good as another. The man will have sworn the *besa,* so maybe that's enough for Yelena's grandfather."

The bratva has the *Vory v Zakone,* the thief's code. The Albanian's call their version the *besa.* It's unlikely Kitty or Yelena know anything more than their names since it's not exactly something members like to broadcast.

"Probably. But it makes her a good source of information. What she doesn't already know, she can find out."

"You think she'll get her boyfriend to tell her? Is her pillow talk that good?"

I can't help my grimace before I answer.

"She makes Nadia look like a virgin. She fucked more members of the Ivankovs than Nadia did, and that was pretty much anyone not related to Maks."

"If she fucked more men than Nadia, does that mean she slept with someone in your family?"

I don't want to look at Kitty. It's more like shame than embarrassment. She stares at me until my gaze meets hers, and I sigh.

"Pasha and I..."

She can't seem to help it when her nose curls and her chin tucks. I can practically hear what she's thinking: Gross.

"It's not like our swords crossed."

Now she tries not to laugh, and I know I sound offended and defensive. The moment of shame is gone, but the embarrassment takes its place.

"You could have had a thousand threesomes with whomever you wanted, Misha. That's your past. Okay, maybe not a thousand. I don't love knowing you even had one. I suspect it happened more than once from your expression."

I shift uncomfortably. Can we please move on?

"Anyway...Damn it, I don't remember what I was just saying."

"That if her boyfriend won't tell her, she's been with enough men that someone'll know something. Are you sure she hasn't changed?"

"Maybe. Anything's possible, but most leopards don't change their spots."

"Fine. When do we leave?"

"As soon as we get the Kutsenko Partners' jet fueled and ready to go. We should go home and pack."

She freezes in fear. I stand and walk around the table to her before I squat beside her chair. She turns to face me as I take her hands.

"*Kiska*, I know it's scary to go back because Yuri clearly knows things he shouldn't. We don't have to stay there tonight. We can come back here, or we can go to one of my cousins' homes. But we need to get our things."

"I know."

She whispers, and I see the idea of going back to the loft is like revisiting the trauma Yuri already inflicted.

"Do you want to stay here with Sergei and Anton while I get stuff for us? Or do you want to go somewhere else?"

"I don't want either of us to go back there."

She clutches my hands as though I might walk away, or worse, someone might take me away. She's holding on so tightly that it actually hurts.

"I've already had the place swept for bugs."

"And?"

"My men found nothing in our loft, but there were listening devices in the one next to ours."

"How do you know that? Did those people let your men in?"

I don't answer out loud, which is an answer in and of itself. There are four lofts on my floor, each occupying the length of the building's walls. I own all four. I have tenants in the other three, but I've considered knocking down walls and combining at least one of the other ones with the unit I live in. However, since meeting Kitty, I've been thinking about renting all four and moving to Queens with her.

"They just broke in?"

"Not exactly. I own those units, so I have keys. I just didn't ask my tenants' permission. And it's just as well. Yuri's men would have stripped the place if I waited to ask, and it would have freaked those tenants out. I'm certain they had no idea anyone else had been in there or that any listening devices were in the adjacent rooms."

"How did he know about my sports bra? He might have heard us having sex and what we do while we are, but how'd he know what I was wearing?"

"You said goodbye to me at the door after I opened it. He must have hacked the security feed because you would have appeared on the hallway camera while we kissed. He didn't hear you moving around in the bedroom, so he must have assumed you hadn't changed."

"I felt safer at my place in the Bronx."

"I know, baby. Do you want to stay here with Sergei and Anton?"

She nods, and I wrap my arms around her. She rests her head on my shoulder with her arms tucked between us as she fists my suit coat.

"Daddy, I'm really scared."

"I know, baby girl. You're safe with my family. My dad and Grigori will come over while I'm gone."

"Don't they guard your mom and Alina?"

"They're at Bogdan and Christina's along with Aunt

Galina. They're babysitting and cooking while Bogdan and Christina go out on a date. It'll be their first one since Lev was born. They know any of our moms would be fine by herself, but I know having all three makes the new parents more comfortable."

"I really don't want you to go back there, Misha. I have a horrible feeling."

"What if I go with some of the others?"

She's slow to nod, but eventually she agrees.

"Take three or four of them, please."

"You really feel that uneasy?"

"Yes."

"Then I'll borrow clothes from Sergei. We can get whatever you want and toothbrushes once we're in Boston."

She appears ready to agree, then her shoulders slump.

"My birth control pills are at the loft."

We stare at each other a long moment, both thinking about the family we've talked about starting. This is not the time, but it's obvious the thought crosses both of our minds.

"Aren't you due to pick up a refill today or tomorrow? Can you start the new pack?"

"It's definitely not ideal, but I could. I'd rather have my period be off by a few days than send you back there right now. But we can't buy me new clothes just because I'm being a pussy about you going back there."

"Yes, we can."

"Misha, I know you're rich. But this is ridiculous and wasteful."

"We have the means, Kitty. It's not like we do this every day."

She looks toward Anton's front door before she sighs.

"All right. I just really don't feel right about either of us going there right now."

"Do you want to spend the night here?"

"Does that mean Sergei's or Anton's place?"

"Same difference. Wherever they put us. Or would you rather go to my parents' or one of my cousins'?"

"Your dad and Grigori are coming here?"

I nod.

"This would be nice. Misha, I know I'm probably making a big deal over nothing, but Yuri terrifies me in a way no one else does."

"Let's find Anton and Sergei. Once we know where they want us to stay, I'll ask my dad to stop by the pharmacy to pick up your prescription and some toothbrushes. We can overnight stuff from Amazon and leave tomorrow."

"Your dad can't—"

Her face flames red, and I cut her off with a kiss.

"As much as my parents are counting on me for grandkids, they don't expect them right this minute. He'll understand. And he doesn't even have to know what he's picking up."

"Fine."

We find my brother and Anton in Anton's gym. Go figure. Sergei likes to lift weights the most out of us, so he's bench pressing something ridiculous while Anton spots him. They tell us which room we can use, and we cross back over to Sergei's place. We'll have it to ourselves tonight since my dad and Grigori will stay in Anton's place. There's an intercom and cameras throughout both places, so I know we're safe even if everyone else is in the other townhouse.

I run us a bath, and Kitty and I soak until the water is cold. We're in bed with the TV on by eight o'clock. We're content to cuddle like an old married couple while Kitty orders some clothes online, and it isn't long before we both fall asleep in the middle of a show.

The flight to Boston is nothing but turbulence, and it sums up how Kitty and I feel. We're traveling with my dad, Sergei, Anton, and Grigori again. Kitty's most comfortable around them, and it means that the rest of the husbands don't have to leave their wives at home. It's not that they won't travel. They still do. But we try not to pull anyone away from their family life if we can avoid it.

It's just over an hour-long flight from the private airfield in New Jersey to the one just outside of Boston. We took off this morning once the items from Amazon arrived. Now we're getting out of the car in front of Yelena's house. It's smaller than what she'd told me she expected, but I'm certain it's filled with plenty of expensive belongings. I hold Kitty's hand as we climb the steps, and I ring the doorbell. The shock on Yelena's face is comical. When she recovers, she sneers at Kitty and glares at me.

"Yelena, don't you remember our teacher, Anya Makarova, used to tell you that your face would stick if you kept making that expression?"

"What do you want, Katerina?"

"Why'd Yuri take my sister?"

Yelena glances at me, then tries to slam the door in our faces. My foot is faster than her and jams between the doorframe and the door. I push it open with my right hand while my left continues to hold Kitty's.

"I don't know anything about your sister, Katerina. And I want absolutely nothing to do with that man. Don't say his name. Don't even think it near me."

"But you can find out, Yelena. You and Larisa were friends when you were kids. You know what Yuri did to me because your grandfather went with my father to find him. He did it to me again, Yelena."

The pain in Kitty's voice tears at me, and I want nothing more than to shield her from having to say any of this. I want to throttle Yelena until she shares every secret she knows.

Yelena won't meet our gaze as she shakes her head.

"He did the same thing to me, Katerina. I never talk about him anymore. I want nothing to do with anything he's connected to. I don't want to remember that."

I speak up.

"When?"

Her glare returns as she lifts her eyes to meet mine.

"Right after Vlad died. I had no one to protect me. I had no one to turn to."

"That isn't true. We might not have been together, but you know damn well that you could have turned to me about something like this. You know Maks would have hunted him down and made sure he never breathed under the same sun as you."

"It didn't feel that way at the time, and it was while I was in Moscow right after Maks killed Vlad. Your cousin wasn't who I wanted to turn to for anything back then. Now I'm with someone who does protect me. I have nothing else to say to either of you."

"He worked with some Cuban in Moscow and kidnapped her. He sold her, Yelena. Who knows what's happened to her between Moscow and Boston? She was in Texas and maybe Mexico. I know she's in Boston now, but I need your help. I need to know everything about Yuri and his connections here. I have to save her. You'd do the same for Nadia or for Inessa."

I remember Inessa is Yelena's younger sister. They weren't close, but some guy tried to intimidate her at school, and Yelena asked me to protect her sister. It was the only altruistic thing she ever asked of me. I made sure the guy couldn't go anywhere near Inessa again.

Yelena stares at Kitty so long that I think she'll just try slamming the door in our faces again, but eventually she nods.

"I'll ask Besnik when he gets home."

"Will he tell Yuri?"

"No. They don't get along, so Besnik won't do anything to help Yuri. Just the opposite. Yuri's father may be *krye*, but the people in the community here think he's a sell out to the Russians. He isn't in town often, but the few times he's come, he's waved his money around and barked orders. It doesn't sit well with people. They're loyal to Besnik, and not many have ties to the old country. Yuri and his father don't impress anyone."

"Thank you."

"Katerina, does Yuri know you're here?"

"He's probably figured it out. He sent me proof Larisa is alive, and it showed she was in Boston. He has to know I would come right away."

"Then expect him to take you, too."

"I'm counting on that."

I've remained silent, but now I squeeze Kitty's hand until her fingers flex. That wasn't what we agreed upon on the flight.

"Take care of yourself, Misha. And take care of Katerina. She's way too good for you."

Before I can respond, Kitty hands Yelena her phone.

"Put your number in and text yourself. Then you'll have mine."

"A burner? Is Yuri tracking you?"

Kitty gives Yelena a look that says don't be stupid. We all come from the same world. Kitty won't use a phone that's easy for someone to trace, especially not when we don't completely trust Yelena.

"Fine. I'll text you again tonight after I talk to Besnik."

Kitty waits for Yelena to send herself a text, then she takes her phone back as she responds.

"Thank you, Yelena. I appreciate it."

I step back, and Yelena closes the door. We'd already driven around the block three times before we stopped. There's a safety detail parked outside of Yelena's house, and one at the end of the street. But her house backs up to another one with no way for Besnik to position guards without the neighbors wondering. It made it easy to drop Anton and Sergei off before my dad pulled up outside Yelena's house.

Kitty and I get back into the car before my dad drives around the block, and we pick up Sergei and Anton. Grigori twists to see all of us from the front passenger seat. He looks at Anton as he speaks.

"Any problems?"

"No. The scan showed no radio frequencies coming from the house. I programmed the jammer just in case and slipped into the walk-out basement. The window was way too easy to jimmy open, and the key was in the door once I was inside. She didn't notice Sergei moving through the house to drop the bugs."

Sergei already has his laptop open while Anton gets his out of his bag. They're sitting next to each other in the second row of the SUV while Kitty and I are in the third. I can only see the back of their heads, but I can see whatever programs they're running. It means nothing to me, but they're typing and clicking away. It makes me think this is how they must have spent many nights during college. They went to UPenn together and studied computer science. They were roommates the entire time, so I don't think I'm exaggerating. They're perfectly nerdy and techie for each other.

Kitty leans forward and taps my brother's shoulder.

"Sergei, what's the range on that? Do we have to stay near here? Or can we go to our hotel?"

"All of it runs off cell towers and Wi-Fi. Between the two, we can keep track from anywhere. I routed the frequencies through so many channels that anyone trying to trace it, if they even find any of the devices, will just spin their wheels."

Kitty sits back as we drive to our hotel. Anton and Sergei put in earbuds to listen to something, but I don't know what since nothing's happening on their computer screens. I can tell Kitty's straining to see what they're doing without breathing down their necks. She finally can't resist.

"Do you hear something?"

Anton looks sheepishly over his shoulder and shakes his head.

"Um, we're listening to the Brazil-Argentina match. Right now, Brazil is up one-nil. I'm winning, and Sergei's annoyed."

"Football?"

Clearly, five years hasn't been long enough to get Kitty to call is soccer. I roll my eyes. I should have known. She glances at me, and I grin.

"My brother never picks the right team. Put me down for a hundred on Brazil."

Grigori laughs and shakes his head.

"Nope. Sergei's right. I have two hundred riding on Argentina. So does Radomir."

"I don't agree with any of you. I put down a hundred that it's a draw."

I look at Kitty, and she shrugs one shoulder.

"I grew up watching it too. Their rivalry is practically as strong as it was thirty years ago. Neither will let the other win. I say it'll be a tie."

We spend the rest of the ride to the hotel discussing soccer teams and the next World Cup. It seems like a good distraction for Kitty, and I can tell she relaxes. But the moment we get to our suite, I can tell it was all for nothing. The men we traveled with are outside the door or sitting at the table inside. It's an immediate reminder.

"I'm going to unpack, Misha. Call me if anything happens."

I watch Kitty go into our bedroom, where our luggage is already waiting for us, and reach into her purse for her phone just before she shuts the door. She made it clear she wants to be alone. I may have an abundance of patience most days; however, forcing myself to give her space might kill me.

Chapter Twenty-Two

Kitty

I need to call my parents and give them an update. I hate that there is so little to tell them after all this time. Something is better than nothing, but I don't want to tell them that Larisa signaled that she's been drugged or beaten, and her captors aren't giving her enough to eat and drink. It won't surprise them, but that doesn't make it any easier to admit.

I know Misha's wondering why I walked away and shut the door on him since I've been practically glued to him throughout all of this. He's asked many times if I need space, and I've always said no. Now, not only do I tell him to leave me alone, I'm the one to walk away. I know he'll respect my wishes, but I know I could have been a little more thoughtful and explained why.

I dial my parents' number, knowing my dad is using burner phones just like I am. It rings so many times I fear they won't answer. It's late at night there, but I assume the phone is near one of them. The longer it takes, the more I fear something's happened to them. So, I nearly cry when I hear my father's voice. We speak Russian in hushed voices. I don't fear Misha or the others hearing me, but I worry about being too loud through the phone and someone hearing me on my father's end.

"Are you and Mama all right?"

"Yes. We're back home. Everyone thinks you've given up and gone back to America."

"And they believe you've given up, too?"

"They believe we've slowed down and are losing hope. But we're still looking, Katerina. We'll always keep looking."

"I know, Papa."

"Do you have news? Are you safe?"

"I'm safe and with Misha. We're in Boston with Radomir, Grigori, Sergei, and Anton. Papa, I have news, but I don't have many answers. Yuri called me yesterday. It was his men who took Larisa from her apartment. He sent me proof that Larisa's alive, and it brought us here. We have someone here with connections to the Albanian community, and we think that person can get us more information. Men Misha knows in New York told us it was a Cuban man who planned Larisa's kidnapping and has had something to do with where she's been since coming here."

"Yuri? Why?"

"He said because he couldn't have me. I don't believe that's all of it. He obviously has connections here in America. He could have come after me long before I met Misha. If it were really about me, then he would have already taken me. With no family in the States, I was an even easier target than in Moscow. I don't know how an Albanian-Russian connected with a Cuban to form this deal. I don't know why a Cuban is interested in Larisa. I'm certain they brought her through Miami because it's an easy entry point for a Cuban and because plenty of people are trafficked through that city. But I don't know how the Cuban or Yuri have connections to Mexican Cartels."

"Cartels? What do they have to do with anything?"

"The men Misha knows in New York told us someone took Larisa to Texas for a while and might have forced her to cross back and forth from Mexico. They would have used her as a drug mule if that's the case."

I don't want to think that they forced her into prostitution, and that's why she went back and forth.

"And now she's in Boston? Are there a lot of Cubans or Mexicans there?"

"I don't know. I don't think so, but I've never been here before. There are other Albanians, though. I saw Yelena today, Papa. She's involved with the Albanian leader here, so she might be able to get me more information. She said the community doesn't like Yuri, but that doesn't change the fact that he has money and influence. I think he's forcing men here to keep Larisa."

"What's next?"

My father is going to lose his shit. Misha's going to lose his shit. But what other choice is there other than waiting and praying?

"I'm going to offer to take Larisa's place."

"No. Absolutely not. I'm not losing both my daughters. It's bad enough that I allowed you to go around Moscow with only that dipshit Semyon to protect you. This is not happening."

"Papa, it's the fastest choice we have. Larisa looked all right in the photo, but she used our code. She's not okay. I don't know what they're doing to her, but I don't think she can last much longer. Yuri will take me, and Misha will kill him. There is no way Misha will let Yuri or anyone else keep me from him. I know this is dangerous, but I know Misha will move Heaven and Earth to protect me. He's going to hate the idea, too. But there just isn't a better way."

"And if Yuri kills you before Misha can rescue you or Larisa?"

"Yuri won't. If I'm dead, he can't torment me. He can't lord his control over me. That's what he really wants."

As I talk to my father, pieces drop into place that were just jumbled in my mind before.

"Papa, can you hold on a moment? I want Misha to hear this. I think I figured something out."

"Of course. You're on a burner, right?"

"Yes. Hold on."

I cross the room and open the door. I should have known Misha would watch it. I wave him over, and he crosses the suite with long strides. I slip my free arm around Misha's waist and hold the phone between us. The cheap thing doesn't have a speaker option, so I turn up the volume all the way.

"Papa, can you hear me?"

"Yes."

It's quieter, but his voice is still clear.

"I don't know why a Cuban was doing business in Russia, but I suspect it was with Yuri. I think the man and his friends met Larisa and her friends in the club because they were there with a purpose. I don't know if this guy was grooming Larisa to take her from the start, and that's why he asked her on the date, or he took her because Larisa rejected him. I think it was the former, and her rejecting him just made him more determined. If he was there looking for women, then maybe that was his business with Yuri. Maybe he asked Yuri for help once he made up his mind about Larisa. I don't know. But Yuri used Albanian men he has in Moscow to take her. Russians would have stayed far away from a bratva daughter. The Cuban had to have paid Yuri, and then the Cuban brought her to America. He sold her or passed her along to the people in Texas. I just don't understand how she wound up in Boston or under Yuri's control."

My dad is mhmming along with me as I speak. I pause to see if he has anything to say.

"Do you think Larisa is just a coincidence Yuri seized upon?"

"Maybe. Larisa is gorgeous, so they both saw the money they could make. But Yuri also saw a way to hurt me yet again. It's a game to him he keeps coming back to play whenever he gets a chance. Maybe he doesn't have as much control as he wants people to think, so he exerts it over me because he thinks he can. Who knows? But he knows I'll do anything to protect my sister, including giving myself up to him. He's baiting me, and I know it. Whether he'll trade Larisa for me or he takes me too, me going to him is the best way to get Larisa back."

"No. Absolutely not. No way."

It's Misha's turn to disagree, and I expected it.

"Misha, I already told my dad that's my plan. I also explained there isn't any chance that you'll let Yuri keep me. You have resources I don't, and neither do my parents. I'm confident you can get both of us out of there."

"If I can get you out, then I can get Larisa out without involving you. You are not turning yourself over to that madman. I can't guarantee he won't hurt you before I can get you both out. And don't you dare say you'll accept whatever happens. I will not."

The resolution in Misha's voice would intimidate most people into obeying, but not me.

"I'm not excited by this idea. But unless something better comes along and soon, then that's the best choice we have."

"To do what? Seriously, Kitty. If you believe I can get you both out, then why can't you believe I can get just Larisa out? What's to be gained from you being there?"

Misha's eyes narrow before he shakes his head.

"No. You want to torture him and kill him? Fine. But I'll take him somewhere secure. You are more likely to die trying without me. I'll give you the ice pick or the thumb screws. Whatever. But thinking you can get to him on your own is just begging for him to rape you again and kill you this time."

"We get Larisa out, *and* we get him, Misha. You might free Larisa, but that doesn't mean we'll have a chance to stop him from coming back again and again. He'll want me personally. When he's near me, then someone—anyone—can kill him. But if I'm not involved, there's no guarantee he'll come out of wherever he's hiding."

Misha knows I'm right. I see it in his expression, but he's going to keep fighting me on this. My dad's been quiet as Misha and I go back and forth. I'm certain he sides with Misha, but he also knows I have a point. There's resignation in his voice when he speaks.

"Misha, what can you do to ensure Katerina's safety if she does this?"

"If I send her to Yuri alone, then there isn't nearly enough I can do. The best I can hope for is to shoot him before he touches Kitty. Without me or someone else guarding her, she's at his mercy. I will not agree to that. He won't believe she's alone, even if it looks that way. Kitty, he could shoot you or snap your neck before anyone can stop him just because he thinks you brought men with you."

"I'm not saying this is the way to do it. I'm saying it's what's likely to work right now. Until we know what Besnik says to Yelena, this is what we have to work with."

"No, it's not. We know where Larisa was yesterday. If Yuri hasn't moved her, then my family and I go in there and free her. You stay here at the hotel. That's what's most likely to work."

"And if he has moved her? How long will it take to find her

again? If I turn myself over to him, then we'll find out much sooner."

"Not if you're dead."

Misha barks his response. He's letting me see how angry I'm making him, but I'm not ready to back down. It's not like I don't know how dangerous this is. It's not like I don't know all the ways in which this could and probably will fail. But no one else has presented a better option. Until something else comes along, this is the best we have.

"Katerina, let Misha plan this. He has far more experience than you do. He's the Ivankov's best *avotoritet*. He leads missions and knows what he's doing. Anton is their best strategist. That's why he's their *obshchak*. I'm not saying you might not have to use your idea after all, but please, let them come up with something else first."

"I will, and that's what I would prefer. But we cannot rule my idea out."

"Kitty, we won't. But I won't agree with it. If you go through with it, it's not because I support it. However, I will do everything I can to keep you safe. When I say everything, you need to know that I don't exaggerate. There are no limits. You may see me do things I wish I could shield you from. You may see the monster I really am."

Admitting that scares the shit out of Misha. I can tell even if he's back to masking his emotions. I know because it's his greatest fear for us. That I won't truly accept all parts of him, and that I'll reject him for the things he can do and has done to other men. He's never said it aloud, but I know it's often on his mind.

"Papa, that's all the news we have right now. I'll call you back when we decide what to do next. I'll make sure you know what's happening."

"Thank you. I'll let Mama know what we've talked about. I hope we hear from you very soon."

"Same. I love you, Papa."

"I love you too. Bye."

"Bye."

I hang up the phone and toss it onto the bed before I wrap my other arm around Misha. I go onto my toes and press a soft kiss to his lips before I cup his left cheek. I kiss along his jaw and other cheek before I come back to his mouth. I pull back and settle on my feet.

"Daddy, I know this scares you, especially the parts where I could get hurt or I could see what you're truly capable of. I think I can guess, but the truth is probably way darker. I know you never want me to see that. But I've known from the start there's that part of you. I tried to get away from this world because I didn't want to be around this type of violence every day for the rest of my life. That was before I met you. My father loves my mother, my sister, and me. He's kind and gentle to us, but I also know his role isn't what yours has been. The men I know who've been enforcers aren't like you at all. They are who I wanted to escape. You don't take any of this lightly. If I see that monster, it's because it's what's necessary. None of this is fun for you. You get no pleasure out of this. Who you are with me is what matters. I can live with the man you have to be sometimes because I love all of you."

"You say that now..."

"Misha, you have skills because Vlad trained you. You do it to protect your people and your family, not for shits and giggles. Vlad might have enjoyed it because he was a psychopath, but he made you who you are to protect what's important in our world. The capacity for that violence isn't limited to just those who learned what you did. That innate drive to protect isn't based on skills. Just because you know how to do things I don't doesn't mean I'm not capable of the same darkness. *She's my sister.* If either of us is a monster to get her back and end Yuri, then so be it. I'll sleep like a baby every night for the rest of my life."

"You say that, *kiska*. But until you see that kind of violence —until you commit that kind of violence—you just don't know."

"Are you scared that I'll see it then be afraid you could do that sort of thing to me?"

"Partly."

"Misha, there isn't a chance in any universe you would ever hurt me. You would send me away before you ever did. You would hide from me before you ever did. If we're talking about the lengths you'd go to protect me, then harming me is the last thing you'd ever do."

"And if you can no longer respect me? Stand to look at me?"

"You don't derive pleasure from this. You might feel satisfied that the threat is gone, but it's not like you get off on hurting people. Even at your darkest, I'm certain you are methodical. You only do what is necessary, no more and no less. If I see this monster in you, it's because that's what's needed. It might terrify me or disgust me in the moment, but it won't stop me from respecting you. What you do, you do because in our world, it's what's right. Most people would call me morally gray and you morally black. But we don't live by those same standards. I will never respect you less for doing whatever you do to protect your family or me."

Misha doesn't look convinced, but he nods. I can't imagine how the other men in his family have had conversations like this with their wives while they were still dating. I can't imagine how the women reacted or how they accepted it. None of them grew up like I did. The "civilized" world sees all of us connected to organized crime as morally ambiguous, at best.

But to us, it's all very clear cut. Right is protecting what's dear to you. Wrong is anyone who threatens what you love. Right is doing any and everything when it's needed. Wrong is giving up or giving in. The other women must understand that, agree with it, because I've seen the couples together. There is no hesitation between the wives and husbands. The love flows unconditionally both ways. I need Misha to understand I feel that way too.

"I hope you can remember that when the times comes, Kitty."

"Have as much faith in me, Daddy, as I have in you."

"I love you, *malyshka*. I never want to lose that."

"Then just don't let go."

Our kiss is slow, but it's like a long fuse that finally explodes into a huge blast. He lifts me off my feet, and I wrap my legs around his waist. He backs me against the wall as I tug at his shirt. I slide my hands underneath and over the scorching skin that covers his chest and abs. He kisses down my throat, then back up to behind my ear.

"Daddy, please. I need you."

I need to show him I have no reservations, that I love and desire him as much now as before he admitted his fears.

He puts me on my feet long enough for us to shed our clothes, then he picks me up again. He carries me to the bathroom and shuts the door. He spins and presses me against it. We're as far from his—our—family as we can get. One arm supports me under my ass while his other hand fists my hair. His kiss is savage as he thrusts into me. He swallows my scream from how rough he is. I'm wet, but not as wet as usual. He doesn't hurt me, and I like the pain that comes from his forcefulness because I know he doesn't intend to harm me. We move together as he pounds into me, my back hitting the door over and over.

"Fucking come, *malyshka*."

"I'm close. Just more."

He does as I wish, and it's the roughest sex we've had that isn't kinky. My fingernails graze his scalp as I pull his hair. He releases mine, so both of his hands can guide me, lifting me up and down his cock.

"I told you to come. Don't make me wait, baby girl. I'm not feeling very patient."

The gravel in his voice is a major turn on. I move, so my clit rubs against him. I explode with a growl that I don't recognize comes from me.

"You better fucking come too, Daddy. Your dick is mine, and I decide it's time for you to come."

"Is that so, baby?"

He pulls out of me, puts me on my feet, and spins me toward the door. He grabs my hips and impales me. Once more, he grabs my hair, and he reaches around to pinch my nipple. He squeezes and twists so hard I whimper. He presses me between him and the door, so I can't move.

"My dick is yours, but you don't give the orders."

"I do today. Your dick, your cum, and everything else is mine. *I* decide what I want and for how long. You are mine for keeps, Daddy. Do not pull away from me. Do not put distance between us, or I will be the one who edges you."

I reach behind me and spread my ass cheeks.

"Fuck me in the ass, Daddy."

"You are a brave little kitten to talk to your Daddy like this."

He pulls out of me and inches his cock into my ass.

"You think you're in control and fucking me, Daddy. Uh-uh. You gave me your dick to fuck. No matter how rough you are, you're inside me. You're giving, and I'm taking, Daddy. I've decided you're mine, Misha. I'm not letting you go. Fuck whether or not you tell me to. You are *mine*."

His hand lands hard on my ass over and over. I push my hips back and take it as he also keeps fucking me. I made my point. I taunted him into this spanking, but I also took some of the burden from him. He knows now that I'm in this for good. I won't back out, no matter what. I've laid my claim, and God help anyone foolish enough to stop me from having a future with Misha.

Chapter Twenty-Three

Misha

I get what Kitty's doing. Normally, I wouldn't be down for the power exchange in her direction, but it's working. I feel better. Not just as I get off hard in her ass. Fuck, she's tight, and it feels amazing. I feel better knowing that she completely accepts me. She won't give up on me just because there's a part of me I loathe. I kiss across her shoulder before I kiss her neck.

"I love you, *kiska*."

"I love you, *papochka*. Are you okay with what I said?"

"Very. Thank you. You understood what I needed."

My arms wrap around her, but it's an affectionate embrace, not one to dominate her. She turns her head and presses a quick kiss to my lips as her hands cover mine over her belly. Just like yesterday when we talked about her birth control, I know we're both thinking about what the future might hold.

I withdraw from her and move to turn on the shower. We don't waste time in there despite the temptation to go another round. We're dressed and back out with the others within five minutes of finishing having mind-blowing sex. It's a wonder that I can ever think straight now that I'm with Kitty. The sex is always mind-blowing.

"We talked to Vadim and let him know what's happening."

I fill the others in on the conversation Kitty and I had with her dad. I can tell the others are as excited at the prospect of Kitty going anywhere near Yuri as Vadim and I were. But when she explains her reasoning, I can see they understand there is some merit to the suggestion. However, it's my dad who puts up a bigger argument than any of us.

"Katerina, I'm not your father, but I hope to be your father-in-law soon. You're an adult, so the decision is yours. But I think this is foolish. I think you're only going to make things worse, and we'll wind up with two people to save instead of one. I'll support you because I care about you and Misha. However, if it were my decision alone, I would forbid it. This is just begging for disaster."

"I understand, but we don't have that many choices if Yelena offers us nothing."

"There are plenty of other choices, and none of them involves you risking your life. We bribe our way in. We force our way in. We sneak our way in. We kill Yuri and leave no reason for those men to do his bidding. We kill the men holding her. We destroy Yuri's businesses and force him to let Larisa go. We threaten whoever is most important to Yuri. We put a hit on his father to force his hand. We tell his father we're going to kill Yuri if he doesn't let Larisa go. We do not have to send you in. We can do all of those things if we have to. But you being within reach of that man is just a bomb waiting to explode in our faces. You may have grown up around the bratva, but you are not bratva. You don't know what we do and what we can do. If you trust Misha, then you need to extend that trust to the rest of us. This is not the first time we've freed hostages."

Kitty stares at my dad for a long time before her lips press between her teeth, and she nods. My dad wraps his arms around her and kisses the top of her head.

"*Dover'tes' nam, pozhaluysta. Ty moya doch', tak chto tvoya sestra mne tozhe kak doch'. My ne poterpim neudachu.*" Trust us, please. You are my daughter, so your sister is like my own daughter, too. We won't fail.

"*Spasibo, otets.*" Thank you, Father.

It's a little formal, but I'm certain she isn't calling my father Dad, Daddy, Papa, or *papochka* any time soon. Two of those names are for her actual father, and two are for me. I wink at her as she looks at me from within my father's embrace. Her cheeks flame. She pulls back and offers my dad a soft smile.

"I will. But I need you to agree to at least consider my idea if it comes to it."

"We will, Katerina. We know it's hard to wait when you feel you're so close, and it's even harder to feel you can't help."

She looks over at Sergei and Anton, who're still at their computers but also still have their earbuds in. She grins at them.

"Am I winning?"

Anton scowls, and Sergei rolls his eyes and shakes his head. Grigori ruffles Anton's hair. It's hilarious to watch since Grigori is hardly small, but Anton easily has thirty pounds on his father and an inch or two. Anton huffs before he answers.

"It's two-two, and it's almost the end of the second half."

"It's not a knockout round, is it?"

"No. So no overtime."

"Pity. I would love to watch a penalty kick shootout."

Kitty laughs as my brother and Anton wear matching scowls. Neither of them is excited to lose their money to Kitty, but the rest of us don't mind. They both went to university on soccer scholarships, so they take the sport even more seriously than your typical European.

"Is the game on TV? Can I watch as I win your money?"

"You know, it's a good thing I always wanted a little sister instead of Misha."

"Ouch, brother."

My dad's reaching for the remote, so I flick Sergei off.

"Mikhail."

I roll my eyes and shake my head.

"Sorry, Papa."

Sergei snickers, so I flick him off again, anyway. Kitty tsks.

"Misha, be nice to your brother. It's not his fault you got all the charm and good looks, and he's as prickly as a porcupine. Let him have his sports."

"Papa, explain to me again why I couldn't have been an only child."

"Have you met your mother and me? Be glad we stopped at just the two of you."

My dad grins, and it's easy to see where Sergei and I get our charm, even if we look more like Mama's side of the family. If I didn't know better, he could be our brother rather than our dad. He looks boyish and roguish when he smiles. I get why Mama fell for him.

Sergei and I respond at the same time.

"Disgusting."

One thing I love most about my family is that we have fun together. We can discuss really heavy shit one moment and tease each other the next. It's what keeps us all sane. If we dwelled on all the darkness in our lives, it would consume us. Instead, we try to be as normal a family as possible most of the time.

Anton and Sergei keep working, presumably listening and watching Yelena's place, while the rest of us watch the soccer match. Kitty stands up and cheers before sticking her hand under my nose. I pretend to snap my teeth at her fingers, but she just wiggles them. She accepts the money I wagered and lost, but she refuses to take anything from my dad or Radomir. She insists that Sergei and Anton concede they were wrong, and she was right. She slips the money back to me after dinner. The rest of the day passes slowly until nine o'clock when Besnik finally comes home.

Anton zooms in on his screen, so we can see a grainy picture of Besnik walking into the bedroom where Yelena is sitting up in bed. Sergei turns up the volume on his computer, so we can hear their conversation.

"I've missed you, *e dashura ime.*"

Sergei's got an Albanian to English translation running subtitles just in case. Besnik calls Yelena his darling. There's sincerity in the man's voice. God bless if he's found anything darling about the woman. I never did.

"*Moya lyubov'*, I need to talk to you." My love.

Is she diving straight into it?

"What's wrong?"

"Apparently, Yuri kidnapped a woman I grew up with."

"Did that bastard contact you? Threaten you? I'll fucking—"

"No, Besnik. I haven't seen or talked to him in years. But he brought the woman to Boston. I don't know how or why. I hoped maybe you'd heard something."

"Yelena, how do you know this?"

"I told you. I grew up with her. I heard about it."

"From whom?"

"I'll tell you, but you need to tell me why you sound so cagey. Did you already know about Larisa?"

"Yes."

"Besnik!"

"It's not my business, Yelena."

We watch Yelena throw back the covers and get out of bed.

"Yes, it is. Anything that fucker does in this city is your business. You're the *krye* here, not him. I don't give a shit who his father is. This is America, not Albania. If you knew about this and did nothing to stop him, then you're no better than him."

"I don't fucking buy and sell people, Yelena. You know that. But I also don't stick my nose in other people's business unless it's good for my people. Getting involved in this shitshow with some Russian woman isn't good for any of us."

"Some Russian woman? I told you I know her. We were friends, Besnik."

"Do you want me to talk to Yuri? Ask him to let her go just because his captive is friends with a woman he once raped? Absolutely not. I will not bring you up to him under any circumstances. I don't want him to think about you. I don't want him to hear about you. I don't want him to know a damn thing about you. It's safer that way. He won't hurt you, and I won't have to kill him."

"Besnik, he took Larisa Vasilieva. Her father is Podolskaya bratva. That's bad enough because my family is too. But it's way—way, way, way—worse than that. Larisa's sister, Katerina, is with Mikhail Andreyev."

"The man you were supposed to marry?"

"Yes. But that's not even remotely my point. Misha is Maksim Kutsenko's cousin. He's Ivankov bratva in New York. Misha was some young guy with potential when I knew him. I don't know his position now, but I guaran-fucking-tee you he's a big deal. He might not be Elite Group—though it wouldn't surprise me if he were—he's probably among the top ranking. If Yuri has his girlfriend's sister, then this is going to explode in all of our faces. I'm assuming Katerina is only his girlfriend. But my guess is she's more likely at least his fiancée, if not his wife. Misha doesn't just date. None of them do. They're either single or married. Nothing in between in that family. That makes Larisa his sister. You will never, ever meet a more protective family. I'm telling you, Besnik, this is really bad. Like we're caught in the middle and likely to die for it bad."

"Shh, sweetheart. I'll see what I can do. But I still don't want Yuri to think you're involved. He knows we're together, and he knows I'll kill him if he comes near you. But I don't want to give him any reason to think he can hurt you again before I kill him. No one is worth that risk to you."

We watch Besnik hug Yelena, and there's genuine affection between the two of them. I realize I'm glad she's found someone to love her. She was manipulative when we were together and has been conniving since I met her. But she's as much a product of her upbringing as I am. Maybe she's changed in the years since I last saw her. I have.

Kitty looks up at me, and I offer her a reassuring smile. At least, it's supposed to be. She looks no more at ease than a moment ago.

"How do you know all of this, Lenka?"

She must love him because she hated any and every diminutive to her name when I knew her. I remember now how Nadia and Inessa used to tease her.

"Katerina and Misha came here today."

"What the fuck, Lenka? You should have told me that first. Stop talking."

"Besnik, they didn't come inside and bug the place."

"No, but they probably distracted you while someone did. Stop talking."

Besnik storms out of the bedroom. We lose the video feed of him, but we can hear him moving around. He works his way through the kitchen and comes dangerously close to a microcamera, but he doesn't see it. He moves into the living room and doesn't look anywhere near where Sergei or Anton put it. It's crazy how close they were to Yelena's back while she talked to us this morning. Freaking cat burglars. Both of them. He storms down to the basement, and we can no longer see him. But it sounds like he's searching practically every inch.

Kitty whispers to my brother and Anton.

"How has he not seen them?"

Sergei speaks over his shoulder.

"The cameras are miniscule. They designed the tech for endoscopies and VR headsets. We put them places that have a clear line of sight, but no one would examine too closely. Besnik is assuming they're way larger than they actually are, so he's not noticing them. Do you see how they're all angled up? It's because they're where the carpet meets the baseboards. Most baseboards are white, so the cameras and microphones are too."

We watch as Besnik leads Yelena back to the bedroom after she followed him downstairs but waited while he searched their place.

"I told you, no one came inside."

"You didn't let anyone inside. I'm still certain they had someone in here while you talked. They wouldn't have come just the two of them."

"There was a car on the street, but I couldn't see who was in it. Maybe someone came in and searched, but you know what to look for, and you've found nothing. You're freaking me out now."

"Lenka, call me immediately if anyone like that comes over again. Any stranger or anyone from your past. I hate the idea that you've been here alone for hours, and someone might have been watching you."

Besnik takes Yelena's hand and kisses her lips. Kitty glances at me each time they kiss, and I know she's wondering if it bothers me to see it. I couldn't give a flying fuck. I slide my hand down the back of her pants and palm her silky skin. She relaxes and leans against me. I don't move my hand while we continue to watch and listen.

"Will you call around and find out where she is? Can you make sure she's still alive? I don't want Katerina and Misha coming back here if something happens to her."

"How did they even know to come here in the first place?"

Yelena sighs.

"Misha knew about Vlad and me."

I didn't know he knew about her and Vlad.

"He knows I don't want my grandfather to find out or anyone who might tell him. He keeps my secret as long as I stay out of his life, or in this case, I cooperate."

"I'll kill the fucker for blackmailing you."

"No. I haven't heard from him in years. He came for Katerina's sake, and I can't blame her for coming. He must have told her about us, and we knew each other before I moved to America. Her English was great, so I think she probably lives in New York now. If this happened to Inessa, I would do the same thing as Katerina. Please make some calls, Bes."

"Fine."

They move to sit on a sofa in their room, and we listen as Besnik makes four calls. The first two wind up going to voicemail. The third one is brief. The person on the other line told Besnik that Yuri's been in town for a couple weeks, but barely anyone has seen him. I can tell Besnik isn't pleased that people kept this from him. It seems he only knew Larisa was here not any details. The fourth call is as close to the jackpot as we get.

"*Krye*, he's been going to an old restaurant on Blue Hill Avenue. Some rotted out, barely standing building. He has men stationed there, but nothing's happening. No one's coming or going. The men sleep there, and Yuri only went once when he first arrived. He hasn't been back."

"How many people are there?"

"Like five or six. One of them's a kid."

"Like a little kid or a teenager?"

"A teenager."

"Are you sure it wasn't a woman, not a teen boy?"

"I guess it could have been a woman. Fuck. If it was, then she's fucked. That isn't somewhere you take a woman you care about. Who is she?"

"Someone of interest. Can you find out if she's alive?"

"Yeah. I'll make sure I'm on tomorrow's garbage pickup. I'll see what I can see. If there's a woman there, what do you want me to do?"

"Just tell me what she looks like and what kind of shape she's in. Don't approach her or anyone there."

"I won't."

"Call me as soon as you're off the street."

"Got it."

We watch Besnik hang up and shove his phone in his pants pocket.

"What can I tell Katerina and Misha?"

"Don't tell them anything. Yelena, you don't owe them any information."

Yelena shakes her head.

"I told them I would speak to you. I'm supposed to text Katerina tonight."

"Tell her I wouldn't help."

"You know it's better for everyone if you cooperate with them. You have influence here, but you aren't New York Russian mafia. I don't want to test Misha because it won't just be him who gets pissed off. I know you don't know Maks well, but you've met him. He's not a forgiving man. Maks will never hurt me because the Kutsenkos and Andreyevs never hurt women. But he'll torture you before breakfast and go on with his day. Please, Bes."

"Only because I don't like how much this is upsetting you."

His hand reaches out and rests on her belly. My eyes almost fall out of my head. Kitty's expression matches mine.

"It's not stress that keeps the IVF from working. It's my body. What did that one nurse call it? I have an inhospitable womb."

"Stress doesn't help. Let's go to bed, my love. We won't solve the world's problems tonight. Let's see what Lorik says tomorrow."

Sergei and Anton will watch and listen to the feeds until they're certain Besnik and Yelena won't say anything else of interest for now. I lead Kitty back to the sofa and sit, pulling her onto my lap.

"How do you feel about what you heard, *malyshka*?"

"Surprised that Yelena would defend Larisa or me at all. Antsy for more news. Worried that Besnik will flake. Scared that Yuri will find out Besnik's asking around, then go after Besnik, Yelena, and Larisa. Unsure of what to do next besides wait some more."

"I feel the same about all of that. But it's progress."

"Is it though?"

"Yes. Did you watch Besnik's expressions and really pay attention to his tone? His fear for Yelena's safety is real. Just like mine is for you. But he hates Yuri, and I think it started well before Besnik found out what happened to Yelena. This is decades-old hate. I don't think he wants to disappoint Yelena by giving her false hope, but I believe he's certain we're listening and watching. He only gave enough to tide us over without giving away anything he thinks we could use against him. Once he knew we'd been there, he was very aware of what he was saying and doing. All of it. From his mannerisms to his tone of voice to what he actually said."

"Do you think he's hiding something?"

"Definitely, but I think it has more to do with his past with Yuri than anything with Larisa."

"Do you think we could have her free by tomorrow afternoon?"

"I don't know, baby girl. But we're one step closer to killing Yuri."

Chapter Twenty-Four

Kitty

I barely slept last night. This is the closest I've been to Larisa yet. I'm certain we're in the same city, and I even know what area she was in last. But I can't go to her. I can't see her or hear her or touch her. I can't promise that she'll be safe soon. The condition we might find her in terrifies me. I know what I was like after each time Yuri assaulted me. I was like a shadow of myself for months afterward. I don't know that there is enough therapy in the world to help my sister. I don't want her to go back to Russia, but I doubt she'll feel comfortable staying in America. Is there anywhere she'll ever feel safe again?

"Did either of you sleep?"

I pass mugs of coffee to Anton and Sergei, who are in the same chairs at the dining table they occupied last night when Misha and I went into our bedroom. Anton takes a sip, and Sergei answers.

"We took shifts. We each got some sleep for a few hours.

Nothing's happened so far, so we both dozed while we were out here."

Sergei stifles a yawn when he finishes speaking. I give him a pointed look, but he just drinks his coffee. I've learned what each of them likes for most meals in a hotel, so I was the one who ordered room service for breakfast. I place the plates in each person's spot while Misha makes me a cup of tea.

We all freeze when we hear a phone ring. It isn't one of ours or the hotel room's. It's coming from the live feed from Besnik and Yelena's bedroom. Besnik steps out of the bathroom naked, so I avert my gaze.

"You can look, Kitty."

Besnik slipped a pair of boxers on, and Yelena's just handed him the phone.

"*Përshëndetje.*" Hello.

Sergei has the subtitles running again on his computer. Thank heavens because Besnik has the entire conversation in Albanian.

"*Krye*, I looked around, but no one is at that old restaurant anymore. If there was a woman there, she's gone now. They moved her. Once I was certain the place was empty, I looked around inside. They swept it. There's not a hint of the people I saw go in there days ago."

"Anyone seen or heard anything?"

"No. They must have left in the middle of the night. No one we have in the neighborhood saw anything, and none of the neighbors reported anything happening. They vanished. What do you want me to do next?"

"Nothing for now. I'll let you know."

We watch Besnik hang up before he looks at Yelena. It surprises me when she speaks Albanian. They've been together longer than I realized because she's obviously fluent.

"Lorik knew nothing?"

"They moved her, but Lorik doesn't know where. It had to be in the middle of the night."

"Moved her? Where?"

"I don't know. Maybe it was Misha and his people. They could have been in and out with no one noticing. They could have the entire place cleaned, and no one would know."

"No. Katerina would have texted me to tell me not to worry about learning anything else. Where could Yuri have taken her?"

"I don't know, but I'm going to ask."

Besnik dials a number and puts the call on speaker. Yelena's wrapped one arm around her middle, and she's got the knuckles of her other hand against her lips. The phone rings three times before I recognize the voice. I fist my hands, and my thumbs are running over my knuckles. I'm trying to soothe myself, but it's not fucking working.

"Good morning, Besnik. Did you sleep well, Yelena?"

Her eyes open with panic as Yuri speaks English. Besnik shakes his head and puts his fingers to his lips.

"You're causing trouble, Yuri. You're messing with a family that I want nothing to do with in my city."

"Your city."

Yuri snorts. Besnik ignores it.

"The Ivankovs leave us alone up here, but I'm not naïve enough to think their reach isn't long enough to strangle us all."

"They have their own problems in New York. They're waging wars against the Colombians, Irish, and Italians right now. They don't have time for your piddly ass."

"Why bother lying to me? I know you know I heard about Larisa Vasilieva. Her sister is practically an Andreyev now. The Kutsenkos weren't going to ignore a kidnapped Russian woman on the East Coast, and they sure as hell aren't going to ignore one who's Misha's sister-in-law."

"Sounds like you've been chatting with some of Yelena's old friends. Let me guess. Katerina and Misha showed up yesterday and filled Yelena's ear, and she put your cock in a vise to talk to me."

"This is bad for business, so it's now my concern. I have other things to do besides make sure you don't bring the bratva to this city. The fucking Irish are more than enough to deal with. They're swinging dicks with the Italians. I don't need both of them taking notice of our community."

"Besnik, I don't give a shit what you do or don't want."

"Then you won't care that I want to kill you. If you fuck things up for me, your daddy won't save you in time."

"You won't do shit to me, you pussy."

"I'll hand you over the Ivankov bratva and let them do whatever fucked-up shit they want."

"You have to catch me. And taking me out means you'll never find the bitch. That's what you really want, isn't it? You want a cut from whatever I make off her. I can make more off her in one night than your skanks make at any of your strip clubs in a week."

"It's only fair you pay your taxes while you're here, Yuri. It's the price of doing business in Boston. I hear you've been here a few weeks. That's a lot of back taxes you owe. I want forty percent of what you've made so far off her."

I glance at Misha, horrified by what I'm hearing.

"He's bluffing, Kitty."

"You're fucking nuts, Bes. I'm not giving you shit."

"Really? Hold on."

I watch Besnik look at his phone. He hits the screen a couple times, then I hear a phone ringing.

"*Çfarë bëri tani ai dreqin?*" What did that fucker do now?

That's not how I expected someone to answer the phone.

"*Thuaj përshëndetje të ndyrës. Ai është në linjë.*" Say hello to the fucker. He's on the line.

This must be Roel, Yuri's father. I struggle to keep up with the subtitles as they continue to speak Albanian. I don't know the language at all.

"Father."

"What did you do, Yuri? Why the fuck is Besnik calling me?"

"I didn't do shit. Besnik's crying to you because he wants money, and I won't give it to him."

"Your son won't pay for doing business in my city. That business is likely to get our community wiped off the map. If you still want our deals to work, Roel, deal with your son."

"Yuri, what did you do?"

"I made money that Besnik isn't entitled to. He's tattling like a little bitch."

"Roel, how's business in New York?"

"Good. Why?"

"Because the pittance you're making now is going to disappear. Everything in New York is going to burn. The Ivankovs are involved in this."

Roel releases a string of curses that make the men I'm with laugh. I don't even understand half of them with the English subtitles to help.

"What the fuck does the bratva have to do with this?"

There's a long pause before Besnik looks like he's ready to hit a wall. Yelena's barely moved since the call started. Besnik snaps at Yuri.

"Tell him, you piece of shit."

Yuri remains silent. Now Roel sounds really pissed.

"You have ten seconds to tell me what the fuck you've done. If the bratva is involved, my guess is you have about five seconds left to live. What did you do? And how much is it going to cost me to fix this? Your mother's sick. If I have to leave her side to come deal with this, I will kill you myself, Yuri."

I don't get the impression that's an empty threat. I think Roel would kill his own son.

"I made a deal with a Cuban to take a woman from Moscow. He paid me to smuggle her out of Russia and into Cuba."

"Who, Yuri?"

"Larisa Vasilieva."

"Why does that name sound familiar?"

"I was involved with her sister, Katerina."

Now I'm the one ready to punch a wall. *Involved?* That motherfucking piece of shit.

"Involved? That's what you call it? You couldn't go back to Russia for two-and-a-half years after you were *involved* with Katerina. If that bullet her father put in you had been an inch to the left, you would have bled out in that warehouse. Why did you go near that family again?"

"Katerina was a good fuck both times. Larisa is far more useful."

I don't even realize what I'm doing until I hear the plate smash against the wall and egg slides down it. I hurl a coffee mug next. The liquid splatters everywhere between the table and the wall. Misha wraps his arms around me, and I fight him.

"Kitty, stop. We can't hear."

I freeze. I'm panting as rage surges through me.

Besnik runs his hand through his hair as he looks at Yelena. He asks what we've all been wondering since the beginning.

"How is she useful?"

"That's not your concern."

"You made it my concern when you brought her to Boston. Answer me."

"I don't owe you shit."

Yuri sounds like a petulant child. When his father speaks, he sounds like he's scolding a kid.

"You owe me everything. Explain to Besnik."

"She knows shit she shouldn't. That knowledge is worth a lot of money."

What the hell does my sister know? She basically went to work and went home. Obviously, she partied a little since she went to that club with Valeriya and Yulia, but she fucking helped college students from Stan countries get into Moscow. What could she have learned from that?

"You're speaking in circles, Yuri. Your father and I aren't interested in listening to you bullshit us. Get on with it."

"No. I'll tell my father when I talk to him without you. You don't need to know."

"Then answer this: where the fuck is she? You had her in some abandoned old restaurant until last night. Where is she now?"

"How do you know where she is or isn't?"

There's an edge to Yuri's voice that sounds like surprise and almost nervousness. I look up at Misha, who's let go of me now that I'm calmer. He shrugs.

"I knew you brought a woman here. I knew her name, but I didn't know who she was connected to until last night. You know Misha and Katerina are here. You did something to tip them off. They're asking questions. I don't like people asking things I don't already know the answer to. Where is she, Yuri?"

"Where I left her. She's at the restaurant."

"No, she isn't. My man swept the place this morning. Said it was like no one had been there. Stop lying."

There's a long pause and some scuffling sound that's super faint. I think it's coming from Yuri's line.

"Dad, I'll call you back. Besnik, go fuck yourself."

Besnik looks down at the phone, so I think Yuri hung up. I hear Roel's voice again.

"What the hell has my son gotten us into?"

"I don't know, Roel. But this shit is going to be worse than anything he's done before. This woman is not only Katerina's sister, but she's probably Misha's sister-in-law. My wife thinks Katerina and Misha might already be married. If they aren't, they will be soon. If the Ivankovs declare war on us, we aren't nearly strong enough to win. The Kutsenkos and Andreyevs are going to make this personal because it is. I don't need my wife stuck in the middle of a battle between Russians and Albanians, especially when she's got ties to those Russians that go back her entire life."

Wife?

All of us look at each other. Yelena and Besnik are married? He couldn't mean someone else, and Yelena's his side piece, could he?

"Look, Besnik. I know what my son did to Yelena and Katerina. I punished him for both. I may threaten him, but you know I can't kill my own son. But I made sure that he will never hurt another woman the way he hurt your wife and Katerina. He physically can't."

"And I'm supposed to give a shit about that? It doesn't undo what he did to Yelena. It doesn't undo how he beat her so badly that we may never have children. You don't have to console my wife every time getting pregnant fails. And if what he did to Katerina Vasilieva is even a fraction of what he did to Yelena, then I'm not going to do a damn thing to keep Misha away from him or stop Katerina from doing whatever she wants when she finds her sister."

"Look. I'm here. You're there. I'll send men to get Yuri and bring him back. But you need to find this woman and get her to

Misha and Katerina before you wind up with a bullet through your skull."

"Thanks for the sage advice, Roel."

"Be pissy later. You need to make calls, and so do I. Tell me when this is over."

Besnik looks at the phone, and I guess Roel hung up too. Yelena's staring at the phone before she looks up at Besnik.

"I've never wanted to run away more, Bes. Why did we have to be the ones born into this life? All I want is a quiet home with you and kids."

"I know, *e dashura ime*." My darling.

It's still hard to imagine anyone speaking so lovingly to Yelena, but she's so different from the woman I knew only a couple years ago. I wish she could have what she wanted. It's what I want.

"Can you find her, Bes?"

"I'm going to have to. Misha wouldn't hurt you. But would Katerina?"

"Yes. If it was between me and her sister, absolutely. But I wouldn't blame her one bit."

"I don't want it to come to that. Would Misha trust me enough to work together?"

"Stranger things have happened. Maybe?"

I glance up at Misha, and he nods.

Besnik looks around the room before he holds up his phone.

"Call whenever you want, Misha. You know the line is free."

"Bes?"

"Lanka, they're all listening. The moment they arrived in Boston, our home was going to be bugged whether or not you answered the door."

Misha pulls out his phone, and Sergei turns down the

volume on his computer. They don't need any feedback. We can still see what's happening on Anton's screen.

"Besnik."

"Misha. You and your family certainly have brass balls coming into my house when my wife was alone."

"I didn't know you were married. I wish you well. We can skip the bullshit since you know I've heard everything since you came home last night. If Larisa isn't at the building on Blue Hill, then where is she most likely?"

"I don't know. You heard Yuri. He wasn't prepared to find out she left there. Whatever's happening isn't under his control anymore."

"Maybe his men made an executive decision and moved her somewhere safer. Where would that be?"

"Fucking Moscow. I don't know. People here don't like him, so those men must be helping him because he's got their families. Money isn't nearly enough for most people to get tangled up with him. They know I won't like it, and they know he's nothing but a shitbag. He is the dog nobody wants to lie down with because they all know they'll get up with fleas."

"Start with those families. Find out who's missing, and you'll know which men were involved."

"No shit, Sherlock. I don't need you to tell me what to do. I already have a pretty good guess since there are some men dumb enough to play cards and lose big to him the last time he was here like six months ago. Give me an hour to make some calls and stop by my office."

I hear as much as see Besnik sigh. He shoots an irritated glance at Yelena as he walks to his closet and pulls out clothes.

"If I help you find your sister-in-law or whoever she is to you, then we're even. I owe you nothing, and I expect nothing from you. We're just done. Go home to New York with your family. Neither of us wants to be in each other's business."

"It's not so simple as that, Besnik, and you know it. If your people are helping Yuri, then you're guilty by association. You aren't keeping a tight enough rein on them if they think they can shit on my family and not feel our wrath."

"These are men who work for hourly wages. They aren't thinking about the mighty Ivankov bratva. They're thinking that they might live long enough to bring home the next paycheck to feed their families. They don't give a fuck about you personally."

"I don't give a fuck about them. I said *you're* guilty. Fix this. Black isn't Yelena's color. Never has been. She'll look washed out when she stands next to your grave."

"Don't threaten—"

"Shut up, Besnik. Yelena's fine. It's you, you should worry about. I'm certain I can find my own abandoned building in that neighborhood. You have an hour."

Misha hangs up. Sergei hurries to turn up the volume.

"You're an asshole, Misha. But I'll take that hour. I'll call you when I know something."

Besnik dresses and kisses Yelena goodbye. We lose him when he's in the hallway, but we all watch him walk out the front door. There's a gunshot and a scream. Besnik bursts back into the house and catches Yelena around the waist as she runs toward him. He hauls her off her feet and carries her to the garage. We can hear the garage door opening, then tires squealing as a group of men flood through the front door.

I look at Misha and the other's shocked faces, and his tone matches their surprise.

"What the ever-loving fuck?"

Chapter Twenty-Five

Misha

What the hell is Carmine Mancinelli doing barging into Besnik's home?

"Search the place. Rip it apart. I want to know if this motherfucker had anything to do with it. Now."

Carmine barks the order, and I recognize Gabriele Mancinelli pointing men in different directions. Carmine and Gabriele were the worthless ones in the family for a long time. Gabriele is some distant relative and Carmine's best friend. Carmine was Salvatore's douchebag nephew for years. A spoiled prick who was basically worthless to Salvatore except for tasks too far below anyone else in the don's family.

If the *Tres J's* have been good actors, then Carmine should win a fucking Oscar. He hasn't been what anyone thought. Which is why I want to know what the fuck he's doing in Besnik's Boston home, issuing orders to men I've never seen before. We can hear them speaking Italian, so these aren't any of Besnik's men who've turned against him. They aren't New

York *Cosa Nostra* either. My guess is men Carmine picked up here in Boston.

"What is he doing here?"

I look at Sergei as he asks what I'm certain everyone but Kitty is wondering. She doesn't know who he is.

"I don't know. Get Maks on the phone."

I watch my brother pull out his phone and dial our cousin.

"*Privet.*" Hello.

Sergei holds the phone up, so we can all hear and any of us can speak clearly. Since Kitty is my girlfriend, and we're here for her, I'm the default leader of this mission, so I explain.

"Maks, we're watching Carmine sweep through Besnik's house after shots were fired as Besnik was leaving. Someone shot at him, or he shot at them, then he rushed back inside. He grabbed Yelena and bolted for the garage. They drove away, and Carmine burst in with Gabriele and men we don't recognize."

"What?"

"We just listened to Besnik on a call with Roel and Yuri. Then I talked to Besnik. Someone moved Larisa last night, and it wasn't Besnik or Yuri. We don't know where. Besnik was leaving to find out what's going on. I thought it was Yuri shooting out there. I didn't expect Carmine."

"What the ever-loving fuck?"

"That's what I said. Are you going to call Salvatore, or can I?"

"You. You're there, but I want a full report."

"Thanks."

My cousin and I end the call, then I dial Salvatore's number. Talk about a fucked-up world. We all have each other on speed dial."

"Misha, you never call. What happened and to who?"

"Hello to you too, Salvatore. Why's Carmine in Boston, breaking into the Albanian *krye's* house?"

There's a long pause before Salvatore answers.

"That's Carmine's business, but I sanctioned it."

"What kind of business? I'm not in the mood to play twenty questions, Salvatore."

"I'm not sure. Something happened a few weeks ago while Carmine and the others were away. I don't know the details. He won't tell anyone, not even his brothers or cousins. I don't think Gabriele knows, but he trusts Carmine enough to stay by my nephew's side."

"And you just let him come up here because he wanted to? When are you going to get control of your fucking family, Salvatore? He's fucking shit up."

"Look, little boy—"

"Salvatore, it's Radomir."

My dad interjects, and Salvatore goes quiet again. I look at my dad, who shrugs.

"Radomir, I don't know why any of you are in Boston or what you're doing with Besnik and his people. I don't care. The Italians and Albanians have their deals that have nothing to do with Russian and Albanian ones. We all prefer it that way. But whatever Carmine is doing is unlike the shit he's caused in the past. I've never seen him like this. He's not causing shit, Radomir. He's trying to fix something that went down while he, Luca, Marco, Mateo, and Lorenzo were out of the country. He's finally being a man instead of an entitled little fucker."

"My future daughter-in-law's sister is missing, Salvatore. Besnik is our strongest chance of finding out where she is. If Carmine fucks that up, then you finally will lose your nephew. It'll be a shame if he's just gotten his head out of his ass."

"Stay away from him."

I speak up again.

"No. Tell Carmine to back off. Whatever he's doing waits until we get Larisa back."

"Fine."

"You are not doing us a favor, Salvatore. And this doesn't make us all right. This is just a time out from our regularly scheduled bullshit."

"I never dreamed it was anything else. Hurry the fuck up with this."

"I expect Carmine out of that house in the next three minutes."

"You're obviously watching Besnik's house from inside. I'm hanging up now. You can watch him take my call."

The call ends, and ten seconds later, we see Carmine pulling his phone from his pocket. It looks like he's going to ignore the call, then he thinks better of it. Sergei hurries to change the settings, so his computer will still give us subtitles but for Italian.

"*Ciao zio.*" Hello, Uncle.

"*Devi andartene subito. E' successo qualcosa e per ora non si può toccare Besnik.*" You need to leave right now. Something's come up. Besnik is off limits for now.

"*Che cosa? No. Abbiamo solo bisogno di altri dieci minuti.*" What? No. We just need another ten minutes.

"*Carmine, e' un ordine.*" Carmine, I'm not asking.

"*Zio Sal, è importante. Te l'avevo detto.Ti spiegherò quando torno. Devo sapere se Besnik è coinvolto in qualcosa che ci fregerà di brutto.*" Uncle Sal, this is important. I told you that. I'll explain when I get back. I need to know if Besnik is involved in a deal that'll fuck us all over.

"*E ti sto dicendo che se non te ne vai subito, saremo più fottuti che mai.*" And I'm telling you that if you don't leave now, we'll be more fucked than ever.

"*Ho bisogno che tu ti fidi di me.*" I need you to trust me.

Salvatore laughs at that. I can see Carmine's frustration. But he brought this on himself. He's been completely untrustworthy since we were all kids.

"*Bene, zio. Ma non incazzarti quando ti dico che te l'avevo detto.*" Fine, Uncle. But don't get pissed when I say I told you so.

Carmine barks out orders for the men to leave. The place is wrecked. They did it to send a message to Besnik as much as they did it to be thorough. He's the last one out of the house, and he looks back, sweeping his gaze over the living room. He hasn't hung up with Salvatore. We can't hear what he says as he puts the phone to his ear and pulls the front door closed.

We're left staring at one another. The house is silent, and nothing moves on Anton's computer screen. My phone doesn't ring, and neither does anyone else's. No one's sure what to make of the past hour. There are way more questions than answers. All of us look at Kitty's hand when her phone buzzes in it.

"Hello?"

She turns up the volume and holds it out, so we can all hear.

"Katerina, I need help."

It's Yelena.

"Besnik says you must have seen what happened. He wants to know if I can come to you. He doesn't believe anywhere else is safe for me."

Kitty answers before I can tell her what to say.

"He's right. I'm sure nowhere else is safe. Why do you think we'll help?"

"Because Besnik won't concentrate on anything else until he knows I'm protected. He doesn't trust anyone now. But I trust you, and I trust Misha. You want your sister back and need Besnik's help. Misha and his family might kill Besnik or any other man, but they won't kill me. I might be on a flight to Siberia before morning, but I'll live."

Kitty looks at me, and I nod.

"We're at the Boston Harbor Hotel."

"Holy shit. That's fifteen-grand a night for the kinda room you must be in."

Kitty's eyes are huge. I nod but signal her to keep the conversation going. My dad points to himself and Grigori, then the door, then straight down.

"Radomir and Grigori will meet you downstairs and bring you up. You come alone, Yelena. None of Besnik's men. You might trust me, but I don't entirely trust you. And I don't know Besnik, so I definitely don't trust him."

"That's fine. Besnik doesn't trust anyone either. Only Besnik will be with me. His only condition is that you let him come up with me, so he can see I'm really safe."

I speak up.

"Besnik, you're in no position to be giving us any conditions. We'll protect Yelena, but I'm not your little bitch to take orders from you."

"Keep my wife safe, Misha. That's the only thing that matters to me. I need to know you'll do that. After that, I'll do what I can to help you."

"She's safe with us. You can come up with my dad and Grigori, but you don't come inside the suite."

I can practically hear him grinding his teeth.

"Fine. Thank you. We'll be there in five minutes."

I hang up, and my dad and Grigori hurry to their rooms. This suite has four bedrooms, so they don't have to share. Kitty's clearly confused when they come out with sweaters instead of their suit coats. My dad lifts his and shows her his bulletproof vest. They put their underarm holsters on before grabbing regular jackets, as though they're headed out into the blustery Boston spring weather. Sergei and Anton hand them earpieces, and we watch them as they hurry out the door.

It feels like forever, but it's only seven or eight minutes tops. Grigori comes in first. Besnik pulls Yelena in for a kiss before he looks at me.

"You understand. Protect her."

"We will."

Then he's gone. Yelena tries to bolt after him, but my dad wraps his arms around her. She sobs against him.

"He's not coming back, is he?"

None of us know the answer to that. Kitty goes over to Yelena and whispers something to her and my dad. He lets go, and Kitty walks with her arm around Yelena as they head to the suite's massive sofa. They sit, and Yelena collapses against her and sobs.

"I didn't have time to tell him the test was finally positive. I found out this morning. We're finally going to have a baby."

Kitty holds her as Yelena sobs, and she looks at me. No one knows what to say. This is not the woman I knew. Carmine is not the man we all knew. Has the world tipped upside down on its axis? What Twilight Zone have we entered?

Kitty comforts Yelena for fifteen minutes before a bout of morning sickness has Yelena running to the half bathroom. She explained that was her first clue, but she'd thought it was just the hormone treatment until that morning. She's napping in Kitty's and my room right now. We've heard nothing from Besnik, but we watched some of his men check out the house. They didn't stay long, said nothing to each other, and must have reported to Besnik after they left. He must have warned them we're watching and listening.

"Have you tracked them yet?"

I'm sitting next to Sergei on the sofa as he works.

"I've tapped into official and unofficial cameras around the city to figure out where they came from and where they went. There are plenty of feeds, but it's not like New York. There are massive parts of the city that aren't properly covered by surveillance I can easily access. It'll take me hours to hack door-bell cameras in their neighborhood. There definitely aren't any in the area around the restaurant. I could spend days trying to hack ones in other parts of the city and find nothing. They didn't fly commercial, and none of the private airfields have records of them. Part of me thinks they drove up from New York. They wouldn't have to arrange for cars, so that's one less record. Anton's calling some of his guys to see if anyone watching Carmine's place saw him leaving with Gabriele in an SUV. Besnik's doorbell camera showed Carmine and his men arrived together, but I couldn't see plates. They parked that way on purpose."

None of that surprises me. It's how we'd roll, too. But it frustrates me because we can't track them. We haven't heard from Besnik. And Yuri went to his hotel and hasn't left since. We have men positioned on all sides of the building and in the underground parking garage.

Kitty's sitting on my lap where I want her. I don't like the idea of her being out of reach. Carmine's caused a lot of shit for my family and endangered more than one woman. Ana was nearly paralyzed because of shit he pulled. Kitty looks up at me.

"Could someone have met Yuri, and we don't know who to look for? Could they have sneaked him out?"

"The sneaking him out isn't likely. Our men have checked out the few trucks and vans coming and going. You saw that from the photos sent to Sergei. As for someone going to see him, it's been quiet in the lobby, so two of our men have been able to follow people. No one's gone into a room where Yuri's waiting."

"How can you be sure? Did they go into the rooms with them?"

"Yes. They're dressed as bellmen. They've been handling luggage and making money on the side. Hopefully, plenty."

"How'd they get the uniforms?"

I shoot Kitty a look that tells her not to ask questions she knows the answer to. She frowns, sighs, rolls her eyes, and shakes her head all at once. Such is our life. That's what her expression tells me. She looks at my brother before she speaks.

"What about Besnik? Sergei, have you tracked him?"

"Yeah. He's at his office. I don't have any bugs in there, so I don't know what's going on beyond he went in and hasn't come out."

It's a waiting game. We all have an abundance of patience. Vlad drilled it into us. A plan is always better than an impulse. Vlad made us recite that creed for hours. That patience has come in handy when prying information out of people you'd like to just be done with.

But Sergei has the most patience. It's like he has our cumulative amount multiplied by a thousand. That's why he's the head of our intelligence gathering. It's not just his skills as a hacker. He can watch hours of video and listen to hours of recordings, whether it's live or playback. He never misses things. He remains hyper focused throughout.

This is new to Kitty, and I can tell the waiting is making her frazzled. She wants to be doing not waiting. Yelena's in our room sleeping, so it's not like I can take Kitty in there and distract her. I sure as hell am not taking my girlfriend into one of the other bedrooms to fuck. I doubt my family would appreciate it.

Grigori and my dad are playing cards, and Anton is

communicating with our men here and the ones we have in New York. Obviously, Sergei is busy. Everyone else is occupied. Even I am because I'm enjoying holding Kitty. But that isn't enough for her.

"*Malyshka,* do you want to change, and I'll take you down to the hotel gym? Would running help? We could go to the pool since it's indoors."

She considers it then looks at Sergei before she shakes her head.

"Sergei will let us know the moment anything happens."

"I don't want Yelena to panic if she wakes up in a place with only four men who don't like her."

"Do you want—"

"Misha, I don't know what the hell I want besides my sister."

Kitty snaps at me, then snaps her mouth shut. She winces at her tone. I know she's thinking about the last time she lashed out at me. Except we have no privacy here for a spanking and sex. But I can feel the same emotions bubbling within her. I don't give a fuck about Yelena or her feelings right now when I see the pain Kitty's in. I move her hair aside and whisper to her.

"*Koshechka,* get changed into workout clothes."

"Misha."

"Now."

I help her stand up. She looks at me doubtfully, but she knows my tone.

"Bring something for me to change into."

She mouths, "Yes, Daddy."

She's gone only a few minutes before she comes out in yoga pants, a sports bra, and tank top. She's carrying a t-shirt and basketball shorts in one hand and socks and my tennis shoes in the other. She's already wearing her tennis shoes.

"Is Yelena still sleeping?"

"Yeah. She barely moved when I went in. I changed in the bathroom, and she didn't move then either."

I duck into Sergei and Anton's room and change. No one appears to pay attention to us, but I know they're all wondering what's going on. I take Kitty's hand and take her toward the door.

"We'll be in the gym. Get us if you need to."

"Misha—"

I shoot her a stare, and she's doesn't argue again. A guard accompanies us down to the gym, and fortunately there's no one there. I look around before turning to Dimitri.

"*Otklyuchite yego.*" Get it turned off.

He knows I mean the security camera. He disappears as I lead Kitty to a treadmill. She really doesn't want to do this, but I tilt my head toward the camera. She suddenly understands that we're not here just for her to run because I'm forcing her. She gets I won't start talking or doing anything else until no one is watching. I see in the mirror when the camera stops flashing a tiny red light. A few minutes later, Dimitri sticks his head in and nods. He closes the door behind him.

"Misha, what are we doing down here?"

"Whatever you want. Run. Lift. Sit quietly. Scream. Lash out at me. Whatever you need. We have privacy now."

"I want to throw things. I want to hit someone. I am so filled with rage I don't know what to do with. I feel so useless, and I hate it. Misha, I'm happy with you. Don't get me wrong. But right now, you're only a distraction for a few minutes among what feels like eons of agony. Being so close and knowing where she was but not getting to her in time is more than I can handle right now. There were times when I wished Semyon would die. There were times when I thought I might kill him. They seem so calm compared to how I feel standing here. I want to hurt someone. I want to be as cruel to them as they're being to my sister, to my family, to me. I want to destroy anything they love, anything they have. I want them to watch as I strip it all from them. Then I want to torture them. And finally, I will kill them. I'm a sick fuck because I want to enjoy every minute."

"We will find who did this, and you will have your vindication, Kitty. I promise you that. You are not a sick fuck for how you feel. Nothing is more important than family. You know how deeply I believe that. You know there is nothing I wouldn't do to protect the people I love. There is nothing wrong with you feeling the same way. But you are one wrong word away from exploding. It can't be at the wrong time or in the wrong place. You need an outlet, and you have it here with me."

I step back and hold my arms out, my hands even with my hips.

"I am not hitting you, Misha."

"Then kick me."

"I am not abusing my boyfriend because I'm bad tempered right now."

"Katerina—"

"Do not call me that, Mikhail."

We stare at one another. We both know I'm the one doing the goading now.

"Sparring with me is not abuse. You're not trying to beat me up to exert your will over me or to control me. You aren't trying to make me fear you. You aren't trying to prove you're superior to me."

"I do not want to hit my boyfriend."

I pause for a moment and dread fills me as I realize just how badly I missed the mark. Fuck me. I'm asking a woman who was abused and raped twice to hit and kick me. She doesn't want to remember what they did to her. She doesn't want to be like them. I'm a fucking bastard. Fuck.

I lower my hands as I take a step closer. She doesn't back away, so I reach for her.

"*Kiska*, I obviously didn't think this all the way through. I'm sorry I reminded you of what's happened to you."

Her brow furrows before her eyebrows shoot up to her hair. She shakes her head as she rests her hands on my chest.

"That wasn't what I was thinking about. Though that might be part of it deep down. Misha, I'm supposed to be—I want to be—the one part of your life that never has anything to do with violence. I want to be your escape from that. I don't want it anywhere near our relationship."

Fuck me even more. She's more worried about me than she is herself. She's putting me ahead of herself. I cup her jaw as I gaze down into her blue-hazel eyes.

"You are, *malyshka*. You are my refuge, my haven from all of that. You're who I feel safe with and at peace with. What I thought I was offering isn't violence. Violence is physical acts meant to hurt, harm, or kill someone or something. That isn't your intention if we spar. If you took a kickboxing class, would you consider that violence?"

"Misha, the entire point of why you're offering this is because I'm ready to blow a gasket, and violence is exactly what I want. You're encouraging me to use you as a scapegoat and do to you what I can't do to these fuckers."

"What do you need from me, *malyshka*?"

"I don't know."

Her answer is a ragged whisper as she trembles. She leans her head against my chest, and I hold her. I glance down and see her eyes are closed. I don't move until she does. When she pulls back, she sighs before she gives me a nod. She's not all right. Not even close, but for my sake, she wants me to think she is. She looks around, then spots something. She lets go of me and goes to a medicine ball rack.

She palms a medium-sized one like a water polo player. I'm not prepared for her to whirl around and hurl it at the wall across the gym. It's a five-pound ball. It weighs more than a discus, but not as much as a shot put. It hits the wall with a loud thud. I jog over and grab it. I move close enough to toss it to her. She catches it with both hands before palming it again. She throws it even harder.

She does this five more times before switching arms. I'm surprised that her left arm is as strong as her right. We remain quiet, the only sound the ball hitting the wall and her more labored breathing. I'm unprepared for her scream.

"Why?!"

I don't answer because I don't think she expects one. She screams again. This is a sound of pure, unadulterated pain. She screams again and again, and it's the most excruciating thing I've ever watched. It's way worse than anything I've inflicted or seen done to someone else. It's worse because I can't make her pain go away. All I can do is watch it. She said she felt useless. I have never felt so out of control. Not the kind that would make me rage. The kind where I feel worthless to Kitty because I can't solve this. I can't protect her from it. I can't fucking make it better.

"Misha, why?"

She looks at me with such anguish, and I have no answer for her yet. *Yet.* I will fucking get an answer, but I have nothing to offer right now.

"I don't know, Kitty."

"Hold me."

I cross to her in four long strides. I pull her against me. She fists my shirt over my pecs. She's not hitting me, but they thump against my chest over and over.

"No one needs to explain to me that life isn't fair. I've known that since I was a child. But I want to know why they took my sister. I want to know who the fuck thought they could do this, and that it was all right."

"I don't know, baby girl. But we will find out."

"Why can't this be something simple that one of your spankings fixes, Daddy?"

I won't say what I'm thinking. I won't say that life has fucked us from the beginning. We were all raised Russian Orthodox, and we all have our complicated relationships with God. None of us believes God abandoned us or that our life is God's fault. We know Man has free will, and that's why our lives are as they are. But all of us are pretty fucking sure that people's belief in redemption and a forgiving God wasn't what He had in mind when that came down from the heavens. We are way too far past any of that, even with the most merciful God.

But I'm praying now. I'm not asking this for myself. I'm asking for His intervention for Kitty's sake and Larisa's. I'm asking Him to protect my future sister-in-law and to strengthen Kitty before she breaks. I'm asking for guidance for how to help Kitty and for how to rescue Larisa.

I start to pull away, but she clings to my shirt, pulling me back.

"Don't let go. I think I'm about to really freak out."

Her breathing comes in short, shallow pants. I feel her break out into a cold sweat. Her back is clammy as I slide my hand beneath her shirt, hoping to soothe her. She's trembling so hard that she's shaking. Goosebumps appear on her arms. I slide my hand around to her belly and up to her chest. Her heart is racing.

"Kitty?"

"My blood sugar dropped because of a surge of stress hormones. The body responds with fight or flight when it tries to pump more epinephrine. It can cause anxiety almost like a panic attack. I need juice or a hard candy, even a soda. It's not serious."

Not serious? I'm the one who's about to really freak out.

"Misha, I can walk back to the elevator. I won't collapse."

I'm not convinced. I scoop her into my arms.

"Daddy."

"Do not argue, *malyshka*."

I walk to the door and struggle but get it open. Dimitri rushes to hold it open enough for me to pass through with Kitty. He hurries ahead and pushes the elevator call button. Because I can't control whether the elevator stops on other floors, I lower Kitty to her feet. She leans against me with her eyes closed. She's breathing better, but she's still in a cold sweat. I pull my phone out and text my dad.

Kitty opens her eyes when the elevator pings, and the doors open. We're on the roof deck. We step outside, and I look around. No one's checked the deck yet, and I regret the impulse to bring her up here for fresh air. There was an incident on Maks's rooftop at his Manhattan penthouse. They shot Sergei.

Dimitri wastes no time sweeping the rooftop before he nods that it's safe. I lift Kitty again and carry her to one of the overstuffed chairs. The elevator pings once more, and it's my dad. He hurries over with a bottle of orange juice that came with our breakfast. He pours a glass and hands it to Kitty. He watches me as much as he does Kitty.

"Radomir, I'm all right. My blood sugar dropped for a moment. It scared Misha, but I'm already feeling better. The orange juice will get me back to normal."

I'm not convinced.

"Are you sure? Should Anton or Sergei check you out?"

She looks at me as though I'm simple, then she laughs.

"I'm a nurse, Misha. I don't need paramedics to check me out. I need the fresh air and orange juice."

"Even doctors need doctors, Kitty."

"Sweet man."

She kisses my cheek, then finishes the glass of orange juice. She holds out the empty glass, and my dad refills it. She gulps it, then tries to climb off my lap. I grit my teeth and let her up. She takes several deep breaths, and I realize she couldn't do that with how tightly I held her. My dad retreats to near the elevator, and Dimitri walks across the deck, patrolling. He's looking at the buildings around us and down at the street.

I pull my phone out and look at the text message from my brother.

SERGEI

Come back. Tres J's called Anton.
Something's up.

Chapter Twenty-Six

Kitty

I feel like shit, yet I feel better. I needed the outlet before I blew. But I didn't love the sudden drop in my blood sugar. That's left me feeling sick and shaken. I followed Misha and the others back to the suite. I look around and find Yelena sitting on the sofa, while Anton's talking quietly to someone on the phone. He's not that far from her, so he's not too concerned about Yelena overhearing.

"They're here. Hold on. I'll pass Katerina the phone."

I walk over to the table with Misha beside me, holding my hand. I accept the phone and look down at it. The screen's asleep, so I don't know which member of the Cartel is on the phone. Then again, they're probably all there.

"Hello?"

"Katerina, it's Javier. I'm here with my brothers."

"Hello."

I don't know what to say, so I repeat myself.

"We've been in touch with our associate. Apparently, the Cuban who brought Larisa to America and sold her to someone in Texas brought her back because Yuri threatened him. Yuri wanted her back because someone offered him ten times what the Texan paid the Cuban. That's what brought her to Boston. Whoever this third or fourth party is, demanded the exchange happens here. I don't know who it is."

"Someone named Carmine showed up this morning at the local Albanian leader's house. He was with a guy called Gabriele. Why are they here?"

"Carmine and Gabriele are there?'

Javier sounds genuinely shocked. I look at Misha. He nods, encouraging me to answer.

"Yeah. We saw them break into Besnik's house and trash the place."

"Misha?"

It's Jorge now. Or at least I think that's who says his name.

"Yeah."

"Did they take anything? Do you know why they went there?"

"No, to both questions. You guys told us the Italians and Albanians have been keeping their distance. Salvatore said Carmine's there for some deal that went wrong. He wouldn't say what kind of deal or what happened. He's convinced Carmine is trying to fix something."

"Carmine fix shit?"

Jorge scoffs, and it seems to match everyone else's opinion of Carmine. What the hell has this guy done in the past?

Misha changes the subject slightly.

"Yeah. Besnik brought his wife here, but he said nothing about why the Italians are after him."

"Wife? Who the fuck would marry Besnik?"

"Yelena."

"Your ex?"

Yelena calls out before Misha can answer.

"Hello, *Tres J's*. If you're helping the bratva, then you aren't the same guys I remember. I'm not the same as back then, either. I had a quiet life here, and I liked it."

Javier speaks up next.

"Do you know anything about your husband's business?"

"Nothing. We preferred it that way. He was my husband when he walked in the door or whenever we went anywhere. He left business behind and shielded me from it."

I walk over to Yelena with the phone, so she doesn't have to strain to talk loudly or to hear. I take a spot on the sofa next to her.

"He might not have told you anything, but did you hear anything? Can you guess why the Italians are involved? Whatever their deal with Besnik is, it's going to get in the way of finding Larisa."

"I truly don't know. When I left New York after Vlad died, I went to Moscow. You know what happened there. I met Besnik while I was in the hospital. He was in Russia for some business deal and was visiting one of his men who'd been in a car accident while drunk. The man was staying on the same floor as me. Besnik would walk with me, and we talked. I don't know why, but I didn't feel like I had to keep any secrets from him. He didn't have to tell me he was Albanian or part of a *fis*. I guessed. But we hit it off. I was there for almost a month to recover from what Yuri did. After that, he invited me to come to Boston. Four months after I moved here, I moved in with Besnik. We got married two months after that. He has protected me ever since we met. He knows I used to want to know everything and use that to manipulate people. He also knows that I will never want that again because that nosiness made me a target to Yuri. Ignorance is bliss, and until you and the Italians showed up, I was blissful."

I take her hand and twist to look in her eyes.

"Yuri said something about Larisa being useful because she knows things. You said wanting to know things or what you knew made you Yuri's target. Could it be the same? What did you know, Yelena?"

She's hesitant, and I fear she's going to shut down completely. She points to the phone and shakes her head. She puts her hand under her chin and waves it side to side. She wants me to cut off the conversation with *Tres J's*.

"Nothing that can help all of you. I'm sorry."

I nod slowly before I turn to find Misha. He comes over and takes the phone from me.

"Javier, keep us posted if you learn anything. We need to find Larisa, and to do that means having Besnik's help. If Carmine's after him, then Besnik can't help. Figure out what the fuck is going on."

"Fine. But if you learn something, don't leave us blowing in the fucking wind for nothing."

The call ends, and Misha hands the phone back to me. I drop it on the sofa beside me and turn back to Yelena.

"What did you learn that you don't want them to know?"

"This is Russian stuff. It doesn't involve the Cartel. There was an oligarch back then who owned major shares of several European soccer teams. He had something to do with the energy industry. I assume oil because it linked him to investments in Kazakhstan. He tried to set up some deals bypassing the Kremlin so he could keep all the money. I don't know the specifics, but Yuri was involved. I overheard him at a bar one night because he was pissed and practically yelling about this falling through. I was just trying to get to the restroom, but he spotted me eavesdropping. He threatened to kill me on the spot. Then he changed his mind. You can guess the rest."

I stare at Yelena as my mind races.

"My sister works with Kazakh and Uzbek students coming to Russia to study. Some of them have wealthy parents, but most don't. Those wealthy parents were all given their Kazakh and Uzbek citizenships after 1991. They were Soviets before that, so citizenship didn't exist for Kazakhstan and Uzbekistan when they were born. Their wealth comes from business dealings through Russia."

"Then my guess is your sister found out something she wasn't supposed to about one of those families. Either they're tied to Yuri, or they hired Yuri to make her go away."

"That would mean Yuri's Russian contacts, not his Albanian ones. Why is Besnik involved, then?"

"Because there isn't a strong bratva presence in Boston. It means Yuri can do business without Russians meddling. Because there are Albanians here, he knows he can force men to work for him. That means Besnik is involved regardless of what he wants. It's like I said last night. It's his business because he's the *krye*."

What Yelena says makes sense. It's what I deduced right after I asked the question. Misha walks around me and perches on the coffee table, so he can see Yelena and me.

"Is he doing business with the *Cosa Nostra*?"

"Maybe. I told you. I stay out of his business. I learned not to be so nosey."

"Have you met any of them?"

"Of course, Misha. We've been married for five years. I've met members of the *Cosa Nostra*, and I know plenty of members of the Irish mob. But that doesn't mean the women and I are having tea and crumpets while swapping recipes and sewing patterns. I'm not calling any of them for a cup of sugar. I see the other syndicate members at events that I attend with Besnik. We all remain civil, and it confuses the hell out of people because we're not going for each other's throats. It's the same as how things work in New York. But we aren't friends, and I do nothing more than look pretty on Besnik's arm for those things."

I spin in my seat at Sergei's voice.

"Besnik's back. He needs to come up."

I strain to see Sergei's computer that has the screen divided to show cameras at various entrances to the hotel. Yelena sees what I do. She's off the sofa and running for the door. I call after her.

"Yelena! He's coming up. Don't go out there."

I catch her and grab her arm. She fights me, but I'm stronger.

"Let go."

"No. He wouldn't want you to leave here. He brought you to us to keep you safe. Whoever did that could still be nearby. We don't know anything yet. He won't forgive you if you endanger yourself. Especially not once he learns about the baby."

The fight drains out of her. We stand together for what feels like an eternity before the suite's door opens. All the men inside draw their weapons. Dimitri and one of the other guards help Besnik into the suite. They're practically dragging him.

Anton and Sergei rush forward, taking over from the guards. They get him to the sofa as I snap orders.

"Get me towels. Get the alcohol out of the minibar. Get any first-aid kits."

I don't notice who's doing what, but people are moving around. Anton and Sergei are helping me strip Besnik, so we can see his wounds. Misha is holding Yelena, who's sobbing. Radomir comes with towels and the little bottles of booze.

Grigori has two first-aid kits that are way more stocked than I expected. These men travel with a mini-ER in their luggage.

The three of us pull on rubber gloves as we pass supplies back and forth. Sergei gets an IV started, and Anton uses a handheld oxygen mask and tank. Radomir holds the bag, and Sergei gets a pulse oximeter onto Besnik's index finger. I use the alcohol and towels to clean the stab wounds as best I can. This is hardly a sterile environment, but it gets enough of the blood away from the wounds that I can see what's happening. I dig in one bag and find iodine and a suture kit. The kit has what I really need, including sterile towels to cover the areas around the wounds.

Sergei and Anton switch places, and Sergei grabs the forceps. I grab the needle while Sergei holds the lacerated flesh together with the forceps. I need to work fast to staunch his bleeding because the one thing we don't have is a way to give Besnik a fucking transfusion. While Sergei and I work, Anton's monitoring Besnik's vitals and keeping the mask on even when he tried to push it away at first. I glanced at the tank more carefully the second time I looked and realized it was nitrous oxide. Besnik was out within a few more breaths, and that's how I could sew him up without him screaming or trashing.

It takes us more than an hour to get Besnik to what I'd consider a barely stable condition. He's lost a shit ton of blood. I have no idea how they're going to explain the mess to house-keeping. The sofa and carpet are ruined. He won't die right this minute, but he really needs a hospital. This is beyond what a nurse and two paramedics should be doing. I stand and realize that I'm covered in blood, too. I peel off my gloves and move, so Yelena can finally get to her husband.

"We don't have what he needs. I don't think they nicked any organs, but I can't be entirely sure. There could be internal bleeding that I have no way to know about. He needs a doctor in a hospital."

"No hospitals!"

Yelena's ready to cover Besnik with her own body, shielding him as though someone might take him from her.

"Yelena, we did everything we could in a hotel room. But this isn't a hospital. There could be more wrong with him than we can see. I know why you don't want him to go, but I'm scared he'll die if you don't."

"What about his vitals? Do they make you think he's dying? I don't know what they mean."

"He's what we'd consider stable for now. But that's because we stopped the bleeding we can see."

"If anything changes, then we take him."

"Yelena, listen to me. If we do that, it may be too late by then."

"No. If you take him to the hospital, then not only the police get called, but it goes into the computer system. Then people can find him. You know that. That's why we don't do hospitals."

I sigh. Anton just gave him a shot of some narcotic pain killer. I didn't look to see what it was, but I'm certain it's strong. But the nitrous is going to wear off in a couple more minutes. Besnik will wake up, and then he can tell us how he feels. Hopefully.

I hurry into the half bathroom and scrub as much blood off me as I can. Misha brings me fresh clothes, but nothing short of a shower will make me feel clean. I walk back over to the sofa just as Besnik's eyes flutter open. He grimaces in pain, and he groans as he tries to move. Anton puts his hand on the man's shoulder and shakes his head.

"Bes."

Yelena's voice is distraught, and she grips Besnik's hand so tightly that it's surely adding to the man's pain.

"Lanka, are you okay?"

"Yes. What happened, *moya lyubov'*?"

"*Cosa Nostra.*"

"Motherfuckers."

I look at Misha as he pulls his phone out of his pocket. I put my hand on his arm.

"Wait."

I turn to Besnik and move to where he can see me without having to turn his head.

"Were they from Boston or New York?"

"Both."

"What did they say when they attacked you?"

"That sucking Russian dick was going to get me killed."

I look at Misha and shrug while I shake my head. I don't understand what that means. Besnik isn't involved with the bratva. It's Grigori who clarifies.

"They mean Yuri. Their issue is with Yuri, but they must have thought Besnik knows something."

"Yes."

Besnik croaks before wincing. He tries to shift on the sofa, but Yelena croons and strokes hair back from his forehead.

"Carmine was looking for Yuri. He said something about already stealing back what they took from him. He wanted to know where Yuri was to keep him from ever stealing again."

Misha is the first to ask what we all wonder.

"What did Yuri steal?"

"I don't know."

Misha unlocks his phone and taps the screen a few times.

"Salvatore, your fuckface nephew—"

"Misha, you need to meet with Carmine."

"Fuck no. Do you know what he did to Besnik? The fuck I'm going near Carmine."

"Besnik wasn't innocent in this. But Carmine isn't the one who's in the wrong. You need to meet with him. He can end all of this. I know why he's there now."

"Just fucking tell me, Salvatore. I'm not in the mood for riddles."

"Do you want Larisa back? Call Carmine."

Chapter Twenty-Seven

Misha

I hang up with Salvatore, but I look at my family before I call Carmine. I don't know what to make of all of this. It's fucking bizarre. Since Yuri is half Russian and half Albanian, I can understand how he got Besnik involved and how he had men to help him in Moscow. But the parts with the Cuban and now Carmine are super confusing. Plus, there's the unaccounted time in Texas.

"Call him, Misha."

I look at Kitty, whose urgent tone matches her expression. Her hand is on my arm and is shaking it. I look at Sergei instead.

"Do you have any idea where Carmine is right now?"

"None. I haven't found a trace of him."

I look at Besnik, who's unconscious again. It's probably for the best, since he must be in agony otherwise. But I never had the chance to ask him what Carmine claimed Yuri stole or why Carmine went after Besnik. Salvatore said Besnik wasn't inno-

353

cent. Of what? Theft? Something to do with Larisa? I hate making this call without at least some information.

"Anton, are we ready to move if Carmine tells us where Larisa is?"

"Yes."

I unlock my phone and once again pull up my contacts. I tap on Carmine's name. I don't automatically put this call on speaker. Kitty's watching me, her brow furrowed. I don't trust Carmine at all. I don't know what to expect when he answers, and I don't want to risk him saying something that'll upset Kitty.

"Misha, she's all right."

"What the fuck do you mean 'all right'?"

Kitty's squeezing my arm, her nails digging into me.

"She's safe, but this shitstorm isn't even remotely over. We're already halfway across Connecticut. You need to come home. I'll meet you at Maks and Laura's."

"Wait a moment. You are pulling over, and we're coming to meet you."

"No. Meet us there. Until Yuri is dead, she's not safe. Neither of us can protect her properly unless we're home and with our families."

Kitty yanks the phone from my hand.

"Carmine? Larisa?"

She puts it on speakerphone.

"I'm here."

"Larisa!"

The pain in Kitty's voice will haunt me for years. Larisa speaks, and I'm surprised at how good her English is. It's not as fluent as Kitty's or mine, but she's easy to understand.

"Katerina, I'm all right. Honestly. Carmine rescued me. He didn't take me. He wants all of us to meet with someone named Maks. We're going to New York."

"No. We'll come get you. Wait for us."

"Carmine said you're involved with Maks's cousin. He said we could trust them."

Kitty looks at me, panicked. I wrap my arm around her as I look at Anton. He gestures twenty, and I know he means that's how long it'll take the pilot to get to the airfield and get the jet going. Sergei is already in their room, and I can see him throwing things in suitcases. Grigori and my dad are doing the same. I look down at Besnik and Yelena. What the fuck are we going to do about them?

"Carmine, I'm calling Maks. If you're halfway across Connecticut, then I'll tell him to expect you in an hour-and-a-half. If you're late—"

"You know I can't control how long it takes to get into the city. I'll call him when we're getting off the 95 and onto the 295 before we cross into Queens."

"We have some things to wrap up here, then we're headed to the airfield."

"You mean dump Besnik's worthless ass somewhere."

Yelena spews a stream of Russian curses that would make a hardened criminal blush. The voices woke Besnik, and he tries to lift his hand to her cheek, but he's in too much pain. We can't leave him here. And the blood. Fuck us. We have to get a crew in here discretely and get this taken care of before the hotel discovers it.

"His value is yet to be determined. He's not your concern anymore. Get Larisa to my cousin. I'll make sure he doesn't have you shot on sight."

"Carmine, I want to speak to my sister again. If she's safe with you, then take us off speakerphone."

"Katerina?"

The sound quality changes, and I'm certain we're not on

speakerphone anymore. But to be cautious, Kitty switches to Russian.

"*Skazhi mne pravdu. Vy v bezopasnosti?*" Tell me the truth. Are you safe?

"*Da. V bol'shey bezopasnosti, chem ya byl s tekh por, kak menya skhvatili lyudi Yuriya.*" Yes. Safer than I have been since Yuri's men took me.

"*Ya videl foto. Ya ponyal kod. Togda ty byl ne v poryadke.*" I saw the photo. I understood the code. You weren't okay then.

"*Ya ne byl togda. Katerina, ya poznakomilas' s nim, kogda tol'ko priyekhala. On znal, chto chto-to ne tak. On pomogayet mne uzhe neskol'ko nedel'. On prosto ne mog osvobodit' menya do proshloy nochi.*" I wasn't then. Katerina, I met him when I first arrived. He knew something was wrong. He's been helping me for weeks. He just couldn't get me free until last night.

Larisa is careful not to use Carmine's name, and I know it's so he doesn't grow even more suspicious. He has to be wondering what they're saying. I wonder if Larisa will tell him. They sound very comfortable together. Not quite old friends, but there's not a note of fear in Larisa's voice when she talks about him.

"*Dom Maksa ogromen. Eto budet vyglyadet' tak, budto vy pod"yezzhayete k rossiyskomu posol'stvu s okhrannikami v chernom i s vintovkami. U nego kol'tsevoy pod"yezd i chetyre garazha. Yesli on uvedet vas kuda-nibud' yeshche, srazhaytes' i ukhodite. Ty ponimayesh'?*" Maks's house is enormous. It'll look like you're pulling up to a Russian embassy with guards in black who carry rifles. It's got a circular drive and four garages. If he takes you anywhere else, fight and get away. Do you understand?

"*Da. Ya lyublyu tebya, i skoro uvidimsya.*" Yes. I love you, and I'll see you soon.

"*Ne skoro. Ya tozhe tebya lyublyu.*" Not soon enough. I love you, too.

Kitty hands the phone back to me.

"Carmine?"

"Yeah, I'm here."

"I will hear you out. All of it. But only if Larisa is unharmed when she gets to Maks's. So, you better tell me now if she has any injuries because if I see a hair out of place, I will kill you."

There's a pause.

"Who can hear me, Misha?"

I look around. I'm certain everyone can hear him, but my family is busy getting ready to leave. I glance down at Besnik and Yelena. They're not paying attention to us, but that doesn't mean they aren't listening.

"Kitty, Besnik, Yelena, and I can."

"*Está más delgada que la primera vez que la vi. Apenas la han alimentado. Probablemente todavía esté deshidratada, aunque bebió tres botellas grandes de agua. Tiene moretones en las muñecas y los tobillos por haber estado sujeta. Pero por lo demás, ella no tiene ninguna lesión.*" She's thinner than the first time I saw her. They've barely fed her. She's probably still dehydrated, even though she drank three big bottles of water. She's got bruises on her wrists and ankles from being restrained. But otherwise, she doesn't have any injuries.

Carmine switches to Spanish since he doesn't speak Russian, and I don't speak Italian. But I watch Kitty, and I can tell she doesn't understand everything.

"*Espera.*" Hold on.

I gesture to my dad when I catch his eye. He comes out to stay with Yelena and Besnik as I take Kitty in our bedroom. I quickly repeat what Carmine said but in English. Then Carmine continues to explain what's happening.

"*Yo sigo con el español, así que ella no sabe de lo que estamos hablando. No quiero molestarla. Intentaré no hablar demasiado rápido, Katerina.*" I'm sticking with Spanish, so she doesn't know what we're talking about. I don't want to upset her. I'll try not to speak too fast, Katerina.

"*Está bien. Sólo dime cómo está mi hermana.*" All right. Just tell me how my sister is.

"*Nadie la obligó a consumir o consumir drogas. Dice que nadie la agredió. Algunos hombres la abofetearon y golpearon, pero nadie hizo más que eso entre Moscú y Boston. Era más confuso que cualquier otra cosa. La hicieron esperar en una casa cara mientras estaba en Texas. No la alimentaron lo suficiente. Pensó que la iban a matar de hambre una vez que estuviera en Boston. Los hombres eran más duros, pero ninguno hacía más que tirarle del pelo y abofetearla. Todos la amenazaron, pero nadie cumplió.*" No one made her take or run drugs. She says no one assaulted her. Some men slapped and hit her, but no one did more than that between Moscow and Boston. It was more confusing than anything else. She was just kept waiting in an expensive house while she was in Texas. They didn't feed her enough. She thought they were going to starve her once she was in Boston. Men were rougher, but none did more than pull her hair and slap her. They all threatened her, but no one followed through.

"*¿Qué tan mal se verá cuando la vea? No quiero que ella vea mi sorpresa.*" How bad will she look when I see her? I don't want her to see my shock.

"*Vy by nikogda ne uznali, chto ona byla v plenu bol'she mesyatsa, yesli by ne sinyaki i khudoba. U neye chistaya odezhda, i proshloy noch'yu ona smogla prinyat' dush v otele..*" You would never know she's been a captive for more than a month, except for the bruises and being thin. She has clean clothes and was able to shower at a hotel last night.

"*Gracias por cuidar de mi hermana.*" Thank you for taking care of my sister.

"*Le he hecho una mierda a la familia de Misha. He causado que las mujeres de su familia resulten heridas y se pongan en peligro. Pero tengo una prima, María, que casi termina en los zapatos de Larisa. Por eso estábamos todos en Miami. Fuimos a buscarla y traerla a casa. No he seguido la regla de no mujeres y niños. Pero tampoco compro y vendo personas. No podía ignorar a tu hermana.*" I've done some fucked up shit to Misha's family. I've caused women in his family to get hurt and be put in danger. But I have a cousin, Maria, who almost wound up in Larisa's shoes. That's why we were all in Miami. We went to find her and bring her home. I haven't followed the no women and children rule. But I don't buy and sell people either. I couldn't ignore your sister.

There's nothing else to say until we get back to New York, and Kitty can see Larisa for herself.

"*Nos vemos en unas horas, Carmine.*" We'll see you in a few hours, Carmine.

"*Hasta pronto.*" See you soon.

I slip my phone back into my pocket before Kitty steps into my embrace.

"Could she really be safe? Can we trust him?"

"I've known Carmine since we were kids. He was a shitbag back then and has been ever since. But this is the sincerest I've ever heard him be about anything. Maria is one of the few people who likes Carmine. His family may love him, but I've always believed it's been out of obligation. She's always felt that way by choice. The only time I've ever not thought he was a waste of space was when we were in high school. She got hurt horseback riding and was in the hospital for three weeks. He would go there every day after school. I heard he tutored her and stayed with her each night until she fell asleep, so she wouldn't be lonely the entire day."

"That sounds really, really sweet. Being in the hospital that long as a kid must have been scary and boring for her. People probably gave him a lot of shit for it, too."

"We all joked that he was the last person who should tutor anyone. We all thought he was a shit student. We assumed he was as dumb as he acted, and that he blew off everything except spending his parents' and his uncle's money. He disappeared for four years and went off to college. No one would say where he went. It was even rumored he wound up in jail, and someone killed him there. Then one day he reappeared. We found out after everything went down with Anastasia that the fucker went to Stanford. He's book smart and manipulative as fuck."

"How the hell did his family keep that a secret for four years? Did he never come home for any holidays? The *Cosa Nostra* really can make people disappear for good."

"It's why I'm wary. But I know he's still close to Maria. I know she wouldn't speak to him while he, Luca, and Gabriele spent some time in Italy. Salvatore sentenced them to some hard labor at a vineyard."

I can't help rolling my eyes at that.

"But we all know they regularly got the shit beaten out of them since it pissed off the owner that Salvatore called in a favor that stuck him with babysitting the three fuckwads."

"All right. I'll choose to trust him for now. You aren't calling everyone under the sun to have him shot right this minute. I know you wouldn't let Larisa stay with him if you thought he was a real danger to her."

"I wouldn't. I don't trust him about most things, but for this I do."

We hurry to pack what we have and head back into the

suite's living room. Yelena looks toward us as Sergei and Anton lift Besnik onto a stretcher.

"He convinced me to let him go to the hospital. He knows he needs it. We know people with a private ambulance company. They'll get him there without drawing attention. He gave Anton the number to cleaners. They'll take care of everything here before the hotel discovers it."

Kitty lets go of her suitcase handle and walks to Yelena.

"What're you going to do?"

"I'm going to Besnik's brother's house. He's on his way back from Chicago already. My sister-in-law will hide me. I trust the men Besnik's assigned to me. They're waiting outside with the ambulance. Your men are making sure no one asks questions about what's going on with the service elevators."

"If they can't keep you safe, call me, Yelena."

I move to stand with the two women and wrap my arm around Kitty's shoulders.

"We've both changed. We aren't those kids anymore. You're married and going to be a mom. Kitty and I have a life to start together. If you need me, I'm here. No questions asked."

"Thank you, Misha. That means a lot to me. I don't know what's going to happen, but I appreciate knowing I have someone outside of Boston I can trust."

Kitty and Yelena embrace tightly, then I give her a loose hug. She follows the stretcher to the door. She looks back and offers such a sad smile that I truly feel badly for her. Since I'm praying again these days, I'll add her to my list.

Grigori walks over to us as he puts his suit coat on.

"We can leave and check out online. That means the cleaners can get in here before anyone notices. We need to go now though. The plane's ready."

As we gather our things, Kitty speaks to all of us.

"What do you think will happen to Besnik? He may survive his wounds, but what then?"

My dad shrugs as he holds the door open for us.

"If he survives, then he continues as he has. You saw his scars. This wasn't the first knife fight he's been in. Once Yuri's dead, then he can breathe easier."

Everyone's lost in thought as we pile into the SUV and make our way to the Boston airfield. Kitty holds my hand but stares out the window silently for the entire flight. Fyodor hasn't even put the SUV in park in Maks's driveway before Kitty is flinging open the door. She practically falls out of the car, forgetting how high it sits off the ground. She bolts to the front door and pounds on it. I rush to catch up, pushing the code into the pad by the door.

"Larisa!"

Chapter Twenty-Eight

Kitty

I don't know what I expected when I ran into Maks and Laura's house, but it wasn't what I found. I take that back. I expected some guy sitting at gunpoint, and my sister running into my arms. Only half of that happened.

"Katerina!"

I fly across the foyer and collide with my sister under the archway to the main living room. We cling to one another, and neither of us can let go. I will never let go. I sense Misha is near me because he kept us from knocking each other over, but nothing exists besides Larisa and him. She and I sob as we rest our heads on each other's shoulder. I don't know how long we stand that way, but it must be awhile.

"Larisa, thank God."

"Katerina, I knew you would find me. I knew you would make sure I was safe."

"I didn't find you."

"Carmine wouldn't have known who to reach out to if you weren't looking for me."

"How'd Carmine know I was?"

I look to the living room as one of the most handsome men I've seen outside of Misha's family approaches us. His deep set, almost black eyes bore into me. I notice two other men who look incredibly like him are watching us.

"I'm Joaquin."

The man sticks his hand out to me, and I release one arm from Larisa long enough to shake his hand.

"I called Carmine when I figured out that he must be involved. It was too coincidental for him to be in Boston and after Besnik at the same time. I told him he needed to call you, Misha."

Another man close to Misha's age steps forward. Larisa pulls away and offers him a kind smile.

"But you called my uncle before I got the chance."

"Katerina, this is Carmine Mancinelli."

Carmine reaches out to shake my hand too.

"Ms. Vasilieva, I'm glad I was able to reunite you with your sister."

He's softer spoken than I expected. Everything about his appearance says he should be brash, but his demeanor seems humble. He steps back and remains quiet.

"Thank you, Mr. Mancinelli."

"Carmine, or you'll get like ten of us. It's the same as the Kutsenkos."

Misha tenses behind me, and I can hear what he's thinking. *Not the fucking same.*

I glance back at Misha, and I know he realizes I read his mind. He drops a kiss on my cheek. Svetlana approaches us, and I release Larisa and fall into her arms. It's like having my mom comfort me. It provides me a support unique from what

Misha can or the relief I feel hugging Larisa. She opens her arms, and Larisa steps into her embrace. The three of us hug as Svetlana strokes our hair.

"Svetlana said she's going to be your mother-in-law soon. Are you engaged?"

"Basically."

I can't help but grin before I twist and look at Misha. His expression matches mine. Svetlana lets go when she's sure Larisa and I are ready. I reach out a hand to Misha, and we entwine our fingers.

"Larisa, this is Misha Andreyev. We met while we were in Moscow. He was there for work, and I was there to—"

"You went to Moscow? Mama and Papa didn't tell me that."

"You've spoken to them?"

"Right after I got off the phone with you."

"I'm glad they know you're safe now."

Larisa's expression drops, and she looks back at Carmine. I don't get the sense that there's anything romantic between them, but she relies on him a bit like I rely on Misha.

"Katerina, I think Larisa and I need to tell everyone what we know. I asked the *Tres J's* to come because I know they're involved. But no one's going to know the full story until we talk."

It's warm enough to move outside. We need the space since everyone is there. I meet Javier and Jorge. I also meet Carmine's cousins Luca, Lorenzo, and Marco. Their friends Gabriele and Matteo are there too. Then there's all of Misha's family. The only ones not outside are the twins and Lev. All three are conveniently napping. It's not long before Carmine has Salvatore on speaker, and Javier calls Enrique and Pablo.

I sit between Misha and Larisa on a patio sofa, holding each of their hands. Larisa looks so fragile, surrounded by all these large men. She's lost a lot of weight. Her cheeks are sunken, and her eyes are more prominent. Her collar bones are sticking out, and her hands appear bonier.

"I went out with a couple of friends to a club one night."

"Yulia and Valeriya. I met them."

"Yes."

I know I surprised her because it takes a moment for her to gather her thoughts.

"I met a man at Bar Disko 50. We hit it off, and he asked me out. He said his name was Fernando Alvarez, and he was in town for a week on business. I didn't want to agree at first. I could tell his friends were bothering mine, but we seemed to have a lot in common. Now I realize he asked me questions and based his responses off my answers to make it seem like we'd be a good match. I went out with him, but his phone rang during dinner. He had it screen down, but the table was glass. I could see the reflection said *esposa*. It wasn't hard to guess that meant wife, especially with how fast he silenced his phone. I insisted I leave. I walked out and blocked his number. I know he came by my place, but I wouldn't answer. He used other phone numbers to call me from, but I hung up on him each time. He scared the shit out of me."

She looks at the ground, lost in thought for a moment.

"I had no idea that him calling would be the least scary part of all of this.

I need to know why, so I ask her.

"Why did he target you?"

She looks around, and I can tell she doesn't want to announce the reason. She doesn't look at Carmine, and he's as curious as everyone else. I suppose. I have never seen so many blank stares in my life. It's like looking at a room filled with male robots. The women's faces convey their emotions, but none of the men do. My new family is far better than the Italians or Colombians, but they're pretty damn good.

Larisa's gaze locks with mine, and I can guess what she's going to say before she switches to Russian.

"*Ya ne znayu, dolzhny li oni znat' ran'she tvoyey sem'i.*" I don't know if they should know before your family.

I'm quick to correct her.

"*Nasha sem'ya.*" Our family.

I look at Carmine, and I wonder how well they've communicated so far. My gaze darts to the *Tres J's.*

"Larisa thinks the explanation is too complicated for her English skills. She may need to switch to Russian, but English is fine for now."

Carmine nose flares for a second, and I wonder if he knows I'm lying.

"*Eto to, chto ya skazal svoyemu spasitelyu.*" That's what I told my rescuer.

Larisa still doesn't want to say Carmine's name and give away that she's talked about him. I can't blame her. Joaquin speaks up next, and once more I think how kind he sounds. Misha hasn't moved since the conversation started, so I can't get a read on him at all. I wish this was one of those times when our telepathy was real.

"Is there anything you can tell us about the Cuban man? We think he's involved in a trafficking ring that's not only connected to Russia but parts of Latin America. The parts where we have interests that don't need interrupting."

"He lives in Miami at least part of the time. I don't know about this ring. I didn't see one."

I think her confusion is genuine, but I don't explain. I want to see what she's willing to say.

"Yuri took me to Fernando's house in Cuba. It was on the coast and easy to get to by boat. They blindfolded me before we got there and when we left. I never saw the outside of the house, and I never saw where we were. But it was salt air, and I know what being on a boat feels like. They didn't blindfold me when we flew. I was at Fernando's Miami home briefly."

She turns to Carmine and offers him a sad smile. I shift my gaze to his relatives. Luca, Lorenzo, Marco, Matteo, and Gabriele have the same simmering rage beneath the surface that I feel rolling off Carmine in waves.

"I met Maria for only a few minutes, but she gave me clothes. I met Carmine while he was there to negotiate with Fernando. He knew I was there against my will, and I knew he could do nothing until his cousin was safe."

Carmine looks at his family before his gaze sweeps over everyone else. He settles on Maks.

"We got to Maria before he could sell her. He drugged her and her friends at a club and took her. Because of who she's related to, he decided to ransom her. He tried to sell Maria's friends. We got there within hours of the bastard taking her because he never found her tracker. He refused the amount we offered, and the negotiations ended. I didn't know who you were. Maria told me about you after we left Fernando's house. She said you were Russian and knew no one here."

"I'd meant I knew no one in Miami. I didn't even know where I was at the time because everyone spoke Spanish. I didn't know if I was in America or what part. I don't know this country's geography well. I never got to tell Maria that my sister lives in New York."

"Luca and I went back for you and offered to buy you from Fernando, but he said someone had already paid. He didn't know that we'd freed Maria and her friends. He thought she was being taken to some warehouse."

"That's where he took me before a woman picked me up. She traveled with some men, and we went to the airport. They slipped me something to make me sleepy. I don't really know how they got me through security with no passport or papers."

I look over at Sergei, and he pushes away from the wall he was leaning against.

"They paid someone off. I saw the footage of you at the Dallas airport when you arrived and left. But I couldn't figure out which flights you took."

Larisa nods as she continues filling in the gaps from Carmine's part of the story. She's doing better than I expected explaining everything in English. I think she'll switch to Russian when she gets to parts about Besnik. Or maybe not. So far she hasn't said anything only Misha's family should know.

"When I got there, the woman held an auction. Some man from Mexico supposedly bought me. But there was an issue with his payment. I guess he was supposed to pay with drugs, but the woman said the quality wasn't good enough. There was a big argument, but I didn't understand it because they switched to Spanish. She told me there would be another auction in a few days. I think she was angry that she didn't know the Mexican man couldn't pay until after all the other bidders left."

Carmine walks over to stand next to Larisa. There's a haunted look in his eyes when he speaks.

"I found out Yuri was involved when I recognized him outside Fernando's house. Marco and Matteo were watching the place. I met him years ago in Boston. Uncle Salvatore sent me up there to deliver a message to some of our guys who were making trouble with the Albanians. That's when I met Besnik, too. Fucker broke my nose before I broke all his fingers. We came to a truce. But Yuri always gave me a bad feeling. He's unpredictable and childish when he doesn't get what he wants."

I lean forward to see Carmine more clearly.

"Someone said something about a deal gone wrong. That Yuri stole something that was already stolen."

"That was Larisa. I offered Yuri ten times what we found out Fernando sold Larisa for. I told him he had to bring Larisa to Boston. I wanted her away from Texas and Florida. He brought her there, but then hid her. He tried to get me to pay five times what I'd already offered. I was done playing. I'd already paid part of what I offered. Larisa, I am so sorry. I have never bought or sold a person in my life. But I didn't know what else to do."

Misha tenses. I turn my head toward him, and he lets me see his shock.

"Carmine, I've known you since we were fourteen. You have never apologized to anyone in your life. Not even your mother. I didn't think you knew the words."

Carmine glares at Misha before he looks down at Larisa again.

"No one should ever be bought or sold. I've committed at least one sin a day for as long as I can remember. I've hurt a lot of people, some of whom are women sitting here with us. The syndicates had an unwritten rule that women and children were off limits. I decided alone that the *Cosa Nostra* would ignore that. I forced Luca and Gabriele in different ways, but I gave them no choice when it came to what I orchestrated with Anastasia. I'm lucky Niko's letting me breathe. I'm a shitty human that it took someone harming my cousin for me to finally grow the fuck up. I didn't know who you were at first, so I didn't know you were someone's sister. But I knew you were someone's daughter. Maybe I could say I paid a ransom for you, but I said the words out loud. I said I wanted to buy you. I'm sorry."

Everyone sits in stunned silence. Clearly, no one who knows Carmine expected any of this. Larisa and I don't know him well enough to know what to expect. It sounds heartfelt to me, but I don't know. I look at Niko, who's sitting with his arm around Anastasia. She's gone white as a sheet. I look at Maks, who's studying Carmine. Laura looks ready to put a gun to Carmine's head. I finally shift my gaze to Misha.

"*Dolzhen li ya verit' yemu?*" Should I believe him?

"*Da.*"

Maks asks the next question, which is good because I'm trying to figure out what Carmine could have done that was so horrible. I look at Anastasia again, and now she's watching Luca. Color is coming back to her cheeks, and she's furious.

"How'd you get Larisa out of the abandoned restaurant?"

"Once Yuri arrived, we followed him. The dumb fuck didn't have nearly enough men with him. The shitbags he hired were worthless. They'd never done this sort of work before. They were lazy. When he wouldn't pay, I went to Besnik's. He shot at me when I got out of the car. Then he ran inside. Next thing we knew, he was peeling out of his driveway. We had to wait a while, but we got him when he left his office."

I speak up again.

"You nearly killed him. A few of those knife wounds were serious. I barely got him stitched in time."

"You?"

Carmine, Luca, and the one I think is Marco ask at the same time.

"I'm a nurse. It's been a long time since I worked in a hospital, but I know what I'm doing. Anton and Sergei helped."

Carmine rakes his hand through his hair and looks at Luca. He lets his cousin take over explaining.

"The Albanians are like you. They keep their communities pretty insular. They stick to doing business with each other in a lot of cases. But you can't do anything in Boston without someone who claims they're Irish."

Something in the air around Misha's family shifts. I look at Laura again, and she's definitely ready to murder someone. Maks's hand is on her forearm to keep her from getting up. I look at Christina, and Bogdan is doing the same thing. Laura and Christina are looking at each other. Maks speaks softly to Laura.

"Let him finish, or we won't know enough."

Enough for what? A strike against the Irish? I feel like I'm watching a tennis match with how my head keeps turning back and forth. I haven't forgotten that there's still shit Larisa needs to tell us, but that has to wait. Luca continues explaining.

"Besnik needed to run some product down to us. That's part of why we suggested Boston. We already needed to be there. He lied and said it was stolen before it made it to him from Mexico. No one stole it. He sold it to Dillan. The Irish wanted to fuck us over. We told Besnik we would forgive that transgression if he told us where the girl—Larisa—was. He refused. We didn't know that he wouldn't tell us because he was trying to help you. The dumb fuck should have mentioned the bratva was involved and trying to get a Russian woman back."

Misha looks at Maks before he speaks.

"Dillan's only involvement was fucking up your shipment?"

The Italians look at each other before Luca speaks again.

"Not exactly."

I'm confused.

"What does not exactly mean? And I don't understand how this involves Larisa anymore. Is it just part of the reason for you picking Boston?"

"Dillan found out there's a—*gjak*—between Besnik and Ardit Hexha. Ardit is the *krye* here in New York."

I look at Misha and mouth, "What's that?"

He answers aloud, and I realize I'm not the only one who must not know. There are five American women who probably don't either. Larisa looks just as confused.

"*Gjak* means blood feud. While members of Albanian organized crime swear to the *bessa*, that's more than just a mafia thing. It means honor in general. It's rooted in the *Kanun*, which is an ancient set of laws about everything. Family, church, civil stuff. A lot of Albanian Americans still believe in it. If someone violates the laws and acts dishonorably, then it can lead to a blood feud."

Carmine continues where Luca left off.

"Besnik and Ardit have been rivals for years, each trying to increase their business with us. When Dillan found out about this, he convinced Besnik to sell to him instead of us. Once he had the shipment, he lied to Ardit and told him that Besnik low-balled him and got a better deal with our uncle. He poured gasoline on the fire between them, hoping Ardit would take out Besnik. That would give Dillan the chance to expand into more of Boston. That's bad for us. That's why we let Besnik live. We only sent a message. We could have killed him."

"How does Yuri play into all of this?"

"The feud started because Yuri killed Ardit's younger brother. Besnik knew, but let Yuri hide in Boston until he could go back to Moscow."

This shit is fucking complicated. I try to work it out in my head.

Yuri killed a New York Albanian and went to hide in Boston. Besnik let him stay there instead of turning him over to the krye here. This caused a feud. This Dillan guy found out about the feud and pit Besnik against Ardit, hoping Besnik would die, so he could get more influence in Boston. The Italians got involved because of a deal that went bad—the deal Dillan meddled in to stir the pot between Besnik and Ardit. I'm still missing something.

"Did Yuri have anything to do with this Dillan guy? Does Dillan have anything to do with what happened to Larisa?"

Carmine inhales deeply. Fuck. Now what? Am I even going to be able to keep up with how fucking twisted this is?

"All of this was going down right after Fernando hired Yuri in Moscow. Yuri threatened Besnik that he would tell Maks it was Besnik who was organizing the trafficking ring. Separately, Yuri promised Dillan that he could get rid of Besnik for him if Ardit didn't. The money Dillan paid Yuri is what Yuri used to buy Larisa back from the Texan, then bring her to Boston and to me. Dillan knew what it was being used for. We found out on the way here that Dillan discovered who Larisa was. That she was a Moscow bratva member's daughter. He planned to kidnap Larisa himself and ransom her to the Podolskaya, saying Maks knew what was happening and didn't stop it."

Jorge, the always quiet one, jumps in.

"That would have been before any of you had heard of Yuri because Misha and Katerina hadn't met yet. Or at least, they hadn't come back here yet. We don't know exact dates for some of this shit. But Maks already knew Besnik. I take it you don't like him much. Is that why Yuri figured you'd believe him over Besnik?"

"Yes."

Strong, silent type. Maks doesn't waste words. No wonder everyone said he was the least chatty before he met Laura.

I try to update things in my mind again.

Okay. I think Dillan and Yuri bribed each other. Or something like that. Dillan paid off Yuri to cause more trouble between Besnik and Ardit, even kill Besnik if needed. Then he was going to kidnap my sister from Yuri anyway to ransom her to my family. And somehow, in all of this, he thought he could blame Maks for doing nothing to protect Larisa. What the moth-erfucking shit was he thinking? I have even more questions than before.

"Wait. I thought everyone near and far knew the Kutsenkos and Andreyevs—so the entire Ivankov bratva—doesn't hurt women and children. I don't understand how Dillan, or anyone, would think people would believe Maks was involved in something like this. It's completely the opposite of every-thing people know about this family. It makes no sense."

"And that is Dillan O'Rourke for you."

I look at Laura, the disgust dripping from each word. She sees my confusion, so she elaborates.

"The O'Rourkes' leadership has relied heavily on sheer muscle and not much cunning until Dillan rose to power. The man is smart. There's no two ways about it. But he also has a charisma that people fall hook, line, and sinker for. People don't realize how conniving he is or how they're being manipulated until he's done. The men he's surrounded by now—Sean, Finn, Shane, Cormac, and Seamus—they're all highly intelligent and well-educated too. None of them have the same gift for strate-gizing as Dillan, but they can implement plans well."

Laura looks into the distance, and I wonder what she's thinking. Or maybe she's remembering something. It's clear that the disdain for the O'Rourkes is something deeply personal to her. It has to go deeper than just them being her in-laws' rivals. She looks back at me.

"I guarantee you they hashed the plan out ages ago. They had a general idea of what they wanted, then they found the players. It's like Dillan sees syndicate life as a chess game. He considers the strategy he wants to implement to get to check-mate. Then it becomes a question of setting up his chess pieces and luring his opponent into moves that don't seem to align. But in truth, he's maneuvered them to their defeat. It's what I did when I still practiced for a large firm. If I was planning a hostile takeover, I would test rivalries to distract my true target. I would make sure that target is large enough that once the acquisition happens, smaller targets understand it's in their best interest not to resist their own merger or acquisition."

Laura turns to Maks and grins before she winks at her husband. Maks's scowl deepens, but I can see his affection for his wife in his gaze. I look away when it turns heated. They're as bad—worse—than Misha and me.

"It's how I got Kutsenko Partners to pay forty-billion-dollars for a merger with a client. When I married Maks and become Kutsenko Partners' in-house legal counsel, I turned around and got them to accept an acquisition for only fifteen billion. It completely devalued the business in the Kutsenkos' favor. Dillan's making sure other organizations in Boston understand that if he can control the Albanians, then it's not worth fighting him. He's also making sure the Boston mob is indebted to him for expanding their influence. But the question is still why. Why is he doing it now? There has to be something he wants, and that's why he's acting now. Find that out, and you find out how to chop the head off the monster."

Everyone remains silent as they consider Laura's rationale. It makes sense the way she put it. The details are still hard to track, but at least now I get the big picture. But the question she poses leads me to my own.

"How do we do that?"

Chapter Twenty-Nine

Misha

The answer to Kitty's question is what we need to consider. But none of the syndicates are going to suggest working together. If this fails, we don't all want to go down with the ship. But neither do we want to have to bow to someone else's successful plan and be reminded of it. Besides, whoever cuts Dillan off at the knees holds power over him, and they assert their dominance across New York's underworld. Actually, internationally. That alone is reason for none of us to want to work together.

Our meeting breaks up quickly, with everyone muttering about thinking on it and getting back to the others. Niko and Aleks walk the Italians and Colombians around the side of the house and out to their cars. We don't continue the conversation until they return. Kitty hugs Larisa again, and the sisters cling to each other once more.

When they pull apart, Kitty wipes Larisa's tears.

"We need to know how this started."

"I know. Yuri actually targeted three students from the same Uzbek family. Their parents are extremely wealthy and moved to Uzbekistan as citizens about four years ago. They were both born there, but because it was still the Soviet Union then, there was no native citizenship to grant them. The husband made millions through oil in Kazakhstan. The wife is a financial planner. There are a lot of investment firms sprouting up in Uzbekistan right now, and it's drawing Russian oligarchs' attention. They see it as a way to increase their wealth while not facing European sanctions for doing business in Russia. Yuri discovered I was handling their university admittance and believed I was privy to the family's financials. I'm not."

"Is that why he kidnapped you? What about Fernando?"

"Fernando was supposed to lure me in and take me himself. Yuri was going to pay him for the chance to get information out of me, then Fernando could do what he wanted with me. That meant selling me. When I rejected Fernando and refused to talk to him, the deal flipped. Fernando paid Yuri to kidnap me. Yuri was supposed to pay Fernando a percentage of whatever he stole from this family in exchange for the time to make me give him the information. Fernando was an idiot to think Yuri would ever pay. But they were already doing business where Yuri arranged for Fernando to meet attractive young women he could kidnap. Basically, Yuri was a—I don't know the English word. *Sutener*."

I supply the translation.

"Pimp."

Kitty's voice is soft the next time she speaks, as though being too demanding might scare Larisa.

"Why this family in particular?"

"It was the pettiest reason. There's a villa in Kazakhstan along the Caspian Sea that Yuri wanted. They outbid him."

Kitty sits back and stares at her sister. I'm as dumbfounded as she is, but I don't remain quiet.

"What the holy fuck? Yuri kidnapped Larisa over a house he didn't get to buy that he'd probably visit once in his life, if that. He targeted Larisa specifically for the financial details she never had. But the rest of the plan had nothing to do with Larisa in particular. It makes me wonder just how many other women Fernando and Yuri smuggled out of Russia."

Maks pulls out his phone as he speaks.

"We have three issues here, and I don't want to deal with all of them if we don't have to. We can finally put Enrique and Salvatore to use. Stupid fucks."

His phone rings on speakerphone.

"Maksim."

"Salvatore, your nephews finally acted like adults. Congratulations. I've gone an hour without wanting to kill any of them. Progress. I'm calling Enrique. Hold on."

The phone rings twice before Enrique answers.

"Maks."

"You're on with Salvatore and me."

"And your whole fucking family. *Hola, Laurita.*"

Laura remains silent.

"Look, we have three enemies right now. Salvatore, Carmine's taken a personal interest in Yuri and the shit he's into. Get rid of the fucker. Enrique, your nephews have their Cuban connections. Get rid of Fernando and anyone associated with him. Dillan and I have some things to work out."

"Are you going to kill him?"

"Salvatore, you know the answer to that."

"You won't tell me."

"He's a little boy who thinks he's allowed at the grown ups' table. He's smart. I will definitely give him that. But he's interrupted the adult conversation one too many times. He needs to be put back in his place."

It's Enrique who chimes in now.

"Just don't burn any of my shit. I appreciate you being careful at the docks last time, but it got a little too close."

Salvatore can't miss his opportunity to bitch, too.

"And don't take out any of my ships. Just because I have a deal with him about the docksides doesn't mean I support him. It's business."

"Salvatore, I'm not interested in your fucking tin cans. Deal with things however you want. I don't give a fuck as long as they go away. You know you'll benefit from whatever I do to put the little prick in his place. He thinks that just because he looked over Donavan's and Declan's shoulders, even whispered in their ears, that he's ready for this. He got off easy with the banking shit. Now he's going to learn what it's like to run with us."

Pasha glances at Sumiko. She's the one who figured out the mob's money laundering scheme. It shocked them to be discovered. They really thought no one would catch on. Dumb fucks. Pasha looks over at Maks before he speaks up.

"That's why he needs to expand. With all the money he lost, he needs more income. His gun runner is dead. Half his products have burned in warehouse fires we've set. He's scrambling right now, and he thought going to Boston would be far enough for us not to notice."

Maks's smile would make most men piss their pants.

"He's going to learn that there's nowhere far enough for us not to notice."

Kitty and Larisa climbed into the bed in my room at Maks and Laura's. They were leaning against each other and watching TV when I left. Kitty didn't ask for any details, and I'm grateful for that. But I could taste her goodbye in our kiss. She knows it could have been our last. I have no intention of that being the case, but as she once pointed out, I can't control everything, even if I am a control freak.

I'm driving the lead SUV right now with Maks, Bogdan, and Niko. Pasha's driving the second one with Aleks, Anton, and Sergei. We're in our black tactical gear, our black balaclavas ready to be pulled down over our faces. People say those of us with the blue eyes look like some type of demon coming at them when we have the rest of our head covered in black. And they say Anton and Pasha are like the devil, their eyes so brown that they seem like empty sockets in the dark. Apparently, they look soulless. We've heard the comparison many times. Always right before the person dies.

"Sergei."

I speak to my brother through the car phone.

"Yeah."

"Where do I pull up? I need more information."

"There's an alley three building to the north. Pull in there. We can go by foot."

"Any cameras to watch for?"

"They're down as of a minute ago."

No city or private property cameras are going to catch us on tape. It doesn't really matter if they do. Our plates aren't real, and we know to keep our heads down to block facial recognition software. People might guess who we are, but we leave no proof.

I glance at my cousin before I speak.

"You still good with me taking point?"

"Of course. Your girlfriend and her family were their targets. This is your op."

Everyone goes silent as I lead the way into the alley. Our headlights have been off for the past two miles. Despite being veritable tanks with reenforced and bulletproof everything, the SUVs drive as silently as hybrids. We ease out, everyone careful not to let the doors make any noise. Bogdan hands out the rifles from our SUV while Aleks does the same for the guys in his car. Once we've all checked our guns—force of habit, not necessity since we all know they're loaded—we put our night vision goggles in place.

We're already in the shadows, so we're not worried about being seen. But the NVGs keep any of us from tripping. Pasha is across from me as our other *avotoritet*. Maks is right behind me. He'll never send someone else into danger without being right there to cover their back. Aleks is across from Maks. Bogdan and Niko are partners, and Anton and Sergei bring up the rear together. It's how we always wind up. There's never any discussion anymore.

I gesture to Pasha to lead us to the backdoor of our target. He gets out his kit and picks the lock. We're inside within a minute. Anton pulled the blueprints for the building, so we know what we're looking for. We break off in pairs, each with a task. Pasha and I head to the office to clear out the safe. Maks and Aleks are going to the display cases to clean them out. Niko and Bogdan are on lookout. Anton and Sergei are going to the fuse box and furnace.

On my mark, we move out. We are synchronized to complete everything and be back out within ten minutes at most. It shouldn't take us more than five. Pasha and I know how to get into any industrial, commercial, or home safe. Most people would think studying such things is a bizarre hobby. We like puzzles.

Maks and Aleks took out the two night guards who were half asleep. We're back in the alleyway in seven minutes. I'm pulling onto the street three minutes later.

The O'Rourkes got into the diamond business a few generations ago. It wasn't easy as Irish immigrants, but they built the business from the ground up. It was their grandmother who made it what it is now. It's a legacy to the other women in their family. It's their security in case anything happens to the core leadership. We will never touch a woman or child, but that doesn't mean we won't take from them.

A while back, a "gas leak"—yes, air quotes and all—blew up their most profitable pub. We can't hit another one because the first won't seem like a fluke, and people will investigate the supposed coincidence. But they have a hotel that is allegedly closed for renovations. It's not. It's their newest place to store meth and heroin since they know their warehouses near the docks aren't safe from us. Actually, they have no warehouses left. Only ones that are midway through completion.

We meet two dozen men a block from the hotel and make our way inside. There are a dozen men working in the basement. They're packaging the heroin, which makes it so much easier for us. We know there's already a truck in the loading bay, so our men help us load everything. We stack the truck to the brim, taking everything in the hotel. Product, equipment, documents. *Everything.* I latch the door closed and slap the back of the truck. Stefan's driving, and he knows what to do. It'll all be on a boat to the Netherlands in thirty minutes.

We clear the building and run back to the SUVs. I glance back and make the call. It triggers the bombs set in the building. We all cover our ears as we pile into the vehicles. Sirens are going off all over the place as we speed away.

Our final destination takes a little longer to get to, but it's worth the drive. There's a house in Yonkers that's been in the family since the O'Rourkes arrived in America in the 1920s. It was the first place they could afford, and three couples lived there with their kids. No one lives there anymore, but it's where they gather for all holidays. It's a shrine to their family, and their most prized family heirlooms apparently sit out to remind them of the greatness they've always imagined.

We park on a parallel street and make our way to the house. No guards here. Why would they need them? No one would ever dare...

Once again, Pasha's in within a minute. Our men are with us for this, too. Unlike a lot of properties, this one has something of a yard. We grab everything that isn't bolted to the floor or the wall that might be of value to them. We take it to the foot of the garden and smash it all. Pieces that are big enough to bother with get thrown in every direction. When we're done decorating the backyard, I head inside alone. I'm no pyro. Fire doesn't fascinate me. I don't get off watching it. But I understand it. I might have studied business in college, but I love science. Maybe that's part of why I enjoy knowing Kitty's a nurse. We have that interest in common.

I work fast in the basement, ensuring the concrete keeps nothing from burning. Then I make my way back up to the main floor. By the time firefighters can get in to investigate, they won't know where the blaze started. They won't figure out the accelerant or where the spark started. We gather again in the backyard, and Maks takes photos. Sergei will get them to Dillan and his family without a trace. But they'll know. I took only one photo before I left. I drew a chalk outline of a bearpaw. We never leave calling cards, but we did this time. We watch it all burn. Then we head home to our wives—or girlfriend—and our beds.

"You're back."

Kitty's eyes flutter open a moment after I come out of the bathroom. I'm standing naked near the window with the plantation shutters closed. Her eyes slide to my dick that's coming to life the longer she looks. Larisa is sleeping in the spare room across the hall. Laura told me just before I came upstairs. She was downstairs when we all returned, warning Maks that he better not wake the twins.

"I am, baby girl."

She pushes back the covers and climbs out of bed. She flicks on the bedside table lamp before she approaches. She trails her fingers over me as she walks around me, examining me for any sign of injury.

"You're all right, Daddy?"

"Yes, *malyshka*."

"Is it done? I mean, at least for now? For tonight?"

"It is. We'll sort out what comes next in the morning."

"Look."

She points toward the window.

"Mr. Bun-Buns is happy to see you."

I look at my rabbit, who's standing on his hind paws and reaching his front paw through the cage. I grin at Kitty before I walk over to the little old man. I run my finger along the pads on his paw before stroking between his ears. Before meeting Kitty, Mr. Bun-Buns was who I looked forward to seeing after a mission. Holding him while watching TV was calming. He's been a little neglected over the past month, even if my cousins have taken excellent care of him. I know Sumiko made sure he was here when I got back from Boston.

"Is Mr. Bun-Buns the only one happy to see me?"

"Of course not."

Kitty wraps her arms around my neck and presses her body

against mine. I gladly wrap my arms around her and devour her as she lifts her chin to accept my kiss. When we stop to catch our breath, I look at my rabbit. It's taking everything for me to remain calm.

"We can't ignore you, my rascally rabbit."

I open his cage and lift him out. I hold him out to Kitty, who smiles and takes him. I know the moment she spots the ribbon I tied loosely around his neck a moment before she stirred. I think the sound of the cage closing might have woken her.

"Misha?"

"Hmm?"

"What this?"

"I asked Mr. Bun-Buns to hold on to something, so I wouldn't lose it."

She cradles my mini lop in her arm as she pulls the ribbon off. I slip the ring into my palm and lower myself on one knee.

"*Malyshka*, I love you. We've had a rollercoaster start to our future together, but we've known from the beginning that this wouldn't be easy. Every day that I have with you makes me feel whole. It pushes the darkness back into a corner and makes every day a little lighter and brighter than before I met you. Will you marry me?"

"*Da.*"

She covers her mouth with her hand as she nods. I put my hand out, and she just stares at it until she realizes I need hers, so I can put the ring on her finger. I know she's barely looked at it because it's the moment that matters to her, not the cut, color, clarity, or carats. But as I slide it onto her ring finger, she notices it in more detail.

"Misha, this is stunning. I've never seen anything like it."

"There's a jewelry store in Manhattan that has become something of a family tradition to use for engagement rings. I was going to wait until morning and ask you with our family there. That's become a bit of a tradition too. But I couldn't wait. I thought this might be sweet."

"It's so sweet, *papochka*. I will never forget this moment."

She strokes one of the rabbit's satiny ears before putting him back in the cage and shutting it. I stand as she tugs at my arms. She strips off the t-shirt and pajama shorts she wore to bed. I lift her off her feet, and she wraps her legs around my waist. We tumble onto the bed, kissing with our hands roaming over every inch we can reach.

"I love you so much, Misha. I never want you to wonder if I fell for you out of necessity. I love you because you are the kindest, most considerate man, with a huge heart. You love with all that you have, whether it's your family or me. I know the rest of the world doesn't understand us and this life. I get why they look down upon us. But I know family, duty, honor, loyalty, and love are what drive you to your core. There is no better man than you. I don't care what the other—"

She silently counts, moving her fingers.

"—Eight women say. They're wrong. I have the best of all of you."

I thrust into her, and we move together as though we've been making love for years not weeks. In my family, we love completely and unconditionally. We know when we meet our soulmate, and we value each moment we share with them from the very beginning.

"Daddy, can we get married tomorrow?"

I chuckle, which makes me twitch inside her. Her moan shoots straight to my dick. Fuck. She's enough to distract a saint.

"We'll see what we can do. It might be the day after."

I know she's joking, but I also know that a large part of her is serious. But I don't want to exclude her parents. And reality is there's going to be fallout tomorrow to deal with.

As our mouths meet again, I sigh. My tongue sweeps the inside of her mouth, and she sucks lightly. I will never get enough of my *kiska*.

"May I come, *papochka*?"

"Yes, baby. As many times as you can."

We spend the next hour tangled together until we're both too spent to remain awake. It feels like I barely closed my eyes when someone pounds on the door.

"Misha, we have to go."

Fucking Maks. I know this isn't an invitation to go to the gym. I glance toward the window, and the sun is up. Kitty's watching me, but I can only shrug.

"Hold on, Maks."

Just like déjà vu, I grab a pair of basketball shorts and open the door a crack.

"I got a text from Pablo. Whatever his cousins arranged happened last night. It was a success, but Salvatore called this morning. Carmine took their jet back up to Boston to deal with Yuri personally. He did, but he got arrested. Besnik narced."

"Motherfucker."

"Which one?"

Maks's sarcasm matches mine.

"Both. What does that mean for us?"

"I don't know yet. We need everyone to meet in my office. I'm going to get my brothers. You get yours and Anton."

"Is it just us?"

"For now. I don't know what's going to come up."

None of the wives or my fiancée—fuck, I love the sound of that—will be at the meeting to protect them from learning anything they shouldn't since I doubt we'll discuss any of our legal ventures. I close the door as Maks moves to the room next to mine.

"Carmine got arrested?"

"Yes. How upset will that make Larisa if she finds out?"

"There's nothing romantic or sexual between them. Neither tried for anything. He truly did just want to help her. But I'm sure she'll feel responsible that he went back up there. What's going to happen to him?"

"My guess is his paperwork will somehow magically disappear. Salvatore will see to it. But I'm also certain Besnik will have called Dillan by now, so that fucker will know what went down in Boston and here. He'll be pissed that he can't gloat about Carmine because he'll have too much to do today."

"Do you think you'll have to leave again?"

"I don't know. Let me go down there and find out what's happening."

"All right."

I hurry to throw on a shirt and walk to my brother's door. I knock, and I hear voices inside.

"We're up."

"Sergei, meet us in the office."

I head downstairs. Maks and Niko are already there. Everyone else filters in. The next thirty minutes feel like an eternity. I didn't need to be here to listen to Salvatore bitch about Besnik and Yuri. But he got Carmine's charges dropped. None of us care about that. We're just glad the little shit hasn't fallen back into his old ways. I know we all worried he would sing like a fucking canary and bring us all down with him.

Maks dials a number and sets the phone back on the desk.

"You've got balls, Kutsenko. You motherfucking, cock sucking, piece of shit."

"See there's your problem, O'Rourke. If you could learn to leave our women alone, then you wouldn't be dealing with the police and fire investigators this morning. You wouldn't be lying to the insurance adjustors. And you wouldn't be explaining to your daddy why the house he grew up in is ashes."

"This isn't over, Maksim."

"But it is, Dillan. Stay away from our women and our children. Act like a man for a fucking day in your life instead of a spoiled brat or a little bitch. Business is between us. Our families stay out of it. You're counting on the fact that we'll never hurt the women and kids in your family, but that doesn't mean we won't strip you of everything your family holds dear. You forget who you're dealing with. America was right to fear the Soviets during the Cold War. We have skills and tactics still in reserve. You had shit cousins and an idiot uncle to train you. Your dad never did more than take orders. You are not a match for us, little boy. Sit your ass down and shut the fuck up before we take it all."

Maks hangs up. I shrug one shoulder.

"Where's he going to hit first?"

"Who knows? He's going to have a hard time getting around without a bus pass or subway tokens. I had all his cars impounded this morning. Somehow, they all wound up parked illegally last night."

No one has a chance to say more because laughter and clapping interrupt. Everyone but me turns toward the door.

"They must be looking at Kitty's ring."

Seven sets of eyes swing back toward me. Now I can't keep from grinning.

"She said yes last night."

"Finally, a sister. About damn time. I've been asking for one for Christmas for the last thirty years."

"I've only been alive for twenty-nine years."

"Yeah, so imagine my disappointment when Mama and Papa brought you home."

"Fuck off."

Sergei wraps me in his arms so tightly that a few vertebrae crack as he lifts me off my feet.

"Congratulations, little brother."

"Thanks, old man. I hope you paid enough attention to know how to be a best man."

"I've always been the better man. You're just finally catching up."

He ruffles my hair and gives me a smacking kiss on the forehead. I pretend to wipe it off before flattening my hair. But no one's fooled. They know I love my brother as much as each of them loves their own brother.

Bogdan waggles his eyebrows at me.

"The baby of the family's finally all grown up."

"Fuck off, dumbass. You're two months older than me."

"That's right. I'm older. Now don't cry to your mama. It won't impress your fiancée."

"Learned that the hard way, did you?"

We move out to the living room where the rest of my family surrounds Kitty. My parents, Grigori and Alina, and Aunt Galina are there, too. I slide my arms around my future wife and press my chest to her back. I kiss her neck as her arms wrap around mine.

Larisa smiles at me, and I realize I might look forward to having a sister, too. Maybe Sergei isn't so wrong. I look over at my brother and shoot him a mocking look.

"You're right. A sister is an upgrade."

Kitty turns in my arms and playfully whacks my chest.

"I told you before. Be nice to your brother. It's not his fault you got all the looks and the charm."

"You thought we were twins, *malyshka*."

"True. Misha?"

Her voice lowers when she says my name, and I know what she's wondering.

"Carmine's on his way home. We'll have to tie up loose ends with Besnik, and Roel will probably have something to say about it, too. We had someone who could have taken care of this for us, but we had a falling out a while ago. The guy's in the wind somewhere."

"In the wind?"

An Americanism Kitty doesn't know.

"It means we don't know where this guy is. I suppose this is a good time to start filling you in on names you need to always be on the look out for. Robert Sims turned out to be way more than a mercenary. He was practically a ghost for nearly twenty years. He's still out there, and we're certain we're going to encounter him again. We just don't know when. With any luck, he'll become Salvatore's or Enrique's problem. But it wouldn't surprise me if he hires himself out to Dillan just out of vengeance."

"This guy sounds horrible."

"He's a mercenary. He is horrible."

"Is there at least a temporary truce between us and the Cartel and the *Cosa Nostra*?"

"I think they finally get that business remains just that. Families are untouchable."

Kitty looks at Larisa, who's joking with Laura and Ana in Russian. She fits in with the family easily.

"Would your parents move here?"

"That's what I'm hoping."

"We can ask later when we tell them about our engagement."

Kitty sighs and rests her head against my chest.

"What's that saying? All's well that ends well?"

"This is just our beginning, *malyshka*. I love you."

"I love you, Daddy."

We join our family as we sit down for breakfast. No one would ever guess we're the senior-most members of the Ivankov brotherhood if they saw us right now. We've been bratva, and we will be for life. But our family is who we are. There'll never be anything more important.

Epilogue

Kitty

I check my mask one more time before we get out of the car. I'm still nervous about anyone seeing me before we go inside. The hood with the kitten ears completely covers my hair, and the mask shields my face. I glance over at Misha, and his hood fully disguises his face, too. I couldn't stop laughing when he first put it on. He's not in leather with metal studs sticking off his clothes, but the hood is definitely what someone would picture a sex dungeon master wearing. But it's fitting I suppose.

"If you change your mind at any time, say so, *kiska*."

"I know, Daddy. Beets. How could I forget?"

I take Misha's hand as we enter the dimly lit building. I'm nervous that someone will recognize Misha. Not someone in a vague sense. I mean a woman he's fucked at a BDSM club before. He admitted that he'd been to one that one of his cousins belonged to several years ago. He'd gone three times but hadn't been that impressed. He knew I worried about that even though I was the one to ask if we could try this.

"The Dungeon Masters have the yellow arm bands marked DM. One of them will show us around. Don't be afraid to ask your questions."

"I won't be. There's just a lot to take in."

I sweep my gaze over the interior. There's a bar in the corner, and what looks like a lounge where people are just mingling. I can see hallways that appear to lead into darkness, but I assume there are private rooms along each of them. Misha found out about some of the roleplaying ones, but none interested either of us.

"Hello. I'm Blanche. I'm one of the Dungeon Masters tonight. There are three other ones on this floor. Dorothy, Sophia, and Rose."

The Golden Girls? I guess she got lucky to be Blanche at a sex club.

"Do you know what interests you?"

I look up at Misha, who nods.

"We want to be watched."

"Do you want anyone to join you?"

"No."

Misha and I answer at the same time and we're both adamant. Blanche smiles and nods.

"We have a few options. If you're exhibitionists, then there is that area across from the bar. If you prefer some privacy and knowing you have voyeurs, then I can take you to a room."

"What happens if we start with one, then decide we'd like to try the other?"

I don't know what to choose. I don't know how I'll feel about this once we start.

"Just find one of us, and we'll set you up somewhere else."

Blanche guides us to a table where we fill out what feels like a mountain of paperwork. Releases of liability and consent forms. I get why these aren't on their website to print and fill out at home. As we walk back toward the bar and lounge, I notice what looks like an ornate chaise lounge. I tap Misha's shoulder and point.

We haven't moved into our new house in Queens yet because we just got back from our honeymoon in Australia two weeks ago. But the one piece of furniture that's already been delivered is our sex chaise. We might not need anything else in the house. The ridiculous number of rooms can stand empty as long as we at least have our chaise. Misha offered to get one for every room.

"Rethinking turning down my offer to get more of them?"

I laugh.

"Mind reader. Maybe a little."

We make our way over to the upholstered bench. There's a fitted sheet folded on one end. Blanche is quick to cover the chaise, and I feel a little better about the public hygiene. That's the one thing that makes me hesitate a little. I try to remind myself that I'm only a nurse from seven-twenty-five a.m. to two-fifty-five p.m. Monday through Friday. But the little voice doesn't always shut up.

"*Malyshka*, you already called and asked about their sanitization process."

"I know. It's not like I'm a germaphobe, but you can't blame me for wondering."

"I know. I would never bring you to a place that I wasn't certain was safe for you."

We thank Blanche and watch her walk away. I know Misha is aware of everyone and everything happening in here. I could blindfold him right now, and he could describe everything in perfect detail down to the color cocktail napkins on the bar across the room from us. That helps set my mind a little more at ease about being watched.

"Come here, *kiska*."

"Yes, Daddy."

He pulls loose the tied belt to my wraparound dress and slides it down my shoulders. He drapes it over the foot of the bench.

"You look beautiful, baby."

I'm wearing a midnight blue lacy bra and panty set. We agreed that we'd both feel more comfortable if I had the underwear on. The material is easy enough to move aside, but it'll let me feel a little covered up if anyone can see me past Misha. We also agreed that he would keep his clothes on. We like the contrast between me nearly naked and him fully clothed. But more importantly, it keeps his very distinguishable and identifiable tats covered.

There's a basket near where we're standing. Misha pulls a broad paddle from it. He guides me around to the high side of the chaise and presses me to lean over it. The chain that connects my nipple clamps to my clit clamp tugs, and I grip the upholstery. My tits are already sensitive from having the clamps on for the past twenty minutes.

"Push your ass out for me, *malyshka*. Let me see that plug."

He pulls my panties aside and twists the sapphire bejeweled plug. I left all my other jewelry at home, including my rings. But the sapphires are real. They're my birthstone, and the plug was a private wedding present from Misha.

"Are you ready?"

"Yes, *papochka*."

I brace myself, but I still jerk forward when the paddle hits my ass. He rubs his hand over my heated flesh. Then he brings the broad end down again. He does it ten times, covering all of my ass. He doesn't miss a spot, and I'm dripping down the inside of my thighs.

"Daddy."

I'm begging.

"Do you want me to stop? You didn't use your safe word."

"No. I want more. Please."

He fists my hair and leans forward to whisper in my ear.

"You know people are watching. You want them to see how you take your daddy's punishment, don't you?"

"Yes."

He helps me up, and I make an annoyed sound to let him know I disagree with this change. His hand lands hard across my ass. That wasn't just for pleasure. I know better, and I did it on purpose. He knows that too because he's smiling. He positions me to lie on my back with my legs up and over the back. He pulls my hips forward, and the chair supports my hips while giving him something to lean over and support his weight. He licks along the inside of my thighs, tasting me before he even gets to my pussy.

He swirls his tongue around my clit before flicking the tip inside me. I wonder when he's going to take the clamp off. Usually, he'd do it now when he starts to eat me out. But only his tongue has touched it. He slides two, then three, then four fingers into me while his other hand tugs the chain connected to the nipple clamps. I fight not to scream. Fuck it hurts. But I don't want him to stop. I squeeze my eyes shut.

"Look around, *kiska*. People are watching me pleasure you. Do you see those men jerking off?"

I open my eyes and turn my head. There are men stroking themselves inside their pants.

"Push your tits together."

"Yes, Daddy."

His tongue flicks the clit clamp, and I writhe.

"Come whenever you want tonight, baby."

"Thank you, Daddy. I need to so badly."

He thrusts his fingers harder, and I moan. Everything

tightens for a moment before the pleasure radiates from my cunt outward.

"Daddy, come over here."

He helps me to sit up, and I pat the highest side of the chair while I kneel in front of it. He climbs onto the chaise and perches against the rolled top of the high back. I unfasten his pants, but I stop with my mouth hanging open.

"*Dah-deee!* What are these?"

"You're wearing panties for the same reason, and you know it."

"I thought I'd thrown all these fucking things away. I bought this lingerie set specifically for tonight."

"And I had to buy this pair just for tonight. Funny how I came home one day, and I didn't have a single pair of boxers or boxer briefs. They just disappeared."

"I told the panty fairy to take them when she came for all my thongs. Move these fucking things out of my way, Daddy."

He pushes down the waistband of the boxer briefs until he springs free. I can admit that seeing him in the snug underwear is fucking hot, so I don't totally mind him wearing them. But I agree that underwear is generally overrated and just in the way.

I wrap my hand around him and stroke him. He fists my hair and keeps my head in one place.

"You will get a private spanking when we get home if you can't remember who decides, *malyshka*."

"I know you decide, Daddy. And I'm cool with that. But it's your fault that you always encourage me to tell you what I'm thinking in and out of bed."

"And I want your opinion—most of the time."

"Daddy, do you see those women?"

"What women, *kiska*?"

"I know you see them. You see everything that's happening here. But thank you. I get your point."

He grins down at me.

"I'm only paying attention to one woman."

"Well, that's not entirely accurate either, but thank you. Do you see how much they wish they were me? Do you see how they're looking at your cock?"

"If you say so, baby."

I sink my head down and take as much of him into my mouth as I can. His grip on my hair tightens to the point of pain for a second. Then it eases as he regains control. I love knowing I do that to him. I love knowing these women wish they were me, sucking Misha off. I love knowing they wish he was going to fuck them tonight. But the thing I love knowing the most is that none of them will ever get what I have. Misha is completely devoted to me, just like I am to him. That makes me enjoy giving him head even more. I want to pleasure him as much as he wants to pleasure me.

"*Koshechka*, let go."

I obey immediately. That deliciously deep tone tells me I'm about to get fucked hard. He's on me before I know what's happening. I squeal as he suddenly spins me and trades places with me. He pushes my legs apart and surges into me. I reach behind me to brace myself as he releases the nipple clamps. Then the clit clamp is gone too. He plays with my left nipple as he sucks the right one. He's pounding into me, and one arm wraps around him to hang on. The blood and sensation rush back into my tender skin, and I come apart. I can't stop—don't want to stop—the scream that comes with this powerful orgasm. I've already heard other people moaning, groaning, and screaming as they come.

"That's right, baby girl. Take all of it. Your body is mine to do with what I want. I will fuck you how I want and when I want. I will make you come until your beg me to stop."

"Never, Daddy."

He wraps my left leg over his hip as he shifts to drive into me ever deeper. I'm only dimly aware that more people are watching us. It's quietly building my excitement, knowing that we're on display. But the way Misha's fucking me has nothing to do with where we are or who's around. This is how it always is. Intense. Consuming. Fulfilling.

We waited six months before we had the wedding. We wanted my parents and Larisa to be here legally. Mama and Papa now live in New Jersey, and Larisa reunited with her ex-girlfriend and is moving to Canada. Misha and I both went back to our regular jobs, and we started a normal-ish life together leading up to the wedding. Our need for each other has only increased during those months while we waited to say I do. And now that we're married, we savor that connection as much as we do the physical fulfillment from joining.

"Daddy, I'm close again. I want to make you come."

"You're going to...Fuck, *kiska*...Yes. Just like that...Fuck."

He's fucking me so hard that the chaise is creaking, and it's skidding along the floor with each of his thrusts. I claw my nails over his shirt, and his back is lucky the material covers him. I'd probably draw blood otherwise. It wouldn't be a first.

"Are you close, *papochka*?"

"I'm about to come."

I shift slightly, and it applies just the right friction for me to detonate. I cling to him as I arch my back and tremble. He pins me in place as he shoots his cum into me. Then he's moving slower. Once more turning us, so he's sitting, and I'm straddling him. Neither of us cares who's watching anymore. We're exchanging soft kisses as we hold each other. His hands are gentle as he caresses my sore ass. He takes the plug out and moves awkwardly to shove it into his pocket along with the chain that connects the clamps.

"Daddy, I'm suddenly so tired and comfy curled around you."

"Do you want to go home, baby girl?"

"Yes, please."

I can barely stifle my yawn. He helps me to stand, then slips my dress back on me. He straightens his clothes as I tie my dress closed. He fixes my mask since it was a bit askew. He reassures me it still hid my face. I slip my hand into his as we head toward the doors.

"Did you enjoy that, *kiska*?"

"Yes. I'm glad we did it. I'm happy to come back here if you want."

"You don't sound as though you'll be suggesting it."

"We satisfied my curiosity, *papochka*. I had a lot of fun, and I would do it again. But I can also live without."

"I feel the same."

"So maybe we don't get a membership after all."

"That's fine by me."

We're almost to the door when I squeeze Misha's hand and wrap the other around his forearm.

"What's wrong, Kitty?"

"Shh. Nothing's wrong. Look. Is that Carmine?"

Misha's head swivels as he follows my gaze.

"It is. But who's he with?"

"I have no idea. But they look like a whole lot more than just fuck buddies."

I heard he was supposed to marry some Italian girl, but he's been avoiding it for years. His body language with this woman doesn't make their relationship look casual. I wonder if he'll be the next of the *Cosa Nostra* to marry. I'll be curious to see how that works out for him.

Stefan's waiting for us with the car. I slide into the back, and Misha follows me. As always, the privacy glass is up. He lifts me onto his lap, and I snuggle against him. I yawn again.

"Misha?"

"Hmm..."

"Thank you."

"For bringing you here tonight?"

"That too. Thank you for sending Semyon away and insisting that you take care of me."

"I'll always take care of you, *malyshka*. You do the same for me. No one could love me better than you do."

"I do love you, Daddy. So much."

"I love you, baby girl."

I'm not as tired as I thought when Misha rolls us, so I'm lying on the seat, and he's thrusting into me. I remember nothing about the ride home except for making love to my husband.

Thank you for reading Bratva Jewel

Sabine Barclay, a nom de plume also writing Historical Romance as Celeste Barclay, lives near the Southern California coast with her husband and sons. Growing up in the Midwest, Celeste enjoyed spending as much time in and on the water as she could. Now she lives near the beach. She's an avid swimmer, a hopeful future surfer, and a former rower. When she's not writing, she's working or being a mom.

Subscribe to Sabine's bimonthly newsletter to receive exclusive insider perks.

www.sabinebarclay.com

Join the fun and get exclusive insider giveaways, sneak peeks, and new release announcements in
Sabine Barclay's Facebook Dubious Dames Group

Do you also enjoy steamy Historical Romance? Discover Sabine's books written as Celeste Barclay.

The Ivankov Brotherhood

Bratva Darling

BOOK ONE SNEAK PEEK

LAURA

As I sit across from the four Kutsenko brothers, I press my lips together to keep from drooling. No four men should be so strikingly handsome. Not all from the same family, anyway. I fight a valiant battle against letting my gaze drift toward the eldest, Maksim, whose ice-blue eyes bore into me. After years of negotiating billion-dollar investment contracts while facing countless ruthless businessmen, I've learned to keep my expression studiously blank. But it's a true struggle today. Instead, I focus my attention on the squirrelly lawyer sitting across the conference table. While he's disingenuous with each comment, he's a good negotiator. But I'm better. How cliché am I?

While I feel Maksim watching me, I focus on Dmitry Yakovitch as he continues to argue the merits of the venture capitalist company I represent, RK Capital Group, merging with Kutsenko Partners. What he means is the merits of Kutsenko Partners acquiring RK Capital Group, then stripping it and making it another money-laundering shell corporation. While most people in New York have little awareness of the Russian mafia, I do. The Kutsenko brothers' names appear on no titles or deeds anywhere in New York City, but it wasn't difficult to determine which shell companies likely belong to them. Their assumption that I'm unfamiliar with them is proving beneficial to me as they continue to whisper amongst themselves in Russian. I think they may even believe they're convincing me that they don't speak much English.

The senior partners of RK Capital Group know who I'm negotiating with, though they may not know I'm aware of these Russians' more nefarious operations. They've given me the go-ahead to agree to a merger with an eventual acquisition, but only for the right price. A price to the tune of twenty billion dollars. Considering an investment firm like Goldman Sachs is worth nearly one-hundred-and-twenty billion dollars, my clients' asking price appears reasonable.

"Mr. Yakovitch, I shall stop you now." I raise my left hand, pen caught between my index and middle fingers. When I have his attention, I lean back in my chair and casually twirl the pen over my index finger and thumb. "Fifty billion is my clients' asking price. You know that. Your clients know that. RK doesn't oppose the merger. What they oppose is the insulting offer you've made. It's nearly noon, and I'm hungry, Mr. Yakovitch. I have a delicious ham sandwich waiting for me. I even have three chocolate chip cookies waiting for me. If we aren't going to make any progress, I shall let you go, so I can move onto my eagerly anticipated lunch."

I cant my head just enough for me to appear as though my gaze rests solely on the opposing attorney's face, but I can see each Kutsenko brothers' reaction. My face battles yet again against showing my emotions as I fight not to smirk. Their muted but surprised expressions confirm what I already know.

"Please tell your clients to make a reasonable counteroffer, or I will conclude this meeting and enjoy my ham sandwich and cookies."

Dmitry glares at me before turning to Maksim and his three brothers. In rapid Russian, he doesn't interpret my suggestion. Oh no. There's no need for that. I can't catch every word because his voice is too low. But I catch something along the lines of "The bitch refuses to budge. What now? A fucking ham sandwich. More like a stick up her ass."

Maksim swivels his chair to look at his brothers. In Russian, he says, "Fifty billion is ridiculous. She's not so stupid or naïve not to know that. My guess is they'll settle for twenty billion. We offer fifteen."

"That's barely better than what we already offered," Aleksei, the second-oldest brother, argues. "She'll be eating the fucking sandwich and dipping her cookies in milk before we walk out the door. We need the buildings."

"We offer twenty, Maks," Bogdan, the youngest, insists.

As I watch the brothers discuss, their voices barely lowered, I pull my lunch sack from the black leather satchel by my feet and set it beside my laptop. It's a ridiculously pink floral bag with an embroidered monogram, the L and D overlapping. It's an empty prop, but they don't know that. I watch as five sets of eyes narrow. I offer a smile that would appear innocent in any setting other than this meeting. It's patronizing, and I know it.

Bratva Sweetheart

Bratva Treasure

Bratva Beauty

Bratva Angel

Bratva Jewel